T0144788

The Great War in England in 1897

The Great War in England in 1897

William Le Queux

MINT EDITIONS

The Great War in England in 1897 was first published in 1894.

This edition published by Mint Editions 2021.

ISBN 9781513281018 | E-ISBN 9781513286037

Published by Mint Editions®

MINT
EDITIONS
minteditionbooks.com

Publishing Director: Jennifer Newens
Design & Production: Rachel Lopez Metzger
Project Manager: Micaela Clark
Typesetting: Westchester Publishing Services

CONTENTS

Book III. The Victory

BOOK I
THE INVASION

I

The Shadow of Moloch

War! *War in England!*

Growled by thoughtful, stern-visaged men, gasped with bated breath by pale-faced, terrified women, the startling news passed quickly round the Avenue Theatre from gallery to boxes. The crisis was swift, complete, crushing. Actors and audience were appalled.

Though it was a gay comic opera that was being performed for the first time, entertainers and entertained lost all interest in each other. They were amazed, dismayed, awestricken. Amusement was nauseating; War, with all its attendant horrors, was actually upon them! The popular tenor, one of the idols of the hour, blundered over his lines and sang terribly out of tune, but the hypercritical first-night audience passed the defect unnoticed. They only thought of what might happen; of the dark cavernous future that lay before.

War had been declared against Britain—Britain, the Empire that had so long rested in placid sea-girt security, confident of immunity from attack, was to be invaded! The assertion seemed preposterous.

Some, after reading eagerly the newspapers still damp from the press, smiled incredulously, half inclined to regard the startling intelligence as a mere fabrication by alarmists, or a perfected phase of the periodical war-scare which sensational journalists annually launch upon the world during what is technically known as the "gooseberry" season.

Other readers, however, recollecting the grave political crises on the Continent, set their teeth firmly, silent and dumfounded. Upon many merchants and City men the news fell like a thunderbolt, for financial ruin stared them in the face.

Evidently a desperate attempt would be made by the enemy to land on English soil. Already the startled playgoers could hear in their excited imagination the clash of arms mingling with the triumphant yell of the victor, and the stifled, despairing cry of the hapless victim. But who, they wondered, would be the victim? Would Britannia ever fall to the dust with broken trident and shattered shield? Would her neck ever lie under the heel of the foreign invader? No, never—while Britons could fight.

The theatre, in its garish blaze of electricity, and crowded with well-dressed men and women, presented a brilliant appearance, which had suddenly become strangely incongruous with the feelings of the audience. In the boxes, where youth and beauty smiled, the bouquets which had been provided by the management gave to the theatre a bright, artistic touch of colour. Yet the pungent odour they diffused had become sickening. Intermingled with other flowers there were many tuberoses. They are funereal blossoms, ineffably emblematic of the grave. There is death in their breath.

When the astounding news fell upon the house the performance was drawing to a close. A moment before, every one had been silent and motionless, listening with rapt attention to the tenor's plaintive love song, and admiring the grace of the fair heroine, but as the terrible truth dawned upon them they rose, amid a scene of the wildest excitement. The few papers that had been purchased at fabulous prices at the doors were eagerly scanned, many of the sheets being torn into shreds in the mad struggle to catch a glimpse of the alarming telegrams they contained. For a few moments the agitation nearly approached a panic, while above the hum and din the hoarse, strident voices of running newsmen could be heard outside, yelling, "War declared against England! Expected landing of the enemy! Extrur-speshal!"

There was a hidden terror in the word "War" that at first held the amazed playgoers breathless and thoughtful. Never before had its significance appeared so grim, so fatal, so fraught with appalling consequences.

War had been actually declared! There was no averting it! It was a stern reality.

No adroit diplomatic negotiations could stem the advancing hordes of foreign invaders; Ministers and ambassadors were as useless pawns, for two great nations had had the audacity to combine in the projected attack upon Great Britain.

It seemed incredible, impossible. True, a Great War had long been predicted, forecasts had been given of coming conflicts, and European nations had for years been gradually strengthening their armies and perfecting their engines of war, in the expectation of being plunged into hostilities. Modern improvements in arms and ammunition had so altered the conditions of war, that there had long been a feeling of insecurity even among those Powers who, a few years before, had felt themselves strong enough to resist any attack, however violent.

WILLIAM LE QUEUX

War-scares had been plentiful, crises in France, Germany, and Russia of frequent occurrence; still, no one dreamed that Moloch was in their midst—that the Great War, so long foreshadowed, had in reality commenced.

Yet on this hot, oppressive Saturday night in August the extra-special editions of the papers contained news that startled the world. It ran as follows:—

INVASION OF ENGLAND.
WAR DECLARED BY FRANCE AND RUSSIA.
HOSTILE FLEETS ADVANCING.
EXTRAORDINARY MANIFESTO BY THE TSAR.
(REUTER'S TELEGRAMS.)

St. Petersburg, *August 14th*, 4 P.M.

The most intense excitement has been caused here by a totally unexpected and amazing announcement made this afternoon by the Minister of Foreign Affairs to the French Ambassador. It appears that the Minister has addressed to the French representative a short note in which the following extraordinary passage occurs:—

"The earnest negotiations between the Imperial Government and Great Britain for a durable pacification of Bosnia not having led to the desired accord, His Majesty the Tsar, my august master, sees himself compelled, to his regret, to have recourse to force of arms. Be therefore so kind as to inform your Government that from to-day Russia considers herself in a state of war with Great Britain, and requests that France will immediately comply with the obligations of the alliance signed by President Carnot on February 23rd, 1892."

A circular note has also been addressed by the Russian Foreign Office to its ambassadors at the principal Courts of Europe, stating that, for reasons assigned, the Tsar has resolved to commence hostilities against Great Britain, and has given his Armies and Navy orders to commence the invasion.

This declaration has, no doubt, been contemplated by the Russian Government for several days. During the past week the French Ambassador has twice had private audience of the

Tsar, and soon after 11 A.M. to-day he had a long interview at the Ministry of Foreign Affairs. It is understood that the Minister of War was also present.

No official notification of the Declaration of War has been given to the British Ambassador. This has created considerable surprise.

5.30 P.M.

Large posters, headed "A Manifesto of His Majesty the Emperor of Russia," and addressed to his subjects, are being posted up in the Nevski Prospekt. In this document the Tsar says—

"Our faithful and beloved subjects know the strong interest which we have constantly felt in the destinies of our Empire. Our desire for the pacification of our western frontier has been shared by the whole Russian nation, which now shows itself ready to bear fresh sacrifices to alleviate the position of those oppressed by British rule. The blood and property of our faithful subjects have always been dear to us, and our whole reign attests our constant solicitude to preserve to Russia the benefits of peace. This solicitude never failed to actuate my father during events which occurred recently in Bulgaria, Austro-Hungary, and Bosnia. Our object, before all, was to effect an amelioration in the position of our people on the frontier by means of pacific negotiations, and in concert with the great European Powers, our allies and friends. Having, however, exhausted our pacific efforts, we are compelled by the haughty obstinacy of Great Britain to proceed to more decisive acts. A feeling of equity and of our own dignity enjoins it. By her recent acts Great Britain places us under the necessity of having recourse to arms. Profoundly convinced of the justice of our cause, we make known to our faithful subjects that we declare war against Great Britain. In now invoking a blessing upon our valiant armies, we give the order for an invasion of England."

This manifesto has excited the greatest enthusiasm. The news has spread rapidly, and dense crowds have assembled in the Nevski, the Izak Platz, and on the English Quay, where the posters are being exhibited.

The British Ambassador has not yet received any communication from the Imperial Government.

Fontainebleau, *Aug. 14th*, 4.30 P.M.
President Felix Faure has received a telegram from the French representative at St. Petersburg, stating that Russia has declared war against Great Britain. The President left immediately for Paris by special train.

Paris, *Aug. 14th*, 4.50 P.M.
An astounding piece of intelligence has this afternoon been received at the Ministry of Foreign Affairs. It is no less than a Declaration of War by Russia against Britain. The telegram containing the announcement was received at the Ministry from the French Ambassador at St. Petersburg soon after three o'clock. The President was at once informed, and the Cabinet immediately summoned. A meeting is now being held for the purpose of deciding upon the course to be pursued with regard to the obligations of France contracted by the Treaty of Alliance made after the Cronstadt incident in 1891. The news of impending hostilities has just been published in a special edition of the *Soir*, and has created the wildest excitement on the Boulevards. Little doubt is entertained that France will join the invading forces, and the result of the deliberations of the Cabinet is anxiously awaited. President Felix Faure has returned from Fountainebleau.

(By Telephone Through Dalziel's Agency.)

6 P.M.
The meeting of the Cabinet has just concluded. It has been resolved that France shall unreservedly render assistance to Russia. There is great activity at the War Office, and troops are already being ordered on active service. The excitement in the streets is increasing.

(Reuter's Telegrams.)

Berlin, *Aug. 14th*, 5.30 P.M.
Telegrams received here from St. Petersburg report that Russia has unexpectedly declared war against Great Britain,

and called upon France to aid her in a combined attack. The report is scarcely credited here, and further details are being eagerly awaited. The Emperor, who was to have left for Bremen this afternoon, has abandoned his journey, and is now in consultation with the Chancellor.

Christiansand, *Aug. 14th*, 7.30 P.M.
The French Channel Squadron, which has been manoeuvring for the past fortnight off the western coast of Norway, anchored outside the fjord here last night. This morning, according to rumour, the Russian Squadron arrived suddenly, and lay about thirty miles off land. Secret telegraphic orders were received at 6 P.M. by the Admirals of both fleets almost simultaneously, and the whole of the vessels left in company half an hour later. They sailed in a southerly direction, but their destination is unknown.

Dieppe, *Aug. 14th*, 8 P.M.
Ten transport vessels are embarking troops for England. Four regiments of cavalry, including the 4th Chasseurs and 16th Guards, are—[1]

---

1. The conclusion of this message has not reached us, all the wires connecting this country with France having been cut.

WILLIAM LE QUEUX

II

A Tottering Empire

The excitement in the theatre had increased, and the curtain had been rung down. Death shadows, grimly apparent, had fallen upon the house, and the scene was an extraordinary and unprecedented one. No such wild restlessness and impetuous agitation had ever before been witnessed within those walls. Some enthusiast of the pit, springing to his feet, and drawing a large red handkerchief from his pocket, waved it, shouting—

"Three cheers for good Old England!" to which, after a moment's silence, the audience responded lustily.

Then, almost before the last sound had died away, another patriot of the people mounted upon his seat, crying—

"No one need fear. The British Lion will quickly hold the French Eagle and the Russian Bear within his jaws. Let the enemy come; we will mow them down like hay."

This raised a combined laugh and cheer, though it sounded forced and hollow. Immediately, however, some buoyant spirits in the gallery commenced singing "Rule, Britannia," the chorus of which was taken up vigorously, the orchestra assisting by playing the last verse.

Outside, the scene in the streets was one of momentarily increasing excitement. The news had spread with marvellous rapidity, and the whole city was agog. An elbowing, waving, stormy crowd surged down the Strand to Trafalgar Square, where an impromptu demonstration was being held, the Government being denounced by its opponents, and spoken of with confidence by its supporters. The Radical, the Socialist, the Anarchist, each aired his views, and through the throng a hoarse threatening murmur condensed into three words, "Down with Russia! Down with France!" The cry, echoed by a thousand throats, mingled weirdly with the shouts of the newsmen and the snatches of patriotic songs.

London was anxious, fevered, and turbulent, that hot, moonless August night. At that hour all the shops were closed, and the streets only lighted by the lamps. From the unlighted windows the indistinct shapes of heads looking out on the scene could be distinguished.

On the pavements of Piccadilly and Knightsbridge knots of people stood arguing and wrangling over the probable turn of events. From uncouth Whitechapel to artistic Kensington, from sylvan Highgate to the villadom of Dulwich, the amazing intelligence had been conveyed by the presses of Fleet Street, which were still belching forth tons of damp news-sheets. At first there was confidence among the people; nevertheless little by little this confidence diminished, and curiosity gave place to surprise. But what could it be? All was shrouded in the darkest gloom. In the atmosphere was a strange and terrible oppression that seemed to weigh down men and crush them. London was, it appeared, walled in by the unknown and the unexpected.

But, after all, England was strong; it was the mighty British Empire; it was the world. What was there to fear? Nothing. So the people continued to shout, "Down with France! Down with the Autocrat! Down with the Tsar!"

A young man, who had been sitting alone in the stalls, had risen, electrified at the alarming news, and rushing out, hailed a passing cab, and drove rapidly away up Northumberland Avenue. This conduct was remarkable, for Geoffrey Engleheart was scarcely the man to flinch when danger threatened. He was a tall, athletic young fellow of twenty-six, with wavy brown hair, a dark, smartly-trimmed moustache, and handsome, well-cut features. He was happy and easy-going, always overflowing with genuine *bonhomie*. As the younger son of a very distinguished officer, he contrived to employ himself for a couple of hours a day at the Foreign Office, where, although a clerk, he held a very responsible position. Belonging to a rather good set, he was a member of several fashionable clubs, and lived in cosy, well-furnished chambers in St. James's Street.

Driving first to the house of his *fiancée*, Violet Vayne, at Rutland Gate, he informed her family of the startling intelligence; then, re-entering the conveyance, he subsequently alighted before the door of his chambers. As he paid the cabman, an ill-clad man pushed a newspaper into his face, crying, "'Ere y'are, sir. Extrur-special edition o' the *People*. Latest details. Serious scandal at the Forrin' Office."

Geoffrey started. He staggered, his heart gave a bound, and his face blanched. Thrusting half a crown into the man's dirty palm, he grasped the paper, and rushing upstairs to his sitting-room, cast himself into a chair. In breathless eagerness he glanced at the front page of the journal, and read the following:—

SCANDAL AT THE FOREIGN OFFICE.
A STATE SECRET DIVULGED.

An extraordinary rumour is going the round of the Service clubs to-night. It is alleged that the present Declaration of War would have been impossible but for the treachery of some person through whose hands the transcript of a secret treaty between England and Germany passed to-day.

A prominent Cabinet Minister, on being questioned by our reporter on the subject, admitted that he had heard the rumour, but declined to make any definite statement whether or not it was true.

There must be a good deal behind the rumour of treachery, inasmuch as none of the prominent men who have already been interviewed gave a denial to the statement.

Geoffrey sat pale and motionless, with eyes fixed upon the printed words. He read and re-read them until the lines danced before his gaze, and he crushed the paper in his hands, and cast it from him.

The little French clock on the mantelshelf chimed the hour of one upon its silvery bell; the lamp spluttered and burned dim. Still he did not move; he was dumfounded, rooted to the spot.

Blacker and blacker grew the crowd outside. The density of the cloud that hung over all portended some direful tragedy. The impending disaster made itself felt. An alarming sense of calmness filled the streets. A silence had suddenly fallen, and was becoming complete and threatening. What was it that was about to issue from these black storm-clouds? Who could tell?

III

Arming for the Struggle

L ondon was amazed.

The provinces were awestricken, paralysed by the startling suddenness with which the appalling news of the invasion had been flashed to them. Bewildered, the people could not believe it.

Only slowly did the vivid and terrible truth dawn individually upon the millions north and south, and then, during the Day of Rest, they crowded to the newspaper and telegraph offices, loudly clamouring for further details of the overwhelming catastrophe that threatened. They sought for information from London; they expected London, the mighty, all-powerful capital, to act.

Through the blazing Sunday the dust rose from the impatient, perspiring crowds in towns and cities, and the cool night brought no rest from a turmoil now incessant. Never before were such scenes of intense enthusiasm witnessed in England, Wales, and Scotland, for this was the first occasion on which the public felt the presence of invaders at their very doors.

A mighty force was on its way to ruin their homes, to sweep from them their hard-earned savings, to crush, to conquer—to kill them!

Fierce antagonism rose spontaneously in every Briton's heart, and during that never-to-be-forgotten day, at every barracks throughout the country, recruiting-sergeants were besieged by all sorts and conditions of men eager to accept the Queen's shilling, and strike for their country's honour. Heedless of danger, of hardship, of the fickle fortune of the fight, the determination to assist in the struggle rose instantly within them.

At York, Chester, Edinburgh, and Portsmouth, volunteers came forward by hundreds. All were enthusiastic, undrilled, but ready to use their guns—genuinely heroic patriots of our land, such as are included in no other nation than the British. Pluck, zeal for the public safety, and an intense partisanship towards their fellows induced thousands to join the colours—many, alas! to sink later beneath a foeman's bullet, unknown, unhonoured heroes!

Already the Cabinet had held a hurried meeting, at which it had been decided to call out the whole of the Reserves. Of this the War Office and Admiralty had been notified, and the Queen had given her sanction to the necessary proclamations, with the result that telegraphic orders had been issued to general officers commanding and to officers commanding Reservists to mobilise instantly.

The posters containing the proclamation, which are always kept in readiness in the hands of officers commanding Regimental Districts, were issued immediately, and exhibited on all public places throughout the kingdom. On the doors of town halls, churches, chapels, police stations, military barracks, and in the windows of post offices, these notices were posted within a few hours. Crowds everywhere collected to read them, and the greatest enthusiasm was displayed. Militia, Yeomanry, Volunteers, all were called out, and men on reading the Mobilisation Order lost no time in obtaining their accoutrements and joining their depôts. The national danger was imminent, and towards their "places of concentration" all categories of Her Majesty's forces were already moving. In every Regimental District the greatest activity was displayed. No country maintains in peace the full complement, or anything approaching the full complement of transport which its Armies require; hence vehicles and horses to complete the Army Service Corps companies, and for the supplemental service, were being immediately requisitioned from far and near.

One of the many anomalies discovered during this critical period was, that while transport could thus be rapidly requisitioned, yet the impressment of civilians as drivers and caretakers of the animals was not permitted by the law; therefore on all hands the organisation of this requisitioned transport was fraught with the utmost difficulty, the majority of owners and employees refusing to come forward voluntarily. Registered horses were quickly collected, but they were far from sufficient for the requirements, and the want of animals caused loud outcries from every Regimental District.

The general scheme was the constitution of a Field Army of four cavalry brigades and three army corps, with behind them a semi-mobile force made up of thirty-three Volunteer infantry brigades and eighty-four Volunteer batteries of position. The garrisons having been provided for, the four cavalry brigades and the 1st and 2nd Army Corps were to be composed entirely of Regulars, the 3rd Army Corps being made up of Regulars, Militia, and Volunteers. Organised in brigades, the Yeomanry were attached to the various infantry brigades or divisions of the Field Army, and the Regular Medical Staff Corps being much too weak, was strengthened from companies of the Volunteer Medical Staff Corps. In brief, the scheme was the formation of a composite Field Army, backed by a second line of partially trained Auxiliaries.

Such a general scheme to set in battle order our land forces for home defence was, no doubt, well devised. Nevertheless, from the first moment the most glaring defects in the working out of details were everywhere manifested. Stores were badly disposed, there was a sad want of clothing, camp equipment, and arms, and the arrangements for the joining of Reservists were throughout defective. Again, the whole Reserve had been left totally untrained from the day the men left the colours; and having in view the fact that all leading authorities in Europe had, times without number, told us that the efficiency of an Army depended on drill, discipline, and shooting, what could be expected from a system which relied in great part for the safety of the country on a Reserve, the members of which were undisciplined, undrilled, and unpractised in shooting for periods ranging from nine years in the Guards to five years in the case of the Line?

On the day of mobilisation not a single regiment in the United Kingdom was ready to move forward to the front as it stood on parade! Not an officer, not a man, was prepared. England had calmly slept for years, while military reforms had been effected in every other European country. Now she had been suddenly and rudely awakened!

Everywhere it was commented upon that no practical peace trial of the mobilisation scheme had ever been made. Little wonder was there, then, that incomplete details hampered rapid movements, or that the carrying out of the definite and distinct programme was prevented by gaps occurring which could not be discovered until the working of the system had been tested by actual experiment.

It was this past apathy of the authorities, amounting to little less than criminal negligence, that formed the text of the vehement outpourings of Anarchists, Socialists, and "No War" partisans. A practical test of the efficiency of the scheme to concentrate our forces should have taken place even at the risk of public expenditure, instead of making the experiment when the enemy were actually at our doors.

Another anomaly which, in the opinion of the public, ought long ago to have been removed, was the fact that the billeting of troops on the march on the inhabitants of the United Kingdom, other than owners of hotels, inns, livery stables, and public-houses, is illegal, while troops when not on the march cannot be billeted at all! At many points of concentration this absurd and antiquated regulation, laid down by the Army Act in 1881, was severely felt. Public buildings, churches, and schools had to be hired for the accommodation of the troops, and those others who could not find private persons hospitable enough to take them in were compelled to bivouac where they could. Of tents they had scarcely any, and many regiments were thus kept homeless and badly fed several days before moving forward!

Was there any wonder, then, that some men should lose heart? Did not such defects portend—nay, invite disaster?

Strange though it may seem, Geoffrey Engleheart was one of but two persons in England who had on that Saturday anticipated this sudden Declaration of War.

Through the hot night, without heed of the wild turbulence outside, regardless of the songs of patriots, of gleeful shouts of Anarchists, that, mingling into a dull roar, penetrated the heavy curtains before the window of his room, he sat with brows knit and gaze transfixed.

Words now and then escaped his compressed lips. They were low and ominous; utterances of blank despair.

IV

The Spy

C ount von Beilstein was a polished cosmopolitan. He was in many ways a very remarkable man.

In London society he was as popular as he had previously been in Paris and in Berlin. Well-preserved and military-looking, he retained the vigour, high spirits, and spruce step of youth, spent his money freely, and led the almost idyllic life of a careless bachelor in the Albany.

Since his partnership with Sir Joseph Vayne, the well-known shipowner, father of Geoffrey's *fiancée*, he had taken up a prominent position in commercial circles, was a member of the London Chamber of Commerce, took an active part in the various deliberations of that body, and in the City was considered a man of considerable importance.

How we of the world, however shrewd, are deceived by outward appearances!

Of the millions in London there were but two men who knew the truth; who were aware of the actual position held by this German landed proprietor. Indeed, the Count's friends little dreamed that under the outward cloak of careless ease induced by wealth there was a mind endowed with a cunning that was extraordinary, and an ingenuity that was marvellous. Truth to tell, Karl von Beilstein, who posed as the owner of the great Beilstein estates, extending along the beautiful valley of the Moselle, between Alf and Cochem, was not an aristocrat at all, and possessed no estate more tangible than the proverbial château in Spain.

Count von Beilstein was a *spy*!

His life had been a strangely varied one; few men perhaps had seen more of the world. His biography was recorded in certain police registers. Born in the Jews' quarter at Frankfort, he had, at an early age, turned adventurer, and for some years was well known at Monte Carlo as a successful gamester. But the Fickle Goddess at last forsook him, and under another name he started a bogus loan office in Brussels. This, however, did not last long, for the police one night made a raid on the place, only to discover that Monsieur had flown. An extensive robbery of diamonds in Amsterdam, a theft of bonds while in transit between Hanover and Berlin, and the forgery of a large quantity of Russian rouble notes, were events which followed in quick succession, and in each of them the police detected the adroit hand of the man who now called himself the Count von Beilstein. At last, by sheer ill-luck, he fell into the grip of the law.

He was in St. Petersburg, where he had opened an office in the Bolshaia, and started as a diamond dealer. After a few genuine transactions he obtained possession of gems worth nearly £20,000, and decamped.

But the Russian police were quickly at his heels, and he was arrested in Riga, being subsequently tried and condemned by the Assize Court at St. Petersburg to twelve years' exile in Siberia. In chains, with a convoy of convicts he crossed the Urals, and tramped for weeks on the snow-covered Siberian Post Road.

His name still appears on the register at the forwarding prison of Tomsk, with a note stating that he was sent on to the silver mines of Nertchinsk, the most dreaded in Asiatic Russia.

Yet, strangely enough, within twelve months of his sentence he appeared at Royat-les-Bains, in Auvergne, posing as a Count, and living expensively at one of the best hotels.

There was a reason for all this. The Russian Government, when he was sentenced, were well aware of his perfect training as a cosmopolitan adventurer, of his acquaintance with persons of rank, and of his cool unscrupulousness. Hence it was that one night while on the march along the Great Post Road to that bourne whence few convicts return, it was hinted to him by the captain of Cossacks, that he might obtain his liberty, and a good income in addition, if he consented to become a secret agent of the Tsar.

The authorities desired him to perform a special duty; would he consent? He could exchange a life of heavy toil in the Nertchinsk mines for one of comparative idleness and ease. The offer was tempting, and he accepted.

That same night it was announced to his fellow-convicts that the Tsar had pardoned him; his leg-fetters were thereupon struck off, and he started upon his return to St. Petersburg to receive instructions as to the delicate mission he was to perform.

It was then, for the first time, that he became the Count von Beilstein, and his subsequent actions all betrayed the most remarkable daring, forethought, and tact. With one object in view he exercised an amount of patience that was almost incredible. One or two minor missions were entrusted to him by his official taskmasters on the banks of the Neva, and in each he acquitted himself satisfactorily. Apparently he was a thoroughly patriotic subject of the Kaiser, with tastes strongly anti-Muscovite, and after his partnership with Sir Joseph Vayne he resided in London, and mixed a good deal with military men, because he had, he said, held a commission in a Hussar regiment in the Fatherland, and took the liveliest interest in all military matters.

Little did those officers dream that the information he gained about improvements in England's defences was forwarded in regular and carefully-written reports to the Russian War Office, or that the Tsar's messenger who carried weekly despatches between the Russian Ambassador in London and his Government frequently took with him a packet containing plans and tracings which bore marginal notes in the angular handwriting of the popular Count von Beilstein!

Early in the morning of this memorable day when the startling news of the Declaration of War had reached England, a telegram had been handed to the Tsar's secret agent while he was still in bed.

He read it through; then stared thoughtfully up at the ceiling.

The message, in code, from Berlin, stated that a draft of a most important treaty between Germany and England had been despatched from the German Foreign Office, and would arrive in London that day. The message concluded with the words, "It is imperative that we should have a copy of this document, or at least a summary of its contents, immediately."

Although sent from Berlin, the Count was well aware that it was an order from the Foreign Minister in St. Petersburg, the message being transmitted to Berlin first, and then retransmitted to London, in order to avoid any suspicion that might arise in the case of messages exchanged direct with the Russian capital. Having read the telegram through several times, he whistled to himself, rose quickly, dressed, and breakfasted. While having his meal, he gave some instructions to Grevel, his valet, and sent him out upon an errand, at the same time expressing his intention of waiting in until his return.

"Remember," the Count said, as his man was going out, "be careful to arouse no suspicion. Simply make your inquiries in the proper quarter, and come back immediately."

At half-past twelve o'clock, as Geoffrey Engleheart was busy writing alone in his room at the Foreign Office, he was interrupted by the opening of the door.

"Hulloa, dear boy! I've found my way up here by myself. Busy, as usual, I see!" cried a cheery voice as the door slowly opened, and Geoffrey looking up saw it was his friend the Count, well groomed and fashionably attired in glossy silk hat, perfect-fitting frock coat, and varnished boots. He called very frequently upon Engleheart, and had long ago placed himself on excellent terms with the messengers and doorkeepers, who looked upon him as a most generous visitor.

"Oh, how are you?" Engleheart exclaimed, rising and shaking his hand. "You must really forgive me, Count, but I quite forgot my appointment with you to-day."

"Oh, don't let me disturb you, pray. I'll have a glance at the paper till you've finished," and casting himself into a chair near the window he took up the *Times* and was soon absorbed in it.

A quarter of an hour went by in silence, while Engleheart wrote on, calmly unconscious that there was a small rent in the newspaper the Count was reading, and that through it he could plainly see each word of the treaty as it was transcribed from the secret code and written down in plain English.

"Will you excuse me for ten minutes?" Geoffrey exclaimed presently. "The Cabinet Council is sitting, and I have to run over to see Lord Stanbury for a moment. After I return I must make another copy of this paper, and then I shall be free."

The Count, casting the newspaper wearily aside, glanced at his watch.

"It's half-past one," he said. "You'll be another half-hour, if not more. After all, I really think, old fellow, I'll go on down to Hurlingham. I arranged to meet the Vaynes at two o'clock."

"All right. I'll run down in a cab as soon as I can get away," answered Engleheart.

"Good. Come on as soon as you can. Violet will be expecting you, you know."

"Of course I shall," replied his unsuspicious friend, and they shook hands, after which the Count put on his hat and sauntered jauntily out.

In Parliament Street he jumped into his phaeton, but instead of driving to Hurlingham gave his man orders to proceed with all speed to the General Post Office, St. Martin's-le-Grand. Within half an hour from the time he had shaken the hand of his unsuspecting friend, a message in code—to all intents and purposes a commercial despatch—was on its way to "Herr Brandt, 116 Friedrich Strasse, Berlin."

That message contained an exact transcript of the secret treaty!

Almost immediately after the Count had left, Geoffrey made a discovery. From the floor he picked up a small gold pencil-case which he knew belonged to von Beilstein.

Engleheart was sorely puzzled to know why the Count should require a pencil if not to write, and it momentarily flashed across his mind that he might have copied portions of the treaty. But the next minute he dismissed the suspicion as ungrounded and preposterous, and placing the pencil in his pocket went in search of Lord Stanbury.

It was only the statement he read in the *People* later, alleging treachery at the Foreign Office, that recalled the incident to his mind. Then the horrible truth dawned upon him. He saw how probable it was that he had been tricked.

He knew that the mine was already laid; that the only thing that had prevented an explosion that would shake the whole world had been the absence of definite knowledge as to the exact terms of the alliance between England, Germany, Italy, and Austria.

V

Bombardment of Newhaven

At sea the night was dark and moonless. A thick mist hung near the land. The Coastguard and Artillery on our southern and eastern shores spent a terribly anxious time, peering from their points of vantage out into the cavernous darkness where no light glimmered. The Harbour Defence Flotilla was in readiness, and under the black cliffs sentinels kept watch with every nerve strained to its highest tension, for the safety of England now depended upon their alertness. The great waves crashed and roared, and the mist, obscuring the light of vessels passing up and down the Channel, seemed to grow more dense as the hours wore on.

In the midst of the feverish excitement that had spread everywhere throughout the length and breadth of the land, the troops were, a couple of hours after the receipt of the alarming news in London, already being mobilised and on their way south and east by special trains. Men, arms, ammunition, and stores were hurried forward to repel attack, and in the War Office and Admiralty, where the staffs had been suddenly called together, the greatest activity prevailed. Messages had been flashed along the wires in every direction giving orders to mobilise and concentrate at certain points, and these instructions were being obeyed with that promptness for which British soldiers and sailors are proverbial.

Yet the high officials at the War Office looked grave, and although affecting unconcern, now and then whispered ominously together. They knew that the situation was critical. An immediate and adequate naval defence was just possible, but the Channel Squadron was manoeuvring off the Irish coast, and both the Coastguard Squadron and the Steam Reserve at the home ports were very weak. It was to our land army that we had to trust, and they were divided in opinion as to the possibility to mobilise a sufficient force in time to bar the advance.

Military experts did not overlook the fact that to Dunkirk, Calais, Boulogne, Dieppe, Fécamp, Havre, Honfleur, and Cherbourg ran excellent lines of railway, with ample rolling-stock, all Government property, and at the beck and call of the French War Minister. In the various ports there was adequate wharf accommodation and plenty of steam tonnage. From the brief official despatches received from Paris before the cutting of the wires, it was apparent that the French War Office had laid its plans with much forethought and cunning, and had provided against any *contretemps*. An army of carpenters and engineers had been put to work in the ports to alter the fittings of such of the merchant steamers as were destined to convey horses, and these fittings, prepared beforehand, were already in position. Four army corps had for several weeks been manoeuvring in Normandy, so that the Reservists had become accustomed to their work, and in excellent condition for war; therefore these facts, coupled with the strong support certain to be rendered by the warships of the Tsar, led experts to regard the outlook as exceedingly gloomy.

For years military and naval men had discussed the possibilities of invasion, haggled over controversial points, but had never arrived at any definite opinion as to the possibility of an enemy's success. Now, however, the defences of the country were to be tested.

Our great Empire was at stake.

The power of steam to cause rapid transit by land and sea, the uncertainty of the place of disembarkment, and the great weight of modern naval artillery, combined to render the defences of England on the coast itself most uncertain and hazardous, and to cause grave doubts to arise in the minds of those who at that critical moment were directing the forward movement of the forces.

The British public, whose national patriotism found vent in expressions of confidence in the Regular Army and Volunteers, were ignorant of the facts. They knew that two great Powers had combined to crush our island stronghold, and were eager that hostilities should commence in order that the enemy should be taught a severe lesson for their presumption.

They, however, knew nothing of the plain truth, that although the 1st Army Corps at Aldershot would be ready to move at a few hours' notice, yet it was hopeless to try and prevent the disembarkation of the French army corps along a long line of unprotected coast by the action of a land force only one-third of their strength.

So, by the water's edge, the lonely posts were kept through the night by patient, keen-sighted sentinels, ready at any moment to raise the alarm. But the dense mist that overhung everything was tantalising, hiding friend and foe alike, and no sound could be heard above the heavy roar of the waters as they rolled in over the rocks.

London, infuriated, enthusiastic, turbulent, knew no sleep that night. The excitement was at fever-heat. At last, soon after daybreak, there came the first news of the enemy. A number of warships had suddenly appeared through the fog off the Sussex coast, and had lost no time in asserting their presence and demanding a large sum from the Mayor of Newhaven.

The French first-class battery cruiser *Tage*, the *Dévastation*, the *Pothuau*, the *Aréthuse* and others, finding that their demand was unheeded, at once commenced shelling the town. Although our Coastguard Squadron and first-class Steam Reserve had mobilised, yet they had received orders and sailed away no one knew whither. The forts replied vigorously, but the fire of the enemy in half an hour had wrought terrible havoc both in the town and in the forts, where several of the guns had been rendered useless and a number of men had been killed. Hostilities had commenced.

Never during the century had such scenes been witnessed in the streets of London as on that memorable Sunday morning. The metropolis was thrilled.

Dawn was spreading, saffron tints were in the sky heralding the sun's coming. Yet Regent Street, Piccadilly, and the Strand, usually entirely deserted at that hour on a Sabbath morning, were crowded as if it were midday.

Everywhere there was excitement. Crowds waited in front of the newspaper offices in Fleet Street, boys with strident voices sold the latest editions of the papers, men continued their snatches of patriotic ballads, while women were blanched and scared, and children clung to their mothers' skirts timidly, vaguely fearing an unknown terror.

The shadow of coming events was black and dim, like a funeral pall. The fate of our Empire hung upon a thread.

Twenty-four hours ago England was smiling, content in the confidence of its perfect safety and immunity from invasion; yet all the horrors of war had, with a startling, appalling suddenness, fallen and bewildered it. The booming of French cannon at Newhaven formed the last salute of many a brave Briton who fell shattered and lifeless.

As the sun rose crimson from the grey misty sea, the work of destruction increased in vigour. From the turrets of the floating monsters smoke and flame poured forth in continuous volume, while shot and shell were hurled into the town of Newhaven, which, it was apparent, was the centre of the enemy's attack, and where, owing to the deepening of the harbour, troops could effect a landing under cover of the fire from the ironclads.

Frightful havoc was wrought by the shells among the houses of the little town, and one falling on board the Brighton Railway Company's mail steamer *Paris*, lying alongside the station quay, set her on fire. In half an hour railway station and quays were blazing furiously, while the flames leaped up about the ship, wrapping themselves about the two white funnels and darting from every porthole.

The Custom House opposite quickly ignited, and the inflammable nature of its contents caused the fire to assume enormous proportions. Meanwhile the bombardment was kept up, the forts on shore still replying with regularity, steadiness, and precision, and the armoured coast train of the 1st Sussex Artillery Volunteers, under Captain Brigden, rendering excellent service. In one of the forts a man was standing in front of a small camera-obscura, on the glass of which were a number of mysterious marks. This glass reflected the water and the ships; and as he stood by calmly with his hand upon a keyboard, he watched the reflections of the hostile vessels moving backwards and forwards over the glass. Suddenly he saw a French gunboat, after a series of smartly-executed manoeuvres, steaming straight over one of the marks, and, quick as lightning, his finger pressed one of the electric keys. A terrific explosion followed, and a column of green water shot up at the same instant. The gunboat *Lavel* had been suddenly blown almost out of the water by a submarine mine! Broken portions of her black hull turned over and sank, and mangled remains of what a second before had been a crew of enthusiastic Frenchmen floated for a few moments on the surface, then disappeared. Not a soul on board escaped.

Along the telegraph line from the signal-station on Beachy Head news of the blowing up of the enemy's gunboat was flashed to London, and when, an hour later, it appeared in the newspapers, the people went half mad with excitement. Alas, how they miscalculated the relative strength of the opposing forces!

They were unaware that our Channel Fleet, our Coastguard Squadron, and our Reserve were steaming away, leaving our southern shores *practically unprotected*!

VI

Landing of the French in Sussex

The Briton is, alas! too prone to underrate his adversary. It is this national egotism, this fatal over-confidence, that has led to most of the reverses we have sustained in recent wars.

The popular belief that one Briton is as good as half a dozen foreigners, is a fallacy which ought to be at once expunged from the minds of every one. The improved and altered conditions under which international hostilities are carried on nowadays scarcely even admit of a hand-to-hand encounter, and the engines of destruction designed by other European Powers being quite as perfect as our own, tact and cunning have now taken the place of pluck and perseverance. The strong arm avails but little in modern warfare; strategy is everything.

Into Brighton, an hour after dawn, the enemy's vessels were pouring volley after volley of deadly missiles. A party had landed from the French flagship, and, summoning the Mayor, had demanded a million pounds. This not being forthcoming, they had commenced shelling the town. The fire was, for the most part, directed against the long line of shops and private residences in King's Road and at Hove, and in half an hour over a hundred houses had been demolished. The palatial Hôtel Métropole stood a great gaunt ruin. Shells had carried large portions of the noble building away, and a part of the ruin had caught fire and was burning unchecked, threatening to consume the whole. Church steeples had been knocked over like ninepins, and explosive missiles dropped in the centre of the town every moment, sweeping the streets with deadly effect. The enemy met with little or no opposition. Our first line of defence, our Navy, was missing! The Admiralty were unaware of the whereabouts of three whole Fleets that had mobilised, and the ships remaining in the Channel, exclusive of the Harbour Defence Flotilla, were practically useless.

At Eastbourne, likewise, where a similar demand had been made, shot fell thick as hail, and shells played fearful havoc with the handsome boarding-houses and hotels that line the sea front. From the redoubt, the Wish Tower, and a battery on the higher ground towards Beachy Head, as well as a number of other hastily constructed earthworks, a reply was made to the enemy's fire, and the guns in the antiquated martello towers, placed at intervals along the beach, now and then sent a shot towards the vessels. But such an attempt to keep the great ironclads at bay was absurdly futile. One after another shells from the monster guns of the Russian ship *Pjotr Velikij*, and the armoured cruisers *Gerzog Edinburskij*, *Krejser*, and *Najezdnik*, crashed into these out-of-date coast defences, and effectually silenced them. In Eastbourne itself the damage wrought was enormous. Every moment shells fell and exploded in Terminus and Seaside Roads, while the aristocratic suburb of Upperton, built on the hill behind the town, was exposed to and bore the full brunt of the fray. The fine modern Queen Anne and Elizabethan residences were soon mere heaps of burning débris. Every moment houses fell, burying their occupants, and those people who rushed out into the roads for safety were, for the most part, either overwhelmed by débris, or had their limbs shattered by flying pieces of shell.

The situation was awful. The incessant thunder of cannon, the screaming of shells whizzing through the air, to burst a moment later and send a dozen or more persons to an untimely grave, the crash of falling walls, the clouds of smoke and dust, and the blazing of ignited wreckage, combined to produce a scene more terrible than any witnessed in England during the present century.

And all this was the outcome of one man's indiscretion and the cunning duplicity of two others!

At high noon Newhaven fell into the hands of the enemy.

The attack had been so entirely unexpected that the troops mobilised and sent there had arrived too late. The town was being sacked, and the harbour was in the possession of the French, who were landing their forces in great numbers. From Dieppe and Havre transports were arriving, and discharging their freights of fighting men and guns under cover of the fire from the French warships lying close in land.

Notwithstanding all the steps taken during the last twenty years to improve the condition of our forces on land and sea, this outbreak of hostilities found us far from being in a state of preparedness for war. England, strangely enough, has never yet fully realised that the conditions of war have entirely changed. In days gone by, when troops and convoys could move but slowly, the difficulty of providing for armies engaged in operations necessarily limited their strength. It is now quite different. Improved communications have given to military operations astonishing rapidity, and the facilities with which large masses of troops, guns, and stores can now be transported to great distances has had the effect of proportionately increasing numbers. As a result of this, with the exception of our own island, Europe was armed to the teeth. Yet a mobilisation arrangement that was faulty and not clearly understood by officers or men, was the cause of the enemy being allowed to land. It is remarkable that the military authorities had not acted upon the one principle admitted on every side, namely, that the only effective defence consists of attack. The attack, to succeed, should have been sudden and opportune, and the Army should have been so organised that on the occurrence of war a force of adequate strength would have been at once available.

In a word, we missed our chance to secure this inestimable advantage afforded by the power of striking the first blow.

There was an old and true saying, that "England's best bulwarks were her wooden walls." They are no longer wooden, but it still remains an admitted fact that England's strongest bulwarks should be her Navy, and that any other nation may be possessed of an equally good one; also that our best bulwark should be equal to, or approach, the fighting power of the bulwarks owned by any two possible hostile nations.

To be strong is to stave off war; to be weak is to invite attack. It was our policy of *laissez faire*, a weak Navy and an Army bound up with red tape, that caused this disastrous invasion of England. Had our Fleet been sufficient for its work, invasion would have remained a threat, and nothing more. Our Navy was not only our first, but our last line of defence from an Imperial point of view; for, as a writer in the *Army and Navy Gazette* pointed out in 1893, it was equally manifest and unquestionable that without land forces to act as the spearhead to the Navy's over-sea shaft, the offensive tactics so essential to a thorough statesmanlike defensive policy could not be carried out. Again, the mobility and efficiency of our Regular Army should have been such that the victory of our Fleet could be speedily and vigorously followed by decisive blows on the enemy's territory.

Already the news of the landing of the enemy had—besides causing a thrill such as had never before been known in our "tight little island"—produced its effect upon the price of food in London as elsewhere. In England we had only five days' bread-stuffs, and as the majority of our supplies came from Russia the price of bread trebled within twelve hours, and the ordinary necessaries of life were proportionately dearer.

But the dice had been thrown, and the sixes lay with Moloch.

VII

Bomb Outrages in London

On that never-to-be-forgotten Sunday, scenes were witnessed in the metropolis which were of the most disgraceful character. The teeming city, from dawn till midnight, was in a feverish turmoil, the throngs in its streets discussing the probable turn of affairs, singing patriotic songs, and giving vent to utterances of heroic intentions interspersed with much horse play.

In Trafalgar Square, the hub of London, a mass meeting of Anarchists and Socialists was held, at which the Government and military authorities were loudly denounced for what was termed their criminal apathy to the interests and welfare of the nation. The Government, it was contended, had betrayed the country by allowing the secret of the German alliance to fall into the hands of its enemies, and the Ministers, adjudged unworthy the confidence of the nation, were by the resolutions adopted called upon to resign immediately. The crisis was an excuse for Anarchism to vent its grievances against law and order, and, unshackled, it had spread with rapidity through the length and breadth of the land. In "The Square" the scarlet flag and the Cap of Liberty were everywhere in evidence, and, notwithstanding the presence of the police, the leaders of Anarchy openly advocated outrage, incendiarism, and murder. At length the police resolved to interfere, and this was the signal for a terrible uprising. The huge mob, which in the mellow sunset filled the great Square and blocked all its approaches, became a seething, surging mass of struggling humanity. The attack by the police, who were ordered to disperse them, only incensed them further against the authorities, whom they blamed for the catastrophe that had befallen our country. Angry and desperate they fought with the police, using both revolvers and knives.

The scene was terrible. The scum of the metropolis had congregated to wage war against their own compatriots whom they classed among enemies, and for an hour in the precincts of the Square the struggle was for life. Dozens of constables were shot dead, hundreds of Anarchists and Socialists received wounds from batons, many succumbing to their injuries, or being trampled to death by the dense mob. It was a repetition of that historic day known as "Bloody Sunday," only the fight was more desperate and the consequences far worse, and such as would disgrace any civilised city.

Before sundown the police had been vanquished; and as no soldiers could be spared, Anarchism ran riot in the Strand, Pall Mall, St. Martin's Lane, Northumberland Avenue, and Parliament Street. Pale, determined men, with faces covered with blood, and others with their clothes in shreds, shouted hoarse cries of victory, as, headed by a torn red flag, they rushed into Pall Mall and commenced breaking down the shutters of shops and looting them. Men were knocked down and murdered, and the rioters, freed from all restraint, commenced sacking all establishments where it was expected spoil could be obtained. At one bank in Pall Mall they succeeded, after some difficulty, in breaking open the strong room with explosives, and some forty or fifty of the rebels with eager greediness shared the gold and notes they stole.

At the Strand corner of the Square a squad of police was being formed, in order to co-operate with some reinforcements which were arriving, when suddenly there was a terrific explosion.

A bomb filled with picric acid had been thrown by an Anarchist, and when the smoke cleared, the shattered remains of thirty-four constables lay strewn upon the roadway!

This was but the first of a series of dastardly outrages. The advice of the Anarchist leaders in their inflammatory speeches had been acted upon, and in half an hour a number of bomb explosions had occurred in the vicinity, each doing enormous damage, and killing numbers of innocent persons. After the petard had been thrown in Trafalgar Square a loud explosion was almost immediately afterwards heard in Parliament Street, and it was soon known that a too successful attempt had been made to blow up the Premier's official residence in Downing Street. The programme of the outrages had apparently been organised, for almost before the truth was known another even more disastrous explosion occurred in the vestibule of the War Office in Pall Mall, which wrecked the lower part of the building, and blew to atoms the sentry on duty, and killed a number of clerks who were busy at their important duties in the apartments on the ground floor.

Through Pall Mall and along Whitehall the mob ran, crying "Down with the Government! Kill the traitors! Kill them!" About three thousand of the more lawless, having looted a number of shops, rushed to the Houses of Parliament, arriving there just in time to witness the frightful havoc caused by the explosion of two terribly powerful bombs that had been placed in St. Stephen's Hall and in Westminster Abbey.

A section of the exultant rioters had gained access to the National Gallery, where they carried on ruthless destruction among the priceless paintings there. Dozens of beautiful works were slashed with knives, others were torn down, and many, cut from their frames, were flung to the howling crowd outside. Suddenly some one screamed, "What do we want with Art? Burn down the useless palace! Burn it! Burn it!"

This cry was taken up by thousands of throats, and on every hand the rebels inside the building were urged to set fire to it. Intoxicated with success, maddened by anger at the action of the police, and confident that they had gained a signal victory over the law, they piled together a number of historic paintings in one of the rooms, and then ignited them. The flames leaped to the ceiling, spread to the woodwork, and thence, with appalling rapidity, to the other apartments. The windows cracked, and clouds of smoke and tongues of fire belched forth from them.

It had now grown dusk. The furious, demoniacal rabble surging in the Square set up loud, prolonged cheering when they saw the long dark building burning. In delight they paused in their work of destruction, watching the flames growing brighter as they burst through the roof, licking the central dome; and while the timber crackled and the fire roared, casting a lurid glare upon the tall buildings round and lighting up the imposing façade of the Grand Hotel, they cheered vociferously and sang the "Marseillaise" until the smoke half choked them and their throats grew hoarse.

These denizens of the slums, these criminal crusaders against the law, were not yet satiated by their wild reckless orgies. Unchecked, they had run riot up and down the Strand, and there was scarcely a man among them who had not in his pocket some of the spoils from jewellers' or from banks. In the glare of the flames the white bloodstained faces wore a determined expression as they stood collecting their energies for some other atrocious outrage against their so-called enemies, the rich.

At the first menace of excesses, dwellers in the locality had left their houses and fled headlong for safety to other parts of the city. The majority escaped, but many fell into the hands of the rioters, and were treated with scant humanity. Men and women were struck down and robbed, even strangled or shot if they resisted. The scene was frightful—a terrible realisation of Anarchist prophecies that had rendered the authorities absolutely helpless. On the one hand, an enemy had landed on our shores with every chance of a successful march to London, while on the other the revolutionary spirit had broken out unmistakably among the criminal class, and lawlessness and murder were everywhere rife.

The homes of the people were threatened by double disaster—by the attack of both enemy and "friend." The terrible bomb outrages and their appalling results had completely disorganised the police, and although reinforcements had been telegraphed for from every division in London, the number of men mustered at Scotland Yard was not yet sufficient to deal effectually with the irate and rapidly increasing mob.

As evening wore on the scenes in the streets around the Square were terrible. Pall Mall was congested by the angry mob who were wrecking the clubs, when suddenly the exultant cries were succeeded by terrified shrieks mingled with fierce oaths. Each man fought with his neighbour, and many men and women, crushed against iron railings, stood half suffocated and helpless. The National Gallery was burning fiercely, flames from the great burning pile shot high in the air, illuminating everything with their flood of crimson light, and the wind, blowing down the crowded thoroughfare, carried smoke, sparks, and heat with it.

Distant shrieks were heard in the direction of the Square, and suddenly the crowd surged wildly forward. Gaol-birds from the purlieus of Drury Lane robbed those who had valuables or money upon them, and committed brutal assaults upon the unprotected. A moment later, however, there was a flash, and the deafening sound of firearms at close quarters was followed by the horrified shrieks of the yelling mob. Again and again the sound was repeated. Around them bullets whistled, and men and women fell forward dead and wounded with terrible curses upon their lips.

The 10th Hussars had just arrived from Hounslow, and having received hurried orders to clear away the rioters, were shooting them down like dogs, without mercy. On every hand cries of agony and despair rose above the tumult. Then a silence followed, for the street was thickly strewn with corpses.

VIII

Fateful Days for the Old Flag

A cloudy moonless night, with a gusty wind which now and then swept the tops of the forest trees, causing the leaves to surge like a summer sea.

Withered branches creaked and groaned, and a dog howled dismally down in Flimwell village, half a mile away. Leaning with his back against the gnarled trunk of a giant oak on the edge of the forest, his ears alert for the slightest sound, his hand upon his loaded magazine rifle, Geoffrey Engleheart stood on outpost duty. Dressed in a rough shooting suit, with a deerstalker hat and an improvised kit strapped upon his back, he was half hidden by the tall bracken. Standing motionless in the deep shadow, with his eyes fixed upon the wide stretch of sloping meadows, he waited, ready, at the slightest appearance of the enemy's scouts, to raise the alarm and call to arms those who were sleeping in the forest after their day's march.

The City Civilian Volunteer Battalion which he had joined was on its way to take part in the conflict, which every one knew would be desperate. Under the command of Major Mansford, an experienced elderly officer who had long since retired from the Lancashire Regiment, but who had at once volunteered to lead the battalion of young patriots, they had left London by train for Maidstone, whence they marched by way of Linton, Marden, and Goudhurst to Frith Wood, where they had bivouacked for the night on the Sussex border.

It was known that Russian scouts had succeeded in getting as far as Wadhurst, and it was expected that one of the French reconnoitring parties must, in their circuitous survey, pass the border of the wood on their way back to their own lines. Up to the present they had been practically unmolested. The British army was now mobilised, and Kent, Sussex, and Hampshire were overrun with soldiers. Every household gave men accommodation voluntarily, every hostelry, from the aristocratic hotels of the watering-places to the unassuming Red Lions of the villages, was full of Britain's brave defenders. The echoes of old-world village streets of thatched houses with quaint gables were awakened night and day by the rumbling of heavy artillery, the shouts of the drivers as they urged along their teams, and the rattle of ammunition carts and of ambulance waggons, while on every high road leading south battalions were on the march, and eager to come within fighting range of the audacious foreigners.

At first the peaceful people of the villages gazed, wondered, and admired, thinking some manoeuvres were about to take place—for military manoeuvres always improve village trade. But they were very quickly disillusioned. When they knew the truth—that the enemy was actually at their doors, that the grey-coated masses of the Russian legions were lying like packs of wolves in the undulating country between Heathfield, Etchingham, and the sea—they were panic-stricken and appalled. They watched the stream of redcoats passing their doors, cheering them, while those who were their guests were treated to the best fare their hosts could provide.

Tommy Atkins was now the idol of the hour.

Apparently the enemy, having established themselves, were by no means anxious to advance with undue haste. Having landed, they were, it was ascertained, awaiting the arrival of further reinforcements and armaments from both Powers; but nothing definite was known of this, except some meagre details that had filtered through the American cables, all direct telegraphic communication with the Continent having now been cut off.

Alas! Moloch had grinned. He had sharpened his sickle for the terrible carnage that was to spread through Albion's peaceful land.

Terrible was the panic that the invasion had produced in the North.

Food had risen to exorbitant prices. In the great manufacturing centres the toiling millions were already feeling the pinch of starvation, for with bread at ninepence a small loaf, meat at a prohibitive figure, and the factories stopped, they were compelled to remain with empty stomachs and idle hands.

Birmingham, Manchester, Liverpool, Newcastle, and the larger towns presented a gloomy, sorry aspect. Business was suspended, the majority of the shops were closed, the banks barred and bolted, and the only establishments where any trade flourished were the taverns and music halls. These were crowded. Drink flowed, gold jingled, and the laughter at wild jest or the thunder of applause which greeted dancing girls and comic vocalists was still as hearty as of old. Everywhere there was a sordid craving for amusement which was a reflex of the war fever.

The people made merry, for ere long they might be cut down by a foeman's steel.

Restless impatience thrilled the community from castle to cottage, intensified by the vain clamourings of Anarchist mobs in the greater towns. As in London, these shock-headed agitators held high revel, protesting against everything and everybody—now railing, now threatening, but always mustering converts to their harebrained doctrines. In Manchester they were particularly strong. A number of serious riots had occurred in Deansgate and in Market Street. The mob wrecked the Queen's Hotel, smashed numbers of windows in Lewis's great emporium, looted the *Guardian* office, and set fire to the Town Hall. A portion of the latter only was burned, the fire brigade managing to subdue the flames before any very serious damage was occasioned. Although the police made hundreds of arrests, and the stipendiary sat from early morning until late at night, Anarchist demonstrations were held every evening in the city and suburbs, always resulting in pillage, incendiarism, and not unfrequently in murder. In grey, money-making Stockport, in grimy Salford, in smoky Pendleton, and even in aristocratic Eccles, these demonstrations were held, and the self-styled "soldiers of the social revolution" marched over the granite roads, headed by a dirty scarlet flag, hounding down the Government, and crying shame upon them for the apathy with which they had regarded the presence of the bearded Caucasian Tcherkesses of the White Tsar.

The kingdom was in wild turmoil, for horror heaped upon horror. Outrages that commenced in London were repeated with appalling frequency in the great towns in the provinces. An attempt had been made to assassinate the Premier while speaking in the Town Hall, Birmingham, the bomb which was thrown having killed two hard-working reporters who were writing near; but the Prime Minister, who seemed to lead a charmed existence, escaped without a scratch.

In Liverpool, where feeling against the War Office ran high, there were several explosions, two of which occurred in Bold Street, and were attended by loss of life, while a number of incendiary fires occurred at the docks. At Bradford the Town Hall was blown up, and the troops were compelled to fire on a huge mob of rioters, who, having assembled at Manningham, were advancing to loot the town.

The cavalry barracks at York was the scene of a terrific explosion, which killed three sentries and maimed twenty other soldiers; while at Warwick Assizes, during the hearing of a murder trial, some unknown scoundrel threw a petard at the judge, killing him instantly on the bench.

These, however, were but few instances of the wild lawlessness and terrible anarchy that prevailed in Britain, for only the most flagrant cases of outrage were reported in the newspapers, their columns being filled with the latest intelligence from the seat of war.

It must be said that over the border the people were more law-abiding. The Scotch, too canny to listen to the fiery declamations of hoarse and shabby agitators, preferred to trust to British pluck and the strong arm of their brawny Highlanders. In Caledonia the seeds of Anarchy fell on stony ground.

In Northern and Midland towns, however, the excitement increased hourly. It extended everywhere. From Ventnor to the Pentlands, from Holyhead to the Humber, from Scilly to the Nore, every man and every woman existed in fearfulness of the crash that was impending.

It was now known throughout the breadth of our land that the Government policy was faulty, that War Office and Admiralty organisation was a rotten make-believe, and, worst of all, that what critics had long ago said as to the inadequacy of our naval defence, even with the ships built under the programme of 1894, had now, alas! proved to be true.

The suspense was awful. Those who were now living in the peaceful atmospheres of their homes, surrounded by neighbours and friends in the centre of a great town, and feeling a sense of security, might within a few days be shot down by French rifles, or mowed down brutally by gleaming Cossack *shushkas*. The advance of the enemy was expected daily, hourly; and the people in the North waited, staggered, breathless, and terrified. Men eagerly scanned the newspapers; women pressed their children to their breasts.

In the mining districts the shock had not inspired the same amount of fear as at the ports and in the manufacturing centres. Possibly it was because work was still proceeding in the pits, and constant work prevents men from becoming restless, or troubling themselves about a nation's woes. Toilers who worked below knew that foreign invaders had landed, and that the Militia and Volunteers had been called out, but they vaguely believed that, the seat of war being away down south—a very long distance in the imagination of most of them—everything would be over before they could be called upon to take part in the struggle. In any case coal and iron must be got, they argued, and while they had work they had little time for uneasiness. Nevertheless, great numbers of stalwart young miners enrolled themselves in the local Volunteer corps, and burned to avenge the affront to their country and their sovereign.

Those were indeed fateful, ever-to-be-remembered days.

Amid this weary, anxious watching, this constant dread of what might next occur, an item of news was circulated which caused the greatest rejoicing everywhere. Intelligence reached New York, by cable from France, that Germany had combined with England against the Franco-Russian alliance, that her vast army had been mobilised, and that already the brave, well-drilled legions of the Emperor William had crossed the Vosges, and passed the frontier into France. A sharp battle had been fought near Givet, and that, as well as several other French frontier towns which fell in 1870, were again in the hands of the Germans.

How different were German methods to those of the British!

With a perfect scheme of attack, every detail of which had been long thought out, and which worked without a hitch, the Kaiser's forces were awaiting the word of command to march onward—to Paris. For years—ever since they taught France that severe lesson in the last disastrous war—it had been the ambition of every German cavalryman to clink his spurs on the asphalte of the Boulevards. Now they were actually on their way towards their goal!

The papers were full of these latest unexpected developments, the details of which, necessarily meagre owing to the lack of direct communication, were eagerly discussed. It was believed that Germany would, in addition to defending her Polish frontier and attacking France, also send a naval squadron from Kiel to England.

The Tsar's spy had been foiled, and Russia and France now knew they had made a false move! Russia's rapid and decisive movement was intended to prevent the signing of the secret alliance, and to bar England and Germany from joining hands. But happily the sly machinations of the Count von Beilstein, the released convict and adventurer, had in a measure failed, for Germany had considered it diplomatic to throw in her fortune with Great Britain in this desperate encounter.

A feeling of thankfulness spread through the land. Nevertheless, it was plain that if Germany intended to wield the double-handled sword of conquest in France, she would have few troops to spare to send to England.

WILLIAM LE QUEUX

But those dark days, full of agonising suspense, dragged on slowly. The French well knew the imminent danger that threatened their own country, yet they could not possibly withdraw. Mad enthusiasts always!

It must be war to the death, they decided. The conflict could not be averted. So Britons unsheathed their steel, and held themselves in readiness for a fierce and desperate fray.

The invasion had indeed been planned by our enemies with marvellous forethought and cunning. There was treachery in the Intelligence Department of the British Admiralty, foul treachery which placed our country at the mercy of the invader, and sacrificed thousands of lives. On the morning following the sudden Declaration of War, the officer in charge of the telegraph bureau at Whitehall, whose duty it had been to send the telegrams ordering the naval mobilisation, was found lying dead beside the telegraph instrument—stabbed to the heart! Inquiries were made, and it was found that one of the clerks, a young Frenchman who had been taken on temporarily at a low salary, was missing. It was further discovered that the murder had been committed hours before, immediately the Mobilisation Orders had been sent; further, that fictitious telegrams had been despatched cancelling them, and ordering the Channel Fleet away to the Mediterranean, the Coastguard Squadron to Land's End, and the first-class Reserve ships to proceed to the North of Scotland in search of the enemy! Thus, owing to these orders sent by the murderer, England was left unprotected.

Immediately the truth was known efforts were made to cancel the forged orders. But, alas! it was too late. Our Fleets had already sailed!

IX

Count Von Beilstein at Home

Karl von Beilstein sat in his own comfortable saddlebag-chair, in his chambers in the Albany, lazily twisting a cigarette.

On a table at his elbow was spread sheet 319 of the Ordnance Survey Map of England, which embraced that part of Sussex where the enemy were encamped. With red and blue pencils he had been making mystic marks upon it, and had at last laid it aside with a smile of satisfaction.

"She thought she had me in her power," he muttered ominously to himself. "The wolf! If she knew everything, she could make me crave again at her feet for mercy. Happily she is in ignorance; therefore that trip to a more salubrious climate that I anticipated is for the present postponed. I have silenced her, and am still master of the situation— still the agent of the Tsar!" Uttering a low laugh, he gave his cigarette a final twist, and then regarded it critically.

The door opened to admit his valet, Grevel.

"A message from the Embassy. The man is waiting," he said.

His master opened the note which was handed to him, read it with contracted brows, and said—

"Tell him that the matter shall be arranged as quickly as possible."

"Nothing else?"

"Nothing. I am leaving London, and shall not be back for a week— perhaps longer."

With a slight yawn he rose and passed into his dressing-room, while his servant went to deliver his message to the man in waiting. The note had produced a marked effect upon the spy. It was an order from his taskmasters in St. Petersburg. He knew it must be obeyed. Every moment was of vital consequence in carrying out the very delicate mission intrusted to him, a mission which it would require all his tact and cunning to execute.

In a quarter of an hour he emerged into his sitting-room again, so completely disguised that even his most intimate acquaintances would have failed to recognise him. Attired in rusty black, with clean shaven face and walking with a scholarly stoop, he had transformed himself from the foppish man-about-town to a needy country parson, whose cheap boots were down at heel, and in the lappel of whose coat was displayed a piece of worn and faded blue.

"Listen, Pierre," he said to his man, who entered at his summons. "While I am away keep your eyes and ears open. If there is a shadow of suspicion in any quarter, burn all my papers, send me warning through the Embassy, and clear out yourself without delay. Should matters assume a really dangerous aspect, you must get down to the Russian lines, where they will pass you through, and put you on board one of our ships."

"Has the Ministry at Petersburg promised us protection at last?"

"Yes; we have nothing to fear. When the game is up among these lambs, we shall calmly go over to the other side and witness the fun."

"In what direction are you now going?"

"I don't know," replied the spy, as he unlocked a drawer in a small cabinet in a niche by the fireplace and took from it a long Circassian knife. Drawing the bright blade from its leathern sheath, he felt its keen double edge with his fingers.

It was like a razor.

"A desperate errand—eh?" queried the valet, with a grin, noticing how carefully the Count placed the murderous weapon in his inner pocket.

"Yes," he answered. "Desperate. A word sometimes means death."

And the simple rural vicar strode out and down the stairs, leaving the crafty Pierre in wonderment.

"Bah!" the latter exclaimed in disgust, when the receding footsteps had died away. "So you vainly imagine, my dear Karl, that you have your heel upon my neck, do you? It is good for me that you don't give me credit for being a little more wideawake, otherwise you would see that you are raking the chestnuts from the fire for me. *Bien!* I am silent, docile, obedient; I merely wait for you to burn your fingers, then the whole of the money will be mine to enjoy, while you will be in the only land where the Tsar does not require secret agents. Vain, avaricious fool! *You'll be in your grave!*"

Von Beilstein meanwhile sped along down the Haymarket and Pall Mall to Whitehall. The clock on the stone tower of the Horse Guards showed it was one o'clock, and, with apparently aimless purpose, he lounged about on the broad pavement outside Old Scotland Yard, immediately opposite the dark façade of the Admiralty. His hawk's eye carefully scrutinised every single person of the busy throng entering or leaving the building. There was great activity at the naval headquarters, and the courtyard was crowded with persons hurrying in and out. Presently, after a short but vigilant watch, he turned quickly so as to be unobserved, and moved slowly away.

The cause of this sudden manoeuvre was the appearance of a well-dressed, dark-bearded man of about forty, having the appearance of a naval officer in mufti, who emerged hastily from the building with a handbag in his hand, and crossed the courtyard to the kerb, where he stood looking up and down the thoroughfare.

"My man!" exclaimed von Beilstein, under his breath. "He wants a cab. I wonder where he's going?"

Five minutes later the naval officer was in a hansom, driving towards Westminster Bridge, while, at a little distance behind, the Tsar's agent was following in another conveyance. Once on the trail, the Count never left his quarry. Crossing the bridge, they drove on rapidly through the crowded, turbulent streets of South London to the Elephant and Castle, and thence down the Old Kent Road to the New Cross Station of the South-Eastern Railway.

As a protest against the action of the Government, and in order to prevent the enemy from establishing direct communication with London in case of British reverses, the lines from the metropolis to the south had been wrecked by the Anarchists. On the Chatham and Dover Railway, Penge tunnel had been blown up, on the Brighton line two bridges near Croydon had been similarly treated, and on the South-Eastern four bridges in Rotherhithe and Bermondsey had been broken up and rendered impassable by dynamite, while at Haysden, outside Tunbridge, the rails had also been torn up for a considerable distance. Therefore traffic to the south from London termini had been suspended, and the few persons travelling were compelled to take train at the stations in the remoter southern suburbs.

As the unsuspecting officer stepped into the booking-office, his attention was not attracted by the quiet and seedy clergyman who lounged near enough to overhear him purchase a first-class ticket for Deal. When he had descended to the platform the spy obtained a third-class ticket to the same destination, and leisurely followed him. Travelling by the same train, they were compelled to alight at Haysden and walk over the wrecked permanent way into Tunbridge, from which place they journeyed to Deal, arriving there about six o'clock. Throughout, it was apparent to the crafty watcher that the man he was following was doing his utmost to escape observation, and this surmise was strengthened by his actions on arriving at the quaint old town, now half ruined; for, instead of going to a first-class hotel, he walked on until he came to Middle Street,—a narrow little thoroughfare, redolent of fish, running parallel with the sea,—and took up quarters at the Mariners' Rest Inn. It was a low, old-fashioned little place, with sanded floors, a smoke-blackened taproom, a rickety time-mellowed bar, with a comfortable little parlour beyond.

In this latter room, used in common by the guests, on the following day the visitor from London first met the shabby parson from Canterbury. The man from the Admiralty seemed in no mood for conversation; nevertheless, after a preliminary chat upon the prospect of the invasion, they exchanged cards, and the vicar gradually became confidential. With a pious air he related how he had been to Canterbury to conduct a revival mission which had turned out marvellously successful, crowds having to be turned away at every service, and how he was now enjoying a week's vacation before returning to his poor but extensive parish in Hertfordshire.

"I came to this inn, because I am bound to practise a most rigid economy," he added. "I am charmed with it. One sees so much character here in these rough toilers of the sea."

"Yes," replied his friend, whose card bore the words "Commander Yerbery, R.N." "Being a sailor myself, I prefer this homely little inn, with its fisher folk as customers, to a more pretentious and less comfortable establishment."

"Are you remaining here long?" asked his clerical friend.

"I—I really don't know," answered the officer hesitatingly. "Possibly a day or so."

The spy did not pursue the subject further, but conducted himself with an amiability which caused his fellow-traveller to regard him as "a real good fellow for a parson." Together they smoked the long clays of the hostelry, they sat in the taproom of an evening and conversed with the fishermen who congregated there, and frequently strolled along by the shore to Walmer, or through the fields to Cottingham Court Farm, or Sholden. Constantly, however, Commander Yerbery kept his eyes seaward. Was he apprehensive lest Russian ironclads should return, and again bombard the little town; or was he expecting some mysterious signal from some ship in the Downs?

X

A Death Draught

On several occasions the spy had, with artful ingenuity, endeavoured to discover the object of Commander Yerbery's sojourn, but upon that point he preserved a silence that was impenetrable. In their wanderings about the town they saw on every side the havoc caused by the bombardment which had taken place three days previously. Whole rows of houses facing the sea had been carried away by the enemy's shells, and the once handsome church spire was now a mere heap of smouldering débris. The barracks, which had been one of the objects of attack, had suffered most severely. Mélinite had been projected into them, exploding with devastating effect, and demolishing the buildings, which fell like packs of cards. Afterwards, the enemy had sailed away, apparently thinking the strategical position of the place worthless.

And all this had been brought about by this despicable villain—the man who had now wrapped himself in the cloak of sanctity, and who, beaming with well-feigned good fellowship, walked arm-in-arm with the man upon whom he was keeping the most vigilant observation! By night sleep scarcely came to his eyes, but in his little room, with its clean old-fashioned dimity blinds and hangings, he lay awake,—scheming, planning, plotting, preparing for the master-stroke.

One morning, after they had been there three days, he stood alone in his bedroom with the door closed. From his inner pocket he drew forth the keen Circassian blade that reposed there, and gazed thoughtfully upon it.

"No," he muttered, suddenly rousing himself, as if a thought had suddenly occurred to him. "He is strong. He might shout, and then I should be caught like a rat in a trap."

Replacing the knife in his pocket, he took from his vest a tiny phial he always carried; then, after noiselessly locking the door, he took from the same pocket a small cube of lump sugar. Standing by the window he uncorked the little bottle, and with steady hand allowed one single drop of the colourless liquid to escape and fall upon the sugar, which quickly absorbed it, leaving a small darkened stain. This sugar he placed in a locked drawer to dry, and, putting away the phial, descended to join his companion.

That night they were sitting together in the private parlour behind the bar, smoking and chatting. It was an old-fashioned, smoke-begrimed room, with low oak ceiling and high wainscot,—a room in which many a seafarer had found rest and comfort after the toils and perils of the deep, a room in which many a stirring tale of the sea has been related, and in which one of our best-known nautical writers has gathered materials for his stirring ocean romances.

Although next the bar, there is no entrance on that side, neither is there any glass, therefore the apartment is entirely secluded from the public portion of the inn. At midnight the hearty Boniface and his wife and servant had retired, and the place was silent, but the officer and his fellow-guest still sat with their pipes. The parson, as became one who exhibited the blue pledge of temperance in his coat, sipped his coffee, while the other had whisky, lemon, and a small jug of hot water beside him. The spy had been using the sugar, and the basin was close to his hand.

His companion presently made a movement to reach it, when the pleasant-spoken vicar took up the tongs quickly, saying—

"Allow me to assist you. One lump?"

"Yes, thanks," replied the other, holding his glass for the small cube to be thrown in. Then he added the lemon, whisky, and hot water. Beilstein, betraying no excitement, continued the conversation, calmly refilled his pipe, and watched his companion sip the deadly potion.

Karl von Beilstein had reduced poisoning to a fine art.

Not a muscle of his face contracted, though his keen eyes never left the other's countenance.

They talked on, the Commander apparently unaffected by the draught; his friend smilingly complacent and confident.

Suddenly, without warning, the officer's face grew ashen pale and serious. A violent tremor shook his stalwart frame.

"I—I feel very strange," he cried, with difficulty. "A most curious sensation has come over me—a sensation as if—as if—ah! heavens! Help, help!—I—I can't breathe!"

The mild-mannered parson jumped to his feet, and stood before his friend, watching the hideous contortions of his face.

"Assistance!" his victim gasped, sinking inertly back in the high-backed Windsor arm-chair. "Fetch me a doctor—quick."

But the man addressed took no heed of the appeal. He stood calmly by, contemplating with satisfaction his villainous work.

"Can't you see—I'm ill?" the dying man cried in a feeble, piteous voice. "My throat and head are burning. Give me water—*water*!"

Still the spy remained motionless.

"You—you refuse to assist me—you scoundrel! Ah!" he cried hoarsely, in dismay. "Ah! I see it all now! *God! You've poisoned me!*"

With a frantic effort he half-raised himself in his chair, but fell back in a heap; his arms hanging helplessly at his side. His breath came and went in short hard gasps; the death-rattle was already in his throat, and with one long deep-drawn sigh the last breath left the body, and the light gradually died out of the agonised face.

Quick as thought the Count unbuttoned the dead man's coat, and searching his pockets took out a large white official envelope bearing in the corner the blue stamp of the Admiralty. It was addressed to "Sir Michael Culme-Seymour, Admiral commanding the Channel Squadron," and was marked "Private."

"Good!" exclaimed the spy, as he tore open the envelope. "I was not mistaken, after all! He was waiting until the flagship came into the Downs to deliver it."

The envelope contained a letter accompanied by a chart of the South Coast, upon which were certain marks at intervals in red with minute directions, as well as a copy of the code of secret signals in which some slight alterations had lately been made.

"What fortune!" cried the Count gleefully, after reading the note. "Their plans and the secret of their signals, too, are now ours! The Embassy were correct in their surmise. With these the French and Russian ships will be able to act swiftly, and sweep the British from the sea. Now for London as quickly as possible, for the information will be absolutely invaluable."

Without a final glance at the corpse, huddled up in its chair, he put on his hat, and stealing noiselessly from the house, set out in the moonlight to walk swiftly by way of Great Mongeham and Waldershare to Shepherd's Well station, whence he could get by train to London.

The immense importance of these secret documents he had not overrated. Their possession would enable the Russian ships to decipher many of the hitherto mysterious British signals.

The spy had accomplished his mission!

WILLIAM LE QUEUX

XI

The Massacre at Eastbourne

Hourly the most alarming reports were being received at the War Office, and at newspaper offices throughout the country, of the rapidly-increasing forces of the invaders, who were still landing in enormous numbers. Vague rumours were also afloat of desperate encounters at sea between our Coastguard Squadron that had returned and the French and Russian ironclads.

Nothing definite, however, was known. News travelled slowly, and was always unreliable.

Mobilisation was being hurried forward with all possible speed. Nevertheless, so sudden had been the descent of the enemy, that Eastbourne, Newhaven, and Seaford had already fallen into their hands. Into the half-wrecked town of Eastbourne regiment after regiment of Russian infantry had been poured by the transports *Samojed* and *Artelscik*, while two regiments of dragoons, one of Cossacks, and many machine-gun sections had also been landed, in addition to a quantity of French infantry from the other vessels. The streets of the usually clean, well-ordered town were strewn with the débris of fallen houses and shops that had been wrecked by Russian shells. The Queen's Hotel at Splash Point, with its tiers of verandahs and central spire, stood out a great gaunt blackened ruin.

Along Terminus Road the grey-coated hordes of the Great White Tsar looted the shops, and showed no quarter to those who fell into their hands. The Grand Hotel, the Burlington, the Cavendish, and others, were quickly transformed into barracks, as well as the half-ruined Town Hall, and the Floral Hall at Devonshire Park.

Robbery, outrage, and murder ran riot in the town, which only a few days before had been a fashionable health resort, crowded by aristocratic idlers. Hundreds of unoffending persons had been killed by the merciless fire from the enemy's battleships, and hundreds more were being shot down in the streets for attempting a feeble resistance. The inhabitants, surrounded on all sides by the enemy, were powerless.

The huge guns of the *Pamyat Azova*, the *Imperator Nicolai I*, the *Pjotr Velikij*, the *Krejser*, the *Najezdnik*, and others, had belched forth their death-dealing missiles with an effect that was appalling.

The thunder of cannon had ceased, but was now succeeded by the sharp cracking of Russian rifles, as those who, desperately guarding their homes and their loved ones, and making a stand against the invaders, were shot down like dogs. A crowd of townspeople collected in the open space outside the railway station, prepared to bar the advance of the Russians towards the Old Town and Upperton. Alas! it was a forlorn hope for an unarmed mob to attempt any such resistance.

A Russian officer suddenly shouted a word of command that brought a company of infantry to the halt, facing the crowd. Another word and a hundred rifles were discharged. Again and again they flashed, and the volley was repeated until the streets were covered with dead and dying, and the few who were not struck turned and fled, leaving the invaders to advance unopposed.

Horrible were the deeds committed that night. English homes were desecrated, ruined, and burned. Babes were murdered before the eyes of their parents, many being impaled by gleaming Russian bayonets; fathers were shot down in the presence of their wives and children, and sons were treated in a similar manner.

The massacre was frightful. Ruin and desolation were on every hand.

The soldiers of the Tsar, savage and inhuman, showed no mercy to the weak and unprotected. They jeered and laughed at piteous appeal, and with fiendish brutality enjoyed the destruction which everywhere they wrought.

Many a cold-blooded murder was committed, many a brave Englishman fell beneath the heavy whirling sabres of Circassian Cossacks, the bayonets of French infantry, or the deadly hail of machine guns. Battalion after battalion of the enemy, fierce and ruthless, clambered on over the débris in Terminus Road, enthusiastic at finding their feet upon English soil. The flames of the burning buildings in various parts of the town illuminated the place with a bright red glare that fell upon dark bearded faces, in every line of which was marked determination and fierce hostility. Landing near Langney Point, many of the battalions entered the town from the east, destroying all the property they came across on their line of advance, and, turning into Terminus Road, then continued through Upperton and out upon the road leading to Willingdon.

The French forces, who came ashore close to Holywell, on the other side of the town, advanced direct over Warren Hill, and struck due north towards Sheep Lands.

At about a mile from the point where the road from Eastdean crosses that to Jevington, the force encamped in a most advantageous position upon Willingdon Hill, while the Russians who advanced direct over St. Anthony's Hill, and those who marched through Eastbourne, united at a point on the Lewes Road near Park Farm, and after occupying Willingdon village, took up a position on the high ground that lies between it and Jevington.

From a strategic point of view the positions of both forces were carefully chosen. The commanding officers were evidently well acquainted with the district, for while the French commanded Eastbourne and a wide stretch of the Downs, the Russians also had before them an extensive tract of country extending in the north to Polegate, in the west to the Fore Down and Lillington, and in the east beyond Willingdon over Pevensey Levels to the sea.

During the night powerful search-lights from the French and Russian ships swept the coast continually, illuminating the surrounding hills and lending additional light to the ruined and burning town. Before the sun rose, however, the majority of the invading vessels had rounded Beachy Head, and had steamed away at full speed down Channel.

Daylight revealed the grim realities of war. It showed Eastbourne with its handsome buildings scorched and ruined, its streets blocked by fallen walls, and trees which had once formed shady boulevards torn up and broken, its shops looted, its tall church steeples blown away, its railway station wrecked, and its people massacred. Alas! their life-blood was wet upon the pavements.

The French and Russian legions, ever increasing, covered the hills. The heavy guns of the French artillery and the lighter but more deadly machine guns of the Russians had already been placed in position, and were awaiting the order to move north and commence the assault on London.

It was too late! Nothing could now be done to improve the rotten state of our defences. The invasion had begun, and Britain, handicapped alike on land and on sea, must arm and fight to the death.

By Tuesday night, three days after the Declaration of War, two French and half a Russian army corps, amounting to 90,000 officers and men, with 10,000 horses and 1500 guns and waggons, had landed, in addition to which reinforcements constantly arrived from the French Channel and Russian Baltic ports, until the number of the enemy on English soil was estimated at over 300,000.

The overwhelming descent on our shores had been secretly planned by the enemy with great forethought, every detail having been most carefully arranged. The steam tonnage in the French harbours was ample and to spare, for many of the vessels, being British, had been at once seized on the outbreak of hostilities. The sudden interruption of the mail and telegraphic services between the two countries left us in total ignorance of the true state of affairs. Nevertheless, for weeks an army of carpenters and engineers had been at work preparing the necessary fittings, which were afterwards placed in position on board the ships destined to convey horses and men to England.

In order to deceive the other Powers, a large number of military transport vessels had been fitted out at Brest for a bogus expedition to Dahomey. These ships actually put to sea on the day previous to the Declaration of War, and on Saturday night, at the hour when the news reached Britain, they had already embarked guns, horses, and waggons at the Channel ports. Immediately after the Tsar's manifesto had been issued the Russian Volunteer Fleet was mobilised, and transports which had long been held in readiness in the Baltic harbours embarked men and guns, and, one after another, steamed away for England without the slightest confusion or any undue haste.

XII

In the Eagle's Talons

M any British military and naval writers had ridiculed the idea of a surprise invasion without any attempt on the part of the enemy to gain more than a partial and temporary control of the Channel. Although an attack on territory without having previously command of the sea had generally been foredoomed to failure, it had been long ago suggested by certain military officers in the course of lectures at the United Service Institution, that under certain conditions such invasion was possible, and that France might ere long be ruled by some ambitious soldier who might be tempted to try a sudden dash on *le perfide Albion*. They pointed out that at worst it would entail on France the loss of three or four army corps, a loss no greater than she would suffer in one short land campaign. But alas! at that time very little notice was taken of such criticisms and illustrations, for Britons had always been prone to cast doubts upon the power of other nations to convey troops by sea, to embark them, or to land them. Thus the many suggestions directed towards increasing the mobility and efficiency of the Army were, like other warnings, cast aside, the prevailing opinion in the country being that sudden invasion was an absolute impossibility.

Predictions of prophets that had so long been scorned, derided, and disregarded by an apathetic British public were rapidly being fulfilled. Coming events had cast dark shadows that had been unheeded, and now the unexpected bursting of the war cloud produced panic through our land.

General Sir Archibald Alison struck an alarming note of warning when he wrote in *Blackwood* in December 1893: "No one can look carefully into the present state of Europe without feeling convinced that it cannot continue long in its present condition. Every country is maintaining an armed force out of all proportion to its resources and population, and the consequent strain upon its monetary system and its industrial population is ever increasing, and must sooner or later become unbearable."

It had never been sufficiently impressed upon the British public, that when mobilised for war, and with all the Reserves called out,

Russia had at her command 2,722,000 officers and men, while France could put 2,715,000 into the field, making a total force of the Franco-Russian Armies of 5,437,000 men, with 9920 field guns and 1,480,000 horses.

This well-equipped force was almost equal to the combined Armies of the Triple Alliance, Germany possessing 2,441,000, Austria 1,590,000, and Italy 1,909,000, a total of 5,940,000 officers and men, with 8184 field guns and 813,996 horses.

Beside these enormous totals, how ridiculously small appeared the British Army, with its Regular forces at home and abroad amounting to only 211,600 of all ranks, 225,400 Volunteers, and 74,000 Reserves, or 511,000 fighting men! Of these, only 63,000 Regulars remained in England and Wales, therefore our Reserves and Volunteers were the chief defenders of our homes.

What a mere handful they appeared side by side with these huge European Armies!

Was it not surprising that in such circumstances the constant warnings regarding the weakness of our Navy—the force upon which the very life of our Empire depended—should have been unheeded by the too confident public?

When we were told plainly by a well-known authority that the number of our war vessels was miserably inadequate, that we were 10,000 men and 1000 officers short, and, among other things, that a French cruiser had, for all practical purposes, three times the fighting efficiency of an English cruiser, no one troubled. Nor was any one aroused from his foolishly apathetic confidence in British supremacy at sea. True, our Navy was strengthened to a certain extent in 1894, but hard facts, solemn warnings, gloomy forebodings, all were, alas! cast aside among the "scares" which crop up periodically in the press during a Parliamentary recess, and which, on the hearing of a murder trial, or a Society scandal, at once fizzle out and are dismissed for ever.

On this rude awakening to the seriousness of the situation, Service men now remembered distinctly the prophetic words of the few students of probable invasion. Once they had regarded them as based on wild improbabilities, but now they admitted that the facts were as represented, and that critics had foreseen catastrophe.

Already active steps had been taken towards the defence of London.

Notwithstanding the serious defects in the mobilisation scheme, the 1st Army Corps, formed at Aldershot under Sir Evelyn Wood, and three cavalry brigades, were now in the field, while the other army corps were being rapidly conveyed southwards.

Independently of the Field Army, the Volunteers had mobilised, and were occupying the lines north and south of the metropolis. This force of Volunteer infantry consisted of 108,300 officers and men, of whom 73,000, with 212 guns, were placed on the line south of the Thames.

It stretched along the hills from Guildford in Surrey to Halstead in Kent, with intermediate concentration points at Box Hill and Caterham. At the latter place an efficient garrison had been established, consisting of 4603 of all ranks of the North London Brigade, 4521 of the West London, 5965 of the South London, 5439 of the Surrey, and 6132 of the Lancashire and Cheshire. This force was backed by eleven 16-pounder batteries of the 1st Norfolk from Yarmouth, the 1st Sussex from Brighton, the 1st Newcastle and the 2nd Durham from Seaham, and ten 40-pounder batteries of the 3rd and 6th Lancashire from Liverpool, the 9th Lancashire from Bolton, the 1st Cheshire from Chester, the 1st Cinque Ports from Dover, and the 2nd Cinque Ports from St. Leonards. At Halstead, on the left flank, there were massed about 20,470 Volunteer infantry, these being made up of the South Wales Brigade 4182, Welsh Border 5192, the North Midland 5225, and the South Midland 5970. The eleven 16-pounder batteries came from the Woolwich Arsenal, Monmouth, Shropshire, and Stafford Corps, and five 40-pounder batteries from the Preston Corps.

To Guildford 4471 infantry in the Home Counties Brigade and 4097 in the Western Counties were assigned, while the guns consisted of four 40-pounder batteries from the York and Leeds Corps, the 16-pounder batteries of the Fife, Highland, and Midlothian Corps being unable, as yet, to get south on account of the congested state of all the northern railways.

For this same reason, too, the force at Box Hill, the remaining post in the south line of defence, was a very weak one. To this the Volunteers assigned were mostly Scottish.

Of the Glasgow Brigade 8000 of all ranks arrived, with 4000 from the South of Scotland Brigade; but the Highland Brigade of 4400 men, all enthusiastically patriotic, and the 16-pounder batteries from Ayr and Lanark, were compelled, to their chagrin, to wait at their headquarters for several days before the railways—every resource of which was strained to their utmost limits—could move them forward to the seat of war.

The five heavy batteries of the Aberdeen and North York Corps succeeded in getting down to their place of concentration early, as likewise did the 16-pounder battery from Galloway. Volunteers also undertook the defences north of the metropolis, and a strong line, consisting of a number of provincial brigades, stretched from Tilbury to Brentwood and Epping.

The British Volunteer holds no romantic notions of "death or glory," but is none the less prepared to do his duty, and is always ready "to do anything, and to go anywhere." Every officer and every man of this great force which had mounted guard north and south of the Thames was resolved to act his part bravely, and, if necessary, lay down his life for his country's honour.

At their posts on the Surrey Hills, ready at any moment to go into action, and firmly determined that no invader should enter the vast Capital of the World, they impatiently awaited the development of the situation, eager to face and annihilate their foreign foe.

Britannia had always been justly proud of her Volunteer forces, although their actual strength in time of invasion had never before been demonstrated. Now, however, the test which had been applied showed that, with an exception of rarest occurrence, every man had responded to this hasty call to arms, and that on active service they were as fearless and courageous as any body of Regulars ever put in the field.

Every man was alive to Britain's danger; every man knew well how terrible would be the combat—the struggle that must result in either victory or death.

The double-headed Eagle had set his talons in British soil!

XIII

Fierce Fighting in the Channel

In the Channel disastrous events of a most exciting character were now rapidly occurring.

Outside Seaford Bay, Pevensey Bay, and off Brighton and the Mares at Cuckmere Haven, the enemy's transports, having landed troops and stores, rode at anchor, forming a line of retreat in case of reverses, while many fast French cruisers steamed up and down, keeping a sharp lookout for any British merchant or mail steamers which, ignorant of the hostilities, entered the Channel.

The officers and crews of these steamers were in most cases so utterly surprised that they fell an easy prey to the marauding vessels, many being captured and taken to French ports without a shot being fired. Other vessels, on endeavouring to escape, were either overhauled or sunk by the heavy fire of pursuing cruisers. One instance was that of the fast mail steamer *Carpathian*, belonging to the Union Steamship Company, which, entering the Channel on a voyage from Cape Town to Southampton, was attacked off the Eddystone by the Russian armoured cruiser *Gerzog Edinburskij*. The panic on board was indescribable, over a hundred steerage passengers being killed or mutilated by the shells from the bow guns of the cruiser, and the captain himself being blown to atoms by an explosion which occurred when a shot struck and carried away the forward funnel. After an exciting chase, the *Carpathian* was sunk near Start Point, and of the five hundred passengers and crew scarcely a single person survived.

This terrible work of destruction accomplished, the Russian cruiser turned westward again to await further prey. As she steamed away, however, another ship rounded the Start following at full speed in her wake. This vessel, which was flying the British flag, was the barbette-ship *Centurion*. Already her captain had witnessed the attack and sinking of the *Carpathian*, but from a distance too great to enable him to assist the defenceless liner, and he was now on his way to attack the Tsar's cruiser. Almost immediately she was noticed by the enemy. Half an hour later she drew within range, and soon the two ships were engaged in a most desperate encounter. The gunners on the *Centurion*, seeing the Russian cross flying defiantly, and knowing the frightful havoc already wrought on land by the enemy, worked with that pluck and indomitable energy characteristic of the Britisher. Shot after shot was exchanged, but hissed and splashed without effect until the ships drew nearer, and then nearly every shell struck home. The rush of flame from the quick-firing guns of the *Centurion* was continuous, and the firing was much more accurate than that of her opponent, nevertheless the latter was manipulated with remarkable skill.

The roar of the guns was deafening. Clouds of smoke rose so thickly that the vessels could scarcely distinguish each other. But the firing was almost continuous, until suddenly a shell struck the *Centurion* abaft the funnel, and for a moment stilled her guns.

This, however, was not for long, for in a few moments she recovered from the shock, and her guns were again sending forth shells with regularity and precision. Again a shell struck the *Centurion*, this time carrying away one of her funnels and killing a large number of men.

The British captain, still as cool as if standing on the hearthrug of the smoking-room of the United Service Club, took his vessel closer, continuing the fire, heedless of the fact that the Russian shells striking his ship were playing such fearful havoc with it. Every preparation had been made for a desperate fight to the death, when suddenly a shot struck the vessel, causing her to reel and shiver.

So well had the Russians directed their fire that the British vessel could not reply. One of her 29-tonners had been blown completely off its carriage, and lay shattered with men dead all around, while two of her quick-firing broadside guns had been rendered useless, and she had sustained other injuries of a very serious character, besides losing nearly half her men.

She was silent, riding to the swell, when wild exultant shouts in Russian went up from the enemy's ship, mingling with the heavy fire they still kept up.

At that moment, however, even while the victorious shouts resounded, the captain of the *Centurion*, still cool and collected, swung round his vessel, and turning, touched one of the electric knobs at his hand. As he did so a long silvery object shot noiselessly from the side of the ship, and plunged with a splash into the rising waves.

Seconds seemed hours. For a whole three minutes the captain waited; then, disappointed, he turned away with an expression of impatience. The torpedo had missed its mark, and every moment lost might determine their fate. With guns still silent he again adroitly manoeuvred his ship. Once again he touched the electric knob, and again a torpedo, released from its tube, sped rapidly through the water.

Suddenly a dull and muffled explosion from the Russian cruiser sounded. Above the dense smoke a flame shot high, with great columns of spray, as the guns suddenly ceased their thunder.

There was a dead stillness, broken only by the wash of the sea.

Then the smoke clearing showed the débris of the *Gerzog Edinburskij* fast sinking beneath the restless waters. Some splinters precipitated into the air had fallen with loud splashes in every direction, and amid the victorious shouts of the British bluejackets the disabled ship, with its fluttering Russian cross, slowly disappeared for ever, carrying down every soul on board.

The torpedo, striking her amidships, had blown an enormous hole right through her double bottom, and torn her transverse bulkheads away so much that her watertight doors were useless for keeping her afloat, even for a few minutes.

Partially crippled as she was, the *Centurion* steamed slowly westward, until at noon on the following day she fell in with a division of the Coastguard Squadron, which, acting under the fictitious telegraphic orders of the French spy, had been to Land's End, but which, now the enemy had landed, had received genuine orders from the Admiralty.

Compared with the number and strength of the French and Russian vessels mustered in the Channel, this force was so small as to appear ludicrous. To send this weak defending division against the mighty power of the invaders was sheer madness, and everybody on board knew it. The vessels were weaker in every detail than those of the enemy.

At full speed the British vessels steamed on throughout that day, until at 8 p.m., when about twenty miles south of Selsey Bill, they were joined by forces from the Solent. These consisted of the turret-ship *Monarch*, the turret-ram *Rupert*, the barbette-ship *Rodney*, the belted cruiser *Aurora*, and the coast defence armour-clads *Cyclops* and *Gorgon*, together with a number of torpedo boats. The night was calm, but moonless, and without delay the vessels all continued the voyage up Channel silently, with lights extinguished.

Two hours later the officers noticed that away on the horizon a light suddenly flashed twice and then disappeared.

One of the enemy's ships had signalled the approach of the defenders!

This caused the British Admiral to alter his course slightly, and the vessels steamed along in the direction the light had shown.

In turrets and in broadside batteries there was a deep hush of expectation. Officers and men standing at their quarters scarcely spoke. All felt the fight must be most desperate.

Presently, in the far distance a small patch of light in the sky showed the direction of Brighton, and almost immediately the Admiral signalled to the cruisers *Aurora*, *Galatea*, and *Narcissus*, and the new battleship *Hannibal*, built under the 1894 programme, to detach themselves with six torpedo boats, and take an easterly course, in order to carry out instructions which he gave. These tactics caused considerable comment.

The orders were to make straight for Eastbourne, and to suddenly attack and destroy any of the hostile transports that were lying there, the object being twofold—firstly, to cut off the enemy's line of retreat, and secondly, to prevent the vessels from being used for the purpose of landing further reinforcements.

Soon after 2 A.M. this gallant little division had, by careful manoeuvring, and assisted by a slight mist which now hung over the sea, rounded Beachy Head without being discovered, and had got outside Pevensey Bay about eight miles from land. Here a number of Russian transports and service steamers were lying, among them being the *Samojed* and *Olaf*, *Krasnaya Gorka* and *Vladimir*, with two smaller ones—the *Dnepr* and the *Artelscik*.

Silently, and without showing any lights, a British torpedo boat sped quickly along to where the dark outline of a ship loomed through the mist, and, having ascertained that it was the *Olaf*, drew up quickly.

A few minutes elapsed, all being quiet. Then suddenly a bright flash was followed by a fearful explosion, and the bottom of the Tsar's vessel being completely ripped up by the torpedo, she commenced to settle down immediately, before any of those on board could save themselves. The enemy had scarcely recovered from their surprise and confusion when three other loud explosions occurred, and in each case transport vessels were blown up. British torpedo boats, darting hither and thither between the Russian ships, were dealing terrible blows from which no vessel could recover. So active were they, indeed, that within the space of fifteen minutes six transports had been blown up, as well as the first-class torpedo boat *Abo*. The loss of life was terrible.

Simultaneously with the first explosion, the guns of the *Aurora*, *Galatea*, and *Narcissus* thundered out a terrible salute. The bright search-lights of the Russian cruisers and of the battleship *Navarin* immediately swept the sea, and through the mist discerned the British ships. The lights served only to show the latter the exact position of the enemy, and again our guns belched forth shot and shell with disastrous effect.

Quickly, however, the Russian vessels replied. Flame flashed continuously from the turret of the *Navarin* and the port guns of the *Opricnik* and the *Najezdnik*, while the search-lights were at the same time shut off.

At first the fire was very ineffectual, but gradually as the vessels crept closer to each other the encounter became more and more desperate.

The Russian torpedo boats *Vzryv*, *Vindava*, and *Kotlinj* were immediately active, and the *Narcissus* had a very narrow escape, a Whitehead torpedo passing right under her bows, while one British torpedo boat, which at the same moment was endeavouring to launch its deadly projectile at the *Navarin*, was sent to the bottom by a single shot from the *Najezdnik*.

The combat was desperate and terrible. That the British had been already successful in surprising and sinking a torpedo boat and six of the hostile transports was true; nevertheless the number of Russian ships lying there was much greater than the British Admiral had anticipated, and, to say the least, the four vessels now found themselves in a most critical position.

The *Navarin* alone was one of the most powerful of the Tsar's battleships, and, in addition to the seven cruisers and nine torpedo boats, comprised an overwhelming force.

Yet the English warships held their own, pouring forth an incessant fire. Each gun's crew knew they were face to face with death, but, inspired by the coolness of their officers, they worked on calmly and indefatigably. Many of their shots went home with frightful effect. One shell which burst over the magazine of the *Lieut. Iljin* ripped up her deck and caused severe loss of life, while in the course of half an hour one of the heavy turret guns of the *Navarin* had been disabled, and two more Russian torpedo boats sunk. Our torpedo boat destroyers operating on the Channel seaboard were performing excellent work, the *Havock*, *Shark*, *Hornet*, *Dart*, *Bruiser*, *Hasty*, *Teaser*, *Janus*, *Surly*, and *Porcupine* all being manoeuvred with splendid success. Several, however, were lost while sweeping out the enemy's torpedo boat shelters, including the *Ardent*, *Charger*, *Boxer*, and *Rocket*.

But the British vessels were now suffering terribly, hemmed in as they were by the enemy, with shells falling upon them every moment, and their decks swept by the withering fire of machine guns. Suddenly, after a shell had burst in the stern of the *Aurora*, she ceased firing and swung round, almost colliding with the *Narcissus*. Her steam steering-gear had, alas! been broken by the shot, and for a few moments her officers lost control over her.

A Russian torpedo boat in shelter behind the *Navarin*, now seeing its chance, darted out and launched its projectile.

The officers of the *Aurora*, aware of their danger, seemed utterly powerless to avert it. It was a terrible moment. A few seconds later the torpedo struck, the cruiser rose as if she had ridden over a volcano, and then, as she gradually settled down, the dark sea rolled over as gallant a crew as ever sailed beneath the White Ensign.

Immediately afterwards the *Navarin* exchanged rapid signals with a number of ships which were approaching with all speed from the direction of Hastings, and the captains of the three remaining British vessels saw that they had fallen into a trap.

The *Narcissus* had been drawn between two fires. Both her funnels had been shot away, two of her broadside guns were useless, and she had sustained damage to her engines; nevertheless, her captain, with the dogged perseverance of a British sailor, continued the desperate combat. With the first flush of dawn the fog had lifted, but there was scarcely sufficient wind to spread out the British ensign, which still waved with lazy defiance.

On one side of her was the ponderous *Navarin*, from the turret of which shells were projected with monotonous regularity, while on the other the British cruiser was attacked vigorously by the *Najezdnik*. The *Narcissus*, however, quickly showed the Russians what she could do against such overwhelming odds, for presently she sent a shot from one of her 20-ton guns right under the turret of the *Navarin*, causing a most disastrous explosion on board that vessel, while, at the same time, her 6-inch breechloaders pounded away at her second antagonist, and sank a torpedo boat manoeuvring near.

Both the *Galatea* and the *Hannibal* were in an equally serious predicament. The enemy's torpedo boats swarmed around them, while the cruisers *Opricnik*, *Admiral Korniloff*, *Rynda*, and several other vessels, kept up a hot, incessant fire, which was returned energetically by the British vessels.

The sight was magnificent, appalling! In the spreading dawn, the great ships manoeuvring smartly, each strove to obtain points of vantage, and vied with each other in their awful work of destruction. The activity of the British torpedo boats, darting here and there, showed that those who manned them were utterly reckless of their lives. As they sped about, it was indeed marvellous how they escaped destruction, for the Russians had more than double the number of boats, and their speed was quite equal to our own.

Nevertheless the British boats followed up their successes by other brilliant deeds of daring, for one of them, with a sudden dash, took the *Rynda* off her guard, and sent a torpedo at her with awful result, while a few moments later two terrific explosions sounded almost simultaneously above the thunder of the guns, and it was then seen that the unprotected cruiser *Asia*, and the last remaining transport the *Krasnaya Gorka*, were both sinking.

It was a ghastly spectacle.

Hoarse despairing shrieks went up from hundreds of Russian sailors who fought and struggled for life in the dark rolling waters, and three British torpedo boats humanely rescued a great number of them. Many, however, sank immediately with their vessels, while some strong swimmers struck out for the distant shore. Yet, without exception, all these succumbed to exhaustion ere they could reach the land, and the long waves closed over them as they threw up their arms and sank into the deep.

During the first few minutes following this sudden disaster to the enemy the firing ceased, and the *Navarin* ran up signals. This action attracted the attention of the officers of the British vessels to the approaching ships, and to their amazement and dismay they discovered that they were a squadron of the enemy who had returned unexpectedly from the direction of Dover.

The British ships, in their half-crippled condition, could not possibly withstand such an onslaught as they knew was about to be made upon them, for the enemy's reinforcements consisted of the steel barbette-ships *Gangut*, *Alexander II*, and *Nicolai I*, of the Baltic Fleet, the great turret-ship *Petr Veliky*, the *Rurik*, a very powerful central-battery belted cruiser of over ten thousand tons, two new cruisers of the same type that had been recently completed, the *Enara* and *Ischma*, with three other cruisers and a large flotilla of torpedo boats. Accompanying them were the French 10,000-ton armoured barbette-ship *Magenta*, the central-battery ship *Richelieu*, the armoured turret-ship *Tonnerre*, and the *Hoche*, one of the finest vessels of our Gallic neighbour's Navy, as well as the torpedo cruisers *Hirondelle* and *Fleurus*, and a number of swift torpedo boats and "catchers."

The captains of the British vessels saw that in the face of such a force defeat was a foregone conclusion; therefore they could do nothing but retreat hastily towards Newhaven, in the hope of finding the division of the British Coastguard Squadron which had gone there for the same purpose as they had rounded Beachy Head, namely, to destroy the enemy's transports.

Without delay the three vessels swung round with all speed and were quickly headed down Channel, while the remaining attendant torpedo boats, noticing this sudden retreat, also darted away. This manoeuvre did not, of course, proceed unchecked, the enemy being determined they should not escape. Signals were immediately made by the *Alexander II*, the flagship, and the *Petr Veliky* and *Enara*, being within range, blazed forth a storm of shell upon the fugitives. The shots, however, fell wide, and ricochetted over the water, sending up huge columns of spray; whereupon the *Narcissus* and *Galatea* replied steadily with their 6-inch guns, while the heavy guns of the *Hannibal* were also quickly brought into play.

In a few minutes the *Magenta* and *Tonnerre* with the *Alger*, *Cécille*, and *Sfax*, started in pursuit, and an intensely exciting chase commenced. The engines of the British vessels were run at the highest possible pressure, but the French ships proved several knots swifter. As they steamed at full speed around Beachy Head towards Seaford Bay the enemy gradually overhauled them. The brisk fire which was being kept up soon began to tell, for all three retreating ships had lost many men, and the scenes of bloodshed on board were frightful.

Eagerly the officers swept the horizon with their glasses to discover signs of friendly aid, but none hove in sight. All three ships were weak, their guns disabled, with whole guns' crews lying dead around, and many of the officers had fallen. In strength, in speed, in armaments—in fact, in everything—they were inferior to their opponents, and they saw it was a question of sheer force, not one of courage.

They would either be compelled to surrender to the Tricolor, or deliberately seek the grave. With such a force bearing down upon them, escape seemed absolutely impossible.

WILLIAM LE QUEUX

XIV

BATTLE OFF BEACHY HEAD

The sun at last broke forth brilliantly, betokoning another blazing day.

Having regard to the fact that both the Channel Fleet and the reserve had been sent on futile errands by our enemy's secret agent, and the superior forces against which the British had all along had to fight, they had most assuredly shown what tact and courage could effect.

Opposite the Belle Tout lighthouse a disaster occurred to the *Narcissus*. During the fight one of her engines had been injured, and this being now strained to its utmost limit had suddenly broken down altogether, with the result that the vessel gradually slackened speed, and the *Sfax* and *Alger* bore down quickly upon her, pouring into her a heavy fire from their 5-tonners. The reply was a weak one from her quick-firing guns, her heavy arms having nearly all been disabled.

Onward steamed the *Galatea* and *Hannibal*, keeping up a running fire with the four vessels pursuing them, while the two cruisers engaging the *Narcissus* continued their strenuous endeavours to silence her guns. The British sailors, however, still undaunted, quickly showed their opponents that all the arms workable would be brought into play by directing a most vigorous fire upon their pursuers, blowing away one of the funnels of the *Alger*, and disabling one of her large bow guns.

Just then, however, while the *Narcissus* was discharging a broadside, a torpedo boat crept under her stern and sent forth its submerged projectile. For a moment there was a hush of expectation, then a dull explosion sounded as the cruiser, apparently rent in twain, plunged stern foremost into the sea, and with her ensign still flying gradually disappeared without a soul on board being able to save himself.

Meanwhile the *Galatea* and *Hannibal*, with their torpedo boats, were sustaining serious injuries from the heavy bow fire, and there seemed every possibility that they too would share the same terrible fate as the *Narcissus*, when suddenly one of the officers of the *Galatea* discovered three vessels approaching. The "demand" was immediately hoisted, and responded to by both vessels running up private signals. With an expression of satisfaction he directed the attention of the captain to the fact, for the flags of the first-named vessel showed her to be the British turret-ship *Monarch*, and those of the second the great barbette-ship *Rodney*, while a moment later it was discerned that the third vessel was the *Gorgon*.

Even as they looked, other masts appeared upon the horizon, and then they knew relief was at hand. Both vessels ran up signals, while the men, encouraged by the knowledge that some powerful British ironclads were bearing down to their aid in indented line ahead, worked with increased vigour to keep the enemy at bay.

It was a fierce, sanguinary fight. Fire vomited from all the vessels' battered works, and the scuppers ran with blood. The French vessels, having apparently also noticed the relief approaching, did not seem inclined to fight, but were nevertheless compelled, and not for a single instant did the firing from the attacked vessels cease. Their guns showed constant bursts of flame.

Soon, however, the *Rodney* drew within range. A puff of white smoke from her barbette, and the *Cécille* received a taste of her quick-firing guns, the shots from which struck her amidships, killing a large number of her men, and tearing up her deck. This was followed by deafening discharges from the four 25-ton guns of the *Monarch*, while the *Gorgon* and a number of other vessels as they approached all took part in the conflict, the engagement quickly becoming general. With great precision the British directed their fire, and the French vessels soon prepared to beat a retreat, when, without warning, a frightful explosion occurred on board the *Hirondelle*, and wreckage mingled with human limbs shot into the air amid a great sheet of flame.

The magazine had exploded! The scene on board the doomed vessel, even as witnessed from the British ships, was awful. Terrified men left their guns, and, rushing hither and thither, sought means of escape. But the boats had already been smashed by shots from the British cruisers, and all knew that death was inevitable.

The burning ship slowly foundered beneath them, and as they rushed about in despair they fell back into the roaring flames. A British torpedo boat rescued about a dozen; but presently, with a heavy list, the warship suddenly swung round, and, bow first, disappeared into the green sunlit sea, leaving only a few poor wretches, who, after struggling vainly on the surface for a few moments, also went down to the unknown.

The carnage was frightful. Hundreds of men were being launched into eternity, while upon the horizon both east and west dozens of ships of both invaders and defenders were rapidly approaching, and all would, ere long, try conclusions.

Before half an hour had passed, a fierce battle, as sanguinary as any in the world's history, had commenced. The cruisers, acting as satellites to the battleships forming the two opposing fighting lines, had quickly commenced a series of fierce skirmishes and duels, all the most destructive engines of modern warfare being brought into play.

The division of our Channel Fleet that had at last returned consisted of the powerful battleship *Royal Sovereign*, flying the Admiral's flag; the barbette-ships *Anson*, *Howe*, *Camperdown*, and *Benbow*; the turret-ships *Thunderer* and *Conqueror*; the cruisers *Mersey*, *Terpsichore*, *Melampus*, *Tribune*, *Latona*, *Immortalité*, and *Barham*; with the torpedo gunboats *Spanker* and *Speedwell*, and nineteen torpedo boats.

The forces of the invaders were more than double that of the British, for, in addition to the vessels already enumerated, the reinforcements consisted of the French battleships *Amiral Baudin*, *Formidable*, *Amiral Duperré*, *Brennus*, *Tréhouart*, *Jemappes*, *Terrible*, *Requin*, *Indomptable*, *Caïman*, *Courbet*, *Dévastation*, *Redoubtable*, and *Furieux*, together with nine cruisers, and thirty-eight *torpilleurs de haute mer*.

From the very commencement the fighting was at close quarters, and the storm of shot and shell caused death on every hand. With such an overwhelming force at his disposal, Admiral Maigret, the French commander, had been enabled to take up a position which boded ill for the defenders, nevertheless the British Admiral on board the *Royal Sovereign* was determined to exert every effort to repulse the enemy.

In the thick of the fight the great flagship steamed along, her compartments closed, her stokeholds screwed down, her four 67-ton guns hurling great shots from her barbettes, and her smaller arms pouring out a continuous deadly fire upon the French ship *Indomptable* on the one side, and the great Russian armoured cruiser *Nicolai I* on the other. Upon the latter the British vessel's shells played with a terribly devastating effect, bringing down the large forward mast and the machine guns in her fighting tops, and then, while the crew worked to get the wreckage clear, the Maxim, Nordenfelt, and Hotchkiss guns of the *Royal Sovereign* suddenly rattled out, sweeping with their metal hail her opponent's deck, and mowing down those who were cutting adrift the fallen rigging. A moment later a shell struck one of the pair of guns in the *Nicolai's* turret, rendering it useless, and then the captain of the *Royal Sovereign*, who had been standing in the conning-tower calmly awaiting his chance, touched three electric knobs in rapid succession. The engines throbbed, the great ship moved along at increasing speed through dense clouds of stifling smoke, and as she did so the captain shouted an order which had the effect of suddenly turning the vessel, and while her great barbette guns roared, the ram of the British vessel crashed into the broadside of the Tsar's ship with a terrific impact which caused her to shiver from stem to stern.

Then, as the big guns in her rear barbette thundered out upon the *Indomptable*, whose engines had broken down, she drew gradually back from the terrible breach her ram had made under the water-line of her opponent, and the latter at once commenced to sink. The force of the impact had been so great that the Russian's hull was absolutely broken in two, and as the iron stretched and rent like paper, she heaved slowly over, "turning turtle," and carrying down with her over three hundred officers and men.

The British captain now turned his attention to the French ship, which had been joined in the attack by the *Brennus*, the fire from whose 58-ton guns at close quarters played great havoc with the British flagship's superstructure. A second later, however, the captain of the *Royal Sovereign* caught the *Indomptable* in an unguarded moment, and, springing towards one of the electric knobs before him, pressed it. This had the effect of ejecting a torpedo from one of the bow tubes, and so well directed was it that a few seconds later there was a deafening report, as part of the stern portion of the French ship was blown away, raising great columns of spray.

The situation was awful, and the loss of life everywhere enormous. Dense, blinding smoke, and the choking fumes of mélinite, obscured the sun, and in the darkness thus caused the flames from the guns shed a lurid light upon decks strewn with dead and dying. The cruisers and scouts by which our battleships were surrounded cut off many of the French torpedo boats, but a large number got right in among the fleet, and some terrible disasters were thus caused. Once inside the circle of British cruisers, all fire directed at the boats was as dangerous to our own ships as to the enemy's boats.

The superiority of the French torpedo boats was, alas! keenly felt by the British, for in the course of the first hour five of our cruisers— the *Terpsichore, Galatea, Melampus, Tribune, Mersey*, the turret-ship *Conqueror*, and the battleships *Hannibal* and *Rodney*, had been blown up. As compared with these losses, those of the enemy were at this stage by no means small. The French had lost two cruisers and four torpedo boats, and the Russians one battleship, three cruisers, and six torpedo boats.

The British, with all these fearful odds against them, still continued a galling fire. The *Camperdown*, *Anson*, and *Benbow*, steaming together in line, belched a storm of shell from their barbettes, which caused wholesale destruction among the crowd of ships engaging them. Yet the withering fire of the enemy was telling terribly upon the comparatively small force of the defenders. Upon all three battleships the casualties were frightful, and on board each one or more of the heavy guns had been disabled. Suddenly a shot, penetrating a weak point in the armour of the *Anson*, entered her engine-room, disabling a portion of her machinery, while a moment later a shell from the *Amiral Duperré* fell close to her broadside torpedo discharge, and a fragment of the shell coming into contact with the striker of a torpedo, just as it was about to leave its tube, caused a terrific and disastrous explosion between the decks. The effect was horrifying. The torpedo contained over 70 lb. of gun-cotton, therefore the devastating nature of the explosion may be readily imagined. Over a hundred men were blown to atoms, and the whole six of the broadside guns were more or less disabled.

A second later, however, a shell from the *Benbow* struck the *Amiral Duperré*, carrying away the greater portion of her conning-tower, and killing her captain instantly, while almost at the same moment a torpedo from one of the British boats struck her bows with a frightful detonation, blowing an enormous hole in them. The catastrophe was complete. The crew of the doomed ship, panic-stricken, left their guns and commenced to launch the only two boats that remained uninjured; but ere this could be accomplished, the *Tréhouart*, which suddenly went astern, apparently to avoid a torpedo, crashed into her, with the result that she heeled right over and quickly disappeared.

The *Camperdown*, fighting fiercely with the *Requin*, the *Terrible*, and the *Courbet*, was suffering terrible damage from bow to stern; nevertheless her guns kept up an incessant torrent of shot, until suddenly, just after one of her shells had struck right under the turret of the *Terrible*, there was a deafening report, the air was filled with dense smoke, and the French ship, with her engines disabled, commenced to fill and sink.

A portion of the shell had penetrated to her magazine, and she had blown up, nearly half her crew being killed by the terrific force of the explosion. Many of the remaining men, however, scrambled on board the *Caïman*, which by some means had come into slight collision with her; but scarcely had the last terrified man left the sinking vessel, when the *Camperdown's* powerful ram entered the *Caïman's* bows, breaking her hull, and she also foundered, carrying down with her not only her own crew, but also the survivors of the *Terrible*.

This success was witnessed with satisfaction by the British Admiral, who nevertheless saw how seriously weakened was his force, and how critical was the position of his few remaining ships. Yet he remained quite cool, for the heavy guns of the steel monster in whose conning-tower he stood continued thundering forth their projectiles, and the White Ensign still loomed defiantly through the dense black smoke, fluttering in the freshening breeze that was now springing up.

Although a number of the enemy's vessels had been sunk, he knew the issue must be fatal to his force, for they were now surrounded by a number of ships so vastly superior to them in armament and speed, that to die fighting was their only course.

Though the cockpits were full, true British indomitable courage was showing itself everywhere on board our ships. Officers by words of encouragement incited their men to splendid heroic deeds, and guns' crews, with dark determined faces, seeing only death ahead, resolved to fight and struggle to the last for the honour of the Union Jack, which should never be surmounted by the Tricolor.

A moment later, the captain, standing with the Admiral, who had just entered the conning-tower of the *Royal Sovereign*, suddenly uttered a cry of dismay, and with transfixed, horrified gaze pointed with his finger to the sea.

Breathlessly the Admiral looked in the direction indicated.

Though one of the bravest men in the Navy, and on his breast he wore the Victoria Cross, his eyes fell upon a sight that appalled him.

It was a critical moment.

A small French vessel, the unarmoured cruiser *Faucon*, had crept up unnoticed. The attention of the British officers had been, until that moment, concentrated upon the three powerful battleships, the *Requin*, the *Dévastation*, and the *Jemappes*, which kept up their hot fire upon the flagship, causing terrible destruction. Now, however, the British Admiral saw himself surrounded by the enemy, and the sight which caused his heart to beat quickly was a distinct line of bubbles upon the water, advancing with terrific speed, showing that a torpedo had been ejected from the *Faucon* directly at his ship!

WILLIAM LE QUEUX

In the conning-tower all knew their danger, but not a man spoke. Both the Admiral and the captain at the same instant saw the death-dealing projectile advancing, and both retained their coolness and presence of mind. The captain, shouting an order, sprang back and touched one of the electric signals, which was instantly responded to.

It was the work of a second. The great engines roared and throbbed, and the huge vessel, propelled backwards by its 13,000 horse-power, swung steadily round just as the torpedo glanced off her bow obliquely. The crew of the *Royal Sovereign* had never been nearer death than at that instant. Had the ironclad not halted in her course, the striker of the torpedo would have come square upon her bows, and one of the finest vessels of the British Navy would have probably gone to the bottom.

The *Faucon* was not given an opportunity to make a second attempt. The captain of the *Anson* had witnessed how narrowly the British flagship had escaped, and immediately turned his great guns upon the little vessel, with the result that her quick-firing guns were quickly rendered useless, her hull was torn up like paper, and she slowly sank without offering resistance.

Shots came from the frowning barbettes of the *Camperdown*, *Benbow*, and the turrets of the *Monarch* rapidly, the damage and loss of life suffered by the enemy now being enormous. The three French battleships engaging the *Royal Sovereign* at close quarters received terrible punishment. One of the 75-ton guns of the *Requin* had been rendered useless, her deck had been torn up, and her bulwarks had been carried away, together with her funnel and forward mast. The rear barbette gun of the *Jemappes* had been thrown off its mounting, and a shell striking the port side battery, had burst against the forward bulkhead, and wrought horrible destruction among the guns' crews.

The three powerful French vessels pouring their fire upon the British flagship, and finding themselves being raked by the heavy fire of their adversary, signalled the *Tonnerre* and *Furieux* to assist them. Both vessels drew nearer, and soon afterwards commenced pounding at the *Royal Sovereign*.

The *Anson*, however, noticed the dangerous position of the British flagship, and, having manoeuvred adroitly, succeeded in getting under way, and with her great forward guns thundering, she crashed her ram into the *Furieux*, and sank her, while almost at the same moment a torpedo, discharged from one of the British boats, struck the *Tonnerre* right amidships, dealing her a blow from which she could never recover. Five minutes later, the *Gangut*, fighting desperately at close quarters with the *Camperdown*, had part of her armoured casemate blown away, and the British battleship followed up this success by directing a torpedo at her in such a manner that, although she drew back quickly to avoid it, she nevertheless received it right under her stern. Some ammunition on board that vessel also exploded, and the effect was frightful, for fragments of wood, iron, and human bodies were precipitated in all directions.

The loss of life, although heavy on the British side, was nevertheless far greater on board the enemy's ships. The continuity and precision of the British fire wrought awful destruction. Between the decks of many of the French and Russian ships the carnage was frightful. Among wrecked guns and mountings lay headless and armless bodies; human limbs shattered by shells were strewn in all directions upon decks slippery with blood. The shrieks of the dying were drowned by the roar and crash of the guns, the deafening explosion of shells, and the rending of iron and steel as the projectiles pierced armourplates, destroying everything with which they came in contact.

The noon had passed, and as the day wore on other catastrophes occurred involving further loss of life. One of these was the accidental ramming of the *Sfax* by the French battleship *Redoubtable*, which managed, however, to save the greater portion of the crew, although her engines broke down.

During the afternoon the fire from the British ships seemed to increase rather than diminish, notwithstanding each vessel flying the White Ensign fought more than one of the enemy's ships, and in doing so constantly received shots that spread death and destruction between the decks. Still, amid the blinding smoke, the din of battle, and the constant roaring of the guns, British bluejackets with smoke-begrimed faces worked enthusiastically for the defence of Old England. Many heroic deeds were performed that memorable afternoon, and many a gallant hero was sent to an untimely grave.

On board the *Royal Sovereign* the destruction was frightful. By four o'clock many of the guns had been disabled, half the crew had perished, and the decks ran with the life-blood of Britain's gallant defenders. The captain had been struck upon the forehead by a flying fragment of shell, causing a fearful wound; yet, with his head enveloped in a hastily improvised bandage, he stuck to his post. He was engaging the *Redoubtable* and getting the worst of it, when suddenly, having manoeuvred once or twice, he turned to his lieutenant, saying, "Lay guns, ahead full speed, and prepare to ram." The officer addressed transmitted the order, and a few moments later, as her guns thundered forth, the bows of the *Royal Sovereign* entered the broadside of the French ship with a loud crash, ripping her almost in half.

Backing again quickly as the *Redoubtable* sank, she suddenly received a shock which made her reel and shiver. A shell from the Russian flagship had struck under her stern barbette, but, failing to penetrate the armour, glanced off into the sea.

Fiercer and more fierce became the fight. A well-directed shot from one of the 67-ton guns on the *Anson's* rear barbette struck the conning-tower of the *Magenta*, blowing it away, killing the captain and those who were directing the vessel.

The sun was sinking, but the battle still raged with unabated fury. Each side struggled desperately for the mastery. The British, fighting nobly against what had all along been overwhelming odds, had succeeded in sinking some of the enemy's finest ships, and inflicting terrible loss upon the crews of the others; yet the British Admiral, on viewing the situation, was compelled to admit that he was outnumbered, and that a continuance of the struggle would inevitably result in the loss of other of his ships. There still remained three of the enemy's vessels to each one of the British. His ships were all more or less crippled, therefore a successful stand against the still overwhelming force would be sheer madness. He was not the sort of man to show the white feather; nevertheless a retreat upon Portsmouth had now become a matter of policy, and the *Royal Sovereign* a few minutes later ran up signals intimating to the other vessels her intention.

As the British Squadron moved away down Channel the hoarse exultant shouts of the enemy filled the air. But the fighting became even more desperate, and for over an hour there was a most exciting chase. The running fire did little harm to the retreating ships, but their stern guns played terrible havoc with the French and Russian torpedo boats, which were picked off one after another with remarkable rapidity.

Off Littlehampton one of the Russian ships ran up signals, and immediately the enemy's ships slackened. Apparently they had no desire to follow further west, for after a few parting shots they turned and stood away up Channel again, while the surviving ships of the British Squadron steamed onward in the blood-red track of the dying day.

At their head was the *Royal Sovereign*, battered, and bearing marks of the deadly strife; but bright against the clear, calm evening sky, the British flag, half of which had been shot away, still fluttered out in the cool breeze of sunset.

The British Lion had shown his teeth. Alas, that our Navy should have been so weak! Several of the ships had had their engines severely damaged or broken, but our margin of additional strength was so small that we had no vessels wherewith to replace those compelled to return to port.

The struggle in this, the first naval battle in the defence of our Empire, had been desperate, and the loss of life appalling.

The First Act of the most sanguinary drama of modern nations had closed.

What would be its *dénouement*?

BOOK II
THE STRUGGLE

XV

THE DOOM OF HULL

In Hull forty-eight long weary hours of anxious suspense and breathless excitement had passed. The night was dark, the sky overcast, and there was in the air that oppressive sultry stillness precursory of a storm.

Church clocks had chimed ten, yet most of the shops were still open, and the well-lighted streets of the drab old Yorkshire town were filled by a pale-faced, terror-stricken crowd surging down the thoroughfares towards the Victoria Pier. A panic had suddenly been created an hour before by the issue of an extra-special edition of the Hull evening paper, the *Daily News*, containing a brief telegram in large type, as follows:—

The Coastguard at Donna Nook report that a strong force of Russian war vessels, including the turret-ship *Sevastopol* and the barbette-ships *Sinope* and *Cizoi Veliky*, have just hove in sight and are making for the Humber. Lloyd's signal station on Spurn Point has also intimated that hostile ships coming from the south are lying-to just beyond the Lightship.

The papers sold more quickly than they could be printed, a shilling each being given for copies by the excited townspeople, who now, for the first time, suddenly realised that the enemy was upon them. Men and boys with bundles of limp papers, damp from the press, rushed along Whitefriargate, away in every direction into the suburbs, shouting the appalling intelligence in hoarse, strident tones that awoke the echoes of the quieter thoroughfares.

Now, even as purchasers of papers read the few lines of print under the dim uncertain light of street lamps, the dull booming of distant guns fell upon their ears, and the populace, wildly excited, made their way with one accord towards the Victoria Pier, to glean the latest news, and ascertain the true significance of the repeated firing.

Was Hull in danger? Would the enemy advance up the river and bombard the town? These all-important questions were on every one's tongue, and as the thousands of all classes rushed hither and thither, wild rumours of the enemy's intentions spread and increased the horror.

Within an hour of the publication of the first intimation of the presence of the invaders the excitement had become intense, and the narrow streets and narrower bridges had become congested by a terror-stricken multitude. Time after time the thunder of heavy guns shook the town, causing windows to clatter, and the people standing on the pier and along the riverside strained their eyes into the cavernous darkness towards the sea. But they could discern nothing. Across at New Holland, two miles away, lamps twinkled, but the many lights—red, white, and green—that stud the broad river for the guidance of the mariner had, since the Declaration of War, been extinguished. The familiar distant lights that had never failed to shine seaward at Salt End and Thorngumbald no longer shed their radiance, and from the revolving lights at Spurn no stream of brilliancy now flashed away upon the rolling waters of the North Sea. The buoys had been cut adrift, the Bull Lightship taken from her moorings, and the entrance to Grimsby harbour was unillumined. Not a star appeared in the sky, for all was dark, black, and threatening. Through the hot, heavy atmosphere the roar of cannon came from the direction of Spurn Point, and as the sounds of the shots fell upon the ears of the anxious watchers, they stood aghast, wondering what would be their destiny.

The suspense was awful. Men, women, and children, with scared faces, stood in groups in the market-place, in Queen Street, and in High Street, discussing the situation. This question, however, was already engaging the attention of the municipal and military authorities, for on hearing the alarming news the Mayor, with shrewd promptitude, walked quickly to the Town Hall, and held a hurried informal consultation with Mr. Charles Wilson, Mr. Arthur Wilson, Mr. Richardson, Major Wellsted, Alderman Woodhouse, and a number of aldermen and councillors. All knew the town was in peril. The enemy could have but one object in entering the Humber. Yet it was agreed that no steps could be taken at such brief notice to defend the place. The guardship *Edinburgh* had been withdrawn to form part of the squadron upon which they would be compelled to rely, with the batteries at Paull and the submarine mines.

It was evident by the firing that an attack upon the British Squadron had commenced. The shadow of impending disaster had fallen.

Working men, hurrying towards the pier, stopped their leader,

Mr. Millington, and tried to learn what was being done, while many of the leading townsfolk were thronged around for information, and were centres of excited groups in Whitefriargate. The boatmen, sharply questioned on every hand, were as ignorant of the state of affairs as those seeking information, so nothing could be done except to wait.

Women and children of the middle and upper classes, regardless of their destination, were being hurried away by anxious fathers. Every train leaving Hull was filled to overflowing by those fleeing from the advance of the Russians, and on the roads inland to Beverley, Selby, and Market Weighton crowds of every class hurried away to seek some place of safety.

Suddenly, just before eleven o'clock, the thousands anxiously peering over the wide, dark waters saw away on the bank, three miles distant, two beams of white light, which slowly swept both reaches of the river.

They were the search-lights of the battery at Paull. Scarcely had the bright streaks shone out and disappeared when they were followed by a terrific cannonade from the forts, and then, for the first time, those standing on the Victoria Pier could discern the enemy's ships. How many there were it was impossible at that moment to tell, but instantly their guns flashed and thundered at the forts in reply. Far away seaward could also be heard low booming. The enemy's vessels were creeping carefully up the Humber, being compelled to take constant soundings on account of the removal of the buoys, and evidently guided by foreign pilots who had for years been permitted to take vessels up and down the river.

Moments dragged on like hours, each bringing the town of Hull nearer its fate. The people knew it, but were powerless. They stood awaiting the unknown.

The Russian force, besides the three vessels already mentioned, included the armoured cruiser *Dimitri Donskoi*, the central-battery ship *Kniaz Pojarski*, the cruiser *Pamyat Merkuriya*, two of the new armoured cruisers, *Mezen* and *Syzran*, of the *Rurik* type, the corvette *Razboynik*, the torpedo gunboats *Griden* and *Gaidamak*, and the armoured gunboat *Gremyastchy*, with several torpedo boats.

The manner in which they had manoeuvred to pass Spurn Point and ascend the river was remarkable, and astounded the officers in the forts at Paull. They, however, were not aware that each captain of those vessels possessed a copy of the British secret code and other important information compiled from the documents filched from the body of the

Admiralty messenger by the Count von Beilstein at the Mariners' Rest at Deal!

The possession of this secret knowledge, which was, of course, unknown to our Admiralty, enabled the captains of the Russian vessels to evade sunken hulks and other obstructions, and take some of their ships slowly up the river, bearing well on the Lincolnshire coast, so as to keep, until the last moment, out of the range of the search-lights at Paull. Then, on the first attack from the batteries, they suddenly replied with such a hail of shell, that from the first moment it was clear that the strength of the fort with its obsolete guns was totally inadequate.

The roar of the cannonade was incessant. Amid the deafening explosions the townspeople of Hull rushed up and down the streets screaming and terrified. Suddenly a great shell fell with a dull thud in Citadel Street, close to a crowd of excited women, and exploding a second later, blew a number of them to atoms, and wrecked the fronts of several houses.

This served to increase the panic. The people were on the verge of madness with fright and despair. Thousands seized their money and jewellery and fled away upon the roads leading to the country. Others hid away their valuables, and preferred to remain; the crisis had come, and as Britons they determined to face it.

While the Russian ships, lying broadside-on in positions carefully selected to avoid the electro-contact mines, poured their terrible fire upon the land battery at Paull, their torpedo boats darted hither and thither with extraordinary rapidity. Several were sunk by shots from the battery, but four piquet boats in the darkness at last managed to creep up, and after searching, seized the cable connecting the mines with the Submarine Mining Station at Paull.

This was discovered just at the critical moment by means of one of the British search-lights, and upon the hostile boats a frightful cascade of projectiles was poured by the quick-firing guns of the battery.

But it was, alas, too late! The cable had been cut. To the whole of the wires a small electric battery had in a moment been attached, and as the guns of the fort crashed out there were a series of dull explosions under the bed of the river across the channel from Foul Holme Sand to Killingholme Haven, and from Paull Coastguard Station to the Skitter.

The dark water rose here and there. The whole of the mines had been simultaneously fired!

Cheers rang out from the Russian vessels, sounding above the heavy cannonade. The destruction of this most important portion of the defences of the Humber had been accomplished by the boats just at the very instant when they were shattered by British shells, and ere the waters grew calm again the last vestige of the boats had disappeared. The officers at Paull worked on with undaunted courage, striving by every means in their power to combat with the superior forces. In a measure, too, they were successful, for such havoc did the shells play with the gunboat *Gremyastchy* that she slowly foundered, and her crew were compelled to abandon her. A portion of the men were rescued by the *Syzran*, but two boatloads were precipitated into the water, and nearly all were drowned. Two of the big guns of the *Dimitri Donskoi* were disabled, and the loss of life on several of the ships was considerable. Nevertheless the firing was still incessant. Time after time the 9-ton guns of the *Kniaz Pojarski* and the four 13½-tonners of the *Mezen* threw their terrible missiles upon the defences at Paull with frightful effect, until at length, after a most desperate, stubborn resistance on the part of the British commander of the battery, and after half the defending force had been killed, the guns suddenly ceased.

Both land and sea defences had been broken down! The Russians were now free to advance upon Hull!

Not a moment was lost. Ten minutes after the guns of Paull had been silenced, the enemy's ships, moving very cautiously forward, opened a withering fire upon the town.

The horrors of that bombardment were frightful. At the moment of the first shots, fired almost simultaneously from the two big guns of the *Syzran*, the panic became indescribable. Both shells burst with loud detonations and frightfully devastating effect. The first, striking one of the domes of the Dock Office, carried it bodily away, at the same time killing several persons; while the other, crashing upon the Exchange, unroofed it, and blew away the colossal statue of Britannia which surmounted the parapet on the corner. Surely this was an omen of impending disaster!

Ere the horrified inhabitants could again draw breath, the air was rent by a terrific crash, as simultaneously flame rushed from the guns of the *Kniaz Pojarski*, the *Pamyat Merkuriya*, and the *Mezen*, and great shells were hurled into the town in every direction. The place trembled and shook as if struck by an earthquake, and everywhere walls fell and buildings collapsed.

Long bright beams of the search-lights swept the town and neighbouring country, lighting up the turbulent streets like day, and as the crowds rushed headlong from the river, shot and shell struck in their midst, killing hundreds of starving toilers and unoffending men, women, and children.

Lying off Salt End, the *Cizoi Veliky*, which had now come up the river in company with two torpedo boats, poured from her barbette a heavy fire upon the Alexandra Dock and Earle's shipbuilding yard, while the other vessels, approaching nearer, wrought terrible destruction with every shot in various other parts of the town. In the course of a quarter of an hour many streets were impassable, owing to the fallen buildings, and in dozens of places the explosion of the mélinite shells had set on fire the ruined houses.

Missiles hurled from such close quarters by such heavy guns wrought the most fearful havoc. Naturally, the Russian gunners, discovering the most prominent buildings with their search-lights, aimed at them and destroyed many of the public edifices.

Among the first prominent structures to topple and fall was the Wilberforce Monument, and then, in rapid succession, shots carried away another dome of the Dock Office, and the great square towers of St. John's and Holy Trinity Churches. The gaudily gilded equestrian statue of King William III was flung from its pedestal and smashed by a heavy shot, which entered a shop opposite, completely wrecking it; and two shells, striking the handsome offices of the Hull Banking Company at the corner of Silver Street, reduced the building to a heap of ruins. Deadly shells fell in quick succession in Paragon Street, and at the North-Eastern Railway Station, where the lines and platforms were torn up, and the Station Hotel, being set on fire, was soon burning fiercely, for the flames spread unchecked here, as in every other quarter. Church spires fell crashing into neighbouring houses, whole rows of shops were demolished in Whitefriargate, High Street, and Saville Street, and roads were everywhere torn up by the enemy's exploding missiles.

Not for a moment was there a pause in this awful work of destruction; not for a moment was the frightful massacre of the inhabitants suspended. The enemy's sole object was apparently to weaken the northern defences of London by drawing back the Volunteer battalions to the north. There was no reason to bombard after the fort had been silenced, yet they had decided to destroy the town and cause the most widespread desolation possible.

Flame flashed from the muzzles of those great desolating guns so quickly as to appear like one brilliant, incessant light. Shells from the *Cizoi Veliky* fell into the warehouses around the Alexandra Dock, and these, with the fine new grain warehouses on each side of the river Hull, were blazing furiously with a terrible roar. High into the air great tongues of flame leaped, their volume increased by the crowd of ships in the dock also igniting in rapid succession, shedding a lurid glare over the terrible scene, and lighting up the red, angry sky. The long range of warehouses, filled with inflammable goods, at the edge of the Albert and William Wright Docks, were on fire, while the warehouses of the Railway Dock, together with a large number of Messrs. Thomas Wilson's fine steamers, were also in flames. Such a hold had the flames obtained that no power could arrest them, and as the glare increased it was seen by those flying for their lives that the whole of the port was now involved.

The great petroleum stores of the Anglo-American Company, struck by a shell, exploded a few moments later with a most terrific and frightful detonation which shook the town. For a moment it seemed as if both town and river were enveloped in one great sheet of flame, then, as blazing oil ran down the gutters on every side, fierce fires showed, and whole streets were alight from end to end.

Hundreds of persons perished in the flames, hundreds were shot down by the fragments of flying missiles, and hundreds more were buried under falling ruins. Everywhere the roar of flames mingled with the shrieks of the dying. Shells striking the Royal Infirmary burst in the wards, killing many patients in their beds, and setting fire to the building, while others, crashing through the roof of the Theatre Royal, carried away one of the walls and caused the place to ignite. One shot from the 13-ton gun of the *Syzran* tore its way into the nave of Holy Trinity Church, and, exploding, blew out the three beautiful windows and wrecked the interior, while another from the same gun demolished one of the corner buildings of the new Market Hall. The handsome tower of the Town Hall, struck by a shell just under the dial, came down with a frightful crash, completely blocking Lowgate with its débris, and almost at the same instant a shot came through the dome of the Council Chamber, totally destroying the apartment.

The Mariners' Hospital and Trinity House suffered terribly, many of the inmates of the former being blown to pieces. One shot completely demolished the Savings Bank at the corner of George Street, and a shell exploding under the portico of the Great Thornton Street Chapel blew out the whole of its dark façade. Another, striking the extensive premises of a firm of lead merchants at the corner of Brook and Paragon Streets, swept away the range of buildings like grass before the scythe.

In the Queen's, Humber, Victoria, and Prince's Docks the congested crowd of idle merchant ships were enveloped in flames that wrapped themselves about the rigging, and, crackling, leaped skyward. The Orphanage at Spring Bank, the Artillery Barracks, and Wilberforce House were all burning; in fact, in the course of the two hours during which the bombardment lasted hardly a building of note escaped.

The houses of the wealthy residents far away up Spring Bank, Anlaby and Beverley Roads, and around Pearson's Park, had been shattered and demolished; the shops in Saville Street had without exception been destroyed, and both the Cannon Street and Pier Stations had been completely wrecked and unroofed.

Soon after two o'clock in the morning, when the Russian war vessels ceased their thunder, the whole town was as one huge furnace, the intense heat and suffocating smoke from which caused the Russian Admiral to move his vessels towards the sea as quickly as the necessary soundings allowed.

The glare lit the sky for many miles around. The immense area of great burning buildings presented a magnificent, appalling spectacle.

It was a terrible national disaster—a frightful holocaust, in which thousands of lives, with property worth millions, had been wantonly destroyed by a ruthless enemy which Britain's defective and obsolete defences were too weak to keep at bay—a devastating catastrophe, swift, complete, awful.

XVI

Terror on the Tyne

E ngland was thrilled, dismayed, petrified. The wholesale massacre at Eastbourne and the terrible details of the bombardment of Hull had spread increased horror everywhere throughout the land.

Terror reigned on the Tyneside. Hospitals, asylums, and public institutions, crowded with affrighted inmates, had no food to distribute. In Newcastle, in Shields, in Jarrow, and in Gateshead the poor were idle and hungry, while the wealthy were feverishly apprehensive. A Sabbath quiet had fallen on the great silent highway of the Tyne. In those blazing days and breathless nights there was an unbroken stillness that portended dire disaster.

In the enormous crowded districts on each side of the river the gaunt spectre Starvation stalked through the cheerless homes of once industrious toilers, and the inmates pined and died. So terrible was the distress already, that domestic pets were being killed and eaten, dogs and cats being no uncommon dish, the very offal thrown aside being greedily devoured by those slowly succumbing to a horrible death. Awful scenes of suffering and blank despair were being witnessed on every side.

Three days after the enemy had ascended the Humber and dealt such a decisive blow at Hull, the port of South Shields was suddenly alarmed by information telegraphed from the Coastguard on Harton Down Hill, about a mile south of the town, to the effect that they had sighted a number of French and Russian ships.

Panic at once ensued. The broad market-place was filled by a terror-stricken crowd of townspeople, while the seafaring population surged down King Street and Ocean Road, across the park to the long South Pier at the entrance to the Tyne, eager to reassure themselves that the enemy had no designs upon their town.

In the dull red afterglow that lit up the broad bay of golden sand between Trow Point and the pier, a huge vessel suddenly loomed dark upon the sky line, and, as she approached, those watching anxiously through glasses made her out as the great steel turret-ship *Lazare Carnot*, flying the French Tricolor. Immediately following her came a number of cruisers, gunboats, and torpedo boats. They included the *Dimitri Donskoi*, the *Kniaz Pojarski*, the *Pamyat Merkuriya*, the *Mezen*, the *Syzran*, the *Griden*, and the *Gaidamak*, all of which had taken part in the attack on Hull, while they had now been joined by the French battleships *Masséna* and *Neptune*, the small cruisers *Cosamo*, *Desaix*, *D'Estaing*, *Coetlogon*, and *Lalande*, the torpedo gunboats *Iberville*, *Lance*, *Léger*, and *Fléche*, and the gun-vessels *Etoile*, *Fulton*, *Gabes*, *Sagittaire*, and *Vipère*, with a large number of torpedo boats and "catchers," in addition to those which were at Hull.

As the vessels steamed onward at full speed, the people rushed from the pier back again into the town in wild disorder, while the Coastguard at Spanish Battery on the north shore of the estuary, having now discovered the presence of the menacing ships, at once telegraphed the intelligence up to Newcastle, where the most profound sensation was immediately caused. The news spread everywhere, and the people on the Tyneside knew that the hand of the oppressor was upon them.

Suddenly, without warning, smoke tumbled over the bows of the *Lazare Carnot*. There was a low boom, and one of the ponderous guns in her turret sent forth an enormous shell, which struck the battery at Trow Point, blowing away a portion of a wall.

A moment later the battery replied with their 9-tonners, sending forth shot after shot, most of which, however, ricochetted away over the glassy sea. It was the signal for a fight which quickly became desperate.

In a few moments half a dozen of the ships lay broadside on, and the great guns of the *Masséna* and *Neptune*, with those of four other vessels, opened a terrible fire upon the fort, casting their shells upon the British gunners with frightful effect.

In the battery the Armstrong disappearing guns were worked to their utmost capacity, and the shots of the defenders played havoc with the smaller craft, three torpedo boats and a "catcher" being sunk in as many minutes.

Meanwhile the *Active*, *Bonaventure*, *Cambrian*, *Canada*, and *Archer* of the Reserve Squadron, now on its way from the north of Scotland in consequence of orders from the Admiralty having reached it, rounded Sharpness Point, and steamed full upon the enemy's ships.

The conflict was fierce, but quickly ended.

Heavy fire was kept up from the fort at Tynemouth, from Spanish Battery, from Trow Battery, and from several new batteries with disappearing guns between the Groyne and the quarry at Trow, that had been constructed and manned since the mobilisation by Volunteers, consisting of the 1st Newcastle Volunteer Engineers, the 3rd Durham Volunteer Artillery, and the 4th Durham Light Infantry from Newcastle. Nevertheless the assistance received by the British ships from the land was of but little avail, for a Russian torpedo boat sent forth its messenger of death at the third-class cruiser *Canada*, blowing her up, while the engines of both the *Active* and *Bonaventure* were so seriously damaged as to be practically useless. Rapid signalling by the semaphore at Spanish Battery had placed the defenders on the alert, and although the British were suffering so heavily on account of their minority, still the enemy were everywhere feeling the effect of the hot and unexpected reception.

Before half an hour had passed two Russian gunboats had been torpedoed, and the French cruiser *D'Estaing*, having caught fire, was burning furiously, many of her crew perishing at their guns.

The *Lazare Carnot* and the *Masséna*, heedless of the fire from the shore, steamed at half speed across the estuary until they were opposite the Tynemouth Battery, when they suddenly opened fire, being quickly joined by six French and Russian cruisers. In the meantime the contact mines were being blown up by piquet boats, who, although suffering heavily from the fire from the shore, nevertheless continued their task. It was then seen how utterly inadequate were the defences of the Tyne, and what negligence had been displayed on the part of the War Office in not providing at Tynemouth adequate means of warding off or successfully coping with an attack.

From behind the tall grey lighthouse a few guns were thundering, but in face of the overwhelming force at sea it was but a sorry attempt. One shot from the battery severely damaged the superstructure of the *Lazare Carnot*, another cut through the funnel of the *Neptune*, carrying it away, and a third entering the magazine of one of the small cruisers caused it to explode with serious loss of life. Yet the devastating effect of the enemy's shells on the obsolete defences of Tynemouth was appalling.

Enclosed in the fortifications were the crumbling ruins of the ancient Priory, with its restored chapel, a graveyard, and an old Castle that had been converted into artillery barracks. As flame and smoke rushed continuously from the barbettes, turrets, and broadsides of the hostile ships, the shots brought down the bare, dark old walls of the Priory, and, crashing into the Castle, played havoc with the building. The lantern of the lighthouse, too, was carried away, probably by a shot flying accidentally wide, and every moment death and desolation was being spread throughout the fort. Such a magnificent natural position, commanding as it did the whole estuary of the Tyne, should have been rendered impregnable, yet, as it remained in 1894, so it stood on this fatal day, a typical example of War Office apathy and shortsightedness.

Its guns were a mere make-believe, that gave the place an appearance of strength that it did not possess. In the North Battery, on the left side, commanding a broad sweep of sea beyond Sharpness, only one gun, a 64-pounder, was mounted, the remaining five rotting platforms being unoccupied! At the extreme point, to command the mouth of the river, a single 5-tonner was placed well forward with great ostentation, its weight, calibre, and other details having been painted up in conspicuous white letters, for the delectation of an admiring public admitted to view the Priory. The South Battery, a trifle stronger, was, nevertheless, a sheer burlesque, its weakness being a disgrace to the British nation. In fact, in the whole of the battery the upper defences had long been known to experts to be obsolete, and the lower ones totally inadequate for the resistance they should have been able to offer.

Was it any wonder, then, that the shells of the enemy should cause such frightful destruction? Among the British artillerymen there was no lack of courage, for they exerted every muscle in their gallant efforts to repulse the foe. Yet, handicapped as they were by lack of efficient arms and properly constructed fortifications, their heroic struggles were futile, and they sacrificed their lives to no purpose. The deadly hail from the floating monsters swept away the whole of the ancient Priory walls, demolishing the old red brick barracks, blowing up the Castle gateway, wrecking the guardroom, and igniting the Priory Chapel. The loss of life was terrible, the whole of the men manning the 5-ton gun pointing seaward having been killed by a single shell that burst among them, while everywhere else men of the Royal Artillery, and those of the Tynemouth Volunteer Artillery, who were assisting, were killed or maimed by the incessant rain of projectiles.

Night clouds gathered black and threatening, and it appeared as if the enemy were carrying all before them. The French battleship *Neptune*, seeing the guns of all three batteries had been considerably weakened, was steaming slowly into the mouth of the Tyne, followed by the Russian cruiser *Syzran*, when suddenly two terrific explosions occurred, shaking both North and South Shields to their very foundations. High into the air the water rose, and it was then seen that two submarine mines had been exploded simultaneously by electric current from the Tynemouth Battery, and that both vessels had been completely blown up. Such was the force of the explosion, that the hull of the *Neptune*, a great armour-clad of over ten thousand tons, had been ripped up like paper, and of her crew scarcely a man escaped, while the cruiser had been completely broken in half, and many of her crew blown to atoms. Scarcely had this success of the defenders been realised when it was followed by another, for a second later a British torpedo boat succeeded in blowing up with all hands the French torpedo gunboat *Lance*.

These reverses, however, caused but little dismay among the invaders, for ere long the British cruisers had been driven off, the guns at Trow had been silenced, while those at Spanish Battery and Tynemouth could only keep up a desultory fire. Then, in the falling gloom, ship after ship, guided by foreign pilots, and carefully evading a number of hulks that had been placed near the estuary, entered the Tyne, pouring forth their heavy monotonous fire into North Shields and South Shields. Skilfully as the despairing defenders managed their submarine mines, they only succeeded in destroying three more of the enemy's ships, the French torpedo gunboats *Iberville* and *Cassini* and the cruiser *Desaix*, the crews perishing.

Not for a moment was there a cessation of the cannonade as the smaller ships of the enemy advanced up the river, and the damage wrought by their shells was enormous. Tynemouth had already suffered heavily, many of the streets being in flames. The tower of St. Saviour's Church had fallen, the conspicuous spire of the Congregational Chapel had been shot away, the Piers Office had been reduced to ruins, and the long building of the Royal Hotel completely wrecked. The houses facing Percy Park had in many cases been shattered, a shell exploding under the archway of the Bath Hotel had demolished it, and the handsome clock tower at the end of the road had been hurled down and scattered.

Slackening opposite the Scarp, the gunboats and cruisers belched forth shot and shell upon North Shields, aiming first at the more conspicuous objects, such as the Sailors' Home, the Custom House, the tall tower of Christ Church, and the Harbour Master's office, either totally destroying them or injuring them irreparably, while the houses on Union Quay and those in Dockway Square and in adjoining streets, from the gasometers down to the Town Hall, were also swept by shells. Resistance was made from Fort Clifford on the one side of the town, from a position occupied by a battery of the Durham Volunteer

Artillery, who had mounted guns on the hill behind Smith's Yard, and also by the submarine mines of the Tyne Division Volunteer Miners; but it was most ineffectual, and, when night fell, hundreds of terror-stricken persons had been killed, and the town was on fire in dozens of places, the flames illuminating the sky with their lurid brilliancy.

In South Shields tragic scenes were being enacted. Shells flying about the town from the river on the one side and the sea on the other exploded in the streets, blowing unfortunate men, women, and children into atoms, wrecking public buildings, and setting fire to the cherished homes of the toilers. The congested blocks of buildings around Panash Point were one huge furnace; the Custom House, the River Police Station, and the Plate Glass Works were wrecked, while a shell exploding in one of the petroleum tanks on the Commissioners' Wharf caused it to burst with fearful effect. The queer old turret of St. Hilda's fell with a crash, the Church of St. Stephen was practically demolished, and the school in the vicinity unroofed. The dome of the Marine School was carried bodily away; nothing remained standing of the Wouldhave Memorial Clock but a few feet of the square lower structure, and the Ingham Infirmary being set on fire, several of the patients lost their lives. Amid this frightful panic, Lieut.-Col. Gowans and Major Carr of the 3rd Durham Artillery, the Mayor, Mr. Readhead, Alderman Rennoldson, Councillors Lisle, Marshall, and Stainton, the Town Clerk, Mr. Hayton, and the Rev. H. E. Savage, were all conspicuous for the coolness they displayed. Courage, however, was unavailing, for South Shields was at the mercy of the invaders, and all defence was feeble and futile. Hundreds of the townspeople were killed by flying fragments of shells, hundreds more were buried in the débris of tottering buildings, while those who survived fled horror-stricken with their valuables away into the country, beyond the range of the enemy's fire.

The horrors of Hull were being repeated. The streets ran with the life-blood of unoffending British citizens.

As evening wore on, the invaders came slowly up the Tyne, heedless of the strenuous opposition with which they were met by Volunteer Artillery, who, having established batteries on various positions between Shields and Newcastle, poured a hot fire upon them. Advancing, their terrible guns spread death and destruction on either bank.

The crowds of idle shipping in the great Tyne Dock at South Shields, and those in the Albert Edward and Northumberland Docks on the north bank, together with the staiths, warehouses, and offices, were blazing furiously, while the Tyne Commissioners' great workshops, Edwards' Shipbuilding Yard, and many other factories and shipbuilding yards, were either set on fire or seriously damaged.

Many of the affrighted inhabitants of North Shields sought refuge in the railway tunnel, and so escaped, but hundreds lost their lives in the neighbourhood of Wallsend and Percy Main.

Shells fell in Swinburne's brass foundry at Carville, destroying the buildings, together with the Carville Hotel and the railway viaduct between that place and Howdon.

The Wallsend Railway Station and the Theatre of Varieties were blown to atoms, and the houses both at High and Low Walker suffered severely, while opposite at Jarrow enormous damage was everywhere caused. At the latter place the 1st Durham Volunteer Engineers rendered excellent defensive service under Lieut.-Col. Price and Major Forneaux, and the Mayor was most energetic in his efforts to insure the safety of the people. A submarine mine had been laid opposite Hebburn, and, being successfully exploded, blew to atoms the French gunboat *Gabes*, and at the same time seriously injured the propeller of the cruiser *Cosamo*. This vessel subsequently broke down, and a second mine fired from the shore destroyed her also. Nevertheless the invaders steadily advanced up the broad river, blowing up obstacles, dealing decisive blows, and destroying human life and valuable property with every shot from their merciless weapons.

The panic that night in Newcastle was terrible. The streets were in a turmoil of excitement, for the reports from Tynemouth had produced the most intense alarm and dismay. On receipt of the first intelligence the Free Library Committee of the City Council happened to be sitting, and the chairman, Alderman H. W. Newton, the popular representative of All Saints' North, formally announced it to his colleagues, among whom was the Mayor. The committee broke up in confusion, and an excited consultation followed, in which Councillors Durnford, Fitzgerald, and Flowers, with Alderman Sutton, took part. Capt. Nicholls, the Chief Constable, Major A. M. Potter of the 1st Northumberland Artillery, Lieut.-Col. Angus of the 1st Newcastle Volunteer Artillery, Lieut.-Col. Palmer and Major Emley of the Volunteer Engineers, Mr. Hill Motum, and Mr. Joseph Cowen also entered the room and engaged in the discussion.

At such a hasty informal meeting, nothing, however, could be done. The Mayor and Councillors were assured by the Volunteer officers that everything possible under the circumstances had been arranged for the defence of the Tyne. Property worth millions was at stake, and now that the news had spread from mouth to mouth the streets around the Town Hall were filled with crowds of excited, breathless citizens, anxious to know what steps were being taken to insure their protection.

So loudly did they demand information, that the Mayor was compelled to appear for a moment and address a few words to them, assuring them that arrangements had been made which he hoped would be found adequate to repel the foe. This appeased them in a measure, and the crowd dispersed; but in the other thoroughfares the excitement was intensified, and famished thousands rushed aimlessly about, many going out upon the High Level and Low Level Bridges and straining their eyes down the river in endeavour to catch a glimpse of the enemy.

Heavy and continuous firing could be heard as the dark evening dragged on, and presently, just before nine o'clock, the anxious ones upon the bridges saw the flash of guns as the invading vessels rounded the sharp bend of the river at the ferry beyond Rotterdam Wharf.

The sight caused the people to rush panic-stricken up into the higher parts of Newcastle or across the bridges into Gateshead, and from both towns a rapid exodus was taking place, thousands fleeing into the country. From gun-vessels, torpedo gunboats, and cruisers, shot and shell poured in continuous streams into the wharves, shipping, and congested masses of houses on either bank.

The houses along City Road, St. Lawrence Road, Quality Row, and Byker Bank, on the outskirts of Newcastle, suffered severely, while shots damaged the great Ouseburn Viaduct, wrecked St. Dominic's Roman Catholic Chapel, and blew away the roof of the new Board School, a prominent feature of the landscape.

Several shells fell and exploded in Jesmond Vale. One burst and set fire to the Sandyford Brewery, and one or two falling in Portland Road caused widespread destruction and terrible loss of life. The London and Hamburg Wharves, with the shipping lying near, were soon blazing furiously, and all along Quay Side, right up to the Guildhall, shops and offices were every moment being destroyed and swept away. New Greenwich and South Shore on the Gateshead side were vigorously attacked, and many shots fired over the Salt Marshes fell in the narrow thoroughfares that lie between Sunderland Road and Brunswick Street.

Upon the enemy's ships the Volunteer batteries on the commanding positions on either side of the high banks poured a galling fire, one battery at the foot of the Swing Bridge on the Gateshead side effecting terrible execution. Their guns had been well laid, and the salvoes of shell played about the French gun-vessels and torpedo boats, causing frightful destruction among the crews. Both Newcastle and Gateshead, lying so much higher than the river, were in a certain measure protected, and the high banks afforded a wide command over the waterway. At various points, including the entrances to the High Level Bridge, at the Side, the Close, New Chatham, and the Rabbit Banks, the Volunteers had opened fire, and were keeping up a terrible cannonade. The dark river reflected the red light which flashed forth every moment from gun muzzles, while search-lights from both ships and shore were constantly streaming forth, and the thunder of war shook the tall factory chimneys to their very foundations.

Heedless of the strenuous opposition, the invading ships kept up a vigorous fire, which, aimed high, fell in the centre of Newcastle with most appalling effect. In the midst of the crowds in Newgate and Pilgrim Streets shells exploded, blowing dozens of British citizens to atoms and tearing out the fronts of shops. One projectile, aimed at the strangely shaped tower of St. Nicholas' Cathedral, struck it, and swept away the thin upper portion, and another, crashing into the sloping roof of the grim, time-mellowed relic Black Gate, shattered it, and tore away part of the walls.

The old castle and the railway bridge were also blown up in the earlier stages of the bombardment, and the square tower of St. John's fell with a sudden crash right across the street, completely blocking it. From end to end Grainger Street was swept by French mélinite shells, which, bursting in rapid succession, filled the air with tiny flying fragments, each as fatal as a bullet fired from a rifle. The French shell is much more formidable than ours, for, while the latter breaks into large pieces, the former is broken up into tiny and exceedingly destructive fragments.

In the midst of this terrible panic a shot cut its way through the Earl Grey Monument, causing it to fall, many persons being crushed to death beneath the stones, while both the Central Exchange and the Theatre Royal were now alight, shedding a brilliant glare skyward.

At this time, too, the whole of Quay Side was a mass of roaring, crackling flames, the thin spire of St. Mary's Roman Catholic Cathedral had been shot away, Bainbridge's great emporium was blazing furiously, and the Art Club premises had taken fire. One shot had fallen at the back of the Town Hall, and torn an enormous hole in the wall, while another, entering the first floor of the County Hotel, had burst with awful force, and carried away the greater part of its gloomy façade.

In the Central Station opposite, dozens of shells had exploded, and it was now on fire, hopelessly involved together with the adjoining Station Hotel. The grey front of the imposing *Chronicle* building had been wrecked by a shell that had descended upon the roof, and a row of dark old-fashioned houses in Eldon Square had been demolished.

The same fate had been shared by the Co-operative Wholesale Society's warehouse, the Fish Market, the *Journal* office, and both the Crown and Métropole Hotels at the bottom of Clayton Street.

Yet the firing continued; the terrified citizens were granted no quarter. The Royal Arcade was blown to atoms, the new red brick buildings of the Prudential Assurance Company were set on fire, and were blazing with increasing fury. The building of the North British and Mercantile Assurance Company, the Savings Bank at the corner of Newgate Street, and the Empire Theatre were wrecked. Along New Bridge Street dozens of houses were blown to pieces, several fine residences in Ellison Place were utterly demolished and blocked the roadway with their débris, and the whole city, from the river up to Brandling Village, was swept time after time by salvoes of devastating shots. Rows of houses fell, and in hundreds the terrified people were massacred. Away over the Nun's Moor shells were hurled and burst, and others were precipitated into the great Armstrong works at Elswick.

Suddenly, in the midst of the incessant thunder, a series of terrific explosions occurred, and the great High Level Bridge collapsed, and fell with an awful crash into the Tyne. The enemy had placed dynamite under the huge brick supports, and blown them up simultaneously. A few moments later the Swing Bridge was treated in similar manner; but the enemy, under the galling fire from the Volunteer batteries, were now losing frightfully. Many of the new guns at the Elswick works were brought into action, and several ironclads in the course of construction afforded cover to those desperately defending their homes.

But this blow of the invaders had been struck at a most inopportune moment, and was evidently the result of an order that had been imperfectly understood. It caused them to suffer a greater disaster than they had anticipated. Six torpedo boats and two gun-vessels had passed under the bridge, and, lying off the Haughs, were firing into the Elswick works at the moment when the bridges were demolished, and the débris, falling across the stream, cut off all means of escape.

The defenders, noticing this, worked on, pounding away at the hostile craft with merciless monotony, until one after another the French and Russians were blown to atoms, and their vessels sank beneath them into the dark, swirling waters.

While this was proceeding, two mines, one opposite Hill Gate, at Gateshead, and the other near the Rotterdam Wharf, on the Newcastle side, were fired by the Volunteer Engineers, who thus succeeded in blowing up two more French gunboats, while the battery at the foot of the Swing Bridge sank two more torpedo boats, and that in front of the Chemical Works at Gateshead sent a shell into the "vitals" of one of the most powerful torpedo gunboats, with the result that she blew up.

Everywhere the enemy were being cut to pieces.

Seeing the trap into which their vessels had fallen above the ruined bridges, and feeling that they had caused sufficient damage, they turned, and with their guns still belching forth flame, steamed at half speed back again towards the sea.

But they were not allowed to escape so easily, for the mines recently laid by the Volunteers were now brought into vigorous play, and in the long reach of the river between High Walker and Wallsend no fewer than six more of the enemy's gun and torpedo boats had their bottoms blown out, and their crews torn limb from limb.

Flashed throughout the land, the news of the enemy's repulse, though gained at such enormous loss, excited a feeling of profound satisfaction.

The injury inflicted on the invaders had been terrible, and from that attack upon the Tyne they had been hurled reeling back the poorer by the loss of a whole fleet of torpedo and gun boats, one of the most effective arms of their squadrons, while the sea had closed over one of France's proudest battleships, the *Neptune*, and no fewer than four of her cruisers.

The surviving vessels, which retreated round the Black Middens and gained the open sea, all more or less had their engines crippled, and not half the men that had manned them escaped alive.

They had wrought incalculable damage, it is true, for part of Newcastle was burning, and the loss of life had been terrible; yet they were driven back by the Volunteers' desperately vigorous fire, and the lives of many thousands in Newcastle and Gateshead had thus been saved at the eleventh hour by British patriots.

Alas, it was a black day in England's history!

Was this to be a turning-point in the wave of disaster which had swept so suddenly upon our land?

XVII

Help from Our Colonies

Days passed—dark, dismal, dispiriting. Grim-visaged War had crushed all joy and gaiety from British hearts, and fierce patriotism and determination to fight on until the bitter end mingled everywhere with hunger, sadness, and despair. British homes had been desecrated, British lives had been sacrificed, and through the land the invaders rushed ravaging with fire and sword.

Whole towns had been overwhelmed and shattered, great tracts of rich land in Sussex and Hampshire had been laid waste, and the people, powerless against the enormous forces sweeping down upon them, had been mercilessly mowed down and butchered by Cossacks, whose brutality was fiendish. Everywhere there were reports of horrible atrocities, of heartless murders, and wholesale slaughter of the helpless and unoffending.

The situation, both in Great Britain and on the Continent, was most critical. The sudden declaration of hostilities by France and Russia had resulted in a great war in which nearly all European nations were involved. Germany had sent her enormous land forces over her frontiers east and west, successfully driving back the French along the Vosges, and occupying Dijon, Chalons-sur-Saône, and Lyons. Valmy, Nancy, and Metz had again been the scenes of sanguinary encounters, and Chaumont and Troyes had both fallen into the hands of the Kaiser's legions. In Poland, however, neither Germans nor Austrians had met with such success. A fierce battle had been fought at Thorn between the Tsar's forces and the Germans, and the former, after a desperate stand, were defeated, and the Uhlans, dragoons, and infantry of the Fatherland had swept onward up the valley of the Vistula to Warsaw. Here the resistance offered by General Bodisco was very formidable, but the city was besieged, while fierce fighting was taking place all across the level country that lay between the Polish capital and the Prussian frontier. Austrians and Hungarians fought fiercely, the Tyrolese Jägers displaying conspicuous bravery at Brody, Cracow, Jaroslav, and along the banks of the San, and they had succeeded up to the present in preventing the Cossacks and Russian infantry from reaching the Carpathians, although an Austrian army corps advancing into Russia along the Styr had been severely cut up and forced to retreat back to Lemberg.

Italy had burst her bonds. Her Bersaglieri, cuirassiers, Piedmontese cavalry, and carabiniers had marched along the Corniche road into Provence, and, having occupied Nice, Cannes, and Draguigan, were on their way to attack Marseilles, while the Alpine infantry, taking the road over Mont Cenis, had, after very severe fighting in the beautiful valley between Susa and Bardonnechia, at last occupied Modane and Chambéry, and now intended joining hands with the Germans at Lyons.

France was now receiving greater punishment than she had anticipated, and even those members of the Cabinet and Deputies who were responsible for the sudden invasion of England were compelled to admit that they had made a false move. The frontiers were being ravaged, and although the territorial regiments remaining were considered sufficient to repel attack, yet the Army of the Saône had already been cut to pieces. In these circumstances, France, knowing the great peril she ran in prolonging the invasion of Britain, was desperately anxious to make the British sue for peace, so that she could turn her attention to events at home, and therefore, although in a measure contravening International Law, she had instructed her Admirals to bombard British seaports and partially-defended towns.

Although the guns of the hostile fleet had wrought such appalling havoc on the Humber, on the Tyne, and along the coast of Kent and Sussex, nevertheless the enemy had only secured a qualified success. The cause of all the disasters that had befallen us, of the many catastrophes on land and sea, was due to the wretchedly inadequate state of our Navy, although the seven new battleships and six cruisers commenced in 1894 were now complete and afloat.

Had we possessed an efficient Navy the enemy could never have approached our shores. We had not a sufficient number of ships to replace casualties. Years behind in nearly every essential point, Britain had failed to give her cruisers either speed or guns equal in strength to those of other nations. Our guns were the worst in the world, no fewer than 47 vessels still mounting 350 old muzzleloaders, weapons discarded by every other European Navy.

For years it had been a race between the hare and the tortoise. We had remained in dreamy unconsciousness of danger, while other nations had quickly taken advantage of all the newly-discovered modes of destruction that make modern warfare so terrible.

Notwithstanding the odds against us in nearly every particular, the British losses had been nothing as compared with those of the enemy. This spoke much for British pluck and pertinacity. With a force against them of treble their strength, British bluejackets had succeeded in sinking a number of the finest and most powerful ships of France and Russia. France had lost the *Amiral Duperré*, a magnificent steel vessel of eleven thousand tons; the *Neptune* and *Redoutable*, a trifle smaller; the *Tonnerre*, the *Terrible*, the *Furieux*, the *Indomptable*, the *Caïman*, all armoured ships, had been lost; while the cruisers *D'Estaing*, *Sfax*, *Desaix*, *Cosamo*, *Faucon*, the despatch-vessel *Hirondelle*, the gunboats *Iberville*, *Gabes*, and *Lance*, and eleven others, together with sixteen torpedo boats and numbers of transports, had been either blown up, burned, or otherwise destroyed.

The losses the Russians had sustained, in addition to the many transports and general service steamers, included the great steel cruiser *Nicolai I*, the vessels *Gerzog Edinburgskij*, *Syzran*, *Rynda*, *Asia*, *Gangut*, *Kranaya Gorka*, *Olaf*, and the torpedo boat *Abo*, with eight others.

The destruction of this enormous force had, of course, not been effected without an infliction of loss upon the defenders, yet the British casualties bore no comparison to those of the enemy. True, the armoured turret-ship *Conqueror* had, alas! been sacrificed; the fine barbette-ships *Centurion* and *Rodney* had gone to the bottom; the splendid first-class cruiser *Aurora* and the cruiser *Narcissus* had been blown up; while the cruisers *Terpsichore*, *Melampus*, *Tribune*, *Galatea*, and *Canada*, with a number of torpedo boats and "catchers," had also been destroyed, yet not before every crew had performed heroic deeds worthy of record in the world's history, and every vessel had shown the French and Russians what genuine British courage could effect.

Still the invaders were striking swift, terrible blows. On the Humber and the Tyne the loss of life had been appalling. The bombardment of Brighton, the sack of Eastbourne, and the occupation of the Downs by the land forces, had been effected only by wholesale rapine and awful bloodshed, and Britain waited breathlessly, wondering in what direction the next catastrophe would occur.

Such newspapers as in these dark days continued to appear reported how great mass meetings were being held all over the United States, denouncing the action of the Franco-Russian forces.

In New York, Chicago, Washington, Philadelphia, Boston, San Francisco, and other cities, resolutions were passed at enormous demonstrations by the enthusiastic public, demanding that the United States Government should give an immediate ultimatum to France that unless she withdrew her troops from British soil, war would be declared against her.

Special sittings of Congress were being held daily at Washington for the purpose of discussing the advisability of such a step; influential deputations waited upon the President, and all the prominent statesmen were interviewed by the various enterprising New York journals, the result showing a great preponderance of feeling that such a measure should be at once taken.

In British colonies throughout the world the greatest indignation and most intense excitement prevailed. Already bodies of Volunteers were on their way from Australia and Cape Town, many of the latter, under Major Scott, having already been in England and shot as competitors at Bisley. From India a number of native regiments had embarked for Southampton, but the Northern frontier stations had been strengthened in anticipation of a movement south by Russia, and the French Indian possessions, Pondichéry and Karikal, were occupied by British troops.

An expedition from Burmah had crossed the Shan States into Tonquin, and with the assistance of the British Squadron on the China Station had, after hard fighting, occupied a portion of the country, while part of the force had gone farther south and commenced operations in French Cochin-China by a vigorous attack on Saigon.

Armed British forces had also landed in Guadaloupe and Martinique, two of the most fertile of the West Indian Islands, and St. Bartholomew had also been occupied by West Indian regiments.

On the outbreak of hostilities intense patriotism spread through Canada, and from the shores of Lake Superior away to far Vancouver a movement was at once made to assist the Mother Country. In Quebec, Montreal, Ottawa, Toronto, and Kingston mass meetings were held, urging the Dominion Government to allow a force of Volunteers to go to England without delay; and this universal demand was the more gratifying when it was remembered that more than a quarter of the population were themselves French. Nevertheless the knowledge that Britain was in danger was sufficient to arouse patriotism everywhere, and within a few days 20,000 Volunteers were enrolled, and these, before a fortnight had passed, were on their way to Liverpool. Great was the enthusiasm when, a few days later, to the strains of "Rule, Britannia," the first detachment landed in the Mersey, and as they marched through the crowded streets, the people, delighted at this practical demonstration of sympathy, wrung the hands of the patriots of the West. Vessel after vessel, escorted by British cruisers, arrived at the landing-stage, and discharged their regiments of men to whom the knowledge of Britain's danger had been sufficient incentive to induce them to act their part as Britons. Then, when the last vessel had arrived, they were formed into a brigade, and set out to march south in the direction of Birmingham.

Meanwhile a great loan was being floated in Australia and the United States. The former colony had but recently passed through a serious financial crisis, but in America a sum of no less than £200,000,000 was taken up, although the issue only continued a few days. In Wall Street the excitement was intense, and the struggle to invest was desperate. No such scenes had ever been witnessed within the memory of the oldest member of the Stock Exchange, for financiers were determined to assist the greatest Power on earth; indeed, apart from the sound security offered, they felt it their duty to do so. Melbourne, Sydney, Brisbane, and Calcutta all contributed in more or less degree, and the loan immediately proved the most successful ever floated.

To Britain on every side a helping hand was outstretched, and, irrespective of politics and party bickerings, assistance was rendered in order that she might crush her enemies. Britannia gathered her strength, and armed herself for the fierce combat which she knew must decide the destiny of her glorious Empire.

London, starving, terror-stricken, and haunted continually by apprehensions of an unknown doom, was in a state of restlessness both night and day. Food supplies had failed, the cheapest bread was sold at 3s. 8d. a small loaf, and neither fish nor meat could be purchased.

In the City the panic was frightful. Business was paralysed, hundreds were being ruined daily, and after the first sensation and headlong rush on the Stock Exchange, transactions remained at a standstill. Then suddenly, when the seriousness of the situation was fully understood, there was a run on the banks.

Crowds, eager and clamouring, surrounded the Bank of England, and establishments in Lombard Street and elsewhere, with cheques in their hands, demanding their deposits in gold. Although weak and half-starved, they desired their money in order to flee and take with them all they possessed before the enemy swept down upon London.

Day and night in all the City banks the cashiers were kept paying out thousands upon thousands in hard shining gold. The clink of coin, the jingle of scales, and the eager shouts of those feverishly anxious for their turn, and fearing the resources would not hold out, formed a loud incessant din.

As the days passed, and the run on the banks continued, one after another of the establishments, both in the City and the West End, unable to withstand the heavy withdrawals, were compelled to close their doors. Many were banks of such high reputation that the very fact of being a depositor was a hall-mark of a man's prosperity, while others were minor establishments, whose business was mainly with small accounts and middle-class customers. One by one they failed to fulfil their obligations, and closed; and the unfortunate ones, including many women who had not been able to struggle successfully to get inside, turned away absolutely ruined!

In the West End the starving poor had formed processions, and marched through Mayfair and Belgravia demanding bread, while Anarchists held council in front of the blackened ruins of the National Gallery, and the Unemployed continued their declamatory oratory on Tower Hill. The starving thousands from the East End ran riot in the aristocratic thoroughfares of Kensington, and, heedless of the police,—who were, in fact, powerless before such superior numbers,—residences of the rich were entered and searched for food, and various acts of violence ensued. The cellars of clubs, hotels, and private houses were broken open and sacked, granaries were emptied, wholesale grocery warehouses were looted, and flour mills searched from roof to basement. If they could not obtain food, they said, they would drink. A desperate starving crowd then forced an entry to the wine vaults at the Docks, and swallowed priceless vintages from pewter pots. Hogsheads of port and sherry were carried up into the streets, and amid scenes of wild disorder were tapped and drunk by the excited and already half-intoxicated multitude.

For days London remained at the mercy of a drunken, frenzied rabble. Murder and incendiarism were committed in every quarter, and many serious and desperate conflicts occurred between the rioters and the law-abiding patriotic citizens.

Enthusiasm was displayed by even the latter, when an infuriated mob one night surrounded Albert Gate House, the French Embassy, and, breaking open the door, entered it, and flung the handsome furniture from the windows.

Those below made a huge pile in the street, and when the whole of the movable effects had been got out, the crowd set fire to them, and also to the great mansion, at the same time cheering lustily, and singing "Rule, Britannia," as they watched the flames leap up and consume both house and furniture.

The servants of the Embassy had fortunately escaped, otherwise they would no doubt have fared badly at the hands of the lawless assembly.

When the fire had burned itself out, however, a suggestion was spread, and the mob with one accord rushed to the Russian Embassy in Chesham Place.

This house was also entered, and the furniture flung pell-mell from the windows, that too large to pass through being broken up in the rooms, and the fragments thrown to the shouting crowd below.

Chairs, tables, ornaments, mirrors, bedding, kitchen utensils, and crockery were thrown out, carpets were taken up, and curtains and cornices torn down by ruthless denizens of Whitechapel and Shoreditch, who, maddened by drink, were determined to destroy everything belonging to the countries which had brought disaster upon them.

Presently, when nearly all the furniture had been removed, some man, wild-haired and excited, emerged into the street, with a great flag he had discovered in one of the attics. With a shout of delight he unfurled it. It was a large yellow one, upon which was depicted a huge black double eagle; the flag that had been hoisted at the Embassy on various State occasions.

Its appearance was greeted by a fearful howl of rage, and the infuriated people, falling upon the man who waved it, tore it into shreds, which they afterwards cast into the bonfire they had made for the Ambassador's furniture.

From the archives the secret papers and reports of spies were taken, and, being torn into fragments, were scattered from an upper window to the winds, until at last, men, snatching up flaring brands from the huge bonfire, rushed into the dismantled mansion, and, having poured petroleum in many of the apartments, ignited them.

Flames quickly spread through the house, belching forth from the windows, and, ascending, had soon burst through the roof, illuminating the neighbourhood with a bright, fitful glare. The mob, as the flames leaped up and crackled, screamed with fiendish delight. From thousands of hoarse throats there went up loud cries of "Down with the Tsar! Down with Russia!" And as the great bonfire died down, and the roof of the Embassy collapsed with a crash, causing the flames to shoot higher and roar more vigorously, they sang with one accord, led by a man who had mounted some railings, the stirring British song, "The Union Jack of Old England."

Although the colonies had shown how zealously they were prepared to guard the interests of the Mother Country, their public spirit was eclipsed by the spontaneous outburst of patriotism which occurred in Ireland. Mass meetings were being held in Belfast, Dublin, Cork, Waterford, Limerick, Londonderry, Sligo, Armagh, Dundalk, Newry, and dozens of other places, at which men of all grades of society unanimously decided by resolution to raise Volunteer regiments to take arms against the foe.

The knowledge of Britain's danger had aroused the patriotic feelings of the people, and they were determined to give their sovereign a proof of their allegiance, cost what it might.

The movement was a general one. Nationalists and Unionists vied in their eagerness to demonstrate their love for the Empire, and that part of it which was now in danger.

Already the Irish Reserve forces had been mobilised and sent to their allotted stations. The 3rd Irish Rifles from Newtownards, the 5th Battalion from Downpatrick, and the 6th from Dundalk, were at Belfast under arms; the Donegal Artillery from Letterkenny had already gone to Harwich to assist in the defence of the east coast; and both the Londonderry and Sligo Artillery had gone to Portsmouth; while the 3rd Irish Fusiliers from Armagh were at Plymouth, and the 4th Battalion from Cavan had left to assist in the defence of the Severn.

Whatever differences of political opinion had previously existed between them on the question of Home Rule, were forgotten by the people in the face of the great danger which threatened the Empire to which they belonged. The national peril welded the people together, and shoulder to shoulder they marched to lay down their lives, if necessary, in the work of driving back the invader.

Within six days of this spontaneous outburst of patriotism, 25,000 Irishmen of all creeds and political opinions were on their way to assist their English comrades. As might have been expected, the greater number of these Volunteers came from the North of Ireland, but every district sent its sons, eager to take part in the great struggle. At the great meetings held at Dublin, Belfast, Cork, Limerick, Wexford, Waterford, Strabane, Newtown-Stewart, Downpatrick, Ballymena, and dozens of other places all over the country, from the Giant's Causeway to Cape Clear, and from Dublin to Galway Bay, the most intense enthusiasm was shown, and men signed their names to the roll in hundreds, many subscribing large sums to defray the cost of equipment and other expenses. Each passenger or mail boat from Larne to Stranraer, from Dublin to Holyhead, every steamer from Belfast to Whitehaven and Liverpool, brought over well-armed contingents of stalwart men, who, after receiving hearty receptions of the most enthusiastic and flattering description, were moved south to Stamford in Lincolnshire as quickly as the disorganised railway service would allow.

The object of the military authorities in concentrating them at this point was to strengthen the great force of defenders now marching south. Detraining at Stamford, the commanding officer had orders to march to Oundle, by way of King's Cliffe and Fotheringhay, and there remain until joined by a brigade of infantry with the Canadians coming from Leicestershire. The great body of men at length mustered, answered the roll, and marched through the quiet old-world streets of Stamford, and out upon the broad highway to King's Cliffe on the first stage of their journey.

It was early morning. In the sunlight the dew still glistened like diamonds on the wayside, as regiment after regiment, with firm, steady step, and shouldering their rifles, bravely passed away through the fields of ripe uncut corn, eager to unite with a force of Regulars, and strike their first blow for their country's liberty.

Sturdy fishermen from the rough shores of Donegal marched side by side with townsmen and artisans from Dublin, Belfast, and Limerick; sons of wealthy manufacturers in Antrim and Down bore arms with stalwart peasantry from Kerry and Tipperary; while men whose poor but cherished cabins overlooked Carlingford Lough, united with fearless patriots from Carlow, Wexford, and Waterford.

Since they landed on English soil, they had met with a boundless welcome.

In the rural districts the distress was not yet so great as in the larger towns; consequently at King's Cliffe, when the first detachment halted for rest in the long straggling street of the typical English village, the bells of the quaint old church were rung, and villagers gave their defenders bread, cheese, and draughts of ale. While the men were standing at ease and eating heartily, two officers entered Bailey's, the village grocery store, which served as post office, and received a cipher telegraphic despatch. They emerged into the roadway immediately, and their faces showed that some unforeseen event had occurred. A third officer was summoned, and a hurried and secret consultation took place as they stood together opposite the Cross Keys Inn.

"But can we do it?" queried the youngest of the trio, aloud, pulling on his gloves, and settling the hang of his sword.

The grave elder man, commander of the brigade, glanced quickly at his watch, with knit brows.

"Do it?" he replied, with a marked Irish accent. "We must. It'll be a dash for life; but the boys are fresh, and as duty calls, we must push onward, even though we may be marching to our doom. Go," he said to the youngest of his two companions, "tell them we are moving, and that our advance guard will reach them at the earliest possible moment."

The young lieutenant hurried over to the little shop, and as he did so the colonel gave an order, and a bugle awoke the echoes of the village.

Quick words of command sounded down the quaint, ancient street, followed by the sharp click of arms. Again officers' voices sounded loud and brief, and at the word "March!" the great body of stern loyalists moved onward over the bridge, and up the School Hill on to the long winding road which led away through Apesthorpe and historic Fotheringhay to Oundle.

The message from the front had been immediately responded to, for a few minutes later the excited villagers stood watching the rearguard disappearing in the cloud of dust raised by the heavy tread of the thousand feet upon the white highway.

XVIII

Russian Advance in the Midlands

Through the land the grey-coated hordes of the White Tsar spread like locusts—their track marked by death and desolation.

Both French and Russian troops had taken up carefully selected positions on the Downs, and, backed by the enormous reinforcements now landed, were slowly advancing. Every detail of the surprise invasion had apparently been carefully considered, for immediately after the fierce battle off Beachy Head a number of French and Russian cruisers were despatched to the Channel ports in order to threaten them, so as to prevent many of the troops in Hampshire, Dorset, and Devon from moving to their place of assembly. Consequently large bodies of British troops were compelled to remain inactive, awaiting probable local attacks.

Meanwhile the invaders lost no time in extending their flanks preparatory to a general advance, and very quickly they were in possession of all the high ground from Polegate to Steyning Down, while Cossack patrols were out on the roads towards Cuckfield and West Grinstead, and demonstrations were made in the direction of Horsham, where a strong force of British troops had hastily collected.

As the long hot days passed, the Volunteers forming the line of defence south of London had not been idle. A brigade of infantry had been pushed forward to Balcombe, and with this the British were now watching the high ground that stretched across to Horsham.

The advance of the enemy had not, of course, been accomplished without terrible bloodshed. A division of the Regulars from Parkhurst, Portsmouth, and Winchester, which had been hurried down to Arundel to occupy a strong defensive position near that town, had come into contact with the enemy, and some desperate fighting ensued. Outposts had been thrown across the river Arun, and about midnight a patrol of the 2nd Cavalry Brigade from Petersfield, supported by infantry, had been suddenly attacked close to Ashington village. Under a vigorous fire they were unfortunately compelled to fall back fighting, and were almost annihilated, for it was only then ascertained that the enemy were moving in great force, evidently with the intention of obtaining possession of the heights as far as Cocking, West Dean, and Chichester, and so threaten Portsmouth from the land.

The survivors of this cavalry patrol succeeded in recrossing the Arun, but their losses were exceedingly heavy.

At daybreak the enemy were visible from Arundel, and shot and shell were poured into them from the batteries established along the hills to Houghton. So heavy was the British fire that the Russians were compelled to seek cover, and their advance in this direction was, for this time, checked.

The defenders, although occupying an excellent position, were, however, not sufficiently strong to successfully cope with the onward rush of invaders, and could do little else beyond watching them.

On the other hand, the Russians, displaying great tactical skill, and led by men who had thoroughly studied the geography of the South of England, had gained a distinct advantage, for they had secured their left flank from attack, so that they could now advance northward to Horsham and Balcombe practically unmolested.

The first general movement commenced at noon, when an advance was made by two enormous columns of the enemy, one of which proceeded by way of Henfield and Partridge Green and the other by Cooksbridge and Keynes, the third column remaining in Sussex to protect the base of operations. Meanwhile, Horsham had been occupied by a portion of the 2nd division of the 1st Army Corps with a 12-pounder, a 9-pounder field battery, and a field company of the Royal Engineers, and had been placed in a state of hasty defence. Walls had been loopholed, fences had been cut down, and various preparations made for holding the town.

Our forces were, nevertheless, sadly lacking in numbers. A cavalry patrol of one of our flying columns was captured by Cossacks at Cowfold, and the neglect on the part of the commander of this column to send out his advance guard sufficiently far, resulted in it being hurled back upon the main body in great disorder. Then, seeing the success everywhere attending their operations, the invaders turned their attention to the British line of communication between Horsham and Arundel, and succeeded in breaking it at Billinghurst and at Petworth.

Fierce fighting spread all over Sussex, and everywhere many lives were being sacrificed for Britain. The defenders, alas! with their weak and totally inadequate forces, could make but a sorry stand against the overwhelming masses of French and Russians, yet they acted with conspicuous bravery to sustain the honour of their native land. Villages and towns were devastated, rural homes were sacked and burned, and everywhere quiet, unoffending, but starving Britons were being put to the sword.

Over Sussex the reign of terror was awful. The pastures were stained by Britons' life-blood, and in all directions our forces, though displaying their characteristic courage, were being routed. At Horsham they were utterly defeated after a fierce and bloody encounter, in which the enemy also lost very heavily; yet the cause of the British reverse was due solely to a defective administration. Hurriedly massed in the town from Aldershot by way of Guildford, they had, owing to the short-sighted policy of the War Office, arrived without a sufficient supply of either transport or ammunition. Night was falling as they detrained, and in the hopeless confusion battalion commanders could not find their brigade headquarters, and brigadiers could not find their staff.

This extraordinary muddle resulted in the fresh troops, instead of being sent forward to reinforce the outposts, being kept in town, while the jaded, ill-fed men, who had already been on the alert many hours, were utterly unable to resist the organised attack which was made before daybreak.

Though they made a gallant stand and fought on with desperate determination, yet at last the whole of them were driven back in confusion, and with appalling loss, upon their supports, and the latter, who held out bravely, were at last also compelled to fall back upon their reserves. The latter, which included half a battery of artillery stationed at Wood's Farm and Toll Bar, held the enemy in temporary check; but when the heavy French artillery was at length brought up, the invaders were enabled to cut the railway, destroy the half battery at Wood's Farm, turn the British right flank, and compel them to retreat hastily from Horsham and fly to defensive positions at Guildford and Dorking.

By this adroit manoeuvre the enemy succeeded in taking over two hundred prisoners, capturing the guns of the 12-pounder field battery,—which had not been brought into play for the simple reason that only ammunition for 9-pounders had been collected in the town,—and seizing a large quantity of stores and ammunition of various kinds.

This success gave the enemy the key to the situation.

As on sea, so on land, our blundering defensive policy had resulted in awful disaster. Sufficient attention had never been paid to detail, and the firm-rooted idea that Britain could never be invaded had caused careless indifference to minor matters of vital importance to the stability of our Empire.

The contrast between the combined tactics of the enemy and those of our forces was especially noticeable when the cavalry patrol of the British flying column was captured on the Cowfield road and the column defeated. The commander of the column, a well-known officer, unfortunately, like many others, had had very little experience of combined tactics, and looked upon cavalry not merely as "the eyes and ears of an army," but as the army itself. It was this defect that was disastrous. For many years past it had never appeared quite clear whether British cavalry were intended to act *en masse* in warfare, or simply as scouts or mounted infantry, therefore their training had been uncertain. The Home establishment of our cavalry was supposed to be about 12,000 men, but owing to a parsimonious administration only about half that number had horses, and in some corps less than a half. Another glaring defect was the division of many regiments into detachments stationed in various towns, the inevitable result of this being that many such detachments were without regimental practice for months, and there were many who had not manoeuvred with a force of all arms *for years*!

Army organisation proved a miserable failure.

The supply of ammunition was totally inadequate, and a disgrace to a nation which held its head above all others. It was true that depôts had been established at various centres, yet with strange oversight no provision had been made for the work of ammunition trains.

Originally it had been intended that men for this most important duty should be found by the Reserves, and that the horses should be those privately registered; nevertheless it was found necessary at the very last moment to weaken our artillery by detailing experienced men for duty with the ammunition column. Many of the horses which were registered for service were found to be totally unfit, and very few of the remainder had been previously trained. In the case of those which were required for the cavalry regiments—nearly six thousand—the best men in the regiments had to be told off at the very beginning of the invasion to hurriedly train and prepare these animals for service, when they should have been available to proceed to any part of the kingdom at twenty-four hours' notice. By such defects mobilisation was foredoomed to failure.

The scheme, instead of being so arranged as to be carried out without confusion, resulted in muddle and farcical humiliation.

WILLIAM LE QUEUX

Again, the infantry, owing to the recent departure of the Indian drafts, had been considerably weakened, many battalions being found on mobilisation very disorganised and inefficient. As an instance, out of one battalion at Aldershot, which was on paper 1000 strong, 200 had been sent away to India, while of the remainder more than half had only seen twelve months' service, and a large percentage were either under eighteen years of age or were "special enlistments," namely, below the minimum standard of height.

Such a battalion compared very unfavourably with the majority of Volunteer regiments,—those of the Stafford Brigade, for instance,— the average service of the men in those regiments being over five years, and the average age twenty-seven years. British officers had long ago foreseen all these defects, and many others, yet they had preserved an enforced silence. They themselves were very inefficiently trained in manoeuvring, for, with one or two exceptions, there were no stations in the kingdom where forces were sufficiently numerous to give the majority of the superior officers practice in handling combined bodies of troops.

Thus in practical experience in the field they were far behind both French and Russians, and it was this very serious deficiency that now became everywhere apparent.

British troops, fighting valiantly, struggled to protect their native land, which they determined should never fall under the thrall of the invader. But alas! their resistance, though stubborn and formidable, was nevertheless futile. Time after time the lines of defence were broken.

The Russian Eagle spread his black wings to the sun, and with joyous shouts the dense grey white masses of the enemy marched on over the dusty Sussex roads northward towards the Thames.

After the battle of Horsham, the gigantic right column of the invaders, consisting mostly of French troops, followed up the defenders to Guildford and Dorking, preparatory to an attack upon London; while the left column, numbering 150,000 French and Russians of all arms, pushed on through Alfold to Haslemere, then through Farnham and Odiham to Swallowfield, all of which towns they sacked and burned, the terrified inhabitants being treated with scant mercy. As the majority of the defenders were massed in Kent, South Surrey, and Sussex, the enemy advanced practically unmolested, and at sunrise one morning a terrible panic was created in Reading by the sudden descent upon the town of a great advance guard of 10,000 Russians.

The people were appalled. They could offer no resistance against the cavalry, who, tearing along the straight high road from Swallowfield, swept down upon them. Along this road the whole gigantic force was moving, and the Cossack skirmishers, spurring on across the town, passed away through the Railway Works, and halted at the bridge that spans the Thames at Caversham. They occupied it at once, in order to prevent it being blown up before the main body arrived, and a brisk fight ensued with the small body of defenders that had still remained at the Brigade depôt on the Purley Road.

Meanwhile, as the French and Russian advance guard came along, they devastated the land with fire and sword. The farms along the road were searched, and afterwards set on fire, while not a house at Three Mile Cross escaped. Entering the town from Whitley Hill, the great mass of troops, working in extended order, came slowly on, and, followed by 140,000 of the main body and 1000 guns, carried everything before them.

No power could stem the advancing tide of the Muscovite legions, and as they poured into the town in dense compact bodies, hundreds of townspeople were shot down ruthlessly, merely because they attempted to defend their homes. From the Avenue Works away to the Cemetery, and from the Railway Station to Leighton Park, the streets swarmed with soldiers of the Tsar, who entered almost every house in search of plunder, and fired out of sheer delight in bloodshed upon hundreds who were flying for their lives.

Men, women, even children, were slaughtered. The massacre was frightful. Neither life nor property was respected; in every thoroughfare brutal outrages and murders were committed, and English homes were rendered desolate.

Almost the first buildings attacked were the great factories of Messrs. Huntley & Palmer, whose 3000 hands were now, alas! idle owing to the famine. The stores were searched for biscuits, and afterwards the whole factory was promptly set on fire. The Great Western, Queen's, and George Hotels were searched from garret to cellar, and the wines and beer found in the latter were drunk in the streets. With the scant provisions found, several of the regiments made merry during the morning, while others pursued their devastating work. The banks were looted, St. Mary's, Greyfriars', and St. Lawrence's Churches were burned, and Sutton & Sons' buildings and the Railway Works shared the same fate, while out in the direction of Prospect Hill Park all the houses were sacked, and those occupants who remained to guard their household treasures were put to the sword.

Everywhere the invaders displayed the most fiendish brutality, and the small force of British troops who had engaged the Russian advance guard were, after a most fiercely contested struggle, completely annihilated, not, however, before they had successfully placed charges of gun-cotton under the bridge and blown it up, together with a number of Cossacks who had taken possession of it.

This, however, only checked the enemy's progress temporarily, for the right flank crossed at Sonning, and as the main body had with them several pontoon sections, by noon the pontoons were in position, and the long line of cavalry, infantry, artillery, and engineers, leaving behind Reading, now in flames, crossed the Thames and wound away along the road to Banbury, which quaint old town, immortalised in nursery rhyme, they sacked and burned, destroying the historic Cross, and regaling themselves upon the ale found in the cellars of the inns, the Red and White Lions. This done, they again continued their march, practically unmolested; while Oxford was also entered and sacked.

True, scouts reported strong forces of the defenders advancing across from Market Harborough, Kettering, and Oundle, and once or twice British outposts had sharp encounters with the Russians along the hills between Ladbrooke and Daventry, resulting in serious losses on both sides; nevertheless the gigantic force of Russians still proceeded, sweeping away every obstacle from their path.

On leaving Banbury, the enemy, marching in column of route, took the road through Stratford-on-Avon to Wootton Wawen, where a halt for twenty-four hours was made in order to mature plans for an organised attack on Birmingham. Wootton Hall, after being looted, was made the headquarters, and from thence was issued an order on the following day which caused Warwick and Leamington to be swept and burned by the invaders, who afterwards broke into two divisions. One body, consisting of 50,000 men, including an advance guard of 5000, took the right-hand road from Wootton to Birmingham, through Sparkbrook; while the remaining 100,000 bore away to the left through Ullenhall and Holt End to the extremity of the Hagley Hills, intending to occupy them. They had already been informed that strong defences had been established at King's Norton, in the immediate vicinity, and knew that severe fighting must inevitably ensue; therefore they lost no time in establishing themselves along the high ground between Redditch and

Barnt Green, in a position commanding the two main roads south from Dudley and Birmingham.

That a most desperate stand would be made for the defence of the Metropolis of the Midlands the Russian commander was well aware. After the long march his troops were jaded, so, bivouacing in Hewell Park, he awaited for nearly two days the reports of his spies. These were not so reassuring as he had anticipated, for it appeared that the high ground south of the city, notably at King's Norton, Northfield, Harborne, Edgbaston, and along the Hagley Road, was occupied by strong bodies of troops and a large number of guns, and that every preparation had been made for a stubborn resistance.

It also appeared that at the entrance to the city at Sparkbrook, which road had been taken by the right column, very little resistance was likely to be offered.

That the positions occupied by the defenders had been very carefully chosen as the most advantageous the Russian commander was bound to admit, and although he possessed such a large body of men it would require considerable tactical skill to dislodge the defenders in order to prevent them covering with their guns the country over which the Russian division, taking the right-hand roads, must travel.

During that day an encounter of a most fierce description occurred between hostile reconnoitring parties on the road between Bromsgrove Lickey and Northfield. The road gradually ascended with a walled-in plantation on either side, and the enemy were proceeding at a comfortable pace when suddenly a number of rifles rattled out simultaneously, and then it was discovered that the wall had been loopholed, and that the British were pouring upon them a deadly hail from which there was no shelter. The walls bristled with rifles, and from them came a storm of bullets that killed and wounded dozens of the invaders.

The latter, however, showed considerable daring, for while the magazine rifles poured forth their deadly shower, they rallied and charged up the hill in the face of the fearful odds against them. For ten minutes or perhaps a quarter of an hour the fighting was a desperate hand-to-hand one, the enemy entering the plantation with a dash that surprised the defenders. Gradually, although outnumbered by the Russians, the British at length, by dint of the most strenuous effort and hard fighting, succeeded in inflicting frightful loss upon the invaders, and the latter, after a most desperate stand, eventually retreated in confusion down into the valley, leaving nearly two-thirds of the party dead or dying.

The British, whose losses were very small, had shown the invaders that they meant to defend Birmingham, and that every inch of ground they gained would have to be won by sheer fighting. An hour later another fierce encounter occurred in the same neighbourhood, and of the 4000 Russians who had advanced along that road not 900 returned to the main body, such havoc the British Maxims caused; while at the same time a further disaster occurred to the enemy in another direction, for away at Tanworth their outposts had been completely annihilated, those who were not killed being taken prisoners by the 3rd South Staffordshire Volunteers, who, under Colonel E. Nayler, acted with conspicuous bravery. In every direction the enemy's outposts and advance guards were being harassed, cut up, and hurled back in disorder with heavy loss, therefore the Russian commander decided that a sudden and rapid movement forward in order to effect a junction with his right column was the only means by which the position could be carried.

In the meantime events were occurring rapidly all over the country south of the city. The commander of the Russian left column, deciding to commence the attack forthwith, moved on his forces just before midnight in order to commence the onslaught before daybreak, knowing the British forces always relieve their outposts at that time. Again, it was necessary to advance under cover of darkness in order to prevent the defenders' artillery, which now commanded the road between Alcester and Moseley, firing upon them.

Having received a message from the right column stating that their advance guard had pushed on to Olton End with outposts at Sheldon and Yardley, and announcing their intention of advancing through Sparkbrook upon the city before dawn, the commanding officer, leaving some artillery at Barnt Green, and sending on cavalry to Stourbridge and Cradley to turn the English flank at Halesowen, manoeuvred rapidly, bringing the main body of cavalry and infantry back to Alvechurch, thence across to Weatheroak, and then striking due north, again marched by the three roads leading to King's Norton.

The high ground here he knew was strongly defended, and it was about a quarter to two o'clock when the British, by means of their search-lights, discovered the great dark masses advancing upon them. Quickly their guns opened fire, and the sullen booming of cannon was answered by the Russian battery near Barnt Green. Over Birmingham the noise was heard, and had volumes of terrible significance for the turbulent crowds who filled the broad thoroughfares. The search-lights used by both invaders and defenders turned night into day, and the battle proceeded.

The enemy had carefully prepared their plans, for almost at the same moment that they assaulted the position at King's Norton, a battery of Russian artillery opened a terrible fire from the hill at Tanner's Green, while the attacking column extended their right across to Colebrook Hall, with intent to push across to Moseley Station, and thus gain the top of the ridge of the ground in the rear of the British positions, and so hem in the British force and allow the right column to advance through Small Heath and Sparkbrook unchecked.

These simultaneous attacks met in the valley separating the parallel ridges held by the Russians and British, and the fighting became at once fierce and stubborn. A furious infantry fire raged for over an hour in the valley between the excellent position held by the defenders at King's Norton and the lower wooded ridge occupied by the Russians, who had succeeded in capturing half a British battery who held it. Owing to the bareness of the slope, the Russians went down into battle without cover, cut up terribly by the British infantry fire, and by the shell fire from the King's Norton batteries. From the British trenches between Broad Meadow and Moundsley Hall a galling fire was poured, and Russian infantry fell in hundreds over the undulating fields between the high road to Alcester and the Blithe River.

From a ridge on the Stratford Road, near Monkspath Street, heavy Russian artillery opened fire just before dawn, and played terrible havoc with the British guns, which on the sky-line opposite afforded a mark. As time crept on there was no cessation in the thunder on either side, while away along the valleys a most bloody encounter was in progress. The whole stretch of country was one huge battlefield. British and Russians fell in hundreds, nay, in thousands.

The losses on every side were appalling; the fortune of war trembled in the balance.

XIX

Fall of Birmingham

The battle outside Birmingham was long, fierce, and furious. No more desperately contested engagement had ever occurred in the history of the British Empire. From the very first moment of the fight it was apparent that the struggle would be a fearful one, both sides possessing advantages; the British by reason of the magnificent defensive positions they occupied, and the Russians by reason of their overwhelming numbers. Against a defending force of 50,000 of all arms, 150,000 invaders—the majority of whom were Russians—were now fighting, and the combat was necessarily long and deadly. British Volunteers were conspicuous everywhere by their bravery; the Canadians rendered most valuable assistance, firing from time to time with excellent precision, and holding their position with splendid courage; while the Irish Brigade, who had moved rapidly from King's Cliffe by train and road, and had arrived in time, now held their own in a position close to Kingsheath House.

Many of the principal buildings in Birmingham had during the past day or two been converted into hospitals, amongst others the Post Office, where the trained nurses received very valuable assistance from the female clerks. A train full of British wounded was captured early in the evening at Barnt Green. It contained regular troops and civilians from the Stratford force which had fallen back to Alcester, and the train had been sent on from there in the hope that it would get through before the enemy were able to cut the line. This, however, was not accomplished, for the Russians inhumanely turned out the wounded and filled the train with their own troops and ammunition. Then, under the guidance of a Birmingham railway man of French nationality who had been acting as spy, the train proceeded to New Street Station. It was impossible for the officials at the station to cope with the enemy, for they had only expected their own wounded, or they would, of course, have wrecked the train by altering the points before it arrived in the station. The Russians therefore detrained, and, led by their spy, made a dash along the subway leading to the lifts ascending to the Post Office. These were secured, and the Office was soon captured by the

Russians, who not only thereby obtained a footing in the very centre of the town from which there was not much chance of dislodging them before Birmingham fell, but they had also obtained possession of the most important telegraph centre for the North and Midland districts of England.

Before the first flush of dawn the whole of the country from Kings Norton right across to Solihull was one huge battlefield, and when the sun rose, bright and glorious, its rays were obscured by the clouds of smoke which hung like a funeral pall over hill and dale. For a long period the principal Russian battery on the Stratford Road was short of ammunition, and, seeing this, the strong British battery at Northfield moved quickly up into a commanding position at Drake's Cross, not, however, before it had been considerably weakened by the Russian fire from Bromsgrove Lickey. During this time, however, detachments of Canadian marksmen had been detailed with no other purpose than to sweep the Russian road at the exposed points of its course, and to fire at everything and everybody exposed on the ridge. This was most effective, and for quite half an hour prevented any supply of ammunition reaching the enemy, thus giving the British battery an opportunity to establish itself. At length, however, both batteries of defenders opened fire simultaneously upon the Russian guns, and so thickly fell the shots, that although ammunition had by this time been brought up, the enemy's power in that quarter was completely broken.

From that time the fierce struggle was confined to cavalry and infantry. Troops of Cossacks, sweeping up the banks of the Arrow, encountered British Hussars and cut into them with frightful effect. The defenders, fighting hard as the day wore on, hindered the enemy from gaining any material advantage, though the latter forced the outer line of the British shelter trenches on the slopes below the position of King's Norton. The Canadians had laid mines in front of their trenches, which were exploded just as the head of the Russian assaulting parties were massed above them, and large numbers of the Tsar's infantry were blown into atoms.

Bullets were singing along the valleys like swarms of angry wasps, and the Russian losses in every direction were enormous.

Hour after hour the fighting continued. The British held good positions, with an inner line of defence across from Selly Oak, Harborne, and Edgbaston, to the high crest on the Hagley Road, close to the Fountain, while the Russians swarmed over the country in overwhelming numbers. The frightful losses the latter were sustaining by reason of the defenders' artillery fire did not, however, disconcert them. But for the huge right column of invaders advancing on Birmingham by way of Acock's Green, it seemed an even match, yet as afternoon passed the firing in the valley swelled in volume, and the mad clamour of battle still surged up into the blue cloudless heavens.

The enemy could see on the sky-line the British reinforcements as they came up from Halesowen by the road close to their battery on the bare spot near the edge of their right flank, and it was decided at four o'clock to deliver a counter flank attack on the left edge of the British position, simultaneously with a renewed strenuous assault by the tirailleurs from below. Soon this desperate manoeuvre was commenced, and although the marching ground was good, the British guns swept them with their terrible fire, and hundreds of the Tsar's soldiers dyed the meadows with their blood.

It was a fierce, mad dash. The British attacked vigorously on every side, fought bravely, straining every nerve to repulse their foe.

The battle had been the most fiercely contested of any during the struggle, and in this desperate assault on King's Norton the Russians had suffered appalling losses. The valleys and slopes were strewn with dead and dying, and a bullet had struck the British commander, mortally wounding him. As he was borne away to the ambulance waggon, the last words on that noble soldier's lips were a fervent wish for good fortune to the arms of the Queen he had served so well.

But the British were, alas! outnumbered, and at last retreating in disorder, were followed over the hills to Halesowen and utterly routed, while the main body of the enemy marching up the Bristol and Pershore Roads, extended their left across to Harborne and Edgbaston. Meanwhile, however, the guns placed on the edge of the city along the Hagley Road near the Fountain, and in Beech Lane close to the Talbot Inn, as well as the Volunteer batteries near St. Augustine's Church and Westfield Road, opened fire upon the advancing legions. The two lower roads taken by the enemy were well commanded by the British guns, and the Volunteers, with the Canadians and Irish, again rendered most valuable assistance, everywhere displaying cool and conspicuous courage. The walls of the new villas along the Hagley Road, Portland Road, and Beech Lane had been placed in a state of hasty defence, and rifles bristled everywhere, but as the sun sank behind the long range of purple hills the fight was in the balance. The British, as they stood, could almost keep back the foe, but, alas! not quite.

There was soon a concentric rush for the hill, and as the cannons thundered and rifles rattled, hundreds of the grey-coats fell back and rolled down the steep slope dead and dying, but the others pushed on in face of the frowning defences, used their bayonets with desperate energy, and a few minutes later loud shouts in Russian told that the ridge had been cleared and the position won. The battle had been long and terrible; the carnage awful!

The British, making a last desperate stand, fought a fierce hand-to-hand struggle, but ere long half their number lay helpless in the newly-made suburban roads, and the remainder were compelled to leave their guns in possession of the enemy and fly north to Sandwell to save themselves. Then, as they fled, the Russians turned the British guns near St. Augustine's upon them, causing havoc in their rear.

The shattered left column of the enemy, having at length broken down the British defences, raised loud victorious yells, and, after reorganising, marched down the Hagley Road upon the city, fighting from house to house the whole way. The gardens in front of these houses, however, aided the defenders greatly in checking the advance.

The sacrifice of human life during those hours from daybreak to sundown had been frightful. The whole country, from Great Packington to Halesowen, was strewn with blood-smeared corpses.

Having regard to the fact that the defending force consisted of only 50,000 men against 100,000 Russians, the losses inflicted upon the latter spoke volumes for British pluck and military skill. Upon the field 10,000 Russians lay dead, 30,000 were wounded, and 2000 were prisoners, while the defenders' total loss in killed and wounded only amounted to 20,000.

Indeed, had it not been for the reinforcements, numbering 50,000, from the right column, which were by this time coming up with all speed from Acock's Green, the Russians, in their terribly jaded and demoralised state, could not have marched upon the city. As it was, however, the occupation commenced as night drew on; the fighting that followed being principally done by the reinforcements.

Leaving no fewer than 42,000 men dead, wounded, and captured, the invaders pushed on into Birmingham. Though the citizens' losses had already been terrific, nevertheless they found that they were still determined to hold out. In all the principal roads leading into the city barricades had been formed, and behind them were bands of desperate men, well equipped, and prepared to fight on to the bitter end.

The first of these in the Hagley Road had been constructed at the junction of Monument Road, and as the skirmishers and advance guard approached, offered a most desperate resistance. In addition to a vigorous rifle fire that poured from the improvised defences, three Maxims were brought into play from the roofs of large houses, and these, commanding the whole road as far as its junction with Beech Lane, literally mowed down the enemy as they approached. Time after time the Russians rushed upon the defenders' position, only to be hurled back again by the leaden hail, which fell so thickly that it was impossible for any body of troops to withstand it. By this the invaders' advance was temporarily checked, but it was not long before they established a battery at the corner of Norfolk Road, and poured shell upon the barricade with frightful effect. Quickly the guns were silenced, and the Russians at last breaking down the barrier, engaged in a conflict at close quarters with the defenders.

The road along to Five Ways was desperately contested. The slaughter on both sides was awful, for a detachment of Russians coming up the Harborne Road had been utterly annihilated and swept away by the rifle fire of defenders concealed behind loopholed walls. At Five Ways the entrance to each of the five broad converging thoroughfares had been strongly barricaded, and as the enemy pressed forward the British machine guns established there caused terrible havoc. Behind those barricades men of Birmingham of every class, armed with all sorts of guns, hastily obtained from Kynoch's and other factories, struggled for the defence of their homes and loved ones, working with a dash and energy that greatly disconcerted the enemy, who had imagined that, in view of their victory in the battle, little resistance would be offered.

In the darkness that had now fallen the scenes in the streets were frightful. The only light was the flash from gun-muzzles and the glare of flames consuming private houses and public buildings. The civilian defenders, reinforced by Regular soldiers, Militia, and Volunteers, had made such excellent preparations for defence, and offered such strenuous opposition, that almost every foot the Russians gained in the direction of the centre of the city was fought for hand to hand. Both right and left Russian columns were now advancing up the Coventry, Stratford, Moseley, Pershore, and Bristol Roads, and in each of those thoroughfares the barricades were strongly constructed, and, being armed with Maxims, wrought frightful execution.

Gradually, however, one after another of these defences fell by reason of the organised attacks by such superior numbers, and the Russians marched on, killing with bayonet and sword.

In the city, as the night passed, the fighting in the streets everywhere was of the fiercest and most sanguinary description. In Corporation Street a huge barricade with machine guns had been constructed opposite the Victoria Law Courts, and, assisted by 200 Volunteers, who, inside the latter building, fired from the windows, the enemy were held in check for several hours.

Time after time shells fell from the Russian guns in the midst of the defenders, and, bursting, decimated them in a horrible manner; yet through the long close night there was never a lack of brave men to step into the breach and take up the arms of their dead comrades. Indeed, it was only when the enemy succeeded in setting fire to the Courts, and compelling the defenders to cease their vigorous rifle fire from the windows, that the position was won; and not until hundreds of Russians lay dead or dying in the street.

In New Street the Irish Volunteers distinguished themselves conspicuously. After the retreat they had been withdrawn with the Canadians into the city, and, waiting in the side thoroughfares at the opposite end of New Street, held themselves in readiness. Suddenly, as the enemy rushed along in their direction, an order was given, and they formed up, and stretching across the street, met them with volley after volley of steady firing; then, rushing onward with fixed bayonets, charged almost before the Russians were aware of their presence.

Without a thought of his own personal safety, every Irishman cast himself into the thick of the fray, and, backed by a strong body of Canadians and fusiliers, they succeeded in cutting their way completely into the invaders, and driving them back into Corporation Street, where they were forced right under the fire of four Maxims that had just at that moment been brought into position outside the Exchange.

Suddenly these guns rattled out simultaneously, and the Russians, unable to advance, and standing at the head of the long broad thoroughfare, were swept down with awful swiftness and with scarcely any resistance. So sudden had been their fate, that of a force over two thousand strong, not more than a dozen escaped, although the defenders were taken in rear by the force of 500 Russians who had occupied the Post Office on the previous night.

From Corporation Street a brilliant, ruddy glow suffused the sky, as both the Law Courts and the Grand Theatre were in flames, while St. Mary's Church and the Market Hall had also been fired by incendiaries.

In the panic and confusion, conflagrations were breaking out everywhere, flames bursting forth from several fine shops in New Street which had already been sacked and wrecked. Maddened by their success, by the thirst for the blood of their enemies, and the rash deeds of incendiaries, the Muscovite legions spread over the whole city, and outrage and murder were common everywhere.

Away up Great Hampton Street and Hockley Hill the jewellery factories were looted, and hundreds of thousands of pounds worth of gems and gold were carried off, while the Mint was entered, afterwards being burned because only copper coins were found there, and the pictures in the Art Gallery were wantonly slashed by sabres and bayonets.

The scenes on that memorable night were awful. Birmingham, one of the most wealthy cities in the kingdom, fell at last, after a most stubborn resistance, for just before day broke the overwhelming forces of Russia occupying the streets commenced to drive out the defenders, and shoot down those who turned to resist. From Bordesley to Handsworth, and from Smethwick to Aston, the city was in the hands of the enemy. The banks in New Street were broken open, and the gold stuffed into the pockets of the uncouth dwellers on the Don and the Volga, Chamberlain's Memorial was wrecked, and Queen's College occupied by infantry. Cossack officers established themselves in the Grand and Queen's Hotels, and their men were billeted at the Midland, Union, Conservative, and other Clubs, and at many minor hotels and buildings.

Before the dawn had spread, whole rows of shops were burning, their brilliant glare illuminating the streets that ran with blood. It was a fearful scene of death and desolation.

The majority of the citizens had fled, leaving everything in the hands of the enemy, who still continued their work of pillage. In the streets the bodies of 10,000 Russians and 3000 British lay unheeded, while no fewer than 9000 of the enemy's infantry had been wounded.

The headquarters of the Russian army had at last been established in a British city, for over the great Council House there now lazily flapped in the fresh morning breeze the great yellow-and-black flag of the Tsar Alexander.

And the Russian General, finding he had lost the enormous force of 61,000 men, spent the grey hours of dawn in nervous anxiousness, pacing the room in which he had installed himself, contemplating the frightful disaster, and undecided how next to act.

An incident illustrative of the fierceness of the fight outside the city was published in the *Times* several days later. It was an extract from a private letter written by Lieut. J. G. Morris of the 3rd Battalion of the York and Lancaster Regiment, and was as follows:—

"The sun that day was blazing and merciless. Throughout the morning our battalion had lost heavily in the valley, when suddenly at about twelve o'clock the enemy apparently received reinforcements, and we were then driven back upon Weatheroak by sheer force of numbers, and afterwards again fell further back towards our position on the high ground in Hagley Road.

"In this hasty retreat I found myself with a sergeant and eighteen men pursued by a large skirmishing party of Russians. All we could do was to fly before them. This we did, until at length, turning into Beech Lane, we found ourselves before a small, low-built ancient hostelry, the King's Head Inn, with a dilapidated and somewhat crude counterfeit presentment of King George II outside. The place was unoccupied, and I decided immediately to enter it. I could count on every one of my men; therefore very soon we were inside, and had barricaded the little place. Scarcely had we accomplished this when the first shots rang out, and in a few moments the space outside where the cross-roads meet literally swarmed with Russians, who quickly extended, and, seeking cover at the junction of each of the five roads, commenced a terrific fusillade. The windows from which we fired were smashed, the woodwork splintered everywhere, and so thickly came the bullets that my men had to exercise the utmost caution in concealing themselves while firing.

"In a quarter of an hour one man had been struck and lay dead by my side, while at the same time the terrible truth suddenly dawned upon me that our ammunition could not last out. Regulating the firing, I rushed to one of the back windows that commanded the valley down to Harborne, and saw advancing along the road in our direction, and raising a cloud of dust, about a thousand Russian cavalry and infantry.

"Back again to the front room I dashed, just in time to witness the enemy make a wild rush towards us. Our slackened fire had deceived them, and as the storming party dashed forward, they were met by vigorous volleys from our magazine rifles, which knocked over dozens, and compelled the remainder to again retire.

"Again the enemy made a desperate onslaught, and again we succeeded in hurling them back, and stretching dead a dozen or more. Meanwhile the great force of Russians was moving slowly up the hill, and I knew that to hold the place much longer would be impossible. From the rear of the building a vigorous attack had now commenced, and moving more men round to the rear, so that our fire would command the sloping approach to the house, I gave an order to fire steadily. A moment later my sergeant and two other men had been severely wounded, and although the former had had his arm broken, and was near fainting from loss of blood, nevertheless he kept up, resting his rifle-barrel upon the shattered window-ledge, and pouring out the deadly contents of his magazine.

"A few minutes afterwards a bullet shattered my left hand, and the man who crouched next to me under the window was a second later shot through the heart, and fell back dead among the disordered furniture.

"Still not a man hesitated, not a word of despair was uttered. We all knew that death stared us in the face, and that to face it bravely was a Briton's duty. Only once I shouted above the din: 'Do your best, boys! Remember we we are all Britons, and those vermin outside have wrecked our homes and killed those we love. Let's have our revenge, even if we die for it!'

"'We'll stick to 'em till the very last, sir, never fear,' cheerily replied one young fellow as he reloaded his gun; but alas! ere he could raise it to fire, a bullet struck him in the throat. He staggered back, and a few moments later was a corpse.

"Undaunted, however, my men determined to sell their lives as dearly as possible, and continued their fire, time after time repelling the attack, and sweeping away the grey-coats as they emerged from behind the low walls.

"Three more men had fallen in as many seconds, and another, staggering back against the wall, held his hand to his breast, where he had received a terrible and mortal wound. Our situation at that moment was most critical. Only two rounds remained to each of my nine brave fellows, yet not a man wavered.

"Looking, I saw in the fading twilight the dark masses of the enemy moving up the steep road, and at that moment a round was fired with effect upon those who had surrounded us. One more round only remained. Then we meant to die fighting. Blinding smoke suddenly filled the half-wrecked room, and we knew that the enemy had succeeded in setting fire to the taproom underneath!

"I stepped forward, and shouted for the last time the order to my brave comrades to fire. Nine rifles rang out simultaneously; but I had, I suppose, showed myself imprudently, for at the same second I felt a sharp twinge in the shoulder, and knew that I had been struck. The rest was all a blank.

"When I regained my senses I found myself lying in Sandwell Hall, with doctors bandaging my wounds, and then I learned that we had been rescued just in time, and that my nine comrades had all escaped the fate they had faced with dogged disregard for their own safety, and such noble devotion to their Queen."

It was a black day for Britain. During the long hours of that fierce, mad struggle many Victoria Crosses were earned, but the majority of those who performed deeds worthy of such decoration, alas! fell to the earth, dead.

XX

Our Revenge in the Mediterranean

M any important events had occurred in the Mediterranean since the outbreak of hostilities. At the moment of the sudden Declaration of War, the ships forming the British Mediterranean Squadron were at Larnaka, Cyprus, and on receipt of the alarming intelligence, the Admiral sailed immediately for Malta. On arrival there, he heard that a strong force of French vessels had been despatched to Gibraltar for the purpose of preventing any British ships from getting out of the Mediterranean in order to strengthen the Channel Squadron. Nevertheless he waited for some days at Malta, in hourly expectation of instructions, which came at length about two o'clock one morning, and an hour later the Squadron sailed westward for an unknown destination.

Our Fleet in those waters was notoriously inadequate in comparison with those of France and Russia. It consisted of three of the battleships constructed under the 1894 programme, the *Jupiter*, *Cæsar*, and *Victorious*, with the cruisers *Diana* and *Dido*; the ironclads *Collingwood*, *Dreadnought*, *Hood*, *Inflexible*, *Nile*, *Ramillies*, *Repulse*, *Sans Pareil*, *Trafalgar*, *Magnificent*, *Empress of India*, and *Revenge*; the cruisers *Arethusa*, *Edgar*, *Fearless*, *Hawke*, *Scout*, *Orlando*, *Undaunted*; the torpedo ram *Polyphemus*; the torpedo gun-vessel *Sandfly*; the sloops *Dolphin*, *Gannet*, *Melita*, and *Bramble*; and the despatch vessel *Surprise*, with twenty-two torpedo boats and six destroyers.

The information received by our Fleet at Malta was to the effect that the French force at Gibraltar was so strong that a successful attack was out of the question; while the Russian Mediterranean and Black Sea Fleets, the strength of which was considerable, were also known to be approaching for the purpose of co-operating with the French.

Notwithstanding the addition of three new battleships and two new cruisers to our force in the Mediterranean, the utter inadequacy of our Navy was still very apparent. For years the British public had demanded that a dozen more new battleships should be constructed in case of casualties, but these demands were unheeded, and during the three years that had passed we had lost our naval supremacy, for France and Russia combined were now considerably stronger. France alone had

150 fighting pennants available along her southern shores, against our 59; and the Tsar's ships were all strong, well-equipped, and armed with guns of the latest type.

As was feared from the outset, the Russian Black Sea Fleet had struck for the Suez Canal, England's highway to the East. Egypt, the Bosphorus, Gibraltar, and Tripoli in the grasp of the enemy, meant supremacy in the East, and a situation that would not be tolerated by either Italy or Austria. Therefore the British Admiral, recognising the seriousness of the situation, and having received instructions to return home and assist in the defence of Britain, mustered his forces and cleared for action. The events that occurred immediately afterwards are best related in the graphic and interesting narrative which was subsequently written to a friend by Captain Neville Reed of the great steel battleship *Ramillies*, and afterwards published, together with the accompanying sketch, in the *Illustrated London News*, as follows:—

"After leaving Malta, we rounded the Adventure Bank off the Sicilian coast, and headed due north past Elba and on to the Gulf of Genoa. From Spezia we received despatches, and after anchoring for twelve hours,—during which time we were busy completing our preparations,—sailed at midnight westward. Off St. Tropez, near the Hyères Islands, in obedience to signals from the flagship, the *Empress of India*, the ironclads *Jupiter*, *Sans Pareil*, *Repulse*, with the cruisers *Edgar*, *Dido*, *Diana*, *Orlando*, *Undaunted*, and *Scout*, the sloop *Gannet*, and five torpedo boats, detached themselves from the Squadron, and after exchanging further signals, bore away due south. Giving the shore a wide offing, we steamed along throughout the afternoon. The Mediterranean had not yet been the scene of any bloody or fatal conflict, but as we cut our way through the calm sunlit waters with a brilliant cerulean sky above, the contrast between our bright and lovely surroundings and the terrible realities of the situation during those breathless hours of suspense still dwells distinctly in my memory.

"It was our duty to fight the enemy, to beat him, and to pass through the Straits of Gibraltar and help our comrades at home. Every man, although totally unaware of his present destination, felt that at last the moment had come when the supreme ambition of his life was to be realised, and he was to strike a blow for his country's honour.

"Apparently our Admiral was in no hurry. He no doubt was awaiting events, for at sunset we lay-to about thirty miles south of La Ciotat, and spent the calm bright night restlessly anxious and keeping a sharp

WILLIAM LE QUEUX

lookout for the enemy. There was a hush of expectation over the ship, and scarcely a sound broke the quiet save the lapping of the water against the smooth sides of the ironclad, and no sign of force except the swish of the waves falling on either side of the formidable and deadly ram.

"Just after seven bells in the morning watch, however, we resumed our voyage, and turning, went north again. Then, for the first time, we knew the Admiral's intentions. An ultimatum had already been given. *We were to bombard Marseilles!*

"Three hours later we came within view of the city. Seen from the sea it has a certain amount of picturesqueness. In the foreground there is the harbour, with a barren group of islands at its entrance, and behind masses of yellow houses covering an extensive valley, and white villas dotted over a semicircle of green hills stretching in the rear. Prominent in the landscape is the church of Nôtre Dame de la Garde, perched on the eminence on the right; while on the left there stands on an island the Château d'If, rendered immortal by the adventures of Monte Cristo; and behind, on the broad Quai de la Joliette, rises the fine Cathedral, built in alternate courses of black and white stone. It is a handsome and wealthy city, with its fine shady boulevard, the Cannebière running through its centre from the Arc de Triomphe right down to the old port whence the mail steamers depart. This city, teeming with life, it was our duty to lay in ruins!

"Knowing how strongly fortified it was, that upon each of those hills were great batteries ready at a given signal to pour out their deadly hail, and that under the blue waters were mines which might be exploded from the shore at any moment, we made preparations for counter-mining, and then cautiously approached within range. Suddenly, however, having got into position and laid our guns, we received the anxiously expected order, and a few moments later opened a terrific and almost simultaneous fire.

"Through my glass I could clearly distinguish the terrible confusion being caused in the streets as our shells fell and burst on the Quai de la Joliette, in the Cannebière, and the Boulevard de l'Empéreur.

"The first taste of our guns had produced a terrible panic, for a shell from the *Dreadnought*, lying next to us, had struck the tower of the Cathedral and brought down a great quantity of masonry, while another shell from one of our 67-ton guns, bursting in the Palais de Justice with terrible effect, had ignited it.

"It was our first shot, and the gun had been well sighted; but ere we fired again such a storm of shell burst upon us that I confess for a moment I stood in my conning-tower motionless in surprise. On all sides the French had apparently established batteries. From the great Fort St. Jean at the entrance to the port, and from the Batterie du Phare on the opposite side, flame and smoke belched from heavy guns continuously. From a small battery in the Château d'If, from another on the rocky promontory on the right known as the Edoume, from a number of smaller ones established on the hills of l'Oriol and the Citadel, as well as from the great fortress of Nôtre Dame de la Garde on the highest hill, a little to the right of the city, there came an incessant thunder, and dozens of shots ricochetted over the placid water towards us.

"In a few moments, however, my 67-tonners were again adding to the deafening roar, my ten 6-inch quick-firing guns were sending out their messengers of death, and my smaller arms, consisting of 3 and 16-pounders, were acting their part in the sudden outburst. We had attacked the town without intention of investment, but simply to destroy it, and as the minutes slipped by, and I peered through my glass, I could see how devastating were our enormous modern shells.

"All our guns were now trained upon the forts, and the bombardment was most vigorous. The six coast-defence ships, which endeavoured to drive us off, we quickly put out of action, capturing one, torpedoing two, and disabling the three others; while up to the present, although a number of shots from the land batteries had struck us, we sustained no serious damage.

"We were avenging Hull and Newcastle. Into the panic-stricken town we were pouring an unceasing storm of shell, which swept away whole streets of handsome buildings, and killed hundreds of those flying for safety into the country. Watching, I saw one shot from one of my bow barbette guns crash into the roof of the fine new Hôtel du Louvre, in the Cannebière. The French Tricolor on the flagstaff toppled over into the street, and a second later the clouds of smoke and the débris which shot up showed plainly the awful results of the bursting shell.

"Time after time my 67-tonners crashed and roared, time after time I pressed my fingers upon the little knobs in the conning-tower, and huge projectiles were discharged right into the forts. In conjunction with the never-ceasing fire of companion ships, we rained iron in a continuous stream that wrought havoc in the defences and destroyed all the buildings that offered targets. In an hour the Arsenal behind the Palais de Justice was laid in ruins, the fine Hôtel de Ville was a mere heap of smouldering débris, the Bourse, and the great Library in the Boulevard du Musée were half wrecked by shells, and the Custom House, the Gendarmerie, and the Prefecture were burning furiously. The Château du Phare on the headland at the entrance to the fort was suffering frightfully, and the shells that had struck the Citadel and the fort of Nôtre Dame had been terribly effective. Every part of the city from the Promenade du Prado to the Botanical Gardens was being swept continuously by our fire, and from the black smoke curling upward in the sunlight we knew that many broad handsome streets were in flames. Excited over their work of revenge, my guns' crews worked on with a contemptuous disregard for the withering fire being poured upon us from the land. They meant, they said, to teach the Frenchmen a lesson, and they certainly did. Around us shots from the batteries fell thickly, sending up huge columns of water. Suddenly a shell struck the *Ramillies* forward in front of the barbette, and burst like the rending of a thundercloud. The deck was torn up, a dozen men were maimed or killed, poor fellows! but the solid face of the barbette held its own, and the muzzles of our two great guns remained untouched.

"Several shots from the Nôtre Dame Fort and the Endoume Battery then struck us in quick succession. One was particularly disastrous, for, crashing into the battery on the port side, it burst, disabling one of the 6-inch guns, and killing the whole gun's crew in an instant. The effect was frightful, for the whole space around was wrecked, and not a man escaped.

"Such are the fortunes of war! A few moments later we turned our heavy guns upon the Endoume Battery, perched up upon the rocky headland, and together with the *Empress of India* and the *Victorious* thundered forth our great projectiles upon it in a manner which must have been terribly disconcerting. The battery replied vigorously at first, but the *Nile*, noticing the direction in which we had turned our attention, trained her guns upon the same fort, and let loose a perfect hail of devastating shell. Without ceasing for a second, we played upon it, and could distinguish even with the naked eye how completely we were destroying it, until half an hour later we found that the Frenchmen had ceased to reply. We had silenced their guns, and, in fact, totally wrecked the fort.

"Several of our vessels were, however, severely feeling the fire from the Nôtre Dame Fortress and that of St. Jean. Nearly one hundred men on board the *Trafalgar* had been killed; while two shots, entering one of the broadside batteries of the flagship, had caused frightful havoc, and had blown to atoms over forty men and three officers. A torpedo boat that had approached the French coast-defence ship just before she was captured had been sunk by a shot, but the crew were fortunately all rescued, after much difficulty, by the sloop *Dolphin*, which had severely suffered herself from the vigorous fire from the Batterie du Phare. The funnel of the *Nile* had been carried away by a shot from the Citadel, while among the more conspicuous British losses was a serious catastrophe which had occurred on board the *Hood* by the premature explosion of a torpedo, by which a sub-lieutenant and thirty-three men were launched into eternity, and sixteen men very severely wounded. The engines of the *Arethusa* were also broken.

"The smoke rising from the bombarded city increased every moment in density, and even in the daylight we could distinguish the flames. The centre of Marseilles was burning furiously, and the fire was now spreading unchecked. One of our objects had been to destroy the immense quantity of war stores, and in this we were entirely successful. We had turned our united efforts upon the Fort St. Jean down at the harbour entrance and that of Nôtre Dame high on the hill. Pounding away at these, time slipped by until the sun sank in a blaze of crimson and gold. Both forts made a gallant defence, but each of our shots went home, and through my glasses I watched the awful result. Suddenly a terrific report caused the whole city to tremble. One of our shots had apparently entered the powder magazine in the Fort St. Jean, and it had blown up, producing an appalling catastrophe from which the fortress could never recover.

"By this time the whole of the shipping in the docks was burning furiously, and the congested part of the city lying between the port and the Lyons Railway Station was like a huge furnace. The sight was one of terrible grandeur.

"Presently, just as the sun sank behind the grey night clouds, we ceased fire, and then gazed with calm satisfaction upon the result of our bombardment. We had treated a French city in the same manner as the French and Russians had treated our own homes, and we could look upon this scene of destruction and death without a pang of remorse. But that was not all. When our guns were silent we could

WILLIAM LE QUEUX

distinctly hear vigorous rifle firing at the back of the city. Then we knew the truth.

"While we had been attacking Marseilles from the sea, the Italians, who a week before had crossed the frontier, and with the Germans occupied Lyons, had co-operated with us on land, and the terror-stricken Marseillais, hemmed in by fire and bullets on either side, had been swept away in thousands.

"The scenes in the streets were, we afterwards learnt, awful; and although the garrison offered a desperate resistance to the Italians along the valley near the Château des Fleurs, most of them were killed, and nearly three thousand of their number taken prisoners. But the Italians were unable to enter Marseilles themselves, as, long before they had succeeded in breaking up the land defences, we had set the place on fire, and now, as night fell, the great city was one mass of flames, the lurid light from which illuminated sky and sea with a bright red glare."

THE BLAZING AFRICAN SUN WAS fading, flooding the calm sapphire Mediterranean with its blood-red afterglow. The air was oppressive, the wind blew hot from the desert, and shoals of tiny green birds were chattering before roosting in the oasis of tall date palms that cast long shadows over the sun-baked stones of the Place du Gouvernement at Algiers. Everything was of a dazzling whiteness, relieved only by the blue sky and sea. The broad, handsome Square was almost deserted, the jalousies of the European houses were still closed, and although a few people were sipping absinthe at the cafés, the siesta was not yet over.

At one corner of the Square the Mosque of Djama-el-Djedid, with its dome and minarets, stood out intensely white against the bright, cloudless sky, its spotless cleanliness causing the white-washed houses of Europeans to appear yellow and dingy; and as the *mueddin* stood on one of the minarets with arms uplifted, calling the Faithful to prayer, idle Moors and Arabs, who had been lying asleep in the shadow during the afternoon, rose quickly, rearranged their burnouses, and entered the Mosque in order to render thanks to Allah.

Darkness crept on after a brief twilight. Moorish women, wrapped in their white *haicks*, wearing their ugly baggy trousers, and veiled to the eyes, waddled along slowly and noiselessly among the palms, and gradually a gay cosmopolitan crowd assembled in the Place to enjoy the *bel fresco* after the terrible heat of the day, and to listen to the fine band of the 1st Zouaves, which had already taken up its stand in the centre of the Square, and was now playing one of Strauss's dreamy waltzes.

The night was bright and starlit, one of those calm, mystic evenings peculiar to North Africa. All was peaceful, but no moon had yet risen. The city wore its gay air of carelessness. White-robed Moors and red-fezzed Arabs, negroes from the Soudan, and Biskris in their blue burnouses, lounged, chattered, and promenaded, while the cafés and bazaars around were full of life, and the warm, balmy air was laden with the scent of flowers.

Suddenly, without warning, the whole place was illuminated by a brilliant light from the sea. Slowly it swept the town, and a few seconds later other bright beams shot forth, lighting up the quays, the terraces of white, flat-roofed houses, and the Moorish city on the hill. Then, before the promenaders could realise the cause, a loud booming was heard at sea, and almost at the same moment a shell fell, and, exploding in the midst of them, blew a dozen Moors and Arabs into atoms.

In a few seconds the cannonade increased, and the battery in the centre of the harbour replied. Then firing seemed to proceed from all quarters, and a storm of shell suddenly crashed upon the town with the most appalling effect.

British war-vessels had crept up within range, and were pouring the vials of Britain's wrath upon the ancient city of the Deys!

The detachment of vessels which, led by the new battleship *Jupiter*, went south from St. Tropez, had received instructions to destroy Algiers and return with all speed to Cagliari, in Sardinia, to await further instructions. The bombardment of the two cities simultaneously was in order to draw off the French Squadron from the position it had taken up near Gibraltar, so that the British could fight and then run past them into the Atlantic.

How far the manoeuvre succeeded is shown in the few interesting details of the bombardment given in the course of an interview which a reporter of the *Daily Telegraph* had with Lieut. George Ingleton, of the first-class cruiser *Edgar*. The officer said:—

"We arrived off Algiers two hours after sundown, and after an inspection with search-lights, began to let fly with our big guns. In a few minutes the Al-Djefna Battery in the centre of the harbour replied, and a moment later a very rigorous fire was poured forth from Fort Neuf on the right and Forts Bab-Azzoun and Conde on the left. All four were very strong, and in conjunction with coast-defence vessels offered a most vigorous resistance. So suddenly did we fire upon the town, that a frightful panic must have been caused. Before we had fired half a dozen times, a shot from one of our 22-tonners crashed into the dome of the Mosque and totally demolished it, while another particularly well-aimed shell struck the Mairie, a big handsome building on the Boulevard de la République, facing the sea, tearing out a portion of the front. Then, turning our guns upon the long row of shops, banks, and hotels which formed the Boulevard, we pounded away most effectively, while several of our other vessels attended to the forts.

"During the first half-hour the four warships of the enemy gave us considerable trouble, but very soon our torpedoes had sunk two of them, and the other two were quickly captured.

"Meanwhile, under the hot fire from the forts, the bombardment grew exciting. Shells were ricochetting on the water all round us, but our search-lights being now shut off, we offered a very indistinct target to the enemy. On nearly all our ships, however, there were some slight casualties. A shell severely damaged the superstructure of the *Jupiter*, while others rendered useless several of her machine guns. A shell penetrated the *Gannet*, unfortunately killing fourteen bluejackets; and had it not been that the deck of the *Edgar* was protected throughout, the consequences to us would also have been very serious. Nevertheless, our two 22-ton guns rendered valuable service, and contributed in no small measure to the demolition of the town.

"From the outset we could see that Algiers was totally unprepared for attack, and, continuing our fire calmly and regularly, we watched the flames bursting forth in every part of the town and leaping skyward. On shore the guns kept up their roaring thunder, although by aid of glasses we could detect how effectual were our shells in wrecking the fortifications and laying in ruins the European quarter. Every moment we were dealing terrible blows which shook the city to its foundations. The formidable city walls availed them nothing, for we could drop our shells anywhere we pleased, either on the hill at Mustapha or upon the pretty Moorish villas that lined the shore at St. Eugène.

"Blazing away at long range upon the town, we spread destruction everywhere. Houses toppled like packs of cards, mosques were blown into the air, and public buildings swept away like grains of sand before the sirocco. Under such a fire thousands of natives and Europeans must have perished, for we were determined to carry out our intentions, and teach the invaders a lesson they were not likely to easily forget. Time after time our heavy guns crashed, while our 6-inch quick-firers kept up their roar, and our machine guns rattled continuously. As the hours went by, and we continued our work of merciless destruction, we were hit once or twice, but beyond the loss of two men and some unimportant damage we escaped further punishment.

"The roar of our guns was deafening, and the smoke hung over the calm sea like a storm-cloud. Still we kept on in the face of the galling fire from the shore, and before midnight had the satisfaction of witnessing a magnificent spectacle, for the isolated conflagrations gradually united and the whole town was in flames.

"We had accomplished our work, so with cheers for Old England we gave a parting shot, and turning were soon steaming away towards the Sicilian coast, leaving Algiers a mass of roaring flame.

"The journey was uneventful until just before noon on the following day. I was at that time on duty, and suddenly, to my surprise, detected a number of ships. By the aid of our glasses, the captain and I found to our dismay that a number of the most powerful vessels of the Russian Fleet were bearing down upon us! All our other vessels had made the same discovery, and I must confess that the meeting was somewhat disconcerting. The strength of the Russian ironclads was such as to cause our hearts to beat more quickly. To engage that great force meant certain defeat, while it was necessary that our Admiral off Marseilles should know of the whereabouts of this hostile squadron, therefore we resolved to get away. But although we altered our course and put on all speed, we were, alas! unsuccessful. At last we determined at all hazards to stick to our guns so long as we were afloat, and as the first of the Tsar's ironclads drew within range, one of our 22-tonners thundered. The white smoke, driven forward, tumbled over our bows. We had spoken the first word of battle!"

XXI

A Naval Fight and Its Consequences

The great naval force of the Tsar, with which we were now face to face," continued Lieutenant Ingleton in his narrative, "consisted of the new battleship *Petropavlovsk* of 10,960 tons, with a speed of 17 knots; the great turret-ship *Dvenadsat Apostoloff* of 8076 tons; the two new barbette-ships *Kama* and *Vologda* of the *Cizoi Veliky* type; the *Tchesmé* of 10,181 tons, the *Gheorghy Pobyednosets* of 10,280 tons, and the powerful *Tria Sviatitelia* of 12,480 tons; the two enormous new cruisers *Tiumen* and *Minsk*, both of 17,000 tons, and running at 20 knots; the *Vladimir Monomach* of 5754 tons; the armoured gunboat *Otvazny*, and the new rams *Admiral Seniavine* and *Admiral Uschakoff*, with thirty torpedo boats, including the *Kodor*, *Reni*, *Anakria*, and *Adler*, the latter being able to run at 27·4 knots.

"Against such a gigantic force as this our small force of vessels and torpedo boats presented but a sorry appearance. Nevertheless we had fired the first shot, and were now determined to die rather than haul down our colours. As our guns thundered, those of the *Jupiter*, *Repulse*, *Sans Pareil*, *Undaunted*, *Orlando*, *Diana*, *Scout*, and *Gannet* joined in noisy chorus. The 12-inch guns in the turrets of the *Petropavlovsk* and the four big guns in the barbettes of the *Tria Sviatitelia* crashed out together, and almost immediately afterwards we found ourselves being swept from stem to stern by the enemy's shells. The Russian battleships were all well armoured, and had a much heavier shell fire than the vessels of either France or Britain. We were both in columns of divisions in line ahead, but from the first moment of the engagement our position was critical.

"A terrific and deadly storm burst upon us from the enemy's tops, while his heavy guns kept up an incessant thunder. With such an enormous force against us, it was apparent to every man on board that disaster was imminent. It had, alas! never been graven sufficiently deep upon the public mind how absurdly weak we were in the Mediterranean. Here, as in all other squadrons, every grade of officer from commander downwards was deficient in numbers, and the ships in commission had for years been so much below their complement that the work had only been carried on with great difficulty. Other ships at home had been obliged to wait until a sufficient number of merchant seamen and half-trained engine-room staff could be scraped together to provide the semblance of a crew. In fact, successive British Governments of both parties had subordinated national necessities to a desire to evade a material increase in taxation, and now at last our Mediterranean Squadron were compelled to face the inevitable.

"The insidious cunning and patient methods to which the Russians resort in order to attain their aims and break their boundaries had once more been illustrated. They had, by dint of extraordinary chicanery, secured absolute possession of the small Turkish peninsula known as Mount Athos. Situated near the entrance of the Gulf of Salonica, it was a paramount strategical position, and its possessor was now enabled to keep watch upon Macedonia, and in the meantime be very near the Dardanelles, and also Asia Minor. The possession was accomplished in a curiously secret manner, showing to what extent Russian foresight and artifice is carried. For years past the *Société Slav de Bienfaisance* had been sending, through a bank in Salonica, large sums of money to further the aim. To the casual observer there was nothing extraordinary about this, for the Russians had established on the lofty heights several monasteries, converting the place into a clerical settlement. This fact was pointed out by the *Pall Mall Gazette* as far back as 1893, but the British public at that time failed to detect any Russian intrigue.

"Gradually, however, Muscovite roubles purchased the surrounding property, and Greek convents were reduced to poverty while Russian institutions flourished and increased. But, strangely enough, the inmates of these monasteries were suddenly discovered to be mock clerics, and then it was disclosed that under the cover of monastic garments and robes were to be found the Tsar's soldiers, performing a three years' special and specific military service!

"Yet, owing to the Sultan's weakness, to the almighty backsheesh, and to the shortsightedness of Turkish statesmen, the Russians were not dislodged, but the position was actually ceded to them, with the result that they had now firmly established themselves where they were enabled to counteract British action and influence. A naval station had been established for their Mediterranean Squadron at Poros, off the eastern coast of the Peloponnesus, some fifteen miles due south of the island of Ægina. Here there were three miles of deep water safe from sea attack, with an arsenal and dockyard, on the very weakest point along the line of our highway between England and India! Such was the manner in which our power in the Mediterranean had been undermined!

"There was, however, no time for reflection amid the deafening roar. This Black Sea Fleet that had burst its bonds and passed through the Dardanelles intended to sweep us from the sea. Yet, notwithstanding the terrible fire pouring upon us from these great and powerful ships, each fully equipped with the latest and most improved arms, fully manned by well-trained men, and fresh for the fray, we held our quarters, determined to show the forces of the Tsar defiance. Even though every man of us might be sent to an untimely grave, the Russian flag should never surmount the White Ensign of Britain. We were determined, so we set our teeth, and showed a firm and vigorous front to the foe.

"Our two 22-tonners rendered admirable service, and the cannonade kept up from our 3 and 6-pounder quick-firing guns was playing havoc with the Russian belted cruiser *Vladimir Monomach* lying on our port quarter. The vessel was slightly larger than ourselves, carrying much heavier armaments, including four 13-ton guns, and twelve 4-tonners. She was indeed a very formidable opponent, nevertheless we did our best, and, blazing away at close quarters, soon succeeded in silencing the starboard 13-tonner nearest us.

"Just at this moment I found we were being attacked on the port bow by the enormous new turret-ship *Petropavlovsk* and the *Dvenadsat Apostoloff*. Two of the heavy 12-inch guns of the former thundered almost simultaneously, and both shells striking us almost amidships, caused us such a shock that for a second I stood breathless.

"In a few moments, however, it was reported that our 'vitals' had fortunately escaped, and we continued firing as if no catastrophe had occurred. As a matter of fact, the damage caused by those two shells was appalling.

"The *Jupiter*, steaming about two miles away on our starboard quarter, was apparently holding her own against the barbette-ships *Tchesmé* and *Gheorghy Pobyednosets*, the cruiser *Tiumen*, one of the largest in the world, and the new ram *Admiral Seniavine*. The four attacking vessels, as seen through the dense smoke, were pouring into the British ship a deadly fire; yet, judging from the fallen tops and disabled engines of the *Gheorghy Pobyednosets* and the wrecked superstructure of the *Tchesmé*, the *Jupiter's* heavy armaments were executing good work, notwithstanding the strength of the *Tchesmé's* six 50-ton guns, admirably arranged in pairs in the centre of the vessel.

"The *Diana* and *Sans Pareil*, lying near to one another, were desperately resisting the vigorous attack made by the *Admiral Uschakoff*, *Minsk*, *Otvazny*, *Kama*, and *Vologda*; and here again, amid smoke and flying débris, I could distinguish that the 67-tonners of the *Repulse*, in co-operation with the lighter weapons of the *Undaunted*, were giving the enemy a taste of what British courage could accomplish.

"The sea around us simply swarmed with Russian torpedo boats, and it required all our vigilance to evade their continued attacks. Before an hour had passed we had succeeded in sinking two by shots from our 6-inch guns, and several more were sent to the bottom by well-aimed projectiles from the *Dido* and *Jupiter*.

"As for ourselves, projectiles were sweeping across our deck like hail, and under the incessant and fearful fire we were suffering frightfully. Over sixty of our men and a sub-lieutenant had been killed, while forty-nine were severely wounded. Once I had occasion to go below, and between decks the sight that met my gaze was awful.

"Around two of the quick-firing guns on our port quarter lay the guns' crews, mutilated by shells from the *Vladimir Monomach*. They had been killed almost instantly while standing bravely at their posts. The scene was appalling. The mangled masses of humanity amid which the surgeons were at work were awful to look upon, and I rushed up again with the terrible scene photographed indelibly upon my memory.

"Meanwhile the ship was in the greatest peril. The continual bursting of shells upon her shook and shattered her, and she trembled violently as, time after time, her own guns uttered their thundering reply to her enemies. Heeling now this way, now that, as the helm was put hard over to avoid a blow, the situation on board was intensely exciting.

"Those were terrible moments. The captain suddenly noticed the movements of the *Vladimir Monomach*, and divined her intentions. She had ceased firing, and by a neatly executed manoeuvre was preparing to ram us. In a moment our helm was put over again, and the *Edgar* answered to it immediately.

"'Ready bow tube!' I heard the captain shout hoarsely. He waited a few moments, allowing the Russian ironclad to partially perform her evolution, then just as she came almost into collision with us he shrieked 'Fire bow tube!' at the same time bringing us over further to port.

"The seconds seemed hours. Suddenly there was a loud explosion, a great column of water rose under the Russian's bow, and we knew the torpedo had struck. At that moment, too, even while the water was still in the air, one of our torpedo boats which had crept up under the *Vladimir Monomach's* stern sent another torpedo at her, which also hit its mark and ripped her up. Turning our guns upon the armoured cruiser, we poured volley after volley into her, but she did not reply, for her men were panic-stricken, and she was sinking fast.

"The *Petropavlovsk*, leaving us, endeavoured to rescue her crew, but ere a dozen men were saved, she settled down bow foremost, and disappeared into the deep, carrying down with her nearly five hundred officers and men.

"The *Dvenadsat Apostoloff* kept up her fire upon us, and a few moments later I witnessed another disaster, for a shot from one of her bow guns struck the torpedo boat that had just assisted us, and sank it. A few minutes later a loud explosion in the direction of the *Sans Pareil* attracted my attention, and, turning, I saw amid the smoke-clouds débris precipitated high into the air. A shot from one of her 111-ton guns had penetrated to the magazine of the *Admiral Seniavine*, which had exploded, causing a frightful disaster on board that vessel, and just at the same moment a cheer from the crew of one of our 6-inch guns prompted me to look for the cause, which I found in the fact that they had shot the Russian colours completely away from the *Dvenadsat Apostoloff*.

"Again another frightful explosion sounded loud above the incessant din, and to my satisfaction I saw a great column of water rise around the *Admiral Uschakoff*, which, fighting at close quarters with the *Dido*, had apparently been torpedoed. Not satisfied with this, the captain of the *Dido*, keeping his machine guns going, turned his vessel and discharged a second Whitehead, which also struck with such terrible effect that the Russian ship began at once to sink, and in a few minutes the blue waves closed for ever over her tops, ere a score or so out of her crew of 300 could be rescued.

"It was nearly three bells, and the sun was setting. A galling fire from the machine guns in the foretop of the *Dvenadsat Apostoloff* suddenly swept our deck, killing a dozen poor fellows who were at work clearing away some débris, and at the same moment a shot from one of her 52-ton guns crashed into our port quarter, and must have caused terrible havoc among the guns' crews. A moment later we were dismayed by the report that our steering-gear had been broken. For a few seconds we were helplessly swinging round under the awful fire which was now pouring from the great guns of the Russian ironclad, and our captain was making strenuous efforts to recover control of the ship, when I saw the torpedo boat *Anakria* shoot suddenly across our bows, then quickly slacken as she got to starboard of us.

"A second later I realised her intention, and shouted frantically. A line of bubbles had appeared on the surface advancing swiftly towards us. She had ejected a torpedo straight at us, and I stood petrified, not daring to breathe.

"A moment later there came a terrific explosion right underneath us, followed by a harsh tearing sound as iron plates were torn asunder like tinfoil, and the ship's side was ripped completely up. The *Edgar* heaved high and plunged heavily, a great column of water rose high above her masts, and the air seemed filled with flying fragments of iron and wood. The vessel rocked and swayed so that we could not keep our feet, and then gradually heeling over, causing her guns to shift, she went down before a soul on board could launch a boat.

"At the moment of the explosion I felt a sharp twinge in the back, and found that I had been struck by a flying splinter of steel. The strain of those hours had been terrible, and of the events that followed I can only recollect two things. I remember finding myself struggling alone in the water with a shower of bullets from the *Dvenadsat Apostoloff's* tops sending up little splashes about me. Then I felt my strength failing, my limbs seemed paralysed, and I could no longer strike out to save myself. Abandoning all hope, I was sinking, when suddenly a rope was flung to me. I remember how frantically I clutched it, and that a few moments later I was hauled aboard a torpedo boat; but for days afterwards I lay hovering 'twixt life and death, oblivious to all. I was one of the thirteen only who were saved out of a crew of 327 brave officers and men."

Such a ghastly disaster could only produce profound dismay among those who manned the remaining British vessels. Straining every nerve to uphold the honour of Britain, the guns' crews of the *Jupiter*, *Sans Pareil*, *Repulse*, and *Undaunted*, with smoke-begrimed hands and faces, worked on with that indomitable energy begotten of despair. Regardless of the awful rain of shot and shell, they reloaded and fired with calm, dogged self-possession, the officers on all four vessels inspiring their men by various deeds of valour, and preserving such discipline under

WILLIAM LE QUEUX

fire as none but British sailors could. The British naval officer is full of undaunted defiance and contempt for his foes; but, above all, he is a strict disciplinarian, and to this our country in a great measure owes the supremacy our Navy has hitherto enjoyed upon the seas. During the fight the vessels had been moving in a north-easterly direction, and although the Russians were unaware of the fact, Her Majesty's ships had therefore continued in their course. Hence, just as a cool breeze sprang up at sundown, soon after the *Edgar* had sunk, a line of low dark cliffs was sighted ahead.

The officers of the *Diana*, watching anxiously through their glasses, distinguished the distant crest of Mount Genargentu gradually appearing against the clear evening sky, and then they knew that they were off Sardinia, outside the Gulf of Oristano.

Altering their course, they headed due north, still keeping up a running fire, but the Russians prevented them making headway.

All our vessels were suffering frightfully, when there was a sudden explosion, and, to the Englishmen's dismay, it was seen that a torpedo had struck the *Undaunted* nearly amidships. Still the doomed vessel managed to evade a second attack, and by a desperate manoeuvre the captain succeeded in turning and heading for land.

The remaining ships, in their terribly crippled condition, would, the Russians anticipated, soon fall an easy prey. Nevertheless, with their crews decimated, their guns disabled, and their machinery damaged, the British vessels still continued firing, the men resolved to go down at their quarters. They knew that escape was hopeless, and every moment they saw their comrades being swept away by the great exploding projectiles of the Tsar's heavy guns. But they were not dismayed. To do their utmost for the defence of Britain, to keep afloat as long as possible, and to die like Britons with faces towards the foe, was their duty. Pale and desperate, they were fighting for their country and their Queen, knowing that only a grave in the deep and the honour of those at home would be the reward of their bravery—that at any moment they might be launched into the unknown.

Suddenly there was a loud shouting on board the *Jupiter*, and signals were, a moment later, run up to her half-wrecked top. The captain of the *Dido*, noticing this, looked to ascertain the cause, and saw away on the horizon to the north, whence the dark night clouds were rising, a number of strange craft. Snatching up his glass, he directed it on the strangers, and discovered that they were Italian warships, and were exchanging rapid signals with the captain. They were promising assistance!

Cheers rang loudly through the British vessels, when, a few minutes later, the truth became known, and the guns' crews worked with redoubled energy, while the Russians, noticing the approaching ships, were apparently undecided how to act. They were given but little time for reflection, however, for within half an hour the first of the great Italian ironclads, the *Lepanto*, opened fire upon the *Petropavlovsk*, and was quickly followed by others, until the action became general all round.

Aid had arrived just in time, and the British vessels, with engines broken, stood away at some distance, leaving matters for the nonce to the powerful Italian Squadron. It was indeed a very formidable one, and its appearance caused the Russian Admiral such misgivings that he gave orders to retreat, a manoeuvre attempted unsuccessfully. The Italian Fleet, as it loomed up in the falling gloom, included no fewer than twenty-six warships and forty-three torpedo boats. The vessels consisted of the barbette-ship *Lepanto* of 15,000 tons; the *Sardegna*, *Sicilia*, and *Re Umberto* of 13,000 tons; the *Andrea Doria*, *Francesca Morosini*, and *Ruggiero di Lauria* of 11,000 tons; the turret-ships *Dandolo* and *Duilio* of the same size; the *Ammeraglio di St. Bon* of 9800 tons; the armoured cruisers *Ancona*, *Castelfidardo*, and *Maria Pia*, and the *San Martino*, each of about 4500 tons; the gun-vessels *Andrea Provana*, *Cariddi*, *Castore*, *Curtatone*; the torpedo gunboats *Aretusa*, *Atlante*, *Euridice*, *Iride*, *Montebello*, and *Monzambano*; the despatch vessels *Galileo* and *Vedetta*; and the first-class torpedo vessels *Aquila*, *Avvoltoio*, *Falco*, *Nibbio*, and *Sparviero*, and thirty-eight others.

With such a force descending upon the Russian ships, which had already been very severely punished by the vigorous fire of the British, there was little wonder that the Tsar's vessels should endeavour to escape. The Italian Fleet had already bombarded and destroyed Ajaccio two days ago, and, steaming south from the Corsican capital, had anchored for twenty-four hours off Cape della Caccia, near Alghero, in the north of Sardinia. Then again taking a southerly course in the expectation of joining hands with the British Mediterranean Squadron, which was on its way from Marseilles to Cagliari, they had fallen in with the three crippled ships.

Without hesitation the powerful Italian ironclads, several of which were among the finest in the world, opened a terrific fire upon the Russian ships, and as darkness fell the sight was one of appalling grandeur. From all sides flame rushed from turrets and barbettes in vivid flashes, while the Maxims in the tops poured out their deadly showers of bullets. The ponderous 105-ton guns of the *Andrea Doria*, *Francesca Morosini*, and *Ruggiero di Lauria* crashed and roared time after time, their great shots causing frightful havoc among the Russian ships, the four 100-tonners of the *Lepanto* and the 67-tonners of the *Re Umberto*, *Sardegna*, and *Sicilia* simply knocking to pieces the *Petropavlovsk*. The Russian ships were receiving terrible blows on every hand. With their search-lights beaming forth in all directions, the ships were fighting fiercely, pounding away at each other with deafening din. It was not long, however, before this vigorous attack of the Italians began to tell, for within an hour of the first shot from the *Lepanto* the fine Russian battleship *Gheorghy Pobyednosets* and the great new cruiser *Minsk* of 17,000 tons had been rammed and sunk, the former by the *Duilio*, and the latter by the *Re Umberto*, while the *Tchesmé* and the gunboat *Otvazny* had been torpedoed, and scarcely a soul saved out of 1500 men who were on board.

Explosions were occurring in quick succession, and red glares flashed momentarily over the sea. Hither and thither as the Italian torpedo boats darted they ejected their missiles, and the rapid and terrible fire from the leviathans of Italy, pouring into every one of the remaining ships of the Tsar, killed hundreds who were striving to defend themselves.

Suddenly the *Sicilia*, which had been fighting the Russian flagship, the *Tria Sviatitelia*, at close quarters, and had blown away her conning-tower and greater portion of her superstructure, performed a neat evolution, and crashed her ram right into her opponent's broadside, breaking her almost in half.

A few moments later there was a terrific explosion on board, and then the doomed vessel sank into the dark rolling sea, carrying with her the Russian Admiral and all hands.

Quickly this success was followed by others—the blowing up of the monster new cruiser *Tiumen*, the sinking of the *Adler* and four other Russian torpedo boats, occurring in rapid succession. Seeing with what rapidity and irresistible force they were being swept from the sea, the remainder of the Tsar's shattered fleet struck their flags and called for quarter, not, however, before the torpedo boat *Kodor* had been sunk. The Russians thus captured were the battleships *Petropavlovsk* of 10,960 tons, the *Dvenadsat Apostoloff* of 8076 tons, the two new barbette-ships,

Kama and *Vologda*, both of whose engines had broken down, and fifteen torpedo boats.

At dawn most of the latter were manned by Italians, while the captured ships, with the Italian colours flying and bearing evidence of the terrible conflict, were on their way due north to Genoa, accompanied by the battered British vessels.

The strongest division of Russia's Fleet had been totally destroyed, and the Tsar's power in the Mediterranean was broken.

XXII

PANIC IN LANCASHIRE

The Russians were within gunshot of Manchester! A profound sensation was caused in that city about eight o'clock on the evening of September 6th, by an announcement made by the *Evening News*—which still appeared in fitful editions—that a Cossack patrol had been seen on the road between Macclesfield and Alderley, and that it was evident, from the manner of the Russian advance, that they meant to attack the city almost immediately.

The utmost alarm was caused, and the streets were everywhere crowded by anxious, starving throngs, eager to ascertain fuller details, but unable to gather anything further beyond the wild conjectures of idle gossip.

The great city which, on the outbreak of war, was one of the most prosperous in the world, was now but a sorry semblance of its former self. Heated, excited, turbulent, its streets echoed with the heartrending wails of despairing crowds, its factories were idle, its shops closed, and its people were succumbing to the horrible, lingering death which is the result of starvation.

Wealth availed them naught. Long ago the last loaf had been devoured, the last sack of flour had been divided, and the rich living in the suburbs now felt the pinch of hunger quite as acutely as factory operatives, who lounged, hands in pockets, about the streets. Manchester, like most other towns in England, had come to the end of her supplies, and death and disease now decimated the more populous districts, while those who had left the city and tramped north had fared no better, and hundreds dropped and died by the roadside.

The situation in Lancashire was terrible. At Liverpool a few vessels were arriving from America, under escort of British cruisers, bringing supplies, but these were mostly purchased at enormously high rates, and sent to London by way of Manchester and Sheffield, railway communication by that route being still open. This fact becoming known in Manchester caused the greatest indignation, and the people, rendered desperate by hunger, succeeded on several occasions in stopping the trains, and appropriating the food they carried. The situation in Manchester was one of constant excitement, and fear that the enemy should repeat the success they had achieved at Birmingham. The hundreds of thousands of hungry ones who flocked Manchester streets and the grimy thoroughfares of Stockport, Ashton, Oldham, Bolton, and other great towns in the vicinity, feared that they, like the people of Birmingham, would be put to the sword by the ruthless invaders.

The week that had elapsed had been an eventful one, fraught with many horrors. After the success of the Russians at Birmingham, the British troops, both Regulars, Volunteers, and improvised, fell back and formed up north of the city, being practically nothing more than a strong line of outposts without reserves, extending from Dudley, through West Bromwich and Sutton Park, to Tamworth. This scheme, however, was ill-devised, for the defenders, in order to act successfully, should have fallen back much further, and concentrated their forces at one or two strategical points on the line to Manchester, as it had been ascertained from spies that a swift and vigorous attack on that city was meditated.

The day following the taking of Birmingham was devoted by the enemy to the reorganisation of their forces, and the rearrangement of their transport and ammunition train. Large quantities of waggons and war stores of all kinds had been found in the town and annexed by the victors, and at Kynoch's Factory at Aston some hundreds of thousands of rounds of ammunition had been seized. These had been made for a foreign government, and fitted both rifles and machine guns of the Russians.

Having thus reorganised, the Russians, leaving 10,000 men in Birmingham as a base, resumed their march north on the third day. The left flank, consisting of 2000 cavalry and 12,000 infantry, took the road through West Bromwich to Wednesbury and Bilston, but quickly found themselves entrapped, for on account of the many canals their cavalry were unable to act, and their transport was cut off. The miners and factory men had armed themselves, and, acting in conjunction with the British troops from Dudley and Great Barr, succeeded, after some hard fighting around Tipton and Coseley, in completely annihilating the enemy, taking 5000 prisoners and killing the remaining 9000.

Meanwhile the right flank had passed out of Birmingham by way of Castle Bromwich, and had advanced without opposition through Wishaw and Tamworth to Lichfield, driving the defenders before them. The Russian main column, however, were not allowed to go north without a most desperate endeavour on the part of our men to hold them in check. Indeed, if ever British courage showed itself it was during those dark days. Advancing through Aston and Perry to Sutton along the ancient highway, Icknield Street, the Russians sent a large force through the woods to the high ground between Wild Green and Maney. Here the British had established strong batteries, but after some desperate fighting these were at length captured, the enemy losing heavily. At the same time, fierce fighting occurred in Sutton Park and across at Aldridge, the defenders making the most strenuous efforts to break the force of the invaders. All was, alas! to no purpose. The British, outnumbered as before, were compelled to fall back fighting, with the result that the enemy's main column, pushing on, effected a junction with its right flank, which had bivouaced on Wittington Heath, near Lichfield, and occupied the barracks there.

On the day following the invaders broke into two columns and marched again north, practically in battle formation, the right column continuing along Icknield Street, through Burton, Derby, Bakewell, and Marple, driving back the defenders, while the left column took a route that lay through the hilly and wooded country near Cannock Chase. Both columns, advancing in échelon of division, with cavalry on their flanks, were constantly harassed in the rear by the British, and in their advance lost numbers of waggons and a large quantity of ammunition; but they succeeded in travelling so quickly north that they were actually marching on Manchester before the people in that city could realise it. Signal acts of bravery were being everywhere reported, but what could individual heroism effect against the fearful odds we had to face?

Thousands of men in Bolton, Bury, Oldham, Wigan, Rochdale, and other neighbouring towns had already armed themselves, and, on hearing that Manchester was threatened, poured into the city to act their part bravely in its defence.

It must be admitted that the British General commanding had, on gaining knowledge of the intentions of the Russians, taken every precaution in his power to prevent an advance on Manchester.

Our troops which had been defeated and driven back from Birmingham, had at once retreated north to the Peak district, and about one-quarter of the number had taken up excellent defensive positions there, while the remainder, with small reinforcements of Regulars drawn from Lancaster, Warrington, Bury, Chester, Wrexham, Burnley, Ashton-under-Lyne, York, Halifax, and as far distant as Carlisle, had, in addition to those from Manchester, been massed along the north bank of the Mersey from Stockport to Flixton, with a line of communication stretching across to Woodley Junction, and thence over Glossop Dale to the Peak.

Thus Manchester was defended by a force of 38,000 cavalry, infantry, Volunteers, and colonials, against the Russian army, consisting of the remaining 65,000 of the force which attacked Birmingham, and reinforcements of 10,000 infantry and 5000 cavalry that had been pushed rapidly forward from Sussex over the ground that the main body had travelled. The total force of Russians was therefore 80,000.

From Stockport, the north bank of the Mersey to its confluence with the Irwell past Flixton was well guarded. Earthworks had been raised, trenches dug, walls had been loopholed, and houses placed in a state of hasty defence. Among the reinforcements now under arms were several portions of battalions of Lancashire Volunteer Artillery who had not gone south to their allotted positions in the defence of London, and five companies of the 1st Cheshire and Carnarvonshire Artillery under Col. H. T. Brown, V.D., together with the Cheshire Yeomanry under Col. P. E. Warburton. The Manchester Brigade was a strong one, consisting of six Volunteer battalions of the Manchester Regiment, the 1st under the Earl of Crawford, V.D., the 2nd under Col. Bridgford, V.D., the 3rd under Col. Eaton, V.D., the 4th under Col. Lynde, V.D., the 5th under Col. Rocca, V.D., and the 6th under Col. Lees; the Cheshire and Lancashire Brigades included three Volunteer battalions of the Lancashire Fusiliers under Colonels Young, Philippi, and Haworth, and two battalions of the South Lancashire Regiment; while the Northern Counties Brigade, composed of one Volunteer battalion of the Royal Lancaster Regiment under Col. Strongitharm, two battalions of the East Lancashire Regiment under Col. A. I. Robinson, V.D., and Col. T. Mitchell, V.D., and two of the Loyal North Lancashire under Col. Widdows and Col. Ormrod, also mustered their forces and performed excellent defensive work. It was here, too, that the Volunteer cyclists were found of the utmost value in scouting and carrying despatches.

The excitement in Manchester on that memorable September night was intense. That a desperate and bloody fray was imminent, every one knew, and the people were trusting to the defensive line on the river bank to protect them from the foreign destroyer. Would they be strong enough to effectively resist? Would they be able to drive back the Russians and defeat them?

The people of Lancashire who condemned our military administration did not do so without cause. It had been claimed by many that England could never be invaded; nevertheless our course should have been to prepare for possible events. Our Army, being small, should have been better equipped and armed, as well as trained to balance weakness in numbers. Again, there had always existed a hideous hindrance to the efficiency of the Auxiliaries—the arms. Many of the Martini-Henrys carried by the Volunteers bore date of a quarter of a century ago, and their barrels were so worn they could not be fired accurately; while others possessed the Snider, which was practically a smoothbore from wear. What was the use of weapons surpassed in power by those of other nations? It was an unpalatable truth that had now at last dawned upon Britain, that in arming her soldiers she was far behind the rest of the world.

While Manchester spent the sultry night in feverish excitement at the knowledge that the enemy had advanced almost to their doors, the British outposts were being harassed by the enemy, who, flushed with success, were advancing gradually onward towards the line of defence. The Russian front had been suddenly widely extended, evidently aiming at a concentric attack on Manchester, and an attempt to wholly envelop the defenders' position by cavalry operating on both flanks.

Some terribly desperate encounters took place during a frightful thunderstorm which lasted a portion of the night, and many a brave Briton fell while performing valiant deeds for the honour of his country. The anxiety within the British lines that hot night was intense.

Reports coming in told of fierce fighting all along the line. Soon after midnight a British patrol, supported by cavalry, that had been sent out from Northenden to Baguley, was suddenly attacked by a party of Russians, who lay in ambush close to Wythenshaw Hall. A short but fierce fight ensued, but the British, knowing that part of the country well, succeeded in totally annihilating their antagonists. The firing, however, attracted attention in the Russian lines, with the result that a second attack was quickly made upon them, compelling them to retire up the hill at Lawton Moor, where they dashed into a small wood, closely pressed by the enemy. The attack was desperate. There is something terrible in a fight in a wood at night. The combatants could see nothing save an occasional flash in the impenetrable darkness, and hoarse cries went up from the mysterious inferno. Neither invader nor defender could distinguish each other, and in the half-hour that followed, many a Russian shot his comrade in mistake for his foe.

At last the defenders, finding that the slightest rustling of boughs brought down a volley from magazine rifles, stood motionless, scarcely daring to breathe, and waited anxiously, until at last the enemy, seeing that their efforts to drive them out were useless, withdrew, and went off towards Baguley.

In another direction, close to Henbury, near Macclesfield, a squadron of British cavalry surprised a small outpost camp of Russians, and cut it up terribly, killing half the number; but pushing on to Marthall, six miles across country, they came into collision with a body of Russian dragoons, and after a very fierce encounter were compelled to fall back again after considerable loss. On the outskirts of Northwich, and on the borders of Delamere Forest, skirmishes occurred, resulting in serious loss on both sides. A reconnoitring party of Russians was totally swept away and every man killed, by a British party who were concealed in an old farm building close to Alderley village; while another engaged in surveying the roads to Altrincham had been forced to retreat, leaving half their number dead or wounded on the edge of Tatton Park.

XXIII

The Eve of Battle

Some idea of the gallant conduct of our Volunteers during the night may be gathered from the following extract from a letter by Lieutenant John Rowling of the 2nd Volunteer Battalion of the East Lancashire Regiment, to a friend a few days afterwards. He wrote—

"You will no doubt have heard something about the warm work we had on the night before the Battle of Manchester. The city, as you know, was covered on the south by a long straggling line of outposts, extending practically from Stockport to Altrincham. Late in the afternoon of September 6th we received an order to proceed to Mere, about four miles from Altrincham, having been detailed to form the section of the outposts from New Tatton to Goodier's Green, and on arrival at Mere half of our force of 600 was left in reserve there; the supports were moved about half a mile down Watling Street, and the remainder was divided into three piquets, No. 1 at Bentley Hurst Farm, No. 2 at Moss Cottage, and No. 3 near Mereplatt Farm, with four double sentry posts out in front of each piquet.

"I was in command of No. 2 picket, with Anderson and Wishton as subs, and as soon as I returned to the piquet, after posting the sentries, I sent the former with two sections to form a detached post at Over Tabley, and instructed him to send a reconnoitring patrol as far down Watling Street as he might consider consistent with safety. Anderson posted his men, and returned to me about ten o'clock with a corporal and two men, bringing in a man who had been pointed out to him at Over Tabley as a suspicious character—in fact, he was said to be a spy. He had been staying at an inn there for two or three days, and had very little luggage. Anderson had examined his portmanteau, but found nothing there; and as the man refused to give any account of himself, he made him a prisoner. Fresh fires were continually breaking out, therefore I thought it best to waste no time questioning him, but took him into a room at Moss Cottage, where he was thoroughly searched. Notes were found upon him from which it was evident that he had been obtaining information for the enemy for some time, and, better still, particulars of their proposed operations for the investment of Manchester, showing that they were advancing in our direction along the old Watling Street.

"I sent the prisoner under escort to the commander of the outposts, and at the same time sent word to Nos. 1 and 3 piquets, after which Anderson and I went down to Over Tabley, leaving Wishton in charge of No. 2. The machine gun that had been allotted to my piquet I also ordered to Over Tabley, and on arrival there we threw up barricades, hastily constructed of barrels, doors, and logs, banked with earth, across the road between the Vicarage and the church. A quantity of barbed wire was found in the village, and this came in very useful, for we stretched several lengths of it across the roads on the off-side of the barricade.

"There were under thirty of us, but every man was determined to do his duty unflinchingly. By this time it was past eleven, and very dark, yet there was just light enough to train the gun on to the centre of the cross-roads by Dairyhouse Farm. Very soon we could hear the enemy approaching, and as their spy had not met them outside, they evidently concluded that the village was unoccupied, and advanced in comparatively close order, Cossacks leading, and the infantry so close that there was practically no division between their vanguard and mainguard. The first section of Cossacks very soon found our first wire, and the whole of their horses came to grief. Those in the rear, thinking probably that there was no other obstruction in the way, spurred their horses and galloped over their friends, only to meet with a similar fate further on.

"The pioneers doubled up, and began to cut the wires, and fearing that the infantry in the rear would soon deploy, I gave the order for independent firing. The Russians stood it for some minutes, and attempted to reply, but not a man of ours was visible, and they soon retreated to Tabley Hall, where I had no means of following them.

"It must be remembered that we were all Volunteers, the Regulars being on the Stockport flank of the outpost line. My men behaved splendidly, and the firing was excellent from first to last."

About the same time as the unsuccessful attack was made on the outposts at Mere, the British line was broken through at Heald Green and Appletree.

A cavalry patrol, supported by infantry, was feeling its way along the road to Wilmslow, and had passed Willow Farm, at which point the road runs beside the railway embankment.

The storm had burst, the thunder rolled incessantly, rain fell in torrents, and the lightning played about them, causing their arms to gleam in its vivid flashes.

Slowly, and without undue noise, the patrol was wending its way up the hill towards Finney Green, when suddenly there was a terrific rattle of musketry, and they discovered to their surprise that the enemy, who were occupying the embankment of the North-Western Railway on their left, were pouring upon them a fire sufficient to blanch the cheek of the bravest among them.

Along the embankment for a mile or more were stationed infantry with magazine rifles, and in addition they had brought two machine guns into play with appalling effect. So sudden did this galling fire open upon them, that men and horses fell without being able to fire a shot in return. British infantry, however, stood their ground, and as the lightning flashed, disclosing the position of the enemy, every Russian who dared to stand up or show himself was promptly picked off. But against the awful rain of deadly bullets ejected from the machine guns, at the rate of 600 a minute, no force could make a successful defence.

Many British heroes fell pierced by a dozen bullets; still their comrades, seeking what shelter they could, continued the defensive.

Meanwhile over the dismal muddy road the survivors of the cavalry galloped back, and quickly reported to the commander of the piquet at Appletree that the enemy were in strong force on the other side of the embankment between Oaklands and Wilmslow Park, and as they had heard a train run into Wilmslow Station and stop, it was evident that the enemy had reopened the line from Crewe, and intended concentrating part of their reinforcements to the general advance. The facts that the enemy had succeeded in cutting all the telegraph lines in the district, and had now obtained complete control over the railway, were most alarming, and the outlook of the defenders was rendered doubly serious by the large force they were compelled to keep east of Stockport, and in the Peak district, to prevent the invaders getting round to attack Manchester from the north.

On receipt of the news of the disaster to the patrol, the commander of the piquet at Appletree immediately sent information to the commander of the piquet posted at the railway station at Cheadle Hulme; but by a strange oversight, due no doubt to the excitement of the moment, sent no report to the commander of the outposts. The infantry engaging the Russians on the embankment, though exhibiting most gallant courage, were so exposed that it was little wonder they were soon completely annihilated, only half a dozen escaping.

The enemy must have detrained a large number of troops at Wilmslow, for the British cavalry scouts were quickly followed up by Cossacks and the Tsar's Dragoons. Quickly the sentries between Heald Green and Appletree were driven back on their piquets, the latter extending in skirmishing order. Such a manoeuvre, however, proved fatal in the darkness and on the heavy ploughed land over which they were fighting. Alas! very few succeeded in reaching the supports, and when they did, they all fell back hurriedly on the reserves at Pimgate.

Then the commander of the piquet at Cheadle Hulme Station, finding that he must inevitably be attacked by road and rail, set the station on fire, and with the assistance of the railway officials blew up a large portion of the permanent way with dynamite, thus cutting off the enemy's means of communication. This accomplished, he fell back upon his supports at Adswood, and they, at about 2 A.M., retreated with the reserves to the embankment of the North-Western Railway which carries the line from Stockport to Whaley Bridge, and took up a strong position to assist in the defence of Stockport.

The latter town was defended on three sides by railway embankments, which were now occupied by strong bodies of Regulars, with several Maxims. One embankment ran from the west boundary of the town to Middlewood Junction, another from Middlewood to Marple, and a third from Marple to Mayercroft. Throughout the night the defenders were in hourly expectation that an attack would be made upon their positions, with the object of investing Stockport as a preliminary to the assault on the defensive lines north of the Mersey; but the enemy apparently had other objects, and the disaster to the British cavalry patrol on the Wilmslow road was, unfortunately, followed by a second and more serious one. The Cossacks and Dragoons that followed the British cavalry scouts overtook them just as they had joined their reserves, a short distance beyond Pimgate, about half-past two. A fierce fight ensued, and the force of British cavalry and infantry was gradually drawn into a cunningly-devised trap, and then there suddenly appeared a great force of Russians, who simply swept down upon them, slaughtering the whole of them with brutal ferocity, not, however, before they had fought desperately, and inflicted enormous loss upon the enemy.

Having totally annihilated that detachment of defenders, the

Russians marched into Cheadle, and, after sacking the little town, burned it, together with the Grange, the Print Works, the railway station, St. Mary's Church, and a number of large mills.

The great army of the Tsar had bivouaced, reserving its strength for a desperate dash upon Manchester. But the British outposts stood wakeful and vigilant, ready at any moment to sound the alarm. To those entrenched beyond the winding Mersey, soaked by the heavy rain, and spending the dark hours in anxiety, there came over the dismal country the sound of distant rifle-firing mingling with the roll of the thunder. Ere long they knew that every man would be fighting for his life against the great hordes of invaders who would descend upon them swiftly and mercilessly. Across the country from the Peak away to Chester, the Briton bravely faced his foe, anxious and vigilant, awaiting breathlessly the progress of events.

Thus passed the stormy, oppressive night, till the grey dawn of a fateful day.

XXIV

MANCHESTER ATTACKED BY RUSSIANS

With the first streak of daylight the anxious, excited crowds of men and women, surging up and down the principal streets of Manchester, were alarmed by the sounds of heavy firing. A terrible panic instantly ensued. The battle had actually commenced!

Half-starved operatives, with pale, wan faces, stood in groups in Deansgate, Market Street, Piccadilly, and London Road, while men, armed with any weapons they could obtain, rushed out along the main roads to the south of the city to assist in its defence. Lancashire men exhibited commendable patriotism, even though they had not hesitated to criticise the administration of our War Department; for now at the critical hour not a man flinched from his duty, both old and young taking up arms for their country's honour.

During the eventful night at all approaches to the city from the south the roads had been thrown into a state of hasty defence. A formidable barricade had been constructed at a point in the Stretford Road close to the Botanical Gardens to prevent the enemy from advancing up the Chester or Stretford New Roads; another was thrown up at the junction of Chorlton Road, Withington Road, Upper Chorlton Road, and Moss Lane West; a third opposite Rusholme Hall prevented any march up the Wilmslow Road; while others of minor strength blocked the Anson Road close to the Elms, the London Road at Longsight, the Hyde Road opposite Belle Vue Prison, and at Ivy Place in the Ashton Old Road.

These had all been raised out of any materials that came to hand. Barrels, brick rubbish, planks, doors, flooring of houses hastily torn up, and scaffold poles lashed together; in fact, the barriers were huge piles of miscellaneous and portable articles, even furniture from neighbouring houses being utilised, while lengths of iron railings and wire torn from fences played an important part in these hastily-built defences. Behind them, armed with rifles, shot-guns, pistols, knives, and any other weapon that came handiest, the men of Manchester waited, breathlessly impatient in the expectation of attack.

As dawn spread bright and rosy, and the mist cleared from the low meadows beside the Mersey, the distant firing was continuous, and the one or two shells that fell and burst in the centre of the city were precursory of an awful sanguinary struggle. Scarcely a person in that densely populated area had slept that night, and the streets were everywhere full, the most exciting and heartrending scenes being witnessed.

A great crowd that assembled in Albert Square was addressed by the Mayor from the steps of the Town Hall, and urged to strain every muscle to drive back the invaders, in order that the disaster at Birmingham should not be repeated. Even as he spoke, in the interval of wild cheering and the energetic singing of the National Anthem and "Rule, Britannia," the distant crackling of rifles and the low booming of field guns could be heard.

It was the din of battle—the catastrophe caused by the cunning spy Von Beilstein, who was still living in luxury in London, and who still posed as the friend of Geoffrey Engleheart and Violet Vayne!

Geoffrey was still with the Volunteers assisting in the defence of London, but the French spy who had sent the forged orders to our Navy had apparently made good his escape.

Here, in Manchester, the sound of the guns aroused that patriotic enthusiasm latent in the heart of every Briton. True, they were weary, famished, ill from lack of food, yet they were fiercely determined that the invader should never tread their streets, nor should incendiaries burn or Russian artillery destroy their handsome buildings—monuments of England's wealth and greatness. In St. Peter's Square, at a mass meeting attended by nearly twelve thousand people, a demonstration was made against the enemy, and it was resolved that every man should act his part in the struggle, and that no quarter should be shown the legions of the Tsar; while at another impromptu meeting held in Piccadilly, in the open space opposite the Infirmary, the conduct of the Russians before Birmingham was denounced; and some speakers, using violent language, lashed their hearers into a frenzy of mad excitement, causing an eager rush to the barricades in readiness for the terrible fray.

As the sun shone out pale and yellow in the stormy sky, the fighting spread quickly down the Mersey banks from Haughton away to Flixton. It became fiercest around Stockport, and over the level pastures the white smoke of rifles puffed from every bush, wall, and fence.

The Russians were the superior force, for, while all were trained soldiers, not more than a third of the defenders had taken the Queen's shilling, and not more than half of them had ever had an hour's drill in their lives. They were simply volunteers who had found their own arms and banded for the defence of their homes.

The soldiers of the Tsar, trained under the most rigorous discipline, had considerably improved in tactics, in drill, and in munitions of war since the Crimea,—a fact overlooked by the majority of Britons,—and they had now taken possession of every strategical position where batteries might be established. After fierce fighting over Lyme Park across to Norbury Hall, in which the Russians lost very heavily owing to the British gun fire from the railway embankment, a great charge was made by an enormous body of infantry, who succeeded, after several futile attempts, in carrying the position, and driving the British artillerymen back to the road which runs from Stockport to Marple.

The embankment which thus fell into the hands of the Muscovite infantry formed one of the strongest defences of Stockport, therefore they at once moved the guns up towards Davenport Station, and commenced shelling the city with the defenders' own guns!

The panic caused in Stockport was awful, when without warning shells commenced to explode in the crowded barricaded streets, but the Russians were not allowed to have things their own way for long. The British batteries on the opposite railway embankment between Heaton Norris and New Mills formed up at the junction almost opposite Davenport, and opened a terrific fire upon the captured guns.

For half an hour this continued, and the Russians, standing in an exposed position right on the sky-line, were being swept away by British shells, when suddenly the enemy were joined by reinforcements, whereupon a small force of British infantry, who had been brought quickly along, unperceived by the enemy from Marple, suddenly swarmed up the embankment at Norbury, and, charging along to the Russian position, added a strong rifle fire to that of their artillery.

The officer commanding the British batteries watched the infantry advance through his field glass, and in a few minutes suddenly ceased his fire, so as to allow the infantry to make the dash for which they were preparing. A heliograph signal was flashed from the batteries, and then, without hesitation, the order was given to charge.

It was a terribly exciting moment. If they succeeded they would in all probability save Stockport. If they were driven back the town was doomed.

With admirable pluck the British rushed upon the guns, and for a few minutes there was a fierce struggle hand to hand. Russians, although making a most desperate stand, were every moment being impaled on British bayonets, or, pierced by bullets, they rolled down the slopes into ditches covered in stagnant slime. Hacked to pieces by the small but gallant force of Britons, the enemy were forced at last to give in and retire, leaving more than half their number killed; but with admirable tact, the fugitives were forced down the bank nearest the British batteries. Thus they fell into a trap, for as soon as they attempted to recover themselves, and make a dash to reorganise their line of communications, two British Maxims uttered their sharp rattle, and the whole force were simply mowed down where they stood.

The fight had been a most desperate one, but, thanks to the heroic charge of the British infantry, Stockport was again safe, and the guns once more in the hands of her defenders.

Meanwhile, fighting of the fiercest possible description was taking place across the meadows lying between Norbury and Bramhall, and the Russians, unable to withstand the withering British fire, were gradually forced back to Cheadle Hulme, where they were surprised by the defenders and utterly routed. So great was the slaughter, that it is estimated that in this engagement alone, after the recapture of the guns by the British, over 4000 Russians were shot down and 3000 taken prisoners!

The Russians, finding how desperate was the resistance, and how heavily they were losing, quickly brought up strong reinforcements upon Cheadle, and, after a fiercely-contested conflict, succeeded in driving back the small British force, they being compelled to retreat back over the Mersey to Parr's Wood and Didsbury, afterwards blowing up the bridges, and keeping up a hot fire from the bank, where a large body of Volunteers were already entrenched. By this means, although they were unable to save Cheadle from being burned, they succeeded, by reason of the excellence of their position and the admirable tactics they displayed, in mowing down another 2000 of the Tsar's soldiers. In this instance the laurels remained with a portion of the Manchester Volunteer Brigade, the effect of whose rifle fire was appalling.

It was now about ten o'clock, and the sky had cleared for a brilliant day. At Chapel-en-le-Frith a large detachment of Cossacks had been swept away by a body of British Hussars who had suddenly descended upon Whitehough, while almost at the same moment a British battery that had been hastily established on Chinley Churn succeeded in wiping out a body of infantry that was advancing with all speed in the neighbourhood of Yeardsley Hall. But one of the most sanguinary portions of the battle was the conflict which spread westward from Cheadle across to Altrincham, Lymm, and Warrington. Already Altrincham had fallen. The fine villas of wealthy Manchester tradesmen and manufacturers, deserted by their owners, had been entered by the uncouth Muscovites and sacked. Every nook and corner had been searched for plate, jewellery, and money, paintings had been ruthlessly torn down, furniture broken and burned, and Russian troopers had made merry in many a handsome drawing-room. Old Field Hall and Timperly Hall had both been ransacked and set on fire with petroleum, while every house at Dunham Massey had been destroyed by incendiaries.

Elated over their successes, the Russians were collecting their forces preparatory to a decisive rush over the Mersey to Stretford, intending to take that place, and advance by that route upon Manchester. The defenders, who had been warned of this through spies, awaited their chance, and suddenly, when the Russians least expected an attack, a body of British cavalry, backed by infantry, crossed the Mersey, and sweeping down the level turnpike road to Sale, came upon their opponents before they were aware of their presence. The effect of this was frightful. A small body of British Hussars, with some Lancashire Yeomanry, made a splendid charge, exhibiting magnificent courage, and cut their way clean through the Russian lines with irresistible force; while the infantry, advancing cautiously, and taking every advantage of the small cover afforded on that level country, poured forth a deadly rifle fire. Indeed, so gallant was this charge, that the Tsar's forces were almost annihilated. They endeavoured to make a stand near the cross-roads leading from Carrington Moss, but the rifle fire of the defenders was so heavy that they dropped by hundreds under the deadly rain of British bullets.

The disaster to the Russians being signalled back by them to their reserves at Tatton Park and around Knutsford, had the effect of bringing up an enormous force of infantry. Signallers were at work in all directions, and those who watched the progress of the action found the next two hours full of exciting moments. It was apparent at once that the Russians had marked out Stretford as the gate by which they intended to enter Manchester, but they must have been misled by their spies as to the strength of the defenders in this direction.

WILLIAM LE QUEUX

Indeed, if they had surveyed the whole of the southern line defending the city, they could not have discovered a point more strongly fortified; therefore it was a somewhat curious fact that they should have concentrated their forces upon that part. Possibly it was because they had formed an opinion by studying their Ordnance Maps—so generously provided for them by the British Department of Agriculture at a cost of one shilling each—that, if they succeeded in breaking the defence at Stretford, they would also secure the road running in a circular direction up to Barton, by which means they could enter Manchester by way of Eccles, Pendleton, and Salford at the same time as the march through Trafford. Such a design was, of course, cleverly planned. It must be admitted that, from a strategical point of view, the taking of Stretford would mean the fall of Manchester, a fact which the Russian commanding officer had not overlooked.

But the soldiers of the Tsar had reckoned without their hosts. They only saw along the Mersey a thin and apparently weak line of defence, a massing of defenders without undue ostentation and without any particular show of strength. A balloon sent up by the Russians to reconnoitre from Sale had been fired at and brought down by the defenders, but with this exception scarcely a shot had been fired north of the Mersey. Britons were watching and waiting. Their foe, ridiculing the idea that a town like Manchester, almost utterly devoid of positions whereon batteries might be established, could be successfully defended, therefore kept up a desultory fire upon the British detachment that had swept away their advance guard, in the meantime covering the massing of their enormous force. This latter consisted of Cossacks, guards, infantry, artillery, and two companies of engineers, with pontoon sections, as well as a ballooning party and two field hospitals.

The British detachment that had crossed the river were, however, unaware of the enemy's intention until too late. The manoeuvres of the Russians were being watched by a British balloon sent up from Old Trafford, but the signals made by the aëronaut were unfortunately unobserved by the party, so desperately were they fighting; otherwise a disaster which befell them on the sudden rush of the enemy towards the river might possibly have been averted. However, no blame could be attached to the officer in charge of the detachment. The men acted their part bravely, and displayed that courage of which the Briton speaks with justifiable pride, even though, alas! they fell, every one of them fighting till the last, their bodies being afterwards frightfully mangled by horses' hoofs, as hundreds of Cossacks rode over them. Not a man of that party escaped, but each one had once more shown the world what pluck and courage could accomplish, and had gone to his grave as a sacrifice for his country and his Queen.

XXV

GALLANT DEEDS BY CYCLISTS

Noon came and went. The fighting grew fiercer around Manchester, and the excitement more intense within the barricaded, starving city. Through the wildly agitated crowds of women of all classes, from manufacturers' wives to factory girls, who moved up and down Deansgate, Market Street, and many other principal thoroughfares, feverishly anxious for the safety of their husbands and brothers manning the improvised defences, rumours of terrible disaster spread like wildfire, and caused loud wailing and lamentation.

Now rumour told of huge British successes away beyond the Mersey, a report which elated the pale-faced hungry ones, but this being followed quickly by a further report that a force of the defenders had been cut up and utterly annihilated outside Eccles, the cheering died away, and give place to deep, long-drawn sighs and murmurings of despair.

Upon the dusty, perspiring throngs the hot noonday sun beat down mercilessly, the low rumbling of artillery sounded gradually closer and more distinct, and the smoke of burning buildings in Sale and Altrincham slowly ascending hung in the clear sky a black ominous cloud.

By about two o'clock the line of defence south of the Mersey had been nearly all withdrawn, leaving, however, the defending line running south-east of Stockport to Buxton and the Peak. Although Cheadle had fallen into the enemy's hands, an English battery, established near the railway at Bamford, commanded the road from Cheadle to Stockport, and British infantry, supported by artillery, were strongly entrenched from Bramhall Moor through Norbury, Poynton, Wardsend, Booth Green, and Bollington, then turning east through Macclesfield Forest to Buxton. This line was being hourly strengthened, and although not strong enough to take the offensive, it was too strong for the Russians to attack.

All the bridges over the Mersey, from Glazebrook to Stockport, had been prepared for demolition, but it was not intended to carry this out except as a last resource. Cavalry and cyclist scouts who were left on the south of the Mersey had withdrawn across the bridges, after exchanging shots with the skirmishers of the advance guards of the enemy who quickly lined the banks. The bridges north of Cheadle were then blown up, and the defenders were well posted in Parr Wood, near where it was believed the enemy would attempt to ford the river. The Russians contented themselves with exchanging a few shots with the defenders until half an hour later, when some of their batteries had been established, and then the passage of the Mersey at Northenden was commenced, under cover of the guns of the Russians near the Convalescent Hospital, north of Cheadle.

As soon as the Russian scouts approached the river three British outposts could be seen in the wood. They were, however, driven in by some Cossacks, who forded the river and attempted to enter the wood, but were all immediately killed by hidden skirmishers. The Russian engineers were meanwhile busy building a pontoon bridge, which they soon completed, and they then crossed after a short opposition, rapidly deploying to right and left in order to surround Didsbury.

This, the first force to cross the Mersey, consisted of two battalions of the Kazan Regiment and two battalions of the Vladimir, with two 9-pounder and one 6-pounder field batteries and 100 cavalry. Didsbury had been put in a state of hasty defence, and was held by two battalions of the defenders, who also established a Volunteer battery at Bank Hall, and lined the railway embankment in force as far as Chorlton-with-Hardy.

The enemy's battery at the Convalescent Home had rendered the wood almost untenable, but it was soon silenced by the well-directed fire of the British Volunteer battery, and the wood was then re-entered by the defenders. By this time, however, a large number of the enemy had taken up positions in it, and the British were once more gradually driven back.

One section, consisting of six cyclists, with a light machine gun mounted on a double cycle, was told off under Sergeant Irons of the Royal Lancaster, to defend a junction of two paths about half-way through the dense wood, and as the latter was still occupied by the defenders, the enemy could only make slow progress, and the cavalry could only move by the paths.

Irons, taking advantage of a bend in the path, dismounted his men, who, having drawn up their cycles under cover, were formed up each side of the road to support the gun. About thirty Russian dragoons, with their infantry, who were working through the wood, were soon upon them, and, seeing such a small force barring the way, the cavalry charged.

They, however, met with such a terribly hot reception that only two reached the guns, and these were immediately shot. The stand made by these seven men was a most noteworthy instance of the indomitable courage of the defenders. In those critical moments they remained calm and collected, obeying the orders of their sergeant as coolly as if they had been drilling in the barrack square. But their position was one of momentarily increasing peril, for bullets whistled about them, and the force against them was an overwhelming one. The Russian horses and men who had fallen blocked the road, and Irons therefore gave the order to fall in, as the sound of firing had now drawn many of the enemy's skirmishers towards the spot.

Irons then re-formed his squad, one of whom had been shot and another wounded, and, taking the wounded man with them, retired. Just as they were moving off the corporal was wounded in the shoulder, and Irons himself received a bullet in the left arm. About two hundred yards nearer Didsbury there was a clearing, with farm buildings on both sides of the road, and these had been loopholed and occupied by a small force of Volunteers. Irons, sending the wounded man on to Didsbury, remained here with his gun, and a few minutes later the position was vigorously attacked.

The conflict which ensued was of the fiercest description. The mere handful of defenders fought with such desperate courage that the great body of Russians which surrounded them were from the first moment gradually swept away by the steady and precise fire from the farm. Around the buildings the enemy swarmed in overwhelming numbers, but every man who showed himself was promptly picked off by Britons shooting almost as coolly as if they were competing for prizes at Bisley.

Sergeant Irons' small machine gun, with its single barrel, rattled out continuously, shedding its rain of lead in all directions, while from muzzles of Martini rifles peeping over walls and from windows there came a continuous stream of bullets, which played frightful havoc with the foe. Within the first ten minutes two men of the defending force had been shot dead and one wounded; still, their comrades never lost heart, for they were determined that their position should never fall into the enemy's hands. The Russian officer who was directing the operations of the attacking party rose and shouted in Russian to encourage his men, but in a moment an English bullet struck him, and, with a loud cry, he fell forward over the body of a dragoon, shot through the heart.

The stand the cyclists and their companions made was unparalleled. They fought on heroically, knowing the importance of the position they held, and how, if it were taken, other and more serious British casualties must follow. Firing steadily and with caution, they displayed such bravery that even the Russians themselves were compelled to secretly admire them; and at last, after nearly half an hour's desperate fighting, the Tsar's soldiers found themselves so terribly cut up that they were forced to retire, leaving more than half their number dead and many wounded.

While this had been in progress, the British battery had totally destroyed the Russian pontoon, and thus all means of retreat for this portion of the invading force were cut off. About ten thousand men had crossed the river at this point, and although they had deployed at first, they had all been gradually driven into the wood by the fire from the railway embankment.

As soon as the pontoon was destroyed, the British commenced to advance through the wood, slowly driving back the Russians, who then endeavoured to make for Stretford along the north bank of the river; but on seeing their intention a brigade of defenders was immediately pushed along the railway, and two regiments of cavalry were hurried down the road to Chorlton.

These succeeded in heading the enemy, and, suddenly swooping down, they destroyed the rest of the Cossacks who had escaped from the wood, as well as the remainder of the force who had attacked the farm.

Another British battery was then hurried forward, and after a stubborn fight the remainder of the invaders who had crossed surrendered.

In this attack alone the Russians lost in killed and wounded 200 cavalry and nearly 2000 infantry and artillery, while Stretford and Stockport still remained safe. But along the long line east and west the battle raged with increasing fierceness. The conflict was a terrible one on every hand.

The town of Lymm had been sacked, and was now burning, while hundreds of unoffending men, women, and children living in the quiet Cheshire villages had been wantonly massacred by the Muscovites. The latter were, however, now suffering well-merited punishment, for in this bloody battle they were falling dead in hundreds.

The Russian Eagle was at last being forced to bite the dust!

XXVI

GREAT BATTLE ON THE MERSEY

The long blazing day was one of many battles and much toilsome combat.

Fighting spread over a front of nearly nine miles, and during the engagement one wing of the Russians was swung across three miles. Hour after hour the tremendous warfare raged between the armies of Queen Victoria and the Tsar, and the bloodshed was everywhere terrible.

Small parties of the Russian Telegraph Corps had ferried over the Ship Canal and the Mersey near Latchford, and wires were run out, and posts established connecting the headquarters at Altrincham, on the south of the river, with the well-advanced guard stations on the Liverpool Road towards Manchester at Woolstone, Hollinfare, and Lower Irlam.

Sending forth a huge division of infantry upon his left, and three brigades of cavalry in the centre, the Russian General struck hard at the British line between Stretford and Chorlton-with-Hardy.

Meanwhile, beyond Ashton-on-Mersey the battle was also growing in intensity, and rifle and cannon were noisily engaged. A strong force of Russian infantry was at once pushed across to Partington, where they succeeded in crossing the Ship Canal and the Mersey, subsequently joining their advance guard at Lower Irlam.

The British reserves at Newton-in-Makerfield, however, swept down upon them, and a terrible fight quickly ensued. The defenders advanced very steadily by section rushes, keeping under good firing discipline as they went, and the enemy were driven on towards Flixton, where they were simply swept away by the 12-pounder batteries established there, while at the same time their wires crossing the Mersey were cut, and communication with their headquarters thus interrupted.

While this was in progress, another and more important attack was being made on Stretford. The heavy artillery fire and the affairs of outposts in the earlier stages of the battle had been followed by a carefully-regulated long-range fire of infantry on both sides.

The tactics the Russians had displayed were as follows:—They had gradually developed their infantry in front of the Stretford position, and brought their pontoons in readiness for a dash over the river. Then, after some tentative movements, designed to feel the strength of our forces massed at this important point, they apparently determined to carry it at any cost.

On their right flank the enemy were losing very heavily. A telegraphic message received at Altrincham gave the headquarters alarming news of constant reverses. A strong force of infantry marching along the banks of the Etherow from Compstall, intending to get to Hyde by way of Mottram and Godley Junction, had been attacked by British infantry and a couple of 9-pounders, and totally annihilated; while at the same time, about a thousand men attacking a British battery on the hill at Charlesworth had been cut up and forced to retreat, being followed by some Lancers right down to Ludworth Houses, where they were nearly all killed or wounded.

Indeed, times without number during that memorable day the Russians made fierce attacks upon our positions on the edge of the Peak district, but on each occasion they were hurled back with fearful loss by the thin line of defenders holding the high ground.

A battery we had established on the crown of the hill at Werneth was charged again and again by Cossacks and Dragoons, but our men, displaying cool courage at the critical moments, fought desperately, and mowed down the foe in a manner that was remarkable.

The Russians, having decided to carry Stretford, were making vigorous demonstrations towards the Peak, and in the direction of Flixton, in order to distract our attention. They occupied us at many points in the vast semicircle, and by thus engaging us all along the line, endeavoured apparently to prevent us from reinforcing the point at Stretford which they intended gaining. Both invaders and defenders gradually extended in order to meet outflanking movements, and this was the cause of another sudden British success. It was a foregone conclusion that such an extension would exceed the limits of defensive power on one side or the other, and then blows would be struck with the object of breaking the too extended line.

What occurred is, perhaps, best related by one of the special correspondents of the *Daily News*, who, in his account of the battle, published two days later, said—

"About three o'clock I was at Barton with the force of infantry who were holding the road to Warrington, when we unexpectedly received telegraphic information from headquarters of a rapid extension of the enemy's left flank. A brigade which I accompanied was pushed on at once down to Hollinfare, where we reinforced those who had been so successful in cutting up the enemy at Lower Irlam half an hour before. We then extended along the Liverpool Road, past Warrington, as far as Widnes. I remained with a small detachment at Hollinfare awaiting developments, when suddenly we were informed that the enemy had thrown a pontoon bridge over the Mersey at its confluence with the Bollin, and that a great body of infantry, with machine guns, had left Lymm, where they had been lying inactive, and were already crossing. There were not more than one hundred of us, mostly men of the Loyal Lancashire from Preston and a few of the Manchester Regiment; but at the word of command we dashed down the road for nearly a mile, and then leaving it, doubled across the fields to Rixton Old Hall, where we obtained cover.

"The Russians had chosen the most advantageous spot they could find to cross, for on the opposite bank there was a small thick wood, and in this they remained quite concealed until they suddenly dashed out and got across. Numbers had already reached our side and were deploying, when our rifles spoke out sharply, and, judging from the manner in which the enemy were exposed, our fire was quite unexpected. About thirty of our men, kneeling behind a wall, kept up a vigorous fire, emptying their magazines with excellent effect upon the grey-coats swarming over the improvised bridge.

"Still it was impossible to keep them back, for the force effecting a passage was very much larger than we had anticipated.

"A few minutes later, having ascertained the extent of the attack, our signallers opened communication with Higher Irlam, and the information was conveyed on to Barton, whence the heliograph flashed the news down to Stretford.

"Suddenly, however, in the midst of a shady clump of trees there was a loud rattle and continuous flashing. The enemy had brought a 10-barrelled Nordenfelt into play, and it was raining bullets upon us at the rate of a thousand a minute!

"The wall behind which I was crouching was struck by a perfect hail of lead, and there was a loud whistling about my ears that was particularly disconcerting. Nevertheless our men had in their sudden dash for the defence secured an excellent position, and only three were killed and five wounded by this sudden outburst.

"The struggle during the next few minutes was the most desperate I have ever witnessed. At the moment of peril our men displayed magnificent pluck. They seemed utterly unconcerned at their imminent danger, and lay or crouched, firing independently with calm precision. A dozen or so fell wounded, however, and a sergeant who knelt next to me, and who was shooting through a hole in the wall, was shot through the heart, and fell dead while in the act of making an observation to me.

"The men who had attacked us were a fierce-looking set, mostly composed of Tchuwakes and Mordwa from the central district of the Volga, and renowned as among the best infantry that the Tsar can command.

"Rifles bristled from every bit of cover around us, and it was really marvellous that we scored such success. Indeed, it was only by reason of the courageous conduct of every individual man that the successful stand was made against such overwhelming numbers. We knew that if the enemy forced the passage and annihilated us, they would then be enabled to outflank our force, and get round to Eccles and Pendlebury—a disaster which might result in the rapid investment of Manchester. Therefore we fought on, determined to do our very utmost to stem the advancing tide of destroyers.

"Time after time our rifles rattled, and time after time the deadly Nordenfelt sent its hail of bullets around us. Presently, however, we heard increased firing on our right, and then welcome signals reached us from Martinscroft Green. We greeted them with loud cheering, for a force of our infantry and cavalry had returned along the road from Warrington, and, working in extended order, were bearing down upon the foe.

"We ceased firing in that direction, and ere long we had the satisfaction of seeing the enemy's pontoon blown up, and then, with their retreat cut off, they became demoralised, and were driven into the open, where we picked them off so rapidly that scarcely one man of the 1500 who had set his foot upon the Lancashire bank survived.

"From first to last our men fought magnificently. The whole engagement was a brilliant and almost unequalled display of genuine British bravery, and all I can hope is that the defenders of London will act their part with equal courage when the decisive struggle comes."

XXVII

The Fate of the Vanquished

While this vigorous attack on the right flank was in progress, the enemy made a sudden dash upon Stretford.

The edge of the town itself—or rather suburb—lies but a short distance from the Mersey, and the turnpike road runs straight away over the river through Sale and Altrincham to Northwich. At the end of the town nearest the river a road leading down from Barton joins the main road, and at the junction is a large red-brick modern hotel, the Old Cock, while adjoining is the Manchester Tramway Company's stable and terminus. At a little distance behind lies a high embankment, which carries the railway from Manchester to Liverpool, while the Mersey itself, though not wide, has steep banks with earthworks thrown up to prevent floods. Hence the force holding this position found ready-made defences which were now of the utmost value.

The defenders here included three batteries of Royal Artillery, one battalion of the Manchester Regiment, the 2nd Volunteer Battalion of the same regiment, and one of the Lancashire Fusiliers, a field company of Engineers, half the 14th (King's) Hussars with their machine gun section, and a company of signallers. Trenches had been dug at various points, and earthworks thrown up all along the line from Chorlton over to Flixton. Across the junction of the two roads opposite the Old Cock a great barricade had been constructed, and behind this was a powerful battery that commanded the level country away towards Altrincham. The bridges carrying the road and railway over the river had both been demolished by engineers, and many other precautions had been taken to prevent the enemy forcing a passage across.

At last, with a swiftness that was surprising, the expected assault was made. Its strength was terrific, and the carnage on both sides appalling.

The first dash across was effected by the Russians from the rifle range near Old Hall, and this was rapidly followed by another from the bank opposite the battery at Stretford, while further down a third attack was made near Mersey House, close to Ashton.

Of the three, the strongest, of course, was that upon Stretford. The enemy had, by a good deal of neat manoeuvring, brought their main body within the triangle bounded on the one side by the road from Cheadle to Altrincham, on the second by the road from the latter place to the river, and the third by the river itself.

Pontoons were floated at many points, and while some cavalry forded the river, infantry and artillery rapidly crossed in the face of a terrific fire which was pouring upon them.

Smokeless powder being used, the positions of the invaders were not obscured, and it could be seen that the British were effecting terrible execution. Hundreds of the foe who were in the act of crossing were picked off, and shells falling upon the pontoons destroyed them. The latter, however, were quickly replaced, and the force of the Tsar, by reason of the overwhelming numbers that had hurled themselves upon Stretford, succeeded, after a desperately-contested fight, in breaking the line of defence between Chorlton-with-Hardy and Fallowfield, and advancing by short rushes upon Manchester.

But the British infantry in their trenches behaved splendidly, and made the roads from Old Hall at Sale right along to Partington quite untenable, so the continuous advance of the enemy cost them very dearly.

Russian shells bursting in Stretford killed and injured large numbers of the defenders. Two of them struck the Old Cock in rapid succession, almost completely demolishing it, but the débris was quickly manned, and rifles soon spoke from its ruined walls. Again, a shell exploding in the large tram stables, set a hay store on fire, and this burned furiously, while away in the centre of the town the Public Library and a number of shops in the vicinity had also been ignited in a similar manner.

At last the thousands of grey-coats swarming over the country fell in such enormous numbers upon the British rifle pits on the Mersey bank, that the first line of defence was at length utterly broken down; but in doing this the enemy's front had become much exposed, whereupon the Maxims on the railway embankment between the river and Barton suddenly burst forth a perfect hail of bullets, and in a short time a whole division of Russian infantry, cavalry, and artillery had been literally swept out of existence.

The batteries down in the Stretford Road, combined with those on the embankment, had up to this moment played greater havoc with the foe than any other. The men of the Manchester Regiment, both Regulars and Volunteers, were displaying the greatest coolness; but unfortunately the Lancashire Fusiliers and the Loyal North Lancashire, who had manned the trenches, had been partially annihilated, the majority lying dead, their bodies scattered over the level fields and roads. Yet, notwithstanding the strenuous opposition of the British batteries at this point, the Russians were bringing up huge reinforcements from Altrincham, Cheadle, and Northenden, and by establishing strong batteries commanding Stretford, they at last, about five o'clock, succeeded in killing nearly half the gallant defenders, and driving back the survivors up the Barton Road.

The tide of grey-coats rushing onward, captured the British guns, and although the batteries on the railway embankment still held out, and the enemy suffered heavily from their Maxims, yet they pressed on into Stretford town, and commenced to sack it. Messrs. Williams, Deacon's Bank, was entered, the safes blown open, and large sums in gold and notes abstracted, shops were entered and looted, and houses ransacked for jewellery.

Thus Stretford fell.

Its streets ran with blood; and on, over the bodies of its brave defenders, the hordes of the Great White Tsar marched towards Manchester.

Meanwhile the British batteries on the railway embankment had also fallen into the hands of the Russians, who were now driving the survivors over towards Barton. They did not, however, retreat without a most desperate resistance. A row of thatched and white-washed cottages at the bend of the road they held for a long time, emptying their magazine rifles with deadly effect upon their pursuers, but at last they were driven north, and half an hour later joined their comrades who had massed at Barton, but who had been attacked in great force and fallen back in good order to Pendleton.

By this time the enemy, having pierced the line of outposts, had occupied Barton and Eccles. At the former place they had set on fire a number of factories, and out of mere desire to cause as much damage to property as possible, they had blown up both the bridge that carried the road over the Ship Canal, and also destroyed the magnificent swinging aqueduct which carried the Bridgewater Canal over the other.

This great triumph of engineering—one of the most successful feats of the decade—was blown into the air by charges of gun-cotton, and now lay across the Ship Canal a heap of fallen masonry and twisted iron cantilevers, while the water from the Bridgewater Canal was pouring out in thousands of tons, threatening to flood the surrounding district, and the church opposite had been wrecked by the terrific force of the explosion.

A frightful panic had been caused in Manchester by these reverses. The scenes in the streets were indescribable. At the barricades, however, the enemy met with a desperate resistance.

Three great columns were marching on Manchester at that moment. The first, having broken the line of defence near Fallowfield, divided into two divisions; one, advancing up the Wilmslow Road, stormed the great barricade opposite Rusholme Hall, while the other appeared on the Withington Road, and commenced to engage the defences that had been thrown across Moss Lane and Chorlton Road. The second column advanced to where Eccles Old Road joins Broad Street at Pendleton; and the third, sweeping along up the Stretford Road, met with a terrific resistance at the Botanic Gardens at Trafford, the walls of which, on either side of the road, were loopholed and manned by infantry and artillery; while opposite, the Blind Asylum was held by a regiment of infantry, and a strong barricade, with a battery of 12-pounders, had been established a little further towards the city, at the junction of the Chester and Stretford New Roads.

The enemy advanced here in enormous force; but, seeing the formidable defences, a number of cavalry and infantry turned off along the Trafford Road, blew up the bridge of the Ship Canal in order to prevent a pursuing force of British cavalry from following, and after setting fire to the great dock warehouses and crowd of idle ships, continued along to Eccles New Road, where, however, they were met by another force of our Hussars, and totally routed and cut up.

From this point the tide of battle turned. It was already half-past five, and the sun was sinking when the Russian forces prepared for their final onslaught. Cossacks and Dragoons charged again and again, and infantry with bayonets fixed rushed onward to the barricades in huge grey legions, only to be met by a sweeping rain of British bullets, which filled the roads with great heaps of dead. In these defences, rendered doubly strong by the patriotic action of the stalwart civilians of Manchester, the invaders could make no breach, and before every one of them they fell in thousands.

The men in the entrenchments saw the foe were falling back, and found the attack growing weaker. Then signals were made, and they raised a long hearty cheer when the truth was flashed to them.

The news was inspiriting, and they fought on with redoubled energy, for they knew that the great body of reserves from Ashton-under-Lyne, Hyde, and Compstall, as well as those who had been occupying the hills on the edge of the Peak, had been pushed right past Stretford to Barton, and were now advancing like a huge fan, outflanking the Russians and attacking them in their rear.

The British tactics were excellent, for while the invaders were attacked by cavalry and infantry on the one side, the defenders manning the barricades made a sudden sortie, cutting their way into them with bayonet rushes which they could not withstand, and which had a terribly fatal effect.

The Tsar's forces, unable to advance or retreat, and being thus completely surrounded, still fought on, and as they refused to surrender, were literally massacred by thousands by British troops, while many guns and horses were captured, thousands of rounds of ammunition seized, and many men taken prisoners.

The fight in that evening hour was the most fiercely contested of any during that day. The fate of Manchester was in the hands of our gallant soldiers, who, although necessarily losing heavily before such an enormous army, behaved with a courage that was magnificent, and which was deserving the highest commendation that could be bestowed.

As dusk gathered into darkness, the enemy were being forced back towards the Mersey over the roads they had so recently travelled, but still fighting, selling their lives dearly. The highways and fields were strewn with their dead and dying, for while infantry fired into their front from the cover of houses and walls, our cavalry, with whirling sabres, fell upon them and hacked them to pieces. Neither Cossacks nor Dragoons proved a match for our Hussars, Lancers, and Yeomanry, and even in face of the machine guns which the Russians brought into play in an endeavour to break the line and escape, our infantry dashed on with grand and magnificent charges, quickly seizing the Nordenfelts, turning their own guns against them, and letting loose a fire that mowed down hundreds.

Across the neighbouring country our forces swept in good attack formation, and all along that great line, nearly six miles in length, the slaughter of Russians was frightful.

In the falling gloom fire flashed from the muzzles of rifles, cannon, and machine guns, and far above the terrible din sounded shrill cries of pain and hoarse shouts of despair as the great Army that had devastated our beloved country with fire and sword was gradually annihilated. In those roads in the south of the city the scenes of bloodshed were awful, as a force of over 20,000 Russians were slaughtered because they would not yield up their arms.

Outside Stretford a last desperate stand was made, but ere long some British cavalry came thundering along, and cut them down in a frightful manner, while about the same time a Russian flying column was annihilated over at Davy-Hulme; away at Carrington a retreating brigade of infantry which had escaped over the river was suddenly pounced upon by the defenders and slaughtered; and at Altrincham the enemy's headquarters were occupied, and the staff taken prisoners. Ere the Russian General could be forced to surrender, however, he placed a revolver to his head, and in full view of a number of his officers, blew his brains out.

Then, when the moon shone out from behind a dark bank of cloud just before midnight, she shed her pale light upon the wide battlefield on both sides of the Mersey, whereon lay the bodies of no fewer than 30,000 Russians and 12,000 British, while 40,000 Russians and 16,000 British lay wounded, nearly 10,000 Russians having been disarmed and marched into the centre of the city as prisoners.

The victory had only been achieved at the eleventh hour by dint of great courage and forethought, and being so swift and effectual it was magnificent.

Manchester was safe, and the public rejoicings throughout that night were unbounded.

The loss of life was too awful for reflection, for 12,000 of Britain's heroes—men who had won the battle—were lying with their white lifeless faces upturned to the twinkling stars.

BOOK III
THE VICTORY

XXVIII

A Shabby Wayfarer

In Sussex the situation was now most critical. The struggle between the French invaders and the line of Volunteers defending London was long and desperate, but our civilian soldiers were bearing their part bravely, showing how Britons could fight, and day after day repelling the repeated assaults with a vigour that at once proved their efficiency.

Three days after the battle at Manchester had been fought and won, a man with slouching gait and woeful countenance, attired in a cheap suit of shabby grey, stood on the steps of the Granton Hotel, at Granton, and with his hands thrust into his pockets gazed thoughtfully out over the broad waters of the Firth of Forth, to where the Fifeshire hills loomed dark upon the horizon. Slowly his keen eyes wandered away eastward to the open sea, an extensive view of which he obtained from the flight of steps whereon he stood, and then with a sigh of disappointment he buttoned his coat, and, grasping his stick, descended, and walked at a leisurely pace along the road through Newhaven to Leith.

"To-night. To-night at sundown!" he muttered to himself, as he bent his head to the wind.

Involuntarily he placed his hand to his hip to reassure himself that a letter he carried was still safe.

"Bah!" he continued, "I declare I feel quite timid to-night. Everything is so quiet here; the houses look deserted, and everybody seems to have left the place. Surely they can have no suspicion, and—and if they had? What does it matter?—eh, what?"

Quickening his pace, he passed down the long, quaint street of Newhaven, lined on each side by ancient fishermen's cottages, and then, crossing the railway, passed under the wall of Leith Fort, whereon a couple of sentries were pacing. Glancing up at the two artillerymen, with the half-dozen obsolete guns behind them, and their background of grass-grown mounds and buildings, the wayfarer smiled. He was thinking how different would be the scene at this spot ere long.

Leith Fort was a sort of fortified back-garden. The railway ran close to the sea, parallel with which was the highway, and upon higher ground at the back was a block of buildings, before which a few black old cannon were placed in formidable array, and in such a position as to be fully exposed to any destructive projectiles fired from the sea.

On went the down-at-heel wayfarer, his shifty eyes ever on the alert, viewing with suspicion the one or two persons he met. Apparently he was expecting the arrival of some craft, for his gaze was constantly turned towards the wide expanse of grey water, eager to detect the smallest speck upon the horizon. Any one who regarded him critically might have noticed something remarkable about his appearance, yet not even his most intimate friends would have recognised in this broken-down, half-starved clerk, who had arrived at Granton that morning, after tramping over from Glasgow, the popular man-about-town, the Count von Beilstein!

"Those fools will soon be swept away into eternity," he muttered to himself, as he glanced back in the direction of the fort. "They will have an opportunity of tasting Russian lead, and of practising with their guns, which are only fit for a museum. They mount guard to defend an attack! Bah! They seek their own destruction, for no force can withstand that which will presently appear to give them a sudden rousing. They will be elevated—blown into the air, together with their miserable guns, their barracks, and the whole of their antiquated paraphernalia. And to me the world owes this national catastrophe! I am the looker-on. These British have a proverb that the looker-on sees most of the game. *Bien! that is full of truth.*"

And he chuckled to himself, pursuing his way at the same pace, now and then glancing back as if to assure himself that no one dogged his footsteps. Darkness had crept on quickly as he passed along through the open country at Fillyside and entered Portobello, the little watering-place so popular with holiday makers from Edinburgh during the summer. Along the deserted promenade he strolled leisurely from end to end, and passing out of the town through Joppa, came at length to that rugged shore between the Salt Pans and Eastfield. The tide was out, so, leaving the road, he walked on in the darkness over the shingles until he came to a small cove, and a moment later two men confronted him.

A few sentences in Russian were rapidly exchanged between the spy and the men, and then the latter at once guided him to where a boat lay in readiness, but concealed. Five minutes later the Count was being rowed swiftly but silently away into the darkness by six stalwart men belonging to one of the Tsar's battleships.

WILLIAM LE QUEUX

The oars dipped regularly as the boat glided onwards, but no word was exchanged, until about twenty minutes later the men suddenly stopped pulling, a rope thrown by a mysterious but vigilant hand whistled over their heads and fell across them, and then they found themselves under the dark side of a huge ironclad. It was the new battleship, *Admiral Orlovski*, which had only just left the Baltic for the first time. Without delay the spy climbed on board, and was conducted at once by a young officer into the Admiral's private cabin.

A bearded, middle-aged man, in handsome naval uniform, who was poring over a chart, rose as he entered. The spy, bowing, said briefly in Russian—

"I desire to see Prince Feodor Mazaroff, Admiral of the Fleet."

"I am at your service, m'sieur," the other replied in French, motioning him to a chair.

The Count, seating himself, tossed his hat carelessly upon the table, explaining that he had been sent by the Russian Intelligence Department as bearer of certain important documents which would materially assist him in his operations.

"Yes," observed the Prince, "I received a telegram from the Ministry at Petersburg before I left Christiansand, telling me to await you here, and that you would furnish various information."

"That I am ready to do as far as lies in my power," replied the Count, taking from his hip pocket a bulky packet, sealed with three great daubs of black wax. This he handed to the Prince, saying, "It contains maps of the country between Edinburgh and Glasgow, specially prepared by our Secret Service, together with a marked chart of the Firth of Forth, and full detailed information regarding the troops remaining to defend this district."

The Admiral broke the seals, and glanced eagerly through the contents, with evident satisfaction.

"Now, what is the general condition of the south of Scotland?" the Prince asked, lounging back, twirling his moustache with a self-satisfied air.

"Totally unprepared. It is not believed that any attack will be made. The military left north of the Cheviots after mobilisation were sent south to assist in the defence of Manchester."

"Let us hope our expedition to-night will meet with success. We are now one mile east of Craig Waugh, and in an hour our big guns will arouse Leith from its lethargy. You will be able to watch the fun from deck, and give us the benefit of your knowledge of the district. Is the fort at Leith likely to offer any formidable resistance?" continued the Admiral. "I see the information here is somewhat vague upon that point."

"The place is useless," replied the spy, as he stretched out his hand and took a pencil and paper from the Prince's writing-table. "See! I will sketch it for you. In the character of a starving workman who desired to volunteer I called there, and succeeded in obtaining a good view of the interior. They have a few modern guns, but the remainder are old muzzleloaders, which against such guns as you have on board here will be worse than useless." And as he spoke he rapidly sketched a plan of the defences in a neat and accurate manner, acquired by long practice. "The most serious resistance will, however, be offered from Inchkeith Island, four miles off Leith. There has lately been established there a new fort, containing guns of the latest type. A plan of the place, which I succeeded in obtaining a few days ago, is, you will find, pinned to the chart of the Firth of Forth."

The Admiral opened out the document indicated, and closely examined the little sketch plan appended. On the chart were a number of small squares marked in scarlet, surrounded by a blue circle to distinguish them more readily from the dots of red which pointed out the position of the lights. These squares, prepared with the utmost care by von Beilstein, showed the position of certain submarine mines, a plan of which he had succeeded in obtaining by one of his marvellous master-strokes of finesse.

"Thanks to you, Count, our preparations are now complete," observed the Prince, offering the spy a cigarette from his silver case, and taking one himself. "Our transports, with three army corps, numbering nearly 60,000 men and 200 guns, are at the present moment lying 12 miles north of the Bass Rock, awaiting orders to enter the Firth, therefore I think when we land we shall"—

A ray of brilliant white light streamed for a moment through the port of the cabin, and then disappeared.

The Prince, jumping to his feet, looked out into the darkness, and saw the long beam sweeping slowly round over the water, lighting up the ships of his squadron in rapid succession.

"The search-lights of Inchkeith!" he gasped, with an imprecation. "I had no idea we were within their range, but now they have discovered us there's no time to be lost. For the present I must leave you. You will, of course, remain on board, and land with us"; and a moment later he rushed on deck, and shouted an order which was promptly obeyed.

Suddenly there was a low booming, and in another second a column of dark water rose as the first shot ricochetted about five hundred yards from their bows. Orders shouted in Russian echoed through the ship, numbers of signals were exchanged rapidly with the other vessels, and the sea suddenly became alive with torpedo boats.

Time after time the British guns sounded like distant thunder, and shots fell in the vicinity of the Russian ships. Suddenly, as soon as the men were at their quarters, electric signals rang from the conning-tower of the *Admiral Orlovski*, and one of her 56-tonners crashed and roared from her turret, and a shot sped away towards where the light showed. The noise immediately became deafening as the guns from nine other ships thundered almost simultaneously, sending a perfect hail of shell upon the island fort. In the darkness the scene was one of most intense excitement.

For the first time the spy found himself amidst the din of battle, and perhaps for the first time in his life his nerves were somewhat shaken as he stood in a convenient corner watching the working of one of the great guns in the turret, which regularly ran out and added its voice to the incessant thunder.

XXIX

Landing of the Enemy at Leith

All the vessels were now under steam and approaching Inchkeith, when suddenly two shells struck the *Admiral Orlovski* amidships, carrying away a portion of her superstructure.

Several of the other vessels were also hit almost at the same moment, and shortly afterwards a torpedo boat under the stern of the flagship was struck by a shell, and sank with all hands. Time after time the Russian vessels poured out their storm of shell upon the fort, now only about a mile and a half distant; but the British fire still continued as vigorous and more effective than at first.

Again the flagship was struck, this time on the port quarter, but the shot glanced off her armour into the sea; while a moment later another shell struck one of her fighting tops, and, bursting, wrecked two of the machine guns, and killed half a dozen unfortunate fellows who had manned them. The débris fell heavily upon the deck, and the disaster, being witnessed by the spy, caused him considerable anxiety for his own safety.

Even as he looked he suddenly noticed a brilliant flash from one of the cruisers lying a little distance away. There was a terrific report, and amid flame and smoke wreckage shot high into the air. An explosion had occurred in the magazine, and it was apparent the ship was doomed! Other disasters to the Russians followed in quick succession. A cruiser which was lying near the Herwit light-buoy blazing away upon the fort, suddenly rolled heavily and gradually heeled over, the water around her being thrown into the air by an explosion beneath the surface. A contact mine had been fired, and the bottom of the ship had been practically blown out, for a few minutes later she went down with nearly every soul on board.

At the moment this disaster occurred, the *Admiral Orlovski*, still discharging her heavy guns, was about half-way between the Briggs and the Pallas Rock, when a search-light illuminated her from the land, and a heavy fire was suddenly opened upon her from Leith Fort.

This was at once replied to, and while five of the vessels kept up their fire upon Inchkeith, the three others turned their attention towards Leith, and commenced to bombard it with common shell.

How effectual were their efforts the spy could at once see, for in the course of a quarter of an hour, notwithstanding the defence offered by Leith Fort and several batteries on Arthur's Seat, at Granton Point, Wardie Bush, and at Seaside Meadows, near Portobello, fires were breaking out in various quarters of the town, and factories and buildings were now burning with increasing fury. The great paraffin refinery had been set on fire, and the flames, leaping high into the air, shed a lurid glare far away over the sea.

Shells, striking the Corn Exchange, wrecked it, and one, flying away over the fort, burst in the Leith Distillery, with the result that the place was set on fire, and soon burned with almost equal fierceness with the paraffin works. The shipping in the Edinburgh, Albert, and Victoria Docks was ablaze, and the drill vessel H.M.S. *Durham* had been shattered and was burning. A great row of houses in Lindsay Road had fallen prey to the flames, while among the other large buildings on fire were the Baltic Hotel, the great goods station of the North British Railway, and the National Bank of Scotland.

In addition to being attacked from the forts on the island, and on land, the Russians were now being vigorously fired upon by the British Coastguard ship *Impérieuse*, which, with the cruiser *Active*, and the gunboat cruisers *Cockchafer*, *Firm*, and *Watchful*, had now come within range. Soon, however, the enemy were reinforced by several powerful vessels, and in the fierce battle that ensued the British ships were driven off. Then by reason of the reinforcements which the Russians brought up, and the great number of transports which were now arriving, the defence, desperate though it had been, alas! broke down, and before midnight the invader set his foot upon Scottish soil.

Ere the sun rose, a huge force of 60,000 men had commenced a march upon Edinburgh and Glasgow!

Events on shore during that never-to-be-forgotten night were well described by Captain Tiller of the Royal Artillery, stationed at Leith Fort, who, in a letter written to his young wife at Carlisle, on the following day, gave the following narrative:—

"Disaster has fallen upon us. The Russians have landed in Scotland, and the remnant of our force which was at Leith has fallen back inland. On Friday, just after nightfall, we were first apprised of our danger by hearing heavy firing from the sea in the direction of Inchkeith Fort, and all civilians were sent on inland, while we prepared for the fight.

"Very soon a number of ships were visible, some of them being evidently transports, and as they were observed taking soundings, it was clear that an immediate landing was intended. Fortunately it was a light night, and while two Volunteer field batteries were sent out along the coast west to Cramond and east to Fisherrow, we completed our arrangements in the fort. With such antiquated weapons as were at our disposal defeat was a foregone conclusion, and we knew that to annoy the enemy and delay their landing would be the extent of our resistance. Some of our guns were, of course, of comparatively recent date, and our supply of ammunition was fair, but the Volunteer guns were antiquated 40-pounder muzzleloaders, which ought to have been withdrawn years ago, and the gunners had had very little field training. The arrangements for horsing the guns were also very inefficient, and they had no waggons or transport. Most of our forces having been drawn south, the only infantry available was a battalion and a half—really a provisional battalion, for it was composed of portions of two Volunteer rifle regiments, with a detachment of Regulars. Our Regular artillery detachment was, unfortunately, very inadequate, for although the armament of the fort had been recently strengthened, the force had been weakened just before the outbreak of war by the despatch of an Indian draft.

"It was apparent that the enemy would not attempt to destroy our position, but land and carry it by assault; therefore, while the Inchkeith guns kept them at bay, we undermined our fort, opened our magazines, and got ready for a little target practice.

"The Volunteer batteries sent eastward had been ordered to do what execution they could, and then, in the case of a reverse, to retire through Portobello and Duddingston to Edinburgh, and those on the west were to go inland to Ratho; while we were resolved to hold the fort as long as possible, and if at last we were compelled to retire we intended to blow up the place before leaving.

"As soon as we found the Russian flagship within range, we opened fire upon her, and this action caused a perfect storm of projectiles to be directed upon us. The town was soon in flames, the shipping in the harbour sank, and the martello tower was blown to pieces. Our search-light was very soon brought into requisition, and by its aid some of the boats of the enemy's transports were sunk, while others came to grief on the Black Rocks.

"By this time the enemy had turned their search-lights in every direction where they could see firing, and very soon our Volunteer batteries were silenced, and then Granton harbour fell into the hands of the enemy's landing parties. Having first rendered their guns useless, the survivors fell back to Corstorphine Hill, outside Edinburgh, and we soon afterwards received intelligence that the Russians were landing at Granton in thousands. Meanwhile, although our garrison was so weak and inexperienced, we nevertheless kept up a vigorous fire.

"We saw how Inchkeith Fort had been silenced, and how our Volunteer batteries had been destroyed, and knew that sooner or later we must share the same fate, and abandon our position. As boatload after boatload of Russians attempted to land, we either sank them by shots from our guns or swept them with a salvo of bullets from our Maxims; yet as soon as we had hurled back one landing party others took its place.

"Many were the heroic deeds our gunners performed that night, as hand to hand they fought, and annihilated the Russians who succeeded in landing; but in this frightful struggle we lost heavily, and at length, when all hope of an effective defence had been abandoned, we placed electric wires in the magazine, and the order was given to retire. This we did, leaving our search-light in position in order to deceive the enemy.

"Half our number had been killed, and we sped across to Bonnington, running out a wire along the ground as we went. The Russians, now landing rapidly in great force, swarmed into the fort and captured the guns and ammunition, while a party of infantry pursued us. But we kept them back for fully a quarter of an hour, until we knew that the fort would be well garrisoned by the invaders; then we sent a current through the wire.

"The explosion that ensued was deafening, and its effect appalling. Never have I witnessed a more awful sight. Hundreds of tons of all sorts of explosives and ammunition were fired simultaneously by the electric spark, and the whole fort, with nearly six hundred of the enemy, who were busy establishing their headquarters, were in an instant blown into the air. For several moments the space around us where we stood seemed filled with flying débris, and the mangled remains of those who a second before had been elated beyond measure by their success.

"Those were terribly exciting moments, and for a few seconds there was a cessation of the firing. Quickly, however, the bombardment was resumed, and although we totally annihilated the force pursuing us, we fell back to Restalrig, and at length gained the battery that had been established on Arthur's Seat, and which was now keeping up a heavy fire upon the Russian transports lying out in the Narrow Deep. Subsequently we went on to Dalkeith. Our situation is most critical in every respect, but we are expecting reinforcements, and a terrible battle is imminent."

Thus the Russians landed three corps of 20,000 each where they were least expected, and at once prepared to invest Edinburgh and Glasgow. Three of the boats which came ashore at Leith that night, after the blowing up of the fort, brought several large mysterious-looking black boxes, which were handled with infinite care by the specially selected detachment of men who had been told off to take charge of them. Upon the locks were the official seals of the Russian War Office; and even the men themselves, unaware of their contents, looked upon them with a certain amount of suspicion, handling them very gingerly, and placing them in waggons which they seized from a builder's yard on the outskirts of the town.

The officers alone knew the character of these mysterious consignments, and as they superintended the landing, whispered together excitedly. The news of the invasion, already telegraphed throughout Scotland from end to end, caused the utmost alarm; but had the people known what those black boxes, the secret of which was so carefully guarded, contained, they would have been dismayed and appalled.

Truth to tell, the Russians were about to try a method of wholesale and awful destruction, which, although vaguely suggested in time of peace, had never yet been tested in the field.

If successful, they knew it would cause death and desolation over an inconceivably wide area, and prove at once a most extraordinary and startling development of modern warfare. The faces of a whole army, however brave, would blanch before its terrific power, and war in every branch, on land and on sea, would become revolutionised.

But the boxes remained locked and guarded. The secret was to be kept until the morrow, when the first trial was ordered to be made, and the officers in charge expressed an opinion between themselves that a blow would then be struck that would at once startle and terrify the whole world.

XXX

Attack on Edinburgh

In attacking Edinburgh the besiegers at once discovered they had a much more difficult task than they had anticipated. The Russian onslaught had been carefully planned. Landing just before dawn, the 1st Corps, consisting of about twenty thousand men, marched direct to Glasgow by way of South Queensferry and Kirkliston, and through Linlithgow, sacking and burning all three towns in the advance.

The 3rd Army Corps succeeded, after some very sharp skirmishing, in occupying the Pentland Hills, in order to protect the flanks of the first force, while a strong detachment was left behind to guard the base at Leith. The 2nd Corps meanwhile marched direct upon Edinburgh.

The defenders, consisting of Militia, Infantry, Artillery, the local Volunteers left behind during the mobilisation, and a large number of civilians from the neighbouring towns, who had hastily armed on hearing the alarming news, were quickly massed in three divisions on the Lammermuir Hills, along the hills near Peebles, and on Tinto Hill, near Lanark.

The Russian army corps which marched from Leith upon Edinburgh about seven o'clock on the following morning met with a most desperate resistance. On Arthur's Seat a strong battery had been established by the City of Edinburgh Artillery, under Col. J. F. Mackay, and the 1st Berwickshire, under Col. A. Johnston; and on the higher parts of the Queen's Drive, overlooking the crooked little village of Duddingston, guns of the 1st Forfarshire, under Col. Stewart-Sandeman, V.D., flashed and shed forth torrents of bullets and shell, which played havoc with the enemy's infantry coming up the Portobello and Musselburgh roads. Batteries on the Braid and Blackford Hills commanded the southern portion of the city; while to the west, the battery on Corstorphine Hill prevented the enemy from pushing along up the high road from Granton.

Between Jock's Lodge and Duddingston Mills the Russians, finding cover, commenced a sharp attack about nine o'clock; but discovering, after an hour's hard fighting, that to attempt to carry the defenders' position was futile, they made a sudden retreat towards Niddry House.

The British commander, observing this, and suspecting their intention to make a circuit and enter the city by way of Newington, immediately set his field telegraph to work, and sent news on to the infantry brigade at Blackford.

This consisted mainly of the Queen's Volunteer Rifle Brigade (Royal Scots), under Col. T. W. Jones, V.D.; the 4th, 5th, 6th, 7th, and 8th Volunteer Battalions of the Royal Scots, under Col. W. U. Martin, V.D., Col. W. I. Macadam, Col. Sir G. D. Clerk, Col. P. Dods, and Col. G. F. Melville respectively, with a company of engineers. The intelligence they received placed them on the alert, and ere long the enemy extended his flank in an endeavour to enter Newington. The bridges already prepared for demolition by the defenders were now promptly blown up, and in the sharp fight that ensued the enemy were repulsed with heavy loss.

Meanwhile the formidable division of the 3rd Russian Army Corps guarding the base at Leith had attacked the Corstorphine position, finding their headquarters untenable under its fire, and although losing several guns and a large number of men, they succeeded, after about an hour's hard fighting, in storming the hill and sweeping away the small but gallant band of defenders.

The fight was long. It was a struggle to the death. Over the whole historic battle-ground from the Tweed to the Forth, fighting spread, and everywhere the loss of life was terrible.

The long autumn day passed slowly, yet hostilities continued as vigorous and sanguinary as they had begun. Before the sun sank many a brave Briton lay dead or dying, but many more Muscovites had been sent to that bourne whence none return.

As it was, the British line of communications was broken between Temple and Eddleston, the outposts at the latter place having been surprised and slaughtered. But although the enemy strove hard to break down the lines of defence and invest Edinburgh, yet time after time they were hurled back with fearful loss. Colinton and Liberton were sacked and burned by the Tsar's forces. On every hand the Russians spread death and destruction; still the defenders held their own, and when the fighting ceased after nightfall Edinburgh was still safe. Strong barricades manned by civilians had been hastily thrown up near the station in Leith Walk, in London Road opposite the Abbey Church, in Inverleith Row, in Clerk Street and Montague Street, while all the bridges over the Water of Leith had been blown up with gun-cotton;

quick-firing guns had been posted on Calton Hill and at the Castle, while in St. Andrew's Square a battery had been established by the 1st Haddington Volunteer Artillery, under Major J. J. Kelly, who had arrived in haste from Dunbar, and this excellent position commanded a wide stretch of country away towards Granton.

At dead of night, under the calm, bright stars, a strange scene might have been witnessed. In the deep shadow cast by the wall of an old and tumble-down barn near the cross-roads at Niddry, about three miles from Edinburgh, two Russian infantry officers were in earnest conversation. They stood leaning upon a broken fence, talking in a half-whisper in French, so that the half-dozen privates might not understand what they said. The six men were busy unpacking several strange black cases, handling the contents with infinite care. Apparently three of the boxes contained a quantity of fine silk, carefully folded, while another contained a number of square, dark-looking packages, which, when taken out, were packed in order upon a strong net which was first spread upon the grass. Ropes were strewn over the ground in various directions, the silk was unfolded, and presently, when all the contents had been minutely inspected by the two officers with lanterns, a small tube was taken from a box that had remained undisturbed, and fastened into an object shaped like a bellows.

Then, when all preparations were satisfactorily completed, the six men threw themselves upon the grass to snatch an hour's repose, while the officers returned to their previous positions, leaning against the broken fence, and gravely discussing their proposals for the morrow's gigantic sensation. The elder of the two was explaining to his companion the nature of the *coup* which they intended to deliver, and the mode in which it would be made. So engrossed were they in the contemplation of the appalling results that would accrue, they did not observe that they were standing beneath a small square hole in the wall of the barn; neither did they notice that from this aperture a dark head protruded for a second and then quick as lightning withdrew. It was only like a shadow, and disappeared instantly!

Ten minutes later a mysterious figure was creeping cautiously along under the hedge of the high road to Newington in the direction of the British lines. Crawling along the grass, and pausing now and then with his ear to the ground, listening, he advanced by short, silent stages, exercising the greatest caution, well aware that death would be his fate should he be discovered. In wading the Braid Burn he almost betrayed himself to a Russian sentry; but at last, after travelling for over an hour, risking discovery at any moment, he at length passed the British outposts beyond Liberton, and ascended the Braid Hills to the headquarters.

The story he told the General commanding was at first looked upon as ludicrous. In the dim candlelight in the General's tent he certainly looked a disreputable derelict, his old and tattered clothes wet through, his hands cut by stones and bleeding, and his face half covered with mud. The three officers who were with the General laughed when he dashed in excitedly, and related the conversation he had overheard; yet when he subsequently went on to describe in detail what he had witnessed, and when they remembered that this tramp was an artilleryman who had long ago been conspicuous by his bravery at El Teb, and an ingenious inventor, their expression of amusement gave way to one of alarm.

The General, who had been writing, thoughtfully tapped the little camp table before him with his pen. "So they intend to destroy us and wreck the city by that means, now that their legitimate tactics have failed! I can scarcely credit that such is their intention; yet if they should be successful—if"—

"But they will not be successful, sir. If you will send some one to assist me, and allow me to act as I think fit, I will frustrate their dastardly design, and the city shall be saved."

"You are at liberty to act as you please. You know their plans, and I have perfect confidence in you, Mackenzie," replied the officer. "Do not, however, mention a word of the enemy's intention to any one. It would terrify the men; and although I do not doubt their bravery, yet the knowledge of such a horrible fate hanging over them must necessarily increase their anxiety, and thus prevent them from doing their best. We are weak, but remember we are all Britons. Now come," he added, "sit there, upon that box, and explain at once what is your scheme of defence against this extraordinary attack."

And the fearless man to whom the General had entrusted the defence of Edinburgh obeyed, and commenced to explain what means he intended to take—a desperate but well-devised plan, which drew forth words of the highest commendation from the commanding officer and those with him. They knew that the fate of Edinburgh hung in the balance, and that if the city were taken it would be the first step towards their downfall.

XXXI

"The Demon of War"

Two hours later, just before the break of day, British bugles sounded, and the camp on the Braid Hills was immediately astir. That the enemy were about to test the efficiency of a new gigantic engine of war was unknown except to the officers and the brave man who had risked his life in order to obtain the secret of the foeman's plans.

To him the British General was trusting, and as with knit brows and anxious face the grey-haired officer stood at the door of his tent gazing across the burn to Blackford Hill, he was wondering whether he had yet obtained his coign of vantage. From the case slung round his shoulder he drew his field glasses and turned them upon a clump of trees near the top of the hill, straining his eyes to discover any movement.

On the crest of the hill two Volunteer artillery batteries were actively preparing for the coming fray, but as yet it was too dark to discern anything among the distant clump of trees; so, replacing his glasses, the commanding officer re-entered his tent and bent for a long time over the Ordnance Map under the glimmering, uncertain light of a guttering candle.

Meanwhile the Russians were busily completing their arrangements for striking an appalling blow.

Concealed by a line of trees and a number of farm buildings, the little section of the enemy had worked indefatigably for the past two hours, and now in the grey dawn the contents of the mysterious boxes, a long dark monster, lay upon the grass, moving restlessly, trying to free itself from its trammels.

It was a huge and curiously-shaped air-ship, and was to be used for dropping great charges of mélinite and steel bombs filled with picric acid into the handsome historic city of Edinburgh! Some of the shells were filled with sulphurous acid, carbon dioxide, and other deadly compounds, the intent being to cause suffocation over wide areas by the volatilisation of liquid gases!

This controllable electric balloon, a perfection of M. Gaston Tissandier's invention a few years before, was, as it lay upon the grass, nearly inflated and ready to ascend, elongated in form, and filled with hydrogen.

It was about 140 feet long, 63 feet in diameter through the middle, and the envelope was of fine cloth coated with an impermeable varnish. On either side were horizontal shafts of flexible walnut laths, fastened with silk belts along the centre, and over the balloon a netting of ribbons was placed, and to this the car was connected. On each of the four sides was a screw propeller 12 feet in diameter, driven by bichromate of potassium batteries and a dynamo-electric motor. The propellers were so arranged that the balloon could keep head to a hurricane, and when proceeding with the wind would deviate immediately from its course by the mere pulling of a lever by the aëronaut.

Carefully packed in the car were large numbers of the most powerful infernal machines, ingeniously designed to effect the most awful destruction if hurled into a thickly-populated centre. Piled in the smallest possible compass were square steel boxes, some filled with mélinite, dynamite, and an explosive strongly resembling cordite, only possessing twice its strength, each with fulminating compounds, while others contained picric acid fitted with glass detonating tubes. Indeed, this gigantic engine, which might totally wreck a city and kill every inhabitant in half an hour while at an altitude of 6½ miles, had rightly been named by the Pole who had perfected Tissandier's invention—"The Demon of War."

While the two officers of the Russian balloon section, both experienced aëronauts, were finally examining minutely every rope, ascertaining that all was ready for the ascent, away on Blackford Hill one man, pale and determined, with coat and vest thrown aside, was preparing a counterblast to the forthcoming attack. Under cover of the clump of trees, but with its muzzle pointing towards Bridgend, a long, thin gun of an altogether strange type had been brought into position. It was about four times the size of a Maxim, which it resembled somewhat in shape, only the barrel was much longer, the store of ammunition being contained in a large steel receptacle at the side, wherein also was some marvellously-contrived mechanism. The six gunners who were assisting Mackenzie at length completed their work, and the gun having been carefully examined by the gallant man in charge and two of the officers who had been in the tent with the General during the midnight consultation, Mackenzie, with a glance in the yet hazy distance where the enemy had bivouaced, pulled over a small lever, which immediately started a dynamo.

"In three minutes we shall be ready for action," he said, glancing at his watch; and then, turning a small wheel which raised the muzzle of the gun so as to point it at a higher angle in the direction of the sky, he waited until the space of time he had mentioned had elapsed.

The officers stood aside conversing in an undertone. This man Mackenzie had invented this strange-looking weapon, and only one had been made. It had some months before been submitted to the War Office, but they had declined to take it up, believing that a patent they already possessed was superior to it; yet Mackenzie had nevertheless thrown his whole soul into his work, and meant now to show his superiors its penetrative powers, and put its capabilities to practical test. Again he glanced at his watch, and quickly pulled back another lever, which caused the motor to revolve at twice the speed, and the gun to emit a low hissing sound, like escaping steam. Then he stepped back to the officers, saying—

"I am now prepared. It will go up as straight and quickly as a rocket, but we must catch it before it ascends two miles, for the clouds hang low, and we may lose it more quickly than we imagine."

The gunners stood in readiness, and the two officers looked away over Craigmillar towards the grey distant sea. Dawn was spreading now, and the haze was gradually clearing. They all knew the attempt would be made ere long, before it grew much lighter, so they stood at their posts in readiness, Mackenzie with his hand upon the lever which would regulate the discharge.

They were moments of breathless expectancy. Minute after minute went by, but not a word was spoken, for every eye was turned upon the crest of a certain ridge nearly three miles away, at a point where the country was well wooded.

A quarter of an hour had thus elapsed, when Mackenzie suddenly shouted, "Look, lads! *There she goes!* Now, let's teach 'em what Scots can do."

As he spoke there rose from behind the ridge a great dark mass, looking almost spectral in the thin morning mist. For a moment it seemed to poise and swing as if uncertain in its flight, then quickly it shot straight up towards the sky.

"Ready?" shouted Mackenzie, his momentary excitement having given place to great coolness. The men at their posts all answered in the affirmative. Mackenzie bent and waited for a few seconds sighting the gun, while the motor hummed with terrific speed. Then shouting "Fire!" he drew back the lever.

The gun discharged, but there was no report, only a sharp hiss as the compressed air released commenced to send charge after charge of dynamite automatically away into space in rapid succession!

None dared to breathe. The excitement was intense. They watched the effect upon the Russian balloon, but to their dismay saw it still rapidly ascending and unharmed!

It had altered its course, and instead of drifting away seaward was now travelling towards Duddingston, and making straight for Edinburgh, passing above the Russian camp.

"Missed! *missed!*" Mackenzie shrieked, turning back the lever and arresting the discharge. "It's four miles off now, and we can carry seven and three-quarters to hit a fixed object. Remember, lads, the fate of Auld Reekie is now in your hands! Ready?"

Again he bent and sighted the gun, raising the muzzle higher than the balloon so as to catch it on the ascent. The motor hummed louder and louder, the escaping air hissed and turned into liquid by the enormous pressure, then with a glance at the gauge he yelled "Fire!" and pulled back the lever.

Dynamite shells, ejected at the rate of 50 a minute, rushed from the muzzle, and sped away.

But the Demon of War, with its whirling propellers, continued on its swift, silent mission of destruction.

"Missed again!" cried one of the men, in despair. "See! it's gone! We've—good heavens!—*why, we've lost it—lost it!*"

Mackenzie, who had been glancing that moment at the gauges, gazed eagerly up, and staggered back as if he had received a blow. "It's disappeared!" he gasped. "*They've outwitted us, the brutes, and nothing now can save Edinburgh from destruction!*"

Officers and men stood aghast, with blanched faces, scarce knowing how to act. The destructive forces in that controllable balloon were more than sufficient to lay the whole of Edinburgh in ruins; and then, no doubt, the enemy would attempt by the same means to destroy the British batteries on the neighbouring hills. Already, along the valleys fighting had begun, for rapid firing could be heard in the direction of Gilmerton, and now and then the British guns on the Braid Hills behind spoke out sharply to the Russians who had occupied Loanhead, and the distant booming of cannon could be heard incessantly from Corstorphine.

Suddenly a loud, exultant cry from Mackenzie caused his companions

WILLIAM LE QUEUX

to strain their eyes away to Duddingston, and there they saw high in the air the monster aërial machine gradually looming through the mist, a vague and shadowy outline. It had passed through a bank of cloud, and was gradually reappearing.

"Quick! There's not a moment to lose!" shrieked Mackenzie, springing to the lever with redoubled enthusiasm, an example followed by the others.

The motor revolved so rapidly that it roared, the gauges ran high, the escaping air hissed so loudly that Mackenzie was compelled to shout at the top of his voice "Ready?" as for a third time he took careful aim at the misty object now six miles distant.

The War Demon was still over the Russian camp, and in a few moments, travelling at that high rate of speed, it would pass over Arthur's Seat, and be enabled to drop its deadly compounds in Princes Street. But Mackenzie set his teeth, and muttered something under his breath.

"*Now!*" he exclaimed, as he suddenly pulled the lever, and for the last time sent forth the automatic shower of destructive shells.

A second later there was a bright flash from above as if the sun itself had burst, and then came a most terrific explosion, which caused the earth to tremble where they stood. The clouds were rent asunder by the frightful detonation, and down upon the Russian camp the débris of their ingenious invention fell in a terrible death-dealing shower. The annihilation of the dastardly plot to wreck the city was complete. Small dynamite shells from Mackenzie's pneumatic gun had struck the car of the balloon, and by the firing of half a ton of explosives the enemy was in an instant hoist with his own petard.

As the débris fell within the Russian lines, some fifty or sixty picric-acid bombs—awful engines of destruction—which had not been exploded in mid-air, crashed into the Muscovite ranks, and, bursting, killed and wounded hundreds of infantrymen and half a regiment of Cossacks. One, bursting in the enemy's headquarters, seriously injured several members of the staff; while another, falling among the Engineers' transport, exploded a great quantity of gun-cotton, which in its turn killed a number of men and horses.

The disaster was awful in its suddenness, appalling in its completeness. The aëronauts, totally unprepared for such an attack, had been blown to atoms just when within an ace of success.

Fortune had favoured Britain, and, thanks to Mackenzie's vigilance and his pneumatic dynamite gun, which the Government had rejected as a worthless weapon, the grey old city of Edinburgh was still safe.

But both Russians and Britons had now mustered their forces, and this, the first note sounded of a second terrific and desperately-fought battle, portended success for Britain's gallant army.

Yet notwithstanding the disaster the enemy sustained by the blowing up of their balloon, their 2nd Army Corps, together with the portion of the 3rd Army Corps operating from their base at Leith, succeeded, after terribly hard fighting and heavy losses, in at length forcing back the defenders from the Braid and Blackford Hills, and the Corstorphine position having already been occupied, they were then enabled to invest Edinburgh. That evening fierce sanguinary fights took place in the streets, for the people held the barricades until the last moment, and the batteries on Calton Hill, in St. Andrew's Square, and at the Castle effected terrible execution in conjunction with those on Arthur's Seat. Still the enemy by their overwhelming numbers gradually broke down these defences, and, after appalling slaughter on both sides, occupied the city. The fighting was fiercest along Princes Street, Lothian Road, and in the neighbourhood of Scotland Street Station, while along Cumberland and Great King Streets the enemy were swept away in hundreds by British Maxims brought to bear from Drummond Place. Along Canongate from Holyrood to Moray House, and in Lauriston Place and the Grassmarket, hand-to-hand struggles took place between the patriotic civilians and the foe. From behind their barricades men of Edinburgh fought valiantly, and everywhere inflicted heavy loss; still the enemy, pressing onward, set fire to a number of public buildings, including the Register Office, the Royal Exchange, the University, the Liberal and New Clubs, and Palace Hotel, with many other buildings in Princes Street. The fires, which broke out rapidly in succession, were caused for the purpose of producing a panic, and in this the enemy were successful, for the city was quickly looted, and the scenes of ruin, death, and desolation that occurred in its streets that night were awful.

In every quarter the homes of loyal Scotsmen were entered by the ruthless invader, who wrecked the cherished household gods, and carried away all the valuables that were portable. Outrage and murder were rife everywhere, and no quarter was shown the weak or unprotected. Through the streets the invader rushed with sword and firebrand, causing destruction, suffering, and death.

The defenders, though straining every nerve to stem the advancing tide, had, alas! been unsuccessful, and ere midnight Edinburgh, one of the proudest and most historic cities in the world, had fallen, and the British standard floating over the Castle was, alas! replaced by the Eagle of the Russian Autocrat.

XXXII

Frightful Slaughter Outside Glasgow

It was a sad misfortune, a national calamity; yet our troops did not lose heart. Commanded as they were by Britons, astute, loyal, and fearless, they, after fighting hard, fell back from Edinburgh in order, and husbanded their force for the morrow.

Indeed, soon after dawn the Russians found themselves severely attacked. Exultant over their success, they had, while sacking Edinburgh, left their base at Leith very inadequately protected, with the result that the defenders, swooping suddenly down upon the town, succeeded, with the assistance of four coast-defence ships and a number of torpedo boats, in blowing up most of the Russian transports, and seizing their ammunition and provisions.

Such an attack was, of course, very vigorously defended, but it was a smart manoeuvre on the part of the British General, and enabled him, after cutting off the enemy's line of retreat, to turn suddenly and attack the Russians who were continuing their destructive campaign through the streets of Edinburgh. This bold move on the part of the defenders was totally unexpected by the foe, which accounted for the frightful loss of life that was sustained on the Russian side, and the subsequent clever tactics which resulted in the driving out of the invaders from Edinburgh, and British troops reoccupying that city.

Meanwhile the 1st Russian Army Corps, which on landing had at once set out towards Glasgow, had marched on in a great extended line, sacking the various towns through which they passed. As they advanced from Linlithgow, Airdrie, and Coatbridge were looted and burned, while further south, Motherwell, Hamilton, and Bothwell shared the same fate. About 20,000 men, together with 11,000 who had been forced to evacuate Edinburgh, had at length advanced a little beyond Coatbridge, and, in preparation for a vigorous siege of Glasgow, halted within seven miles of the city, with flanks extended away south to Motherwell and on to Wishaw, and north as far as Chryston and Kirkintilloch.

In Glasgow the excitement was intense, and surging crowds filled the streets night and day. The fall of Edinburgh had produced the

WILLIAM LE QUEUX

greatest sensation, and the meagre news of the disaster telegraphed had scarcely been supplemented when the report of the retaking of "Auld Reekie" came to hand, causing great rejoicing. Nevertheless, it was known that over thirty thousand trained soldiers were on their way to the banks of the Clyde, and Glasgow was fevered and turbulent. The scanty business that had lately been done was now at a standstill, and the meagre supplies that reached there from America not being half sufficient for the enormous population, the city was already starving. But, as in other towns, great barricades had been thrown up, and those in Gallowgate and Duke Street, thoroughfares by which Glasgow might be entered by way of Parkhead and Dennistoun, were soon manned by loyal and patriotic bands of civilians. Other barriers were constructed at St. Rollox Station, in Canning Street, in Monteith Row, and in Great Western, Dumbarton, and Govan Roads.

South of the river, Eglinton Street and the roads at Crosshill were barricaded, and in New City and Garscube Roads in the north there were also strong defences. All were held by enthusiastic bodies of men who had hastily armed themselves, confident in the belief that our Volunteers and the small body of Regulars would not allow the invader to march in force upon their city without a most determined resistance.

Now, however, the alarming news reached Glasgow that the enemy had actually sacked and burned Coatbridge. In an hour they could commence looting the shops in Gallowgate, and their heavy tramp would be heard on the granite of Trongate and Argyle Street! Throughout the city the feeling of insecurity increased, and hourly the panic assumed greater proportions.

The sun that day was obscured by dark thunder-clouds, the swirling Clyde flowed on black beneath its many bridges, and the outlook was everywhere gloomy and ominous.

Still, away on the hills to southward, our small force of soldiers and Volunteers had narrowly watched the onward tide of destroyers, and carefully laid their plans. The manner in which the defensive operations were conducted is perhaps best related in a letter written by Captain Boyd Drummond of the 1st Battalion Princess Louise's (Argyll and Sutherland) Highlanders, to a friend in London, and which was published with the accompanying sketch in the *Daily Graphic*.

He wrote as follows:—"On the second day after the Russians had landed, Colonel Cumberland of 'Ours' received orders to move us from Lanark, and reconnoitre as far as possible along the Carluke road, with a view to taking up a position to cover the advance of the division, which had during the morning been considerably reinforced by nearly half the centre division from Peebles. In addition to our battalion with two machine guns, Colonel Cumberland was in command of the 1st, 2nd, 3rd, and 4th Volunteer Battalions from Greenock, Paisley, Pollokshaws, and Stirling respectively, the 1st Dumbarton from Helensburgh, the Highland Borderers, and the Renfrew Militia, together with a section of field artillery, a field company of Royal Engineers, and about forty cavalry and cyclists. Arriving at Carluke early in the afternoon, we awaited the return of scouts, who had been pushed on in advance to beyond Wishaw, in the direction of the enemy. They having reported that the Russians had withdrawn from Wishaw, we at once moved on to Law Junction, about a mile from that town, and finally took up a position for the night near Waterloo, commanding Wishaw and Overtown.

"Beyond the junction, towards Glasgow, the railway, which the enemy evidently did not intend to use, had been destroyed, but scouts from Morningside reported that the line to Edinburgh had not been cut, and that the permanent way remained uninjured. Colonel Cumberland therefore told off the right half battalion, with a machine gun, a section of Engineers, and six cyclists, to take up a position near the road between Newmains and Morningside, with instructions to form piquets and patrol the roads north and east. I was with No. 1 Company, but, being senior captain present, the chief gave me command of this detachment. It was the first time such a responsibility had been conferred upon me; therefore I was determined not to be caught napping.

"As soon as we arrived at our ground, I sent two cyclists out to Newmains and two to Morningside, with orders to glean what information they could, and to wait in the villages until further orders, unless they sighted the enemy's outposts, or discovered anything important. As soon as I had sent out my piquets, I took my own company and six of the Engineers down to Morningside. Some of the villagers, who had escaped when a portion of the invaders passed through on the previous night, had returned, and the cyclists gathered from them that we were close upon the heels of the Russian rearguard.

"As the railway had not been destroyed, I thought that possibly the invaders intended to use the line *viâ* Mid-Calder, and therefore examined the station closely. While engaged in this, one of the Engineers suddenly discovered a wire very carefully concealed along the line, and as we followed it up 500 yards each way, and could find no connection with the instrument at the station office, I at once concluded that it was the enemy's field telegraph, forming means of communication between their headquarters at Airdrie and the division that still remained in the Pentlands.

"Cutting the wire, and attaching the ends to the instrument in the station, I left three Engineers, all expert telegraphists, to tap the wire, and they, with the right half company, under Lieutenant Compton, formed a detached post at this point. I also left the cyclists to convey to me any messages which might be received on the instrument, and then proceeded to Newmains. The place was now a mere heap of smouldering ruins; but, as at Morningside, some of the terrified villagers had returned, and they stated that early in the morning they had seen small detachments of Russian cavalry pass through from Bankle, and proceed north along the Cleland road.

"Leaving the left half company here with the other Engineers and the two cyclists, under Lieutenant Planck, with orders to block the road and railway bridge, I returned to my piquet line. A few minutes later, however, a cyclist rode up with a copy of a message which had been sent from the Russian headquarters on the Pentlands to the Glasgow investing force. The message was in cipher, but, thanks to the information furnished by the spy who was captured near Manchester, we were now aware of some of the codes used by the invaders, and I sent the messenger on to the Colonel at once. One of his staff was able to transcribe it sufficiently to show that some disaster had occurred to the enemy on the Pentlands, for it concluded with an order withdrawing the troops from Glasgow, in order to reinforce the 3rd Army Corps in the fierce battle that was now proceeding. It was also stated in the message that despatches followed, so at once we were all on the alert.

"Almost immediately afterwards news was received over our own telegraph from Carstairs, stating that a terrific battle had been fought along the valleys between Leadburn, Linton, and Dolphinton, in which we had suffered very severely, but we had nevertheless gained a decisive victory, for from dawn until the time of telegraphing it was estimated that no fewer than 12,000 Russians had been killed or wounded.

"It appeared that our forces on the Lammermuirs had moved quickly, and, extending along the ridges, through Tynehead, and thence to Heriot, and on to Peebles, joined hands with the division at that place before dawn, and, when it grew light, had made a sudden and desperate attack. The enemy, who had imagined himself in a safe position, was unprepared, and from the first moment of the attack the slaughter was awful. As noon wore on the battle had increased, until now the invaders had been outflanked, and mowed down in such a frightful manner, that the survivors, numbering nearly six thousand of all ranks, had, finding their urgent appeal to their forces at Airdrie met with no response, and imagining that they too had been defeated, at last surrendered, and were taken prisoners.

"On receipt of this intelligence, Colonel Cumberland executed a manoeuvre that was a marvel of forethought and smartness. The appeal to Airdrie for help had, of course, not been received, but in its place he ordered a message in Russian to be sent along the enemy's field telegraph to the force advancing on Glasgow in the following words: 'Remain at Airdrie. Do not advance on Glasgow before we join you. The defenders are defeated with heavy losses everywhere. Our advance guard will be with you in twenty-four hours. Signed— Drukovitch.'

"This having been despatched, he reported by telegraph to the headquarters at Carstairs what he had done, and then our whole force immediately moved as far as Bellshill, in the direction of Glasgow. Here we came across the Russian outposts, and a sharp fight ensued. After half an hour, however, we succeeded in cutting them off and totally annihilating them, afterwards establishing ourselves in Bellshill until reinforcements could arrive. We were now only six miles from the Russian headquarters at Airdrie, and they, on receipt of our fictitious message, had withdrawn from the Clyde bank, and extended farther north over the hills as far as Milngavie.

"We were thus enabled to watch and wait in Bellshill undisturbed throughout the night; and while the enemy were eagerly expecting their legions of infantry who were to swoop down and conquer Glasgow, we remained content in the knowledge that the hour of conquest was close at hand.

"A short, hasty rest, and we were astir again long before the dawn. Just at daybreak, however, the advance guard of our force from Carstairs, which had been on the march during the night, came into touch with us, and in an hour the combined right and centre divisions of the British had opened the battle.

"Our fighting front extended from Wishaw right across to Condorrat, with batteries on Torrance and the hill at New Monkland, while another strong line was pushed across from Cambuslang to Parkhead, and thence to Millerston, for the protection of Glasgow.

"Thus, almost before our guns uttered their voice of defiance, we had surrounded the enemy, and throughout the morning the fighting was most sanguinary and desperate. Our batteries did excellent service; still, it must be remembered we had attacked a well-trained force of over thirty thousand men, and they had many more guns than we possessed. No doubt the fictitious despatch we had sent had prevented the Russian commander from advancing on Glasgow during the night, as he had intended; and now, finding himself so vigorously attacked by two divisions which he believed had been cut up and annihilated, all his calculations were completely upset.

"It was well for us that this was so, otherwise we might have fared much worse than we did. As it was, Cossacks and Dragoons wrought frightful havoc among our infantry; while, on the other hand, the fire discipline of the latter was magnificent. Every bit of cover on the hills seem to bristle with hidden rifles, that emptied their magazines without smoke and with fatal effect. Many a gallant dash was made by our men, the Volunteers especially displaying conspicuous courage. The 1st Dumbartonshire Volunteers, under Col. Thomson, V.D., the 1st Renfrewshire, under Col. Lamont, V.D., and the 4th Battalion Argyll and Sutherland Highlanders, under Col. D. M'Fayden, V.D., operated together with magnificent success, for they completely cut up a strong Russian detachment on the Glasgow road beyond Uddingston, driving them out of the wood near Daldowie, and there annihilating them, and afterwards holding their own on the banks of the North Calder without suffering very much loss. They handled their Maxims as smartly as any body of Regulars; and indeed, throughout the day their performances everywhere were marked by steady discipline and cool courage that was in the highest degree commendable.

"About two o'clock in the afternoon the battle was at its height. Under the blazing sun that beat down upon us mercilessly, my battalion fought on, feeling confident that the enemy were gradually being defeated. The slaughter everywhere was frightful, and the green hillsides and fields were covered with dead and dying soldiers of the Tsar. The grey coats were soaked with blood, and dark, ugly stains dyed the grass of the fertile meadows beside the winding Clyde. Since their sudden landing in Scotland, the enemy's early successes had been followed by defeat after defeat. Their transports had been destroyed, their ammunition and stores seized, both their 2nd and 3rd Army Corps had been totally annihilated, leaving nearly twelve thousand men in our hands as prisoners, and now the defeat of this force of picked regiments, who had, on landing, immediately marched straight across Scotland, would effect a crushing and decisive blow.

"But the struggle was terrific, the din deafening, the wholesale butchery appalling. Our men knew they were fighting for Caledonia and their Queen, and their conduct, from the first moment of hostilities, until stray bullets laid them low one after another, was magnificent; they were splendid examples of the true, loyal, and fearless Briton, who will fight on even while his life-blood ebbs.

"Evening fell, but the continuous firing did not cease. The sun sank red and angry into dark storm-clouds behind the long range of purple hills beyond the Clyde, but the clash of arms continued over hill and dale on the east of Glasgow, and we, exerting every effort in our successful attempt to hold the five converging roads near Broomhouse, knew not which side were victors.

"Suddenly I received orders to send over a small detachment to block the two roads at Baillieston, the one a main road leading up from Coatbridge, and the other from the hilly country around Old Monkland, where the struggle was fiercest. Sending Lieutenant Planck over immediately with a detachment and several cyclists, I followed as soon as possible, and found he had blocked both roads in the centre of the little Scotch village, and had occupied the inn situated between the two roads, leaving just sufficient space for his cyclists to pass. Looking towards the city we could see that the hills on our left were occupied by British redcoats. In the village the quaint little low-built cottages, with their stairs outside, were all closed and deserted, and the place seemed strangely quiet after the exciting scenes and ceaseless deafening din.

"Taking six of Planck's men and the cyclists about a mile towards Coatbridge, I posted them at the cross-roads beyond Rhind House, sending the cyclists out along the valley to Dikehead. All was quiet in our immediate vicinity for some time, until suddenly we discerned the cyclists coming back. They reported that they had seen cavalry. This, then, must be a detachment of the enemy, who in all probability were retreating. I at once sent the cyclists back to inform Planck, and to tell him we should not take a hand in the game until we had allowed them to pass and they had discovered his barricade. In a few minutes we could distinctly hear them approaching. We were all well under cover, but I was surprised to find that it was only an escort.

"They were galloping, and had evidently come a long distance by some circuitous route, and had not taken part in the fighting. I counted five—two Cossacks in advance, then about forty yards behind a shabbily-dressed civilian on horseback, and about forty yards behind him two more Cossacks. They appeared to expect no interruption, and it occurred to me that the Cossacks were escorting the civilian over to the Russian position away beyond Hogganfield Loch. As soon as they were clear, I formed my men up on each side of the road to await events.

"We had no occasion to remain long in expectation, for soon afterwards the stillness was broken by shouts and a few rapid shots, and then we could hear two horses galloping back. One was riderless, and a corporal who attempted to stop it was knocked down and seriously injured; but the other had a rider, and as he neared us I could see he was the civilian. I knew I must stop him at all costs.

"So, ordering the men on the opposite side of the road to lie down, we gave him a section volley from one side as he rushed past. The horse was badly hit, and stumbled, throwing its rider, who was at once secured. To prevent him from disposing of anything, we bound him securely. Two of the Cossacks had been shot and the other two captured. Upon the civilian, and in his saddle-bags, we found a number of cipher despatches, elaborate plans showing how Glasgow was defended, and an autograph letter from the Russian General Drukovitch, giving him instructions to enter Glasgow alone by way of Partick, and to await him there until the city fell.

"But the city was never invested. An hour after we had sent this mysterious civilian—who spoke English with a foreign accent—over to the Colonel, our onslaught became doubly desperate. In the dusk, regiment after regiment of Russians were simply swept away by the cool and deliberate fire of the British, who, being reinforced by my battalion and others, wrought splendid execution in the enemy's main body, forced back upon us at Baillieston.

"Then, as night fell, a report was spread that General Drukovitch had surrendered. This proved true. With his 2nd and 3rd Army Corps annihilated, and his transports and base in our hands, he was compelled to acknowledge himself vanquished; therefore, by nine o'clock hostilities had ceased, and during that night nearly six thousand survivors of the 1st Russian Army Corps were taken prisoners, and marched in triumph into Glasgow amid the wildest excitement of the populace. This desperate attempt to invest Glasgow had cost the Russians no fewer than 25,000 men in killed and wounded.

"The capture we effected near Baillieston turned out to be of a most important character. When searched at headquarters, a visiting-card was found concealed upon the man, and this gave our Colonel a clue. The man has since been identified by one of his intimate friends as a person well known in London society, who poses as a wealthy German, the Count von Beilstein! It is alleged that he has for several years been living in the metropolis and acting as an expert spy in the Secret Service of the Tsar. He was sent handcuffed, under a strong escort, to London a few days after the battle, and if all I hear be true, some highly sensational disclosures will be made regarding his adventurous career.

"But throughout Caledonia there is now unbounded joy. Our beloved country is safe; for, thanks to the gallant heroism of our Volunteers, the Muscovite invaders have been completely wiped out, and Scotland again proudly rears her head."

XXXIII

MARCH OF THE FRENCH ON LONDON

South of the Thames, where the gigantic force of French and Russians, numbering nearly two hundred thousand of all arms, had been prevented from attacking London by our Volunteers and Regulars massed along the Surrey Hills, the slaughter on both sides had been frightful. The struggle was indeed not for a dynasty, but for the very existence of Britain as an independent nation.

Sussex had been devastated, but Kent still held out, and Chatham remained in the possession of the defenders.

The rout of the British at Horsham prior to the march of the left column of invaders to Birmingham was succeeded by defeat after defeat, the engagements each day illustrating painfully that by force of overwhelming numbers the invaders were gradually nearing their goal—the mighty Capital of our Empire.

Gallant stands were made by our Regulars at East Grinstead, Crawley, Alfold, and from Haslemere across Hind Head Common to Frensham. At each of these places, long, desperately-fought battles with the French had taken place through the hot September days,—our Regular forces confident in the stubborn resistance that would be offered by the long unbroken line of Volunteers occupying the range of hills behind. Our signallers had formed a long line of stations from Reculvers and Star Hill, south of the Medway Fortress, to Blue Bell Hill, between Chatham and Maidstone, thence through Snodland, Wrotham, Westerham, and Limpsfield to Caterham, and from there on through Reigate Park, Boxhill, St. Martha's, and over the Hog's Back to Aldershot. With flags in day and lamps by night messages constantly passed, and communication was thus maintained by this means as well as by the field telegraph, which, however, on several occasions had been cut by the enemy.

Yet although our soldiers fought day after day with that pluck characteristic of the true Briton, fortune nevertheless seemed to have forsaken us, and even although we inflicted frightful losses upon the French all round, still they gradually forced back the defenders over the Surrey border. Terror, ruin, and death had been spread by the invading

Gauls. English homes were sacked, French soldiers bivouaced in Sussex pastures, and the ripening corn was trodden down and stained with blood. The white dusty highways leading from London to the sea were piled with unheeded corpses that were fearful to gaze upon, yet Britannia toiled on undaunted in this desperate struggle for the retention of her Empire.

After our defeat at Horsham, the Russians had contented themselves by merely driving back the defenders to a line of resistance from Aldershot to the north of Bagshot, and then they had marched onward to Birmingham. From Horsham, however, two columns of the invaders, mostly French, and numbering over twenty thousand each, had advanced on Guildford and Dorking. At the same time, a strong demonstration was made by the enemy in the country north of Eastbourne and Hailsham, by which the whole of the district in the triangle from Bexhill to Heathfield, and thence to Cuckfield and Steyning, fell into their hands. The British, however, had massed a strong force to prevent the enemy making their way into West Kent, and still held their own along the hills stretching from Crowborough to Ticehurst, and from Etchingham, through Brightling and Ashburnham, down to Battle and Hastings.

The north of London had during the weeks of hostilities been strongly guarded by Volunteers and Regulars, for information of a contemplated landing in Essex had been received; and although the defenders had not yet fired a shot, they were eagerly looking forward to a chance of proving their worth, as their comrades in other parts of England had already done.

At first the tactics of the invaders could not be understood, for it had been concluded that they would naturally follow up their successes on landing with a rapid advance on London.

It was, of course, evident that the vigorous demonstrations made in the North and other parts of Britain were intended with a view to drawing as many troops as possible from the defence of London, and dispose of them in detail before surrounding the capital. Yet, to the dismay of the enemy, no blow they delivered in other parts of our country had had the desired effect of weakening the defensive lines around London. At the opening of the campaign it had been the enemy's intention to reduce London by a blockade, which could perhaps have been successfully carried out had they landed a strong force in Essex. The troops who were intended to land there were, however, sent to Scotland instead, and the fact that they had been annihilated outside Glasgow resulted in a decision to march at once upon the metropolis.

Advancing from Horsham, the French right column, numbering 20,000 men with about 70 guns, had, after desperate fighting, at last reached Leatherhead, having left a battalion in support at Dorking. The British had resolutely contested every step the French had advanced, and the slaughter around Dorking had been awful, while the fighting across Fetcham Downs and around Ockley and Bear Green had resulted in frightful loss on both sides.

Our Regulars and Volunteers, notwithstanding their gallantry, were, alas! gradually driven back by the enormous numbers that had commenced the onslaught, and were at last thrown back westward in disorder, halting at Ripley. Here the survivors snatched a hasty rest, and they were during the night reinforced by a contingent of Regulars who had come over from Windsor and Hounslow. On the arrival of these reinforcements, the Colonel, well knowing how serious was the situation now our first line of defence had been broken, sent out a flying column from Ripley, while the main body marched to Great Bookham, with the result that Leatherhead, now in the occupation of the French, was from both sides vigorously attacked. The British flying column threatening the enemy from the north was, however, quickly checked by the French guns, and in the transmission of an order a most serious blunder occurred, leading to the impossibility of a retreat upon Ripley, for unfortunately the order, wrongly given, resulted in the blowing up by mistake of the bridges over the river Mole by which they had crossed, and which they wanted to use again.

Thus it was that for a time this force was compelled to remain, at terrible cost, right under the fire of the French entrenched position at Leatherhead; but the enemy were fortunately not strong enough to follow up this advantage, and as they occupied a strong strategical position they were content to await the arrival of their huge main body, now on the move, and which they expected would reach Leatherhead during that night. After more fierce fighting, lasting one whole breathless day, the defenders were annihilated, while their main body approaching from the south also fell into a trap. For several hours a fierce battle also raged between Dorking and Mickleham. The British battery on Box Hill wrought awful havoc in the French lines, yet gradually the enemy silenced our guns and cut up our forces.

The invaders were now advancing in open order over the whole of Sussex and the west of Kent, and on the same day as the battle was fought at Leatherhead, the high ground south of Sevenoaks, extending from Wimlet Hill to Chart Common, fell into their hands, the British suffering severely; while two of our Volunteer batteries in the vicinity were surprised and seized by a French flying column.

In the meantime, another French column, numbering nearly twenty thousand infantry and cavalry, had advanced from Alfold, burning Ewhurst and Cranley, and after a desperately-contested engagement they captured the British batteries on the hills at Hascombe and Hambledon.

On the same day the French advance guard, though suffering terrible loss, successfully attacked the battery of Regulars on the hill at Wonersh, and Godalming having been invested, they commenced another vigorous attack upon the strong line of British Regulars and Volunteers at Guildford, where about fourteen thousand men were massed.

On the hills from Gomshall to Seale our brave civilian defenders had remained throughout the hostilities ready to repel any attack. Indeed, as the days passed, and no demonstration had been made in their direction, they had grown impatient, until at length this sudden and ferocious onslaught had been made, and they found themselves face to face with an advancing army of almost thrice their strength. Among the Volunteer battalions holding the position were the 1st Bucks, under Lord Addington, V.D.; the 2nd Oxfordshire Light Infantry, under Col. H. S. Hall; the 1st, 2nd, and 3rd Bedfordshire Regiment, under Col. A. M. Blake, Lieut.-Col. Rumball, and Col. J. T. Green, V.D.; the 1st Royal Berkshire, under Col. J. C. Carter; the 1st Somersetshire Light Infantry, under Col. H. M. Skrine, V.D.; and the 1st and 2nd Wiltshire, under the Earl of Pembroke, V.D., and Col. E. B. Merriman, V.D. Strong batteries had been established between Guildford and Seale by the 1st Fifeshire Artillery, under Col. J. W. Johnston, V.D., and the Highland Artillery, under Col. W. Fraser, V.D.; while batteries on the left were held by the 1st Midlothian, under Col. Kinnear, V.D.; the 1st East Riding, under Col. R. G. Smith, V.D.; and the 1st West Riding, under Col. T. W. Harding, V.D.

Commencing before dawn, the battle was fierce and sanguinary almost from the time the first shots were exchanged. The eight 60-pounder guns in the new fort at the top of Pewley Hill, manned by the Royal Artillery, commanded the valleys lying away to the south, and effected splendid defensive work.

Indeed, it was this redoubt, with three new ones between Guildford and Gomshall, and another on the Hog's Back, which held the enemy in check for a considerable time; and had there been a larger number of a similar strength, it is doubtful whether the French would ever have accomplished their design upon Guildford.

The Pewley Fort, built in the solid chalk, and surrounded by a wide ditch, kept up a continuous fire upon the dense masses of the enemy, and swept away hundreds of unfortunate fellows as they rushed madly onward; while the Volunteer batteries and the Maxims of the infantry battalions poured upon the invaders a devastating hail of lead.

From Farnham, the line through Odiham and Aldershot was held by a force increasing hourly in strength; therefore the enemy were unable to get over to Farnborough to outflank the defenders. Through that brilliant, sunny September day the slaughter was terrible in every part of the enemy's column, and it was about noon believed that they would find their positions at Wonersh and Godalming untenable.

Nevertheless, with a dogged persistency unusual to our Gallic neighbours, they continued to fight with unquelled vigour. The 2nd Oxfordshire Light Infantry and the 1st and 2nd Wiltshire, holding very important ground over against Puttenham, bore their part with magnificent courage, but were at length cut up in a most horrible manner; while the 1st Bedfordshire, who, with a body of Regulars valiantly held the road running over the hills from Gomshall to Merrow, fought splendidly; but they too were, alas! subsequently annihilated.

Over hill and dale, stretching away to the Sussex border, the rattle and din of war sounded incessantly, and as hour after hour passed, hundreds of Britons and Frenchmen dyed the brown, sun-baked grass with their blood. The struggle was frightful. Volunteer battalions who had manoeuvred over that ground at many an Eastertide had little dreamed that they would have one day to raise their rifles in earnest for the defence of their home and Queen. Yet the practice they had had now served them well, for in one instance the 1st Berkshire succeeded by a very smart manoeuvre in totally sweeping away several troops of Cuirassiers, while a quarter of an hour later half an infantry battalion of Regulars attacked a large force of Zouaves on the Compton Road, and fought them successfully almost hand to hand.

Through the long, toilsome day the battle continued with unabated fury, and as the sun went down there was no cessation of hostilities. A force of our Regulars, extending from Farnham over Hind Head Common, fell suddenly upon a large body of French infantry, and, outflanking them, managed—after a most frightful encounter, in which they lost nearly half their men—to totally annihilate them.

In connection with this incident, a squadron of the 5th Dragoon Guards made a magnificent charge up a steep hill literally to the muzzles of the guns of a French battery, and by their magnificent pluck captured it. Still, notwithstanding the bravery of our defenders, and their fierce determination to sweep away their foe, it seemed when the sun finally disappeared that the fortunes of war were once more against us, for the French had now received huge reinforcements, and Dorking and Leatherhead having already passed into their hands two days previously, they were enabled to make their final assault a most savage and terrific one.

It was frightful; it crushed us! In the falling gloom our men fought desperately for their lives, but, alas! one after another our positions were carried by the invaders literally at the point of the bayonet, and ere the moon rose Guildford had fallen into the enemy's hands, and our depleted battalions had been compelled to retire in disorder east to Effingham and west to Farnham. Those who went to Effingham joined at midnight the column who had made an unsuccessful effort to recover Leatherhead, and then bivouaced in Oldlands Copse. The number of wounded in the battles of Guildford and Leatherhead was enormous. At Mickleham the British hospital flag floated over St. Michael's Church, the Priory at Cherkley, Chapel Farm, and on Mickleham Hall, a portion of which still remained intact, although the building had been looted by Zouaves. In Leatherhead the French had established hospitals at Givons Grove, Vale Lodge, Elmbank, and in the Church of St. Mary and the parish church at Fetcham. At Guildford, in addition to the field hospitals on Albury Downs and behind St. Catherine's Hill, Holden, Warren, and Tyting Farms, Sutton Place and Loseley were filled with wounded French infantrymen and British prisoners, and many schools and buildings, including the Guildhall in Guildford town, bore the red cross.

At two most important strategic points the first line defending London had now been broken, and the British officers knew that it would require every effort on our part to recover our lost advantages.

The metropolis was now seriously threatened; for soon after dawn on the following day two great French columns, one from Guildford and the other from Leatherhead, were advancing north towards the Thames! The enemy had established telegraphic communication between the two towns, and balloons that had been sent up from Guildford and Ashstead to reconnoitre had reported that the second line of the British defence had been formed from Kingston, through Wimbledon, Tooting, Streatham, and Upper Norwood, and thence across *viâ* Sydenham to Lewisham and Greenwich.

It was upon this second line of defence that the French, with their enormous force of artillery, now marched. The Leatherhead column, with their main body about one day's march behind, took the route through Epsom to Mitcham, while the troops from Guildford pushed on through Ripley, Cobham, and Esher.

This advance occupied a day, and when a halt was made for the night the enemy's front extended from Walton to Thames Ditton, thence across Kingston Common and Malden to Mitcham. Bivouacing, they faced the British second line of defence, and waited for the morrow to commence their onslaught. In London the alarming news of the enemy's success caused a panic such as had never before been experienced in the metropolis. During the long anxious weeks that the enemy had been held within bounds by our Volunteers, London had never fully realised what bombardment would mean. While the French were beyond the Surrey Hills, Londoners felt secure; and the intelligence received of the enemy's utter rout at Newcastle, Manchester, Edinburgh, and Glasgow added considerably to this sense of security.

London, alas! was starving. Business was suspended; trains no longer left the termini; omnibuses, trams, and cabs had ceased running, the horses having been pressed into military service, and those which had not had been killed and eaten. The outlook everywhere, even during those blazing sunny days and clear moonlit nights, was cheerless and dispiriting. The bright sun seemed strangely incongruous with the black war-clouds that overhung the gigantic city, with its helpless, starving, breathless millions.

In the sun-baked, dusty streets the roar of traffic no longer sounded, but up and down the principal thoroughfares of the City and the West End the people prowled, lean and hungry—emaciated victims of this awful struggle between nations—seeking vainly for food to satisfy the terrible pangs consuming them. The hollow cheek, the thin, sharp nose, the dark-ringed glassy eye of one and all, told too plainly of the widespread suffering, and little surprise was felt at the great mortality in every quarter.

In Kensington and Belgravia the distress was quite as keen as in Whitechapel and Hackney, and both rich and poor mingled in the gloomy, dismal streets, wandering aimlessly over the great Modern Babylon, which the enemy were now plotting to destroy.

The horrors of those intensely anxious days of terror were unspeakable. The whole machinery of life in the Great City had been disorganised, and now London lay like an octopus, with her long arms extended in every direction, north and south of the Thames, inert, helpless, trembling. Over the gigantic Capital of the World hung the dark Shadow of Death. By day and by night its ghastly presence could be felt; its hideous realities crushed the heart from those who would face the situation with smiling countenance. London's wealth availed her not in this critical hour.

Grim, spectral, unseen, the Destroying Angel held the sword over her, ready to strike!

XXXIV

LOOTING IN THE SUBURBS

While famished men crept into Hyde Park and Kensington Gardens and there expired under the trees of absolute hunger, and starving women with babes at their breasts sank upon doorsteps and died, the more robust Londoners had, on hearing of the enemy's march on the metropolis, gone south to augment the second line of defence. For several weeks huge barricades had been thrown up in the principal roads approaching London from the south. The strongest of these were opposite the Convalescent Home on Kingston Hill, in Coombe Lane close to Raynes Park Station, in the Morden Road at Merton Abbey, opposite Lynwood in the Tooting Road; while nearer London, on the same road, there was a strong one with machine guns on the crest of Balham Hill, and another in Clapham Road. At Streatham Hill, about one hundred yards from the hospital, earthworks had been thrown up, and several guns brought into position; while at Beulah Hill, Norwood, opposite the Post Office at Upper Sydenham, at the Half Moon at Herne Hill, and in many of the roads between Honor Oak and Denmark Hill, barricades had been constructed and banked up with bags and baskets filled with earth.

Though these defences were held by enthusiastic civilians of all classes,—professional men, artisans, and tradesmen,—yet our second line of defence, distinct, of course, from the local barricades, was a very weak one. We had relied upon our magnificent strategic positions on the Surrey Hills, and had not made sufficient provision in case of a sudden reverse. Our second line, stretching from Croydon up to South Norwood, thence to Streatham and along the railway line to Wimbledon and Kingston, was composed of a few battalions of Volunteers, detachments of Metropolitan police, Berks and Bucks constabulary, London firemen and postmen, the Corps of Commissionaires—in fact, every body of drilled men who could be requisitioned to handle revolver or rifle. These were backed by great bodies of civilians, and behind stood the barricades with their insignificant-looking but terribly deadly machine guns.

The railways had, on the first news of the enemy's success at Leatherhead and Guildford, all been cut up, and in each of the many bridges spanning the Thames between Kingston and the Tower great charges of gun-cotton had been placed, so that they might be blown up at any instant, and thus prevent the enemy from investing the city.

Day dawned again at last—dull and grey. It had rained during the night, and the roads, wet and muddy, were unutterably gloomy as our civilian defenders looked out upon them, well knowing that ere long a fierce attack would be made. In the night the enemy had been busy laying a field telegraph from Mitcham to Kingston, through which messages were now being continually flashed.

Suddenly, just as the British outposts were being relieved, the French commenced a vigorous attack, and in a quarter of an hour fighting extended along the whole line. Volunteers, firemen, policemen, Commissionaires, and civilians all fought bravely, trusting to one hope, namely, that before they were defeated the enemy would be outflanked and attacked in their rear by a British force from the Surrey Hills. They well knew that to effectually bar the advance of this great body of French was out of all question, yet they fought on with creditable tact, and in many instances inflicted serious loss upon the enemy's infantry.

Soon, however, French field guns were trained upon them, and amid the roar of artillery line after line of heroic Britons fell shattered to earth. Amid the rattle of musketry, the crackling of the machine guns, and the booming of 16-pounders, brave Londoners struggled valiantly against the masses of wildly excited Frenchmen; yet every moment the line became slowly weakened, and the defenders were gradually forced back upon their barricades. The resistance which the French met with was much more determined than they had anticipated; in fact, a small force of Volunteers holding the Mitcham Road, at Streatham, fought with such splendid bravery, that they succeeded alone and unaided in completely wiping out a battalion of French infantry, and capturing two field guns and a quantity of ammunition. For this success, however, they, alas! paid dearly, for a quarter of an hour later a large body of cavalry and infantry coming over from Woodlands descended upon them and totally annihilated them, with the result that Streatham fell into the hands of the French, and a few guns placed in the high road soon made short work of the earthworks near the hospital. Under the thick hail of bursting shells the brave band who manned the guns were at last compelled to abandon them, and the enemy were soon marching unchecked into Stockwell and Brixton, extending their right, with the majority of their artillery, across Herne Hill, Dulwich, and Honor Oak.

In the meantime a desperate battle was being fought around Kingston. The barricade on Kingston Hill held out for nearly three hours, but was at last captured by the invaders, and of those who had manned it not a man survived. Mitcham and Tooting had fallen in the first hour of the engagement, the barricade at Lynwood had been taken, and hundreds of the houses in Balham had been looted by the enemy in their advance into Clapham.

Nearly the whole morning it rained in torrents, and both invaders and defenders were wet to the skin, and covered with blood and mud. Everywhere British pluck showed itself in this desperate resistance on the part of these partially-trained defenders. At the smaller barricades in the suburban jerry-built streets, Britons held their own and checked the advance with remarkable coolness; yet, as the dark, stormy day wore on, the street defences were one after another broken down and destroyed.

Indeed, by three o'clock that afternoon the enemy ran riot through the whole district, from Lower Sydenham to Kingston. Around the larger houses on Sydenham Hill one of the fiercest fights occurred, but at length the defenders were driven down into Lordship Lane, and the houses on the hill were sacked, and some of them burned. While this was proceeding, a great force of French artillery came over from Streatham, and before dusk five great batteries had been established along the Parade in front of the Crystal Palace, and on Sydenham Hill and One Tree Hill; while other smaller batteries were brought into position at Forest Hill, Gipsy Hill, Tulse Hill, Streatham Hill, and Herne Hill; and further towards London about twenty French 12-pounders and a number of new quick-firing weapons of long range and a very destructive character were placed along the top of Camberwell Grove and Denmark Hill.

The defences of London had been broken. The track of the invaders was marked by ruined homes and heaps of corpses, and London's millions knew on this eventful night that the enemy were now actually at their doors. In Fleet Street, in the Strand, in Piccadilly, the news spread from mouth to mouth as darkness fell that the enemy were preparing to launch their deadly shells into the City. This increased the panic. The people were in a mad frenzy of excitement, and the scenes everywhere were terrible. Women wept and wailed, men uttered words of blank despair, and children screamed at an unknown terror.

The situation was terrible. From the Embankment away on the Surrey side could be seen a lurid glare in the sky. It was the reflection of a great fire in Vassall Road, Brixton, the whole street being burned by the enemy, together with the great block of houses lying between the Cowley and Brixton Roads.

London waited. Dark storm-clouds scudded across the moon. The chill wind swept up the river, and moaned mournfully in doors and chimneys.

At last, without warning, just as Big Ben had boomed forth one o'clock, the thunder of artillery shook the windows, and startled the excited crowds. Great shells crashed into the streets, remained for a second, and then burst with deafening report and appalling effect.

In Trafalgar Square, Fleet Street, and the Strand the deadly projectiles commenced to fall thickly, wrecking the shops, playing havoc with the public buildings, and sweeping hundreds of men and women into eternity. Nothing could withstand their awful force, and the people, rushing madly about like frightened sheep, felt that this was indeed their last hour.

In Ludgate Hill the scene was awful. Shots fell with monotonous regularity, bursting everywhere, and blowing buildings and men into atoms. The French shells were terribly devastating; the reek of mélinite poisoned the air. Shells striking St. Paul's Cathedral brought down the right-hand tower, and crashed into the dome; while others set on fire a long range of huge drapery warehouses behind it, the glare of the roaring flames causing the great black Cathedral to stand out in bold relief.

The bombardment had actually commenced! London, the proud Capital of the World, was threatened with destruction!

XXXV

London Bombarded

The Hand of the Destroyer had reached England's mighty metropolis. The lurid scene was appalling.

In the stormy sky the red glare from hundreds of burning buildings grew brighter, and in every quarter flames leaped up and black smoke curled slowly away in increasing volume.

The people were unaware of the events that had occurred in Surrey that day. Exhausted, emaciated, and ashen pale, the hungry people had endured every torture. Panic-stricken, they rushed hither and thither in thousands up and down the principal thoroughfares, and as they tore headlong away in this *sauve qui peut* to the northern suburbs, the weaker fell and were trodden under foot.

Men fought for their wives and families, dragging them away out of the range of the enemy's fire, which apparently did not extend beyond the line formed by the Hackney Road, City Road, Pentonville Road, Euston Road, and Westbourne Park. But in that terrible rush to escape many delicate ladies were crushed to death, and numbers of others, with their children, sank exhausted, and perished beneath the feet of the fleeing millions.

Never before had such alarm been spread through London; never before had such awful scenes of destruction been witnessed. The French Commander-in-chief, who was senior to his Russian colleague, had been killed, and his successor being unwilling to act in concert with the Muscovite staff, a quarrel ensued. It was this quarrel which caused the bombardment of London, totally against the instructions of their respective Governments. The bombardment was, in fact, wholly unnecessary, and was in a great measure due to some confused orders received by the French General from his Commander-in-chief. Into the midst of the surging, terrified crowds that congested the streets on each side of the Thames, shells filled with mélinite dropped, and, bursting, blew hundreds of despairing Londoners to atoms. Houses were shattered and fell, public buildings were demolished, factories were set alight, and the powerful exploding projectiles caused the Great City to reel and quake. Above the constant crash of bursting shells, the dull roar of the flames, and the crackling of burning timbers, terrific detonations now and then were heard, as buildings, filled with combustibles, were struck by shots, and, exploding, spread death and ruin over wide areas. The centre of commerce, of wealth, of intellectual and moral life was being ruthlessly wrecked, and its inhabitants massacred. Apparently it was not the intention of the enemy to invest the city at present, fearing perhaps that the force that had penetrated the defences was not sufficiently large to accomplish such a gigantic task; therefore they had commenced this terrible bombardment as a preliminary measure.

Through the streets of South London the people rushed along, all footsteps being bent towards the bridges; but on every one of them the crush was frightful—indeed, so great was it that in several instances the stone balustrades were broken, and many helpless, shrieking persons were forced over into the dark swirling waters below. The booming of the batteries was continuous, the bursting of the shells was deafening, and every moment was one of increasing horror. Men saw their homes swept away, and trembling women clung to their husbands, speechless with fear. In the City, in the Strand, in Westminster, and West End streets the ruin was even greater, and the destruction of property enormous.

Westward, both great stations at Victoria, with the adjoining furniture repositories and the Grosvenor Hotel, were burning fiercely; while the Wellington Barracks had been partially demolished, and the roof of St. Peter's Church blown away. Two shells falling in the quadrangle of Buckingham Palace had smashed every window and wrecked some of the ground-floor apartments, but nevertheless upon the flagstaff, amidst the dense smoke and showers of sparks flying upward, there still floated the Royal Standard. St. James's Palace, Marlborough House, Stafford House, and Clarence House, standing in exposed positions, were being all more or less damaged; several houses in Carlton House Terrace had been partially demolished, and a shell striking the Duke of York's Column soon after the commencement of the bombardment, caused it to fall, blocking Waterloo Place.

Time after time shells whistled above and fell with a crash and explosion, some in the centre of the road, tearing up the paving, and others striking the clubs in Pall Mall, blowing out many of those noble time-mellowed walls. The portico of the Athenæum had been torn away like pasteboard, the rear premises of the War Office had been pulverised, and the Carlton, Reform, and United Service Clubs suffered terrible damage. Two shells striking the Junior Carlton crashed through the roof, and exploding almost simultaneously, brought down an enormous heap of masonry, which fell across the roadway, making an effectual barricade; while at the same moment shells began to fall thickly in Grosvenor Place and Belgrave Square, igniting many houses, and killing some of those who remained in their homes petrified by fear.

Up Regent Street shells were sweeping with frightful effect. The Café Monico and the whole block of buildings surrounding it was burning, and the flames leaping high, presented a magnificent though appalling spectacle. The front of the London Pavilion had been partially blown away, and of the two uniform rows of shops forming the Quadrant many had been wrecked. From Air Street to Oxford Circus, and along Piccadilly to Knightsbridge, there fell a perfect hail of shell and bullets. Devonshire House had been wrecked, and the Burlington Arcade destroyed. The thin pointed spire of St. James's Church had fallen, every window in the Albany was shattered, several houses in Grosvenor Place had suffered considerably, and a shell that struck the southern side of St. George's Hospital had ignited it, and now at 2 A.M., in the midst of this awful scene of destruction and disaster, the helpless sick were being removed into the open streets, where bullets whistled about them and fragments of explosive shells whizzed past.

As the night wore on London trembled and fell. Once Mistress of the World, she was now, alas! sinking under the iron hand of the invader. Upon her there poured a rain of deadly missiles that caused appalling slaughter and desolation. The newly introduced long-range guns, and the terrific power of the explosives with which the French shells were charged, added to the horrors of the bombardment; for although the batteries were so far away as to be out of sight, yet the unfortunate people, overtaken by their doom, were torn limb from limb by the bursting bombs.

Over the roads lay men of London, poor and rich, weltering in their blood, their lower limbs shattered or blown completely away. With wide-open haggard eyes, in their death agony they gazed around at the burning buildings, at the falling débris, and upward at the brilliantly-illumined sky. With their last breath they gasped prayers for those they loved, and sank to the grave, hapless victims of Babylon's downfall.

Every moment the Great City was being devastated, every moment the catastrophe was more complete, more awful. In the poorer quarters of South London whole streets were swept away, and families overwhelmed by their own demolished homes. Along the principal thoroughfares shop fronts were shivered, and the goods displayed in the windows strewn about the roadway.

About half-past three a frightful disaster occurred at Battersea. Very few shells had dropped in that district, when suddenly one fell right in the very centre of a great petroleum store. The effect was frightful. With a noise that was heard for twenty miles around, the whole of the great store of oil exploded, blowing the stores themselves high into the air, and levelling all the buildings in the vicinity. In every direction burning oil was projected over the roofs of neighbouring houses, dozens of which at once caught fire, while down the streets there ran great streams of blazing oil, which spread the conflagration in every direction. Showers of sparks flew upwards, the flames roared and crackled, and soon fires were breaking out in all quarters.

Just as the clocks were striking a quarter to four, a great shell struck the Victoria Tower of the Houses of Parliament, bringing it down with a terrific crash. This disaster was quickly followed by a series of others. A shell fell through the roof of Westminster Abbey, setting the grand old historic building on fire; another tore away the columns from the front of the Royal Exchange; and a third carried away one of the square twin towers of St. Mary Woolnoth, at the corner of Lombard Street.

Along this latter thoroughfare banks were wrecked, and offices set on fire; while opposite, in the thick walls of the Bank of England, great breaches were being made. The Mansion House escaped any very serious injury, but the dome of the Stock Exchange was carried away; and in Queen Victoria Street, from end to end, enormous damage was caused to the rows of fine business premises; while further east the Monument, broken in half, came down with a noise like thunder, demolishing many houses on Fish Street Hill.

The great drapery warehouses in Wood Street, Bread Street, Friday Street, Foster Lane, and St. Paul's Churchyard suffered more or less. Ryland's, Morley's, and Cook's were all alight and burning fiercely; while others were wrecked and shattered, and their contents blown out into the streets. The quaint spire of St. Bride's had fallen, and its bells lay among the débris in the adjoining courts; both the half-wrecked offices of the *Daily Telegraph* and the *Daily Chronicle* were being consumed.

The great clock-tower of the Law Courts fell about four o'clock with a terrific crash, completely blocking the Strand at Temple Bar, and demolishing the much-abused Griffin Memorial; while at the same moment two large holes were torn in the roof of the Great Hall, the

WILLIAM LE QUEUX

small black turret above fell, and the whole of the glass in the building was shivered into fragments.

It was amazing how widespread was the ruin caused by each of the explosive missiles. Considering the number of guns employed by the French in this cruel and wanton destruction of property, the desolation they were causing was enormous. This was owing to the rapid extension of their batteries over the high ground from One Tree Hill through Peckham to Greenwich, and more especially to the wide ranges of their guns and the terrific power of their shells. In addition to the ordinary projectiles filled with mélinite, charges of that extremely powerful substance lignine dynamite were hurled into the city, and, exploded by a detonator, swept away whole streets, and laid many great public buildings in ruins; while steel shells, filled with some arrangement of liquid oxygen and blasting gelatine, produced frightful effects, for nothing could withstand them.

One of these, discharged from the battery on Denmark Hill, fell in the quadrangle behind Burlington House, and levelled the Royal Academy and the surrounding buildings. Again a terrific explosion sounded, and as the smoke cleared it was seen that a gelatine shell had fallen among the many turrets of the Natural History Museum, and the front of the building fell out with a deafening crash, completely blocking the Cromwell Road.

London lay at the mercy of the invaders. So swiftly had the enemy cut their way through the defences and opened their hail of destroying missiles, that the excited, starving populace were unaware of what had occurred until dynamite began to rain upon them. Newspapers had ceased to appear; and although telegraphic communication was kept up with the defenders on the Surrey Hills by the War Office, yet no details of the events occurring there had been made public for fear of spies. Londoners had remained in ignorance, and, alas! had awaited their doom. Through the long sultry night the situation was one of indescribable panic and disaster.

The sky had grown a brighter red, and the streets within the range of the enemy's guns, now deserted, were in most cases blocked by burning ruins and fallen telegraph wires; while about the roadways lay the shattered corpses of men, women, and children, upon whom the shells had wrought their frightful work.

The bodies, mutilated, torn limb from limb, were sickening to gaze upon.

XXXVI

Babylon Burning

Dynamite had shattered Charing Cross Station and the Hotel, for its smoke-begrimed façade had been torn out, and the station yard was filled with a huge pile of smouldering débris. On either side of the Strand from Villiers Street to Temple Bar scarcely a window had been left intact, and the roadway itself was quite impassable, for dozens of buildings had been overthrown by shells, and what in many cases had been handsome shops were now heaps of bricks, slates, furniture, and twisted girders. The rain of fire continued. Dense black smoke rising in a huge column from St. Martin's Church showed plainly what was the fate of that noble edifice, while fire had now broken out at the Tivoli Music Hall, and the clubs on Adelphi Terrace were also falling a prey to the flames.

The burning of Babylon was a sight of awful, appalling grandeur.

The few people remaining in the vicinity of the Strand who escaped the flying missiles and falling buildings, sought what shelter they could, and stood petrified by terror, knowing that every moment might be their last, not daring to fly into the streets leading to Holborn, where they could see the enemy's shells were still falling with unabated regularity and frightful result, their courses marked by crashing buildings and blazing ruins.

Looking from Charing Cross, the Strand seemed one huge glaring furnace. Flames belched from windows on either side, and, bursting through roofs, great tongues of fire shot upwards; blazing timbers fell into the street; and as the buildings became gutted, and the fury of the devouring element was spent, shattered walls tottered and fell into the roadway. The terrific heat, the roar of the flames, the blinding smoke, the stifling fumes of dynamite, the pungent, poisonous odour of mélinite, the clouds of dust, the splinters of stone and steel, and the constant bursting of shells, combined to render the scene the most awful ever witnessed in a single thoroughfare during the history of the world.

From Kensington to Bow, from Camberwell to Somers Town, from Clapham to Deptford, the vast area of congested houses and tortuous streets was being swept continually. South of the Thames the loss of life was enormous, for thousands were unable to get beyond the zone of fire, and many in Brixton, Clapham, Camberwell, and Kennington were either maimed by flying fragments of shell, buried in the débris of their homes, or burned to death. The disasters wrought by the Frenchmen's improved long-range weapons were frightful.

London, the all-powerful metropolis, which had egotistically considered herself the impregnable Citadel of the World, fell to pieces and was consumed. She was frozen by terror, and lifeless. Her ancient monuments were swept away, her wealth melted in her coffers, her priceless objects of art were torn up and broken, and her streets ran with the blood of her starving toilers.

Day dawned grey, with stormlight gloom. Rain-clouds scudded swiftly across the leaden sky. Along the road in front of the Crystal Palace, where the French batteries were established, the deafening discharges that had continued incessantly during the night, and had smashed nearly all the glass in the sides and roof of the Palace, suddenly ceased.

The officers were holding a consultation over despatches received from the batteries at Tulse Hill, Streatham, Red Post Hill, One Tree Hill, and Greenwich, all of which stated that ammunition had run short, and they were therefore unable to continue the bombardment.

Neither of the ammunition trains of the two columns of the enemy had arrived, for, although the bombarding batteries were unaware of it, both had been captured and blown up by British Volunteers.

It was owing to this that the hostile guns were at last compelled to cease their thunder, and to this fact also was due the fortunes of the defenders in the events immediately following.

Our Volunteers occupying the line of defence north of London, through Epping and Brentwood to Tilbury, had for the past three weeks been in daily expectation of an attempt on the part of the invaders to land in Essex, and were amazed at witnessing this sudden bombardment. From their positions on the northern heights they could distinctly see how disastrous was the enemy's fire, and although they had been informed by telegraph of the reverses we had sustained at Guildford and Leatherhead, yet they had no idea that the actual attack on the metropolis would be made so swiftly. However, they lost not a moment. It was evident that the enemy had no intention of effecting a landing in Essex; therefore, with commendable promptitude, they decided to move across the Thames immediately, to reinforce their comrades in Surrey. Leaving the 2nd and 4th West Riding Artillery, under Col. Hoffmann and Col. N. Creswick, V.D., at Tilbury, and the Lincolnshire, Essex, and Worcestershire Volunteer Artillery, under Col. G. M. Hutton, V.D., Col. S. L. Howard, V.D., and Col. W. Ottley, the greater part of the Norfolk, Staffordshire, Tay, Aberdeen, Manchester, and Northern Counties Field Brigades moved south with all possible speed. From Brentwood, the 1st, 2nd, 3rd, and 4th Volunteer Battalions of the Norfolk Regiment, under Col. A. C. Dawson, Col. E. H. H. Combe, Col. H. E. Hyde, V.D., and Col. C. W. J. Unthank, V.D.; the 1st and 2nd North Staffordshire, under Col. W. H. Dutton, V.D., and Col. F. D. Mort, V.D.; and the 1st, 2nd, and 3rd South Staffordshire, under Col. J. B. Cochrane, V.D., Col. T. T. Fisher, V.D., and Col. E. Nayler, V.D.; the 2nd, 4th, 5th, and 6th Royal Highlanders, under Col. W. A. Gordon, V.D., Col. Sir R. D. Moncreiffe, Col. Sir R. Menzies, V.D., and Col. Erskine; the 7th Argyll and Sutherland Highlanders, under Col. J. Porteous, V.D.; the 3rd, 4th, and 5th Gordon Highlanders, under Col. A. D. Fordyce, Col. G. Jackson, V.D., and Col. J. Johnston—were, as early as 2 A.M., on their way to London.

At this critical hour the Engineer and Railway Volunteer Staff Corps rendered invaluable services. Under the direction of Col. William Birt, trains held in readiness by the Great Eastern Railway brought the brigades rapidly to Liverpool Street, whence they marched by a circuitous route beyond the zone of fire by way of Marylebone, Paddington, Kensington Gardens, Walham Green, and across Wandsworth Bridge, thence to Upper Tooting, where they fell in with a large force of our Regular infantry and cavalry, who were on their way to outflank the enemy.

Attacking a detachment of the French at Tooting, they captured several guns, destroyed the enemy's field telegraph, and proceeded at once to Streatham, where the most desperate resistance was offered. A fierce fight occurred across Streatham Common, and over to Lower Norwood and Gipsy Hill, in which both sides lost very heavily. Nevertheless our Volunteers from Essex, although they had been on the march the greater part of the night, fought bravely, and inflicted terrible punishment upon their foe. The 3rd and 4th Volunteer Battalions of the Gordon Highlanders and the 1st Norfolk, attacking a French position near the mouth of the railway tunnel, displayed conspicuous bravery, and succeeded in completely annihilating their opponents; while in an opposite direction, towards Tooting, several troops of French cavalry were cut up and taken prisoners by two battalions of Royal Highlanders.

The batteries on Streatham Hill having been assaulted and taken, the force of defenders pushed quickly onward to Upper Norwood, where our cavalry, sweeping along Westow Hill and Church Street, fell upon the battery in front of the Crystal Palace. The enemy, owing to the interruption of their field telegraph, were unaware of their presence, and were completely surprised. Nevertheless French infantrymen rushed into the Crystal Palace Hotel, the White Swan, Stanton Harcourt, the Knoll, Rocklands, and other houses at both ends of the Parade, and from the windows poured forth withering volleys from their Lebels. Our cavalry, riding down the broad Parade, used their sabres upon the artillerymen, and the whole of the French troops were quickly in a confused mass, unable to act with effect, and suffering appallingly from the steady fire of our Volunteers, who very soon cleared the enemy from the White Swan, and, having been drawn up outside, poured forth a galling rifle fire right along the enemy's position. Suddenly there was loud shouting, and the British "Cease fire" sounded. The French, though fighting hard, were falling back gradually down the hill towards Sydenham Station, when suddenly shots were heard, and turbaned cavalry came riding into them at a terrific pace from the rear.

The British officers recognised the new-comers as a squadron of Bengal Lancers! At last India had sent us help, and our men sent up a loud cheer. A large force of cavalry and infantry, together with two regiments of Goorkas, had, it appeared, been landed at Sheerness. They had contemplated landing in Hampshire, but, more unfortunate than some of their compatriots who had effected a landing near Southampton, they were driven through the Straits of Dover by the enemy's cruisers. Marching north in company with a force from Chatham, they had earlier that morning attacked and routed the enemy's right flank at Blackheath, and, after capturing the battery of the foe at Greenwich, greater part of the escort of which had been sent over to Lewisham an hour before, they slaughtered a battalion of Zouaves, and had then extended across to Denmark Hill, where a sanguinary struggle occurred.

The French on Dog Kennel, Red Post, Herne, and Tulse Hills turned their deadly machine guns upon them, and for a long time all the positions held out. At length, however, by reason of a splendid charge made by the Bengal Lancers, the battery at Red Post Hill was taken and the enemy slaughtered. During the next half-hour a fierce hand-to-hand struggle took place up Dog Kennel Hill from St. Saviour's Infirmary, and presently, when the defenders gained the spur of the hill, they fought the enemy gallantly in Grove Lane, Private Road, Bromar Road, Camberwell Grove, and adjoining roads. Time after time the Indian cavalry charged, and the Goorkas, with their keen knives, hacked their way into those of the enemy who rallied. For nearly an hour the struggle continued desperately, showers of bullets from magazine rifles sweeping along the usually quiet suburban thoroughfares, until the roads were heaped with dead and dying, and the houses on either side bore evidence of the bloody fray. Then at last the guns placed along the hills all fell into our hands, and the French were almost completely swept out of existence.

Many were the terrible scenes witnessed in the gardens of the quaint last-century houses on Denmark Hill. Around those old-world residences, standing along the road leading down to Half Moon Lane, time-mellowed relics of an age bygone, Indians fought with Zouaves, and British Volunteers struggled fiercely hand to hand with French infantrymen. The quiet old-fashioned quarter, that was an aristocratic retreat when Camberwell was but a sylvan village with an old toll gate, when cows chewed the cud upon Walworth Common, and when the Walworth Road had not a house in the whole of it, was now the scene of a frightful massacre. The deafening explosions of cordite from magazine rifles, the exultant shouts of the victors and the hoarse shrieks of the dying, awakened the echoes in those quaint old gardens, with their Dutch-cut zigzag walks, enclosed by ancient red brick walls, moss-grown, lichen covered, and half hidden by ivy, honeysuckle, and creepers. Those spacious grounds, where men were now being mercilessly slaughtered, had been the scene of many a brilliant *fête champêtre*, where splendid satin-coated *beaux*, all smiles and *ailes de pigeon*, whispered scandal behind the fans of dainty dames in high-dressed wigs and patches, or, clad as Watteau shepherds, had danced the *al fresco* minuet with similarly attired shepherdesses, and later on played *piquet* and drank champagne till dawn.

In the good old Georgian days, when Johnson walked daily under the trees in Gough Square, when Macklin was playing the "Man of the World," and when traitors' heads blackened on Temple Bar, this colony was one of the most rural, exclusive, and gay in the vicinity of London. Alas, how it has decayed! Cheap "desirable residences" have sprung up around it, the hand of the jerry-building Vandal has touched it, the sound of traffic roars about it; yet still there is a charm in those quaint old gardens of a forgotten era. From under the dark yew hedges the jonquils still peep out early—the flowers themselves are those old-fashioned sweet ones beloved of our grandmothers—and the tea roses still blossom on the crumbling walls and fill the air with their fragrance. But in this terrible struggle the walls were used as defences, the bushes were torn down and trampled under foot, and the flowers hung broken on their stalks, bespattered with men's blood!

Proceeding south again, the defenders successfully attacked the strong batteries on One Tree Hill at Honor Oak, and on Sydenham Hill and Forest Hill, and then extending across to the Crystal Palace, had joined hands with our Volunteers from Essex, where they were now wreaking vengeance for the ruthless destruction caused in London.

The bloodshed along the Crystal Palace Parade was fearful. The French infantry and artillery, overwhelmed by the onward rush of the defenders, and now under the British crossfire, fell in hundreds. Dark-faced Bengal Lancers and Goorkas, with British Hussars and Volunteers, descended upon them with appalling swiftness; and so complete was the slaughter, that of the whole force that had effected that terribly effectual bombardment from Sydenham, not more than a dozen survived.

By noon many of the shops on Westow Hill and private residences on College Hill and Sydenham Hill had been wantonly ignited by the enemy; but when the firing ceased some hours later, the roads were heaped with the corpses of those whose mission it had been to destroy London.

Of all those batteries which had caused such frightful desolation and loss of life during the night, not one now remained. The two French columns had been swiftly wiped out of existence; and although our forces had suffered very considerably, they nevertheless were able to go south to Croydon later that afternoon, in order to take part in resisting the vigorous and desperate attack which they knew would sooner or later be made by the whole French army massed beyond the Surrey Hills. The sun was on the horizon, and the shadows were already deepening.

Assistance had arrived tardily, for the damage to property in London during the night had been enormous; nevertheless at this the eleventh hour we had inflicted upon the French a crushing defeat, and now England waited, trembling and breathless, wondering what would be the final outcome of this fierce, bloody struggle for our national existence.

XXXVII

Fighting on the Surrey Hills

Our valiant defenders were striking swift, decisive blows for England's honour. The French, demoralised by their severe defeat in the south of London, and suffering considerable loss in every other direction, fought desperately during the two days following the disastrous bombardment.

In darkness and sunlight fierce contests took place along the Surrey Hills, where our Volunteers, under Major-Gen. Lord Methuen, were still entrenched. Every copse bristled with rifles; red coats gleamed among the foliage, and winding highways were, alas! strewn with corpses. Guildford had again been reoccupied by our Regulars, who were reorganising; and Leatherhead, holding out for another day, was retaken, after a terribly hard-fought battle, by the Highland, South of Scotland, and Glasgow Brigades, with the 1st Ayrshire and Galloway Artillery, under Col. J. G. Sturrock, V.D.; 1st Lanarkshire, under Col. R. J. Bennett, V.D.; 1st Aberdeenshire, under Col. J. Ogston, V.D.; and 1st North Riding Yorkshire Volunteer Artillery, under Major C. L. Bell. In such a splendid and gallant manner had our comparatively small force manoeuvred, that on the second night following the bombardment the whole of the invaders who had penetrated beyond our line of defence towards the metropolis had been completely wiped out, in addition to which the breach in our line had been filled up by strong reinforcements, and the enemy driven from the high ground between Box Hill and Guildford.

The invaders, finding how vigorously we repelled any attack, made terrific onslaughts on our position at various points they believed were vulnerable, but everywhere they were hurled back with appalling slaughter. Volunteers from Australia and the Cape, in addition to the other contingent of 10,000 Indian native troops, had been landed near Southampton, and had advanced to assist in this terrific struggle, upon the result of which the future of our Empire depended. Among these Colonials were 500 Victorian Rangers, 900 Victoria Mounted Rifles, and seven companies of Queensland Mounted Infantry, with two ambulance corps.

The Indians landed in splendid form, having brought their full war equipment with them without any contribution whatever from the Home Government, as it will be remembered they did when they landed at Malta during Lord Beaconsfield's administration. Having received intelligence of the movements of the two columns of the enemy that had gone to London after taking Leatherhead and Guildford, they pushed on to Petworth. By the time they arrived there, however, both towns had been recaptured by the British, who were then being severely harassed by the enemy massed along the south side of our defensive line. Although numerically inferior to the enemy occupying that part of the country, the Indians were already well accustomed to actual warfare, the majority having been engaged in operations against the hill tribes; therefore the commander decided to push on at once, and endeavour to outflank the large French force who with some Russian infantry had again attacked Guildford, and the manner in which this was accomplished was a single illustration of the valuable assistance the Indians rendered us in these days of bloodshed and despair.

One of the native officers of a Sikh regiment, the Subadar Banerji Singh, having served with Sir Peter Lumsden's expeditionary force some years before, had frequently come into contact with the Russians, and could speak Russian better than some of the soldiers of the Tsar's Asiatic corps. The commander of the Indian force, determined that his men should strike their blow and sustain their reputation, advanced with great caution from Petworth, and late in the afternoon of the second evening after the bombardment of London, two Sikhs scouting in front of the advance guard sighted a Russian bivouac on the road on the other side of the Wye Canal beyond Loxwood Bridge, which latter had been demolished. The Indians were thereupon halted on the road which runs through the wood near Plaistow, and the officers held council. Their information was unfortunately very meagre and their knowledge of the country necessarily vague; but the Subadar Banerji Singh, who was of unusually fair complexion, volunteered to don a Russian uniform, which had been taken with other property from a dead officer found upon the road, and endeavour in that disguise to penetrate the enemy's lines.

Towards dusk he set out on his perilous journey, and, on arriving at the wrecked bridge, shouted over to two Russian sentries, explaining that he had been wounded and left behind after the fight at Haslemere, and requesting their assistance to enable him to cross. Believing him to be one of their infantry officers, they told him there were no means of crossing unless he could swim, as their engineers had sounded the canal before blowing up the bridge, and had found it twenty feet deep.

Banerji Singh questioned them artfully as to the position of their column, which they said intended, in co-operation with a great force of French cavalry and infantry, to again attack Guildford at dawn; and further, they told him in confidence that the rearguard to which they belonged only numbered about two thousand men, who had halted for the night with the transport waggons on the Guildford road, about two miles north of Alfold.

Then, after further confidences, they suggested that he should continue along the canal bank for about a mile and a half, where there was a bridge still intact, and near which he would find the rearguard.

Thanking them, he withdrew into the falling gloom, and a quarter of an hour later entered the presence of his commanding officer, who, of course, was delighted with the information thus elicited. The Subadar had carefully noted all the features of the canal bank and broken bridge, and the valuable knowledge he had obtained was at once put to account, and the General at once formed his force into two divisions. Then, after issuing instructions for the following day, he gave orders for a bivouac for the night.

The pioneers, however, were far from idle. During the night they worked with unflagging energy, quietly preparing a position for the guns to cover the contemplated passage at Loxwood Bridge, and before day broke the guns were mounted, and the Engineers were ready for action. As soon as there was sufficient light the laying of the pontoon commenced, but was at once noticed by the Russians, who opened fire, and very soon it was evident that information had been conveyed to the enemy's rearguard, and that they were returning to contest the passage.

In the meantime one division of the Indians, setting out before daybreak, had been cautiously working round to the main road crossing the canal north of Alfold, and succeeded in getting over soon after the majority of the Russian rearguard had left for the assistance of the detachment at Loxwood Bridge, and, after a sharp, decisive fight, succeeded in capturing the whole of the transport waggons. The Engineers, with the Indians, had in the meantime succeeded in completing their pontoon under cover of the guns, and the second division of the Indians, dark-faced, daring fellows, rushed across to the opposite bank, and descended upon the enemy with frightful effect.

In the hot engagement that followed, the Russians, now attacked in both front and rear, were totally annihilated, and thus the whole of the reserve ammunition of the force assaulting Guildford fell into our hands.

This victory on the enemy's left flank caused the tide of events to turn in our favour, for the huge Russian and French columns that intended to again carry the hills from Dorking to Guildford were hampered by want of ammunition, and so vigorously did our Volunteers along the hills defend the repeated attacks, that the invaders were again driven back. Then, as they drew south to recover themselves, they were attacked on their left by a large body of our Regulars, and in the rear by the Indians and Australians. Over the country stretching across from Cranley through Ewhurst, Ockley, Capel, and Newdigate to Horley, the fighting spread, as each side struggled desperately for the mastery.

The fate of England, nay, of our vast British Empire, was in the hands of those of her stalwart sons of many races who were now wielding valiantly the rifle and the sword. Through that blazing September day, while the people of London wailed among the ruins of their homes, and, breathlessly anxious, awaited news of their victory or their doom, the whole of East Kent, the southern portion of Surrey and northern Sussex, became one huge battlefield. Of the vast bodies of troops massed over hill and dale every regiment became engaged.

The butchery was awful.

XXXVIII

Naval Battle off Dungeness

On sea England was now showing the world how she still could fight. Following the desperate struggle off Sardinia, in which Italy had rendered us such valuable help, our Mediterranean Squadron attacked the French Fleet off Cape Tresforcas, on the coast of Morocco, and after a terrific battle, extending over two days, defeated them with heavy loss, several of the enemy's vessels being torpedoed and sunk, two of them rammed, and one so badly damaged that her captain ran her ashore on Alboran Island.

After this hard-earned victory, our Squadron passed out of the Mediterranean, and, returning home, had joined hands with the battered remnant of our Channel Fleet, now reinforced by several vessels recalled from foreign stations. Therefore, while the enemy marched upon London, we had collected our naval strength on the south coast, and at length made a final descent upon the enemy in British waters. The British vessels that passed Beachy Head coming up Channel on the night of the bombardment of London included the *Empress of India, Inflexible, Nile, Trafalgar, Magnificent, Hood, Warspite, Dreadnought, Camperdown, Blenheim, Barham, Benbow, Monarch, Anson, Immortalité,* and *Royal Sovereign*, with four of the new cruisers built under the Spencer programme, viz. the *Terrible, Powerful, Doris,* and *Isis*, and a number of smaller vessels, torpedo boats, and "destroyers."

At the same hour that our vessels were passing Beachy Head, the Coastguard at Sandwich Battery were suddenly alarmed by electric signals being flashed from a number of warships that were slowly passing the Gull Stream revolving light towards the Downs. The sensation these lights caused among the Coastguard and Artillery was immediately dispelled when it was discovered that the warships were not hostile, but friendly; that the Kaiser had sent a German Squadron, in two divisions, to assist us, and that these vessels were on their way to unite with our own Fleet. The first division, it was ascertained, consisted of the *Baden*, flying the flag of Vice-Admiral Koester; the *Sachen*, commanded by Prince Henry of Prussia; the *Würtemberg*, and the *Bayern*—all of 7400 tons, and each carrying 18 guns and nearly

400 men; while the despatch boat *Pfeil*, the new dynamite cruiser *Trier*, and a number of torpedo boats, accompanied them. The second division, under Rear-Admiral von Diederichs on board the *König Wilhelm*, consisted of the *Brandenburg*, *Kürfurst Friedrich Wilhelm*, and *Woerth*, each of 10,300 tons, and carrying 32 guns; the *Deutschland* and the *Friedrich der Grosse*, with the despatch vessel *Wacht*, and several torpedo gunboats and other craft.

Before dawn, the British and German Fleets united near South Sand Head light, off the South Foreland, and it was decided to commence the attack without delay. Turning west again, the British ships, accompanied by those of the Emperor William, proceeded slowly down Channel in search of the enemy, which they were informed by signal had been sighted by the Coastguard at East Wear, near Folkestone, earlier in the night. Just as day broke, however, when the defenders were opposite Dymchurch, about eight miles from land, the enemy were discovered in force. Apparently the French and Russian Fleets had combined, and were preparing for a final descent upon Dover, or an assault upon the Thames defences; and it could be seen that, with both forces so strong, the fight would inevitably be one to the death.

Little time was occupied in preliminaries. Soon our ships were within range in fighting formation in single column in line abreast, while the French, under Admiral le Bourgeois, advanced in single column in line ahead. The French flagship, leading, was within 2000 yards of the British line, and had not disclosed the nature of her attack. The enemy's Admiral had signalled to the ships astern of him to follow his motions together, as nearly as possible to concentrate their guns at point blank, right ahead, and to pour their shot on the instant of passing our ships. He had but three minutes to decide upon the attack, and as he apparently elected to pierce the centre of our line, the British had no time to counteract him. The French Admiral therefore continued his course, and as he passed between the *Camperdown* and *Blenheim*, he discharged his guns, receiving the British broadsides and bow fire at the same time. In a few minutes, however, it was seen that the French attack had been frustrated, and as dawn spread the fighting increased, and the lines became broken. The ponderous guns of the battleships thundered, and ere long the whole of the great naval force was engaged in this final struggle for England's freedom. The three powerful French battleships, *Jauréguiberry*, *Jemappes*, and *Dévastation*, and the submarine torpedo boat *Gustave Zédé*, fiercely attacked the *Brandenburg* and the *König Wilhelm*;

while the *Camperdown*, *Anson*, *Dreadnought*, and *Warspite* fought desperately with half a dozen of the enemy's battleships, all of which suffered considerably. Our torpedo boats, darting swiftly hither and thither, performed much effective service, and many smart manoeuvres were carried out by astute officers in command of those wasps of the sea. In one instance a torpedo boat, which had designs upon a Russian ironclad, obtained cover by sending in front of her a gunboat which emitted an immense quantity of dense smoke. This of course obscured from view the torpedo boat under the gunboat's stern, and those on board the Tsar's battleship pounded away at the gunboat, unconscious of the presence of the dangerous little craft. Just as the gunboat got level with the battleship, however, the torpedo boat emerged from the cloud of smoke, and, darting along, ejected its Whitehead with such precision that five minutes later the Russian leviathan sank beneath the dark green waters. Almost at the same moment, the new German dynamite cruiser destroyed a French cruiser, and a fierce and sanguinary encounter took place between the *Immortalité* and the *Tréhouart*. The former's pair of 22-tonners, in combination with her ten 6-inch guns, wrought awful havoc on board the French vessel; nevertheless, from the turret of her opponent there came a deadly fire which spread death and destruction through the ship. Suddenly the Frenchman swung round, and with her quick-firing guns shedding a deadly storm of projectiles, came full upon the British vessel. The impact and the angle at which she was struck was not, however, sufficient to ram her, consequently the two vessels became entangled, and amid the rain of bullets the Frenchmen made a desperate attempt to board our ship. A few who managed to spring upon the *Immortalité's* deck were cut down instantly, but a couple of hundred fully armed men were preparing to make a rush to overpower our bluejackets. On board the British cruiser, however, the enemy's intentions had been divined, and certain precautions taken. The *Fusiliers Marins*, armed with Lebels and cutlasses, suddenly made a desperate, headlong rush upon the British cruiser's deck, but just as fifty of them gained their goal, a great hose attached to one of the boilers was brought into play, and scalding water poured upon the enemy. This, in addition to some hand charges at that moment thrown, proved successful in repelling the attack; but just as the survivors retreated in disorder there was a dull explosion, and then it was evident, from the confusion on board the French ship, that she had been torpedoed by a German boat, and was sinking.

Humanely, our vessel, the *Immortalité* rescued the whole of her opponent's men ere she sank; but it was found that in the engagement her captain and half her crew had been killed. On every hand the fight continued with unabated fierceness; every gun was worked to its utmost capacity, and amid the smoke and din every vessel was swept from stem to stern. As morning wore on, the enemy met with one or two successes. Our two new cruisers *Terrible* and *Powerful* had been sunk by French torpedoes; the *Hood* had been rammed by the *Amiral Baudin*, and gone to the bottom with nearly every soul on board; while the German despatch boat *Wacht* had been captured, and seven of our torpedo boats had been destroyed. During the progress of the fight, the vessels came gradually nearer Dungeness, and at eleven o'clock they were still firing at each other, with appalling results on either side. At such close quarters did this great battle occur, that the loss of life was awful, and throughout the ships the destruction was widespread and frightful. About noon the enemy experienced two reverses. The French battleship *Formidable* blew up with a terrific report, filling the air with débris, her magazine having exploded; while just at that moment the *Courbet*, whose 48-tonners had caused serious damage to the *Warspite*, was suddenly rammed and sunk by the *Empress of India*.

This, the decisive battle, was the most vigorously contested naval fight during the whole of the hostilities. The scene was terrible. The steel leviathans of the sea were being rent asunder and pulverised by the terribly destructive modern arms, and amid the roar and crashing of the guns, shells were bursting everywhere, carrying away funnels, fighting tops, and superstructures, and wrecking the crowded spaces between the decks. Turrets and barbettes were torn away, guns dismounted by the enormous shells from heavy guns; steel armour was torn up and thrown aside like paper, and many shots entering broadsides, passed clean through and out at the other side. Whitehead torpedoes, carrying heavy charges of gun-cotton, exploded now and then under the enemy's ships; while both British and French torpedo boat "destroyers," running at the speed of an ordinary train, were sinking or capturing where they could.

Through the dull, gloomy afternoon the battle continued. Time after time our ships met with serious reverses, for the *Anson* was sunk by the Russian flagship *Alexander II*, assisted by two French cruisers, and this catastrophe was followed almost immediately by the torpedoing of the new British cruiser *Doris*, and the capture of the new German dynamite cruiser *Trier*.

By this time, however, the vessels had approached within three miles of Dungeness, and the *Camperdown*, *Empress of India*, *Royal Sovereign*, *Inflexible*, and *Warspite*, lying near one another, fought nine of the enemy's vessels, inflicting upon them terrible punishment. Shots from the 67-tonners of the *Empress of India*, *Royal Sovereign*, and *Camperdown*, combined with those from the 22-tonners of the *Warspite*, swept the enemy's vessels with devastating effect, and during the three-quarters of an hour that the fight between these vessels lasted, the scene of destruction was appalling. Suddenly, with a brilliant flash and deafening detonation, the Russian flagship *Alexander II*, one of the vessels now engaging the five British ships, blew up and sank, and ere the enemy could recover from the surprise this disaster caused them, the *Camperdown* rammed the *Amiral Baudin*, while the *Warspite* sank the French cruiser *Cécille*, the submarine boat *Gustave Zédé*, and afterwards captured the torpedo gunboat *Bombe*.

This rapid series of terrible disasters apparently demoralised the enemy. They fought recklessly, and amid the din and confusion two Russian vessels collided, and were so seriously damaged that both settled down, their crews being rescued by British torpedo boats. Immediately afterwards, however, a frightful explosion rent the air with a deafening sound that dwarfed into insignificance the roar of the heavy guns, and the French battleship *Jauréguiberry* was completely broken into fragments, scarcely any of her hull remaining. The enemy were amazed. A few moments later another explosion occurred, even louder than the first. For a second the French battleship *Dévastation*, which had been engaging the *Royal Sovereign*, was obscured by a brilliant flash, then, as fragments of steel and human limbs were precipitated on every side, it was seen that that vessel also had been completely blown out of the water!

The enemy stood appalled. The defenders themselves were at first dumfounded. A few moments later, however, it became known throughout the British ships that the battery at Dungeness, two miles and a half distant, were rendering assistance with the new pneumatic gun, the secret of which the Government had guarded so long and so well. Five years before, this frightfully deadly weapon had been tested, and proved so successful that the one gun made was broken up and the plans preserved with the utmost secrecy in a safe at the War Office. Now, however, several of the weapons had been constructed, and one of them had been placed in the battery at Dungeness. The British vessels drew off to watch the awful effect of the fire from these marvellous and terribly destructive engines of modern warfare. The enemy would not surrender, so time after time the deafening explosions sounded, and time after time the hostile ships were shattered into fragments.

Each shot fired by this new pneumatic gun contained 900 lbs. of dynamite, which could strike effectively at four miles! The result of such a charge exploding on a ship was appalling; the force was terrific, and could not be withstood by the strongest vessel ever constructed. Indeed, the great armoured vessels were being pulverised as easily as glass balls struck by bullets, and every moment hundreds of poor fellows were being hurled into eternity. At last the enemy discovered the distant source of the fire, and prepared to escape beyond range; but in this they were unsuccessful, for, after a renewed and terrific fight, in which three French ironclads were sunk and two of our cruisers were torpedoed, our force and our allies the Germans succeeded in capturing the remainder of the hostile ships and torpedo boats.

The struggle had been frightful, but the victory was magnificent.

That same night the British ships steamed along the Sussex coast and captured the whole of the French and Russian transports, the majority of which were British vessels that had been seized while lying in French and Russian ports at the time war was declared. The vessels were lying between Beachy Head and Selsey Bill, and by their capture the enemy's means of retreat were at once totally cut off.

Thus, at the eleventh hour, the British Navy had shown itself worthy of its reputation, and England regained the supremacy of the seas.

XXXIX

The Day of Reckoning

The Day of Reckoning dawned.

On land the battle was terrific; the struggle was the most fierce and bloody of any during the invasion. The British Regulars holding the high ground along from Crowborough to Ticehurst, and from Etchingham, through Brightling and Ashburnham, down to Battle, advanced in a huge fighting line upon the enemy's base around Eastbourne. The onslaught was vigorously repelled, and the battle across the Sussex Downs quickly became a most wild and sanguinary one; but as the day passed, although the defenders were numerically very weak, they nevertheless gradually effected terrible slaughter, capturing the whole of the enemy's stores, and taking nearly five thousand prisoners.

In Kent the French had advanced from East Grinstead through Edenbridge, extending along the hills south of Westerham, and in consequence of these rapid successes the depôt of stores and ammunition which had been maintained at Sevenoaks was being removed to Bromley by rail; but as the officer commanding the British troops at Eynsford could see that it would most probably be impossible to get them all away before Sevenoaks was attacked, orders were issued that at a certain hour the remainder should be destroyed. The force covering the removal only consisted of two battalions of the Duke of Cambridge's Own (Middlesex) Regiment and half a squadron of the 9th Lancers; but the hills north of Sevenoaks from Luddesdown through Stanstead, Otford, Shoreham, Halstead, Farnborough, and Keston were still held by our Volunteers. These infantry battalions included the 1st and 2nd Derbyshire Regiment (Sherwood Foresters), under Col. A. Buchanan, V.D., and Col. E. Hall, V.D.; the 1st Nottinghamshire, under Col. A. Cantrell-Hubbersty; the 4th Derbyshire, under Lord Newark; the 1st and 2nd Lincolnshire, under Col. J. G. Williams, V.D., and Col. R. G. Ellison; the 1st Leicestershire, under Col. S. Davis, V.D.; the 1st Northamptonshire, under Col. T. J. Walker, V.D.; the 1st and 2nd Shropshire Light Infantry, under Col. J. A. Anstice, V.D., and Col. R. T. Masefield; the 1st Herefordshire, under Col. T. H. Purser, V.D.; the 1st, 3rd, and 4th South Wales Borderers, under

Col. T. Wood, Col. J. A. Bradney, and Col. H. Burton, V.D.; the 1st and 2nd Warwickshire, under Col. W. S. Jervis and Col. L. V. Loyd; the 1st and 2nd Welsh Fusiliers, under Col. C. S. Mainwaring and Col. B. G. D. Cooke, V.D.; the 2nd Welsh Regiment, under Col. A. P. Vivian, V.D.; the 3rd Glamorganshire, under Col. J. C. Richardson, V.D.; and the 1st Worcestershire, under Col. W. H. Talbot, V.D.; while the artillery consisted of the 3rd Kent, under Col. Hozier; the 1st Monmouthshire, under Col. C. T. Wallis; the 1st Shropshire and Staffordshire, under Col. J. Strick, V.D.; and the 5th Lancashire, under Col. W. H. Hunt.

The events which occurred outside Sevenoaks are perhaps best described by Capt. A. E. Brown, of the 4th V.B. West Surrey Regiment, who was acting as one of the special correspondents of the *Standard*. He wrote—

"I was in command of a piquet consisting of fifty men of my regiment at Turvan's Farm, and about three hours before the time to destroy the remainder of the stores at Sevenoaks my sentries were suddenly driven in by the enemy, who were advancing from the direction of Froghall. As I had orders to hold the farm at any cost, we immediately prepared for action. Fortunately we had a fair supply of provisions and plenty of ammunition, for since War had broken out the place had been utilised as a kind of outlying fort, although at this time only my force occupied it. Our equipment included two machine guns, and it was mainly by the aid of these we were saved.

"The strength of the attacking force appeared to be about four battalions of French infantry and a battalion of Zouaves, with two squadrons of Cuirassiers. Their intention was, no doubt, to cut the railway line near Twitton, and thus prevent the removal of the Sevenoaks stores. As soon as the cavalry scouts came within range we gave them a few sharp volleys, and those who were able immediately retired in disorder. Soon afterwards, however, the farm was surrounded, but I had previously sent information to our reserves, and suggested that a sharp watch should be kept upon the line from Twitton to Sevenoaks, for of course I could do nothing with my small force. Dusk was now creeping on, and as the enemy remained quiet for a short time it seemed as though they intended to assault our position when it grew dark.

"Before night set in, however, my messenger, who had managed to elude the vigilance of the enemy, returned, with a letter from a brother officer stating that a great naval battle had been fought in the Channel;

and further, that the enemy's retreat had been cut off, and that the Kentish defenders had already retaken the invaders' base at Eastbourne. If we could, therefore, still hold the Surrey Hills, there was yet a chance of thoroughly defeating the French and Russians, even though one strong body was reported as having taken Guildford and Leatherhead, and was now marching upon London.

"As evening drew on we could hear heavy firing in the direction of Sevenoaks, but as we also heard a train running it became evident that we still held the station. Nevertheless, soon after dark there was a brilliant flash which for a second lit up the country around like day, and a terrific report followed. We knew the remainder of our stores and ammunition had been demolished in order that it should not fall into the enemy's hands!

"Shortly afterwards we were vigorously attacked, and our position quickly became almost untenable by the dozens of bullets projected in every direction where the flash of our rifles could be seen. Very soon some of the farm outbuildings fell into the hands of the Frenchmen, and they set them on fire, together with a number of haystacks, in order to burn us out. This move, however, proved pretty disastrous to them, for the leaping flames quickly rendered it light as day, and showed them up, while at the same time flashes from our muzzles were almost invisible to them. Thus we were enabled to bring our two machine guns into action, and break up every party of Frenchmen who showed themselves. Away over Sevenoaks there was a glare in the sky, for the enemy were looting and burning the town. Meanwhile, however, our men who had been defending the place had retreated to Dunton Green after blowing up the stores, and there they re-formed and were quickly moving off in the direction of Twitton. Fortunately they had heard the commencement of the attack on us, and the commander, halting his force, had sent out scouts towards Chevening, and it appeared they reached us just at the moment the enemy had fired the stacks. They worked splendidly, and, after going nearly all round the enemy's position, returned and reported to their Colonel, who at once resolved to relieve us.

"As may be imagined, we were in a most critical position by this time, especially as we were unaware that assistance was so near. We had been ordered to hold the farm, and we meant to do it as long as breath remained in our bodies. All my men worked magnificently, and displayed remarkable coolness, even at the moment when death stared us in the face. The reports of the scouts enabled their Colonel to make

WILLIAM LE QUEUX

his disposition very carefully, and it was not long before the enemy were almost completely surrounded. We afterwards learnt that our reserves at Stockholm Wood had sent out a battalion, which fortunately came in touch with the survivors of the Sevenoaks force just as they opened a desperate onslaught upon the enemy.

"With the fierce flames and blinding smoke from the burning stacks belching in our faces, we fought on with fire around us on every side. As the fire drew nearer to us the heat became intense, the showers of sparks galled us almost as much as the enemy's bullets, and some of us had our eyebrows and hair singed by the fierce flames. Indeed, it was as much as we could do to keep our ammunition from exploding; nevertheless we kept up our stream of lead, pouring volley after volley upon those who had attacked us. Nevertheless, with such a barrier of flame and obscuring smoke between us we could see but little in the darkness beyond, and we all knew that if we emerged from cover we should be picked off easily and not a man would survive. The odds were against us. More than twenty of my brave fellows had fired their last shot, and now lay with their dead upturned faces looking ghastly in the brilliant glare, while a number of others had sunk back wounded. The heat was frightful, the smoke stifling, and I had just given up all hope of relief, and had set my teeth, determined to die like an Englishman should, when we heard a terrific volley of musketry at close quarters, and immediately afterwards a dozen British bugles sounded the charge. The scene of carnage that followed was terrible. Our comrades gave one volley from their magazines rifles, and then charged with the bayonet, taking the enemy completely by surprise.

"The Frenchmen tried to rally, but in vain, and among those huge burning barns and blazing ricks they all fell or were captured. Dozens of them struggled valiantly till the last; but, refusing to surrender, they were slaughtered amid a most frightful scene of blood and fire. The events of that night were horrible, and the true extent of the losses on both sides was only revealed when the flames died down and the parting clouds above heralded another grey and toilsome day."

Late on the previous evening the advance guard of the enemy proceeding north towards Caterham came in touch with the defenders north of Godstone. The French cavalry had seized Red Hill Junction Station at sundown, and some of their scouts suddenly came upon a detached post of the 17th Middlesex Volunteers at Tyler's Green, close to Godstone. A very sharp skirmish ensued, but the Volunteers, although suffering severe losses, held their own, and the cavalry went off along the Oxted Road. This being reported to the British General, special orders were at once sent to Col. Trotter, the commander of this section of the outpost line.

From the reports of the inhabitants and of scouts sent out in plain clothes, it was believed that the French intended massing near Tandridge, and that they would therefore wait for supports before attempting to break through our outpost line, which still remained intact from the high ground east of Leatherhead to the hills north of Sevenoaks. During the night Oxted and Godstone were occupied by the enemy, and early in the morning their advance guard, consisting of four battalions of infantry, a squadron of cavalry, a battalion of Zouaves, and a section of field artillery, proceeded north in two columns, one along the Roman road leading past Rook's Nest, and the other past Flinthall Farm.

At the latter place the sentries of the 17th Middlesex fell back upon their piquets, and both columns of the enemy came into action simultaneously. The French infantry on the high road soon succeeded in driving back the Volunteer piquet upon the supports, under Lieut. Michaelis, stationed at the junction of the Roman road with that leading to Godstone Quarry. A strong barricade with two deep trenches in front had here been constructed, and as soon as the survivors of the piquet got under cover, two of the defenders' machine guns opened fire from behind the barricade, assisted at the same moment by a battery on Gravelly Hill.

The French artillery had gone on towards Flinthall Farm, but in passing the north edge of Rook's Nest Park their horses were shot by some Inniskilling Fusiliers lying in ambush, and by these two reverses, combined with the deadly fire from the two machine guns at the farm, the column was very quickly thrown into confusion. It was then decided to make a counter attack, and the available companies at this section of the outpost line, under Col. Brown and Col. Roche, succeeded, after nearly two hours' hard fighting, in retaking Godstone and Oxted, compelling the few survivors of the enemy's advance guard to fall back to Blindley Heath.

In the meantime our troops occupying the line from Halstead to Chatham and Maidstone went down into battle, attacking the French right wing at the same time as the Indians were attacking their left, while the Volunteers from the Surrey Hills engaged the main body. The day was blazing hot, the roads dusty, and there was scarce a breath of wind. So hot, indeed, was it, that many on both sides fell from hunger, thirst, and sheer starvation. Yet, although the force of the invaders was nearly twice the numerical strength of the defenders, the latter fought on with undaunted courage, striking their swift, decisive blows for England and their Queen.

The enemy, now driven into a triangle, fought with demoniacal strength, and that frenzied courage begotten of despair. On the hills around Sevenoaks and across to the valley at Otford, the slaughter of the French was fearful. Britons fighting for their homes and their country were determined that Britannia should still be Ruler of the World.

From Wimlet Hill the enemy were by noon totally cut up and routed by the 12th Middlesex (Civil Service), under Lord Bury; the 25th (Bank), under Capt. W. J. Coe, V.D.; the 13th (Queen's), under Col. J. W. Comerford; the 21st Middlesex, under Col. H. B. Deane, V.D.; and the 22nd, under Col. W. J. Alt, V.D. Over at Oxted, however, they rallied, and some brilliant charges by Cossacks, the slaughter of a portion of our advance guard, and the capture of one of our Volunteer batteries on Botley Hill, checked our advance.

The French, finding their right flank being so terribly cut up, had suddenly altered their tactics, and were now concentrating their forces upon the Volunteer position at Caterham in an endeavour to break through our defensive line.

But the hills about that position held by the North London, West London, South London, Surrey, and Cheshire Brigades were well defended, and the General had his finger upon the pulse of his command. Most of the positions had been excellently chosen. Strong batteries were established at Gravelly Hill by the 9th Lancashire Volunteer Artillery, under Col. F. Ainsworth, V.D.; at Harestone Farm by the 1st Cinque Ports, under Col. P. S. Court, V.D.; at White Hill by the 1st Northumberland and the 1st Norfolk, under Col. P. Watts and Col. T. Wilson, V.D.; at Botley Hill by the 6th Lancashire, under Col. H. J. Robinson, V.D.; at Tandridge Hill by the 3rd Lancashire, under Col. R. W. Thom, V.D.; at Chaldon by the 1st Newcastle, under Col. W. M. Angus, V.D., who had come south after the victory at the Tyneside; at Warlingham village by the 1st Cheshire, commanded by Col. H. T. Brown, V.D.; at Warlingham Court by the 2nd Durham, under Col. J. B. Eminson, V.D.; on the Sanderstead road, near King's Wood, by the 2nd Cinque Ports, under Col. W. Taylor, V.D.; and on the railway near Woldingham the 1st Sussex had stationed their armoured train with 40-pounder breech-loading Armstrongs, which they fired very effectively from the permanent way.

Through Limpsfield, Oxted, Godstone, Bletchingley, and Nutsfield, towards Reigate, Frenchmen and Britons fought almost hand to hand. The defenders suffered severely, owing to the repeated charges of the French Dragoons along the highway between Oxted and Godstone, nevertheless the batteries of the 6th Lancashire on Tandridge Hill, which commanded a wide area of country occupied by the enemy, wrought frightful execution in their ranks. In this they were assisted by the 17th Middlesex, under Col. W. J. Brown, V.D., who with four Maxims at one period of the fight surprised and practically annihilated a whole battalion of French infantry. But into this attack on Caterham the enemy put his whole strength, and from noon until four o'clock the fighting along the valley was a fierce combat to the death.

With every bit of cover bristling with magazine rifles, and every available artillery position shedding forth a storm of bullets and shell, the loss of life was awful. Invaders and defenders fell in hundreds, and with burning brow and dry parched throat expired in agony. The London Irish, under Col. J. Ward, V.D.; the Post Office Corps, under Col. J. Du Plat Taylor, V.D., and Col. S. R. Thompson, V.D.; the Inns of Court, under Col. C. H. Russell, V.D.; and the Cyclists, led by Major T. De B. Holmes, performed many gallant deeds, and served their country well. The long, dusty highways were quickly covered with the bodies of the unfortunate victims, who lay with blanched, bloodless faces and sightless eyes turned upward to the burning sun. On over them rode madly French cavalry and Cossacks, cutting their way into the British infantry, never to return.

Just, however, as they prepared for another terrific onslaught, the guns of the 1st Cheshire battery at Warlingham village thundered, and with smart section volleys added by detachments of the London Scottish, under Major W. Brodie, V.D., and the Artists, under Capt. W. L. Duffield and Lieut. Pott, the road was in a few minutes strewn with horses and men dead and dying.

Still onward there rushed along the valley great masses of French infantry, but the 1st, 2nd, and 3rd Volunteer Battalions of the Royal Fusiliers, under Col. G. C. Clark, V.D., Col. A. L. Keller, and Col. L. Whewell respectively; the 2nd V. B. Middlesex Regiment, under Col. G. Brodie Clark, V.D.; the 3rd Middlesex, under Col. R Hennell, D.S.O., late of the Indian Army; and the 1st, 2nd, 3rd, and 4th West

Surrey, under Col. J. Freeland, V.D., Col. G. Drewitt, V.D., Col. S. B. Bevington, V.D., and Col. F. W. Haddan, V.D., engaged them, and by dint of desperate effort, losing heavily all the time, they defeated them, drove them back, and slaughtered them in a manner that to a non-combatant was horrible and appalling. Time after time, the enemy, still being harassed by the British Regulars on their right, charged up the valley, in order to take the battery at Harestone Farm; but on each occasion few of those who dashed forward survived. The dusty roads, the grassy slopes, and the ploughed lands were covered with corpses, and blood draining into the springs and rivulets tinged their crystal waters.

As afternoon passed and the battle continued, it was by no means certain that success in this fierce final struggle would lie with us. Having regard to the enormous body of invaders now concentrated on the Surrey border, and striving by every device to force a passage through our lines, our forces, spread over such a wide area and outflanking them, were necessarily weak. It was therefore only by the excellent tactics displayed by our officers, and the magnificent courage of the men themselves, that we had been enabled to hold back these overwhelming masses, which had already desolated Sussex with fire and sword.

Our Regulars operating along the old Roman highway through Blindley Heath—where the invaders were making a desperate stand—and over to Lingfield, succeeded, after very hard fighting, in clearing the enemy off the railway embankment from Crowhurst along to South Park Farm, and following them up, annihilated them.

Gradually, just at sundown, a strong division of the enemy were outflanked at Godstone, and, refusing to lay down their arms, were simply swept out of existence, scarcely a single man escaping. Thus forced back from, perhaps, the most vulnerable point in our defences, the main body of the enemy were then driven away upon Redhill, still fighting fiercely. Over Redstone Hill, through Mead Vale, and across Reigate Park to the Heath, the enemy were shot down in hundreds by our Regulars; while our Volunteers, whose courage never deserted them, engaged the French in hand-to-hand encounters through the streets of Redhill and Reigate, as far as Underhill Park.

In Hartswood a company of the 4th East Surrey Rifles, under Major S. B. Wheaton, V.D., were lying in ambush, when suddenly among the trees they caught glimpses of red, baggy trousers, and scarlet, black-tasselled fezes, and a few seconds later they found that a large force of Zouaves were working through the wood. A few moments elapsed, and the combat commenced. The Algerians fought like demons, and with bullet and bayonet inflicted terrible punishment upon us; but as they emerged into the road preparatory to firing a volley into the thickets, they were surprised by a company of the 2nd Volunteer Battalion of the East Surrey Regiment, under Capt. Pott, who killed and wounded half their number, and took the remainder prisoners.

Gradually our Volunteer brigades occupying the long range of hills united with our Regulars still on the enemy's right from Reigate to Crawley, and closed down upon the foe, slowly narrowing the sphere of their operations, and by degrees forcing them back due westward. Russians and French, who had attacked Dorking, had by this time been defeated with heavy loss, and by dusk the main body had been thrown back to Newdigate, where in Reffold's Copse one or two very sanguinary encounters occurred. These, however, were not always in our favour, for the Civil Service Volunteers here sustained very heavy losses. On the railway embankment, and on the road running along the crest of the hill to Dorking, the French made a stand, and there wrought frightful execution among our men with their machine guns. Around Beare Green, Trout's Farm, and behind the "White Hart" at Holmwood, the enemy rapidly brought their guns into play, and occupied such strong strategic positions that as night drew on it became evident that they intended to remain there until the morrow.

The defenders had but little cover, and consequently felt the withering fire of the French very severely. The latter had entrenched themselves, and now in the darkness it was difficult for our men to discern their exact position. Indeed, the situation of our forces became very serious and unsafe as night proceeded; but at length, about ten o'clock, a strong force of British Regulars, including the Sikhs and a detachment of Australians, swept along the road from Dorking, and came suddenly upon the French patrols. These were slaughtered with little resistance, and almost before the enemy were aware of it, the whole position was completely surrounded.

Our men then used their field search-lights with very great advantage; for, as the enemy were driven out into the open, they were blinded by the glare, and fell an easy prey to British rifles; while the Frenchmen's own machine guns were turned upon them with frightful effect, their battalions being literally mowed down by the awful hail of bullets.

XL

"FOR ENGLAND!"

Through the whole night the battle still raged furiously. The enemy fought on with reckless, unparalleled daring. Chasseurs and Zouaves, Cuirassiers, Dragoons, and infantry from the Loire and the Rhone struggled desperately, contesting every step, and confident of ultimate victory.

But the enemy had at last, by the splendid tactics of the defenders, been forced into a gradually contracting square, bounded by Dorking and Guildford in the north, and Horsham and Billinghurst in the south, and soon after midnight, with a concentric movement from each of the four corners, British Regulars and Volunteers advanced steadily upon the foe, surrounding and slaughtering them.

The horrors of that night were frightful; the loss of life on every hand enormous. Britannia had husbanded her full strength until this critical moment; for now, when the fate of her Empire hung upon a single thread, she sent forth her valiant sons, who fell upon those who had desecrated and destroyed their homes, and wreaked a terrible vengeance.

Through the dark, sultry hours this awful destruction of life continued with unabated fury, and many a Briton closed with his foe in death embrace, or fell forward mortally wounded. Of British heroes there were many that night, for true pluck showed itself everywhere, and Englishmen performed many deeds worthy their traditions as the most courageous and undaunted among nations.

Although the French Commander-in-chief had been killed, yet the enemy still fought on tenaciously, holding their ground on Leith Hill and through Pasture Wood to Wotton and Abinger, until at length, when the saffron streak in the sky heralded another blazing day, the straggling, exhausted remnant of the once-powerful legions of France and Russia, perspiring, dust-covered, and bloodstained, finding they stood alone, and that the whole of Sussex and Surrey had been swept and their comrades slaughtered, laid down their arms and eventually surrendered.

After these three breathless days of butchery and bloodshed England was at last victorious!

In this final struggle for Britain's freedom the invader had been crushed and his power broken; for, thanks to our gallant citizen soldiers, the enemy that had for weeks overrun our smiling land like packs of hungry wolves, wantonly burning our homes and massacring the innocent and unprotected, had at length met with their well-merited deserts, and now lay spread over the miles of pastures, cornfields, and forests, stark, cold, and dead.

Britain had at last vanquished the two powerful nations that had sought by ingenious conspiracy to accomplish her downfall.

Thousands of her brave sons had, alas! fallen while fighting under the British flag. Many of the principal streets of her gigantic capital were only parallel lines of gaunt, blackened ruins, and many of her finest cities lay wrecked, shattered, and desolate; yet this terrible ordeal had happily not weakened her power one iota, nor had she been ousted from her proud position as chief among the mighty Empires of the world.

Three days after the great and decisive battle of Caterham, the British troops, with their compatriots from the Cape, Australia, Canada, and India, entered London triumphantly, bringing with them some thousands of French and Russian prisoners. In the streets, as, ragged and dusty, Britain's defenders passed through on their way to a great Open-Air Thanksgiving Service in Hyde Park, there were scenes of the wildest enthusiasm. With heartfelt gratitude, the people, scrambling over the débris heaped each side of the streets, cheered themselves hoarse; the men grasping the hands of Volunteers and veterans, and the women, weeping for joy, raising the soldiers' hands to their lips. The glad tidings of victory caused rejoicings everywhere. England, feeling herself free, breathed again. In every church and chapel through the United Kingdom special Services of Thanksgiving for deliverance from the invaders' thrall were held, while in every town popular fêtes were organised, and delighted Britons gaily celebrated their magnificent and overwhelming triumph.

In this disastrous struggle between nations France had suffered frightfully. Paris, bombarded and burning, capitulated on the day following the battle of Caterham, and the legions of the Kaiser marched up the Boulevards with their brilliant cavalry uniforms flashing in the sun. Over the Hotel de Ville, the Government buildings on the Quai d'Orsay, and the Ministries of War and Marine, the German flag was hoisted, and waved lazily in the autumn breeze, while the Emperor

William himself had an interview with the French President at the Elysée.

That evening all France knew that Paris had fallen. In a few days England was already shipping back to Dieppe and Riga her prisoners of war, and negotiations for peace had commenced. As security against any further attempts on England, Italian troops were occupying the whole of Southern France from Grenoble to Bordeaux; and the Germans, in addition to occupying Paris, had established their headquarters in Moghilev, and driven back the Army of the Tsar far beyond the Dnieper.

From both France and Russia, Germany demanded huge indemnities, as well as a large tract of territory in Poland, and the whole of the vast Champagne country from Givet, on the Belgian frontier, down to the Sâone.

Ten days later France was forced to accept the preliminaries of a treaty which we proposed. This included the cession to us of Algiers, with its docks and harbour, so that we might establish another naval station in the Mediterranean, and the payment of an indemnity of £250,000,000. Our demands upon Russia at the same time were that she should withdraw all her troops from Bokhara, and should cede to us the whole of that portion of the Trans-Caspian territory lying between the mouths of the Oxus and Kizil Arvat, thence along the Persian frontier to Zulfikai, along the Afghan frontier to Karki, and from there up the bank of the Oxus to the Aral Sea. This vast area of land included the cities of Khiva and Merv, the many towns around Kara Khum, the country of the Kara Turkomans, the Tekeh and the Yomuts, and the annexation of it by Britain would effectually prevent the Russians ever advancing upon India.

Upon these huge demands, in addition to the smaller ones by Italy and Austria, a Peace Conference was opened at Brussels without delay, and at length France and her Muscovite ally, both vanquished and ruined, were compelled to accept the proposals of Britain and Germany.

Hence, on November 16th, 1897, the Treaty of Peace was signed, and eight days later was ratified. Then the huge forces of the Kaiser gradually withdrew into Germany, and the soldiers of King Humbert recrossed the Alps, while we shipped back the remainder of our prisoners, reopened our trade routes, and commenced rebuilding our shattered cities.

XLI

Dawn

A raw, cold December morning in London. With the exception of a statuesque sentry on the Horse Guards' Parade, the wide open space was deserted. It had not long been light, and a heavy yellow mist still hung over the grass in St. James's Park.

A bell clanged mournfully. Big Ben chimed the hour, and then boomed forth eight o'clock. An icy wind swept across the gravelled square. The bare, black branches of the stunted trees creaked and groaned, and the lonely sentry standing at ease before his box rubbed his hands and shivered.

Suddenly a side door opened, and there emerged a small procession. Slowly there walked in front a clergyman bare-headed, reciting with solemn intonation the Burial Service. Behind him, with unsteady step and bent shoulders, a trembling man with blanched, haggard face, and a wild look of terror in his dark, deep-sunken eyes. He wore a shabby morning-coat tightly buttoned, and his hands in bracelets of steel were behind his back.

Glancing furtively around at the grey dismal landscape, he shuddered. Beside and behind him soldiers tramped on in silence.

The officer's sword grated along the gravel.

Suddenly a word of command caused them to halt against a wall, and a sergeant, stepping forward, took a handkerchief and tied it over the eyes of the quivering culprit, who now stood with his back against the wall. Another word from the officer, and the party receded some distance, leaving the man alone. The monotonous nasal utterances of the chaplain still sounded as four privates advanced, and, halting, stood in single rank before the prisoner.

THEY RAISED THEIR RIFLES. THERE was a momentary pause. In the distance a dog howled dismally.

A sharp word of command broke the quiet.

Then, a second later, as four rifles rang out simultaneously, the condemned man tottered forward and fell heavily on the gravel, shot through the heart.

It was the spy and murderer, Karl von Beilstein!

He had been brought from Glasgow to London in order that certain information might be elicited from him, and after his actions had been thoroughly investigated by a military court, he had been sentenced to death. The whole of his past was revealed by his valet Grevel, and it was proved that, in addition to bringing the great disaster upon England, he had also betrayed the country whose roubles purchased his cunningly-obtained secrets.

Geoffrey Engleheart, although gallantly assisting in the fight outside Leatherhead, and subsequently showing conspicuous bravery during the Battle of Caterham, fortunately escaped with nothing more severe than a bullet wound in the arm. During the searching private inquiry held at the Foreign Office after peace was restored, he explained the whole of the circumstances, and was severely reprimanded for his indiscretion; but as no suspicion of von Beilstein's real motive had been aroused prior to the Declaration of War, and as it was proved that Geoffrey was entirely innocent of any complicity in the affair, he was, at the urgent request of Lord Stanbury, allowed to resume his duties. Shortly afterwards he was married to Violet Vayne, and Sir Joseph, having recovered those of his ships that had been seized by the Russian Government, was thereby enabled to give his daughter a handsome dowry.

The young French clerk who had been engaged at the Admiralty, and who had committed murder for gold, escaped to Spain, and, after being hunted by English and Spanish detectives for many weeks, he became apparently overwhelmed by remorse. Not daring to show himself by day, nor to claim the money that had been promised him, he had tramped on through the snow from village to village in the unfrequented valleys of Lerida, while his description was being circulated throughout the Continent. Cold, weary, and hungry, he one night entered the Posada de las Pijorras at the little town of Oliana, at the foot of the Sierra del Cadi. Calling for wine, he took up a dirty crumpled copy of the Madrid *Globo*, three days old. A paragraph, headed "The Missing Spy," caught his eyes, and, reading eagerly, he found to his dismay that the police were aware that he had been in Huesca a week before, and were now using bloodhounds to track him!

The paper fell from his nerveless grasp. The wine at his elbow he swallowed at one gulp, and, tossing down his last real upon the table, he rose and stumbled away blindly into the darkness.

When the wintry dawn spread in that silent, distant valley, it showed a corpse lying in the snow with face upturned. In the white wrinkled brow was a small dark-blue hole from which blood had oozed over the pallid cheek, leaving an ugly stain. The staring eyes were wide open, with a look of unutterable horror in them, and beside the thin clenched hand lay a revolver, one chamber of which had been discharged!

THE DREARY GLOOM OF WINTER passed, and there dawned a new era of prosperity for England.

Dark days were succeeded by a period of happiness and rejoicing, and Britannia, grasping her trident again, seated herself on her shield beside the sea, Ruler of the Waves, Queen of Nations, and Empress of the World.

THE END

A Note About the Author

William Le Queux (1864–1927) was an Anglo-French journalist, novelist, and radio broadcaster. Born in London to a French father and English mother, Le Queux studied art in Paris and embarked on a walking tour of Europe before finding work as a reporter for various French newspapers. Towards the end of the 1880s, he returned to London where he edited *Gossip* and *Piccadilly* before being hired as a reporter for *The Globe* in 1891. After several unhappy years, he left journalism to pursue his creative interests. Le Queux made a name for himself as a leading writer of popular fiction with such espionage thrillers as *The Great War in England in 1897* (1894) and *The Invasion of 1910* (1906). In addition to his writing, Le Queux was a notable pioneer of early aviation and radio communication, interests he maintained while publishing around 150 novels over his decades long career.

A Note from the Publisher

Spanning many genres, from non-fiction essays to literature classics to children's books and lyric poetry, Mint Edition books showcase the master works of our time in a modern new package. The text is freshly typeset, is clean and easy to read, and features a new note about the author in each volume. Many books also include exclusive new introductory material. Every book boasts a striking new cover, which makes it as appropriate for collecting as it is for gift giving. Mint Edition books are only printed when a reader orders them, so natural resources are not wasted. We're proud that our books are never manufactured in excess and exist only in the exact quantity they need to be read and enjoyed.

bookfinity™

Discover more of your favorite classics with Bookfinity™.

- Track your reading with custom book lists.
- Get great book recommendations for your personalized Reader Type.
- Add reviews for your favorite books.
- AND MUCH MORE!

Visit **bookfinity.com** and take the fun Reader Type quiz to get started.

Enjoy our classic and modern companion pairings!

Bookfinity is a registered trademark of Ingram Book Group LLC. © 2023 Bookfinity. All rights reserved.

Printed in the USA
CPSIA information can be obtained
at www.ICGtesting.com
JSHW022218140824
68134JS00018B/1137

9 781513 281018